*Northern Russia 1924:* The Red Army is eliminating those who resist the fledgling Soviet government. At the Battle of the Plutonian Plain, the White Russian forces, aided by wily American Edgar Rice Burroughs, do not fall, instead retreating into the dangers of Pellucidar. Comrade Trotsky, the Soviet leader, sends his troops to hunt them down and destroy them.

Mikhail Kirillivitch Kirov, a young conscript caught up in this mad scheme, is fascinated by this new world. Formerly a student anthropologist, he finds Pellucidar's Stone Age landscape and inhabitants a revelation—until he's grabbed by a mammoth Skal and flown back to its aerie to feed its giant offspring.

Thus begins Kirov's astounding adventure in the Northern environs of Pellucidar, rife with incredible Paleolithic animal life, including Skals, Trals and Dyals, tremendous birds with sharp talons and fierce beaks; Ryths, the huge Stone Age cave bears whose claws can tear a man apart; and the vicious Jaloks, hyaenodons whose wild packs slaughter their prey mercilessly. These and other fantastic beasts stalk Kirov as he navigates the complex world of Pellucidar's most dangerous predator: Man.

To survive, Kirov must escape slavery from the Beautiful Ala and her mighty Black Birdriders, foster a civil war, impress the natives with his "inventions," conquer the terrifying Pulka Horde, and become a warlord of several tribes as they flee the Soviet invaders. It's a tale in the grand tradition of Edgar Rice Burroughs' epic adventures at the Earth's Core.

# UNTAMED PELLUCIDAR™

One claw swept Kirov off his steed, his feet ripping out of his stirrups. He flew brutally sideways, landing in the mud and water of the wava's canal. Fire wracked his side. The other claw slashed into the dyal's thick body. Feathers flew and muscles shredded under the giant cave bear's attack.

THE WILD ADVENTURES OF EDGAR RICE BURROUGHS® SERIES

# UNTAMED PELLUCIDAR™

LEE STRONG

COVER & INTERIOR ILLUSTRATIONS

BY DOUGLAS KLAUBA

EDGAR RICE BURROUGHS, Inc.

*Publishers*

TARZANA        CALIFORNIA

*Untamed Pellucidar*
*First Edition*

Special thanks to Bob Garcia, Gary A.
Buckingham, Greg Funke, Jim Gerlach,
Scott Tracy Griffin, and Tyler Wilbanks for their
valuable assistance in producing this novel.

Number 7 in the Series

Library of Congress CIP (Cataloging-in-Publication) Data
ISBN-13:
978-1-945462-15-3

- 9 8 7 6 5 4 3 2 1 -

For
George T. McWhorter,
Order of the Burroughs Empire,
Collector, Curator, Inspiration, and Friend

# Table of Contents

# INTRODUCTION

Edgar Rice Burroughs introduced us to the savage land of Pellucidar in the year 1914 when AT THE EARTH'S CORE appeared serialized in the pulp magazine ALL-STORY WEEKLY. Burroughs' exciting story-telling thrilled readers, and his fantastic, primordial world was like no other. Over the years, Burroughs wrote six additional books in the series: PELLUCIDAR, TANAR OF PELLUCIDAR, TARZAN AT THE EARTH'S CORE, BACK TO THE STONE AGE, LAND OF TERROR, and SAVAGE PELLUCIDAR. Those are the stories that I cannot forget. Then in 1976 John Eric Holmes' authorized novel MAHARS OF PELLUCIDAR was published, introducing new characters and subhuman races. Now, 42 years later, Lee Strong is carrying on Burroughs' grand tradition with this new Pellucidar novel.

What is it about this savage world that has so captivated readers young and old? What draws us back to this place again and again?

I was a young boy haunting the paperback racks when my eyes fell upon those cover illustrations by Roy Krenkel and Frank Frazetta. I had no idea who Edgar Rice Burroughs was, but those covers were the reason I bought those first books. When I got home and began reading BACK TO THE STONE AGE, the open-mouth wonder began. Yep, I was lost in Pellucidar.

It's a fascinating concept that 500 miles below the Earth's surface another world exists on the inner surface of Earth's hollow sphere. The science is just believable enough.

i

An interior sun hangs in the exact center of the sky and pours down its torrid rays on the exotic land. With no relative movement, it's always daytime, or high noon; night doesn't exist in Pellucidar. This leads to one of Burroughs' most intriguing ideas. Under the perpetual midday sun, the passage of time is impossible to calculate and so may not exist. Time passes differently for different people. For an individual experiencing many adventures, a lot of time has passed, while for another, it may seem that hardly any time has passed at all. This timelessness also has the peculiar effect of slowing down the aging process. A place sheltered from time and change is quite appealing.

Pellucidar has a moon in its sky that revolves with the Earth, remaining always a mile above the same spot. The area of perpetual darkness beneath the moon is called the Land of Awful Shadow. Unlike the rest of Pellucidar, the vegetation there is stunted, sparse, and colorless.

Burroughs populated his world with prehistoric tribes, leftovers from earlier stages of human evolution, and weird, preternatural races. No doubt my eyes were wide while first reading about the Horibs, grotesque reptile-men atop their strange, swift steeds. And then there were the cold-blooded Mahars that held sway over the local hominid tribes, and the Korsars, colorful pirates whose ancestors came through the polar opening to Pellucidar. Of course there are scantily-clad cave women and dinosaurs! What's not to love about this place?

The idea of a hollow earth has been around for a long time. In 1692, English astronomer Edmond Halley of Halley's Comet fame attempted to explain the reason for the movement in the Earth's magnetic poles. He proposed that within the Earth were three independently turning concentric spheres, each illuminated and possibly inhabited. As in the Pellucidar series, Halley speculated that the Earth's crust was 500 miles thick.

In 1818, Captain John Cleves Symmes of Ohio proposed that the Earth contained concentric spheres nestled inside each other, with the potential for life on both the concave and convex surfaces of each sphere. He stated that common sense says this must be so as the good Lord would not waste space. Symmes advanced Halley's theory by suggesting the existence of polar openings. He believed the holes were 4,000 miles in diameter, large enough to emit light to the inner world. The descent into one of the holes would be so gradual that an explorer might not realize that he was entering the Earth. In the fourth book of the Pellucidar series, Jason Gridley's rescue mission enters the savage land via the northern polar opening. In this new book, author Lee Strong launches his Russian invasion through this same hole in the pole.

With the backing of a Kentucky senator, Symmes unsuccessfully petitioned Congress to fund a polar expedition to prove his theories. He tried twice more over the years and at one point the motion received twenty-three affirmative votes, not enough.

In 1869, Cyrus Teed began to preach his unique ideas. He believed we were on the inside, on the concave surface of the Earth, held in place by centrifugal force, the entire universe contained within the 25,000 mile circumference of the inside-out Earth. Teed built an instrument called the Rectilineator and measured the concavity of the Earth. Sure enough, the results of that experiment satisfied Teed that he was right.

In 1886, Mormon writer Frederick Culmer discussed the theories of Symmes and provided theological evidence. He further speculated that the lost tribes of Israel were living in our hollow Earth. "They shall come forth again when the Father sees fit." Wild stuff, yet the existence of a hollow Earth was an idea that refused to be buried.

Burroughs was not the first author to write subterranean fiction. The first true hollow Earth novel was THE JOURNEY OF NIELS KLIM TO THE WORLD UNDERGROUND by Baron Ludvig Holberg in 1741. Klim falls through a shaft in Norway and tumbles onto a world inside a world, at the center of the Earth. Here the intelligent life forms are walking, talking trees. Klim also visits the underside of the Earth's crust where he encounters a race of intelligent apes. After twelve years below, Klim falls back up the same hole he fell down in the beginning.

One of the best known stories is Jules Verne's JOURNEY TO THE CENTER OF THE EARTH (1864). It's a deep cave system story, not a hollow Earth story. It's perhaps the first to involve prehistoric animals and men. It also contains the first dinosaur fight in literature. Three travelers follow the path of an ancient explorer into an extinct volcano in Iceland. Forty-five days of journeying finds them about 105 miles down, still within the Earth's crust, in an immense cavern, and on the shore of an underground sea. They try to blast open a blocked tunnel but this causes them to be ejected upward out of a volcano in Italy.

Edward Bulwer-Lytton wrote THE COMING RACE in 1871. The author is known for his novel, THE LAST DAYS OF POMPEII, but perhaps better known for the opening line of PAUL CLIFFORD, "It was a dark and stormy night..." Like the Verne novel, this is a deep cave system yarn that takes place within the Earth's crust. The protagonist falls into a vast chasm and discovers a utopia inhabited by an ancient, highly evolved race. Their ancestors lived on the surface during ante-diluvian times but fled below to escape a global catastrophe. Now, through the use of "vril power," they are able to influence the weather and the minds of surface people. They plan on taking over the exterior world, hence the name of the story. There were those that took this book as more than just a piece of fiction, including Adolf Hitler, who some claimed searched for the polar openings and yearned to harness vril power.

MIZORA by Mary E. Bradley Lane was published in 1890. A Russian noblewoman, Vera Zarovitch, is shipwrecked in northern waters and eventually arrives in an unknown world in the Earth's interior. Its inhabitants are all lovely blonde women who allowed the men to die out 3000 years ago when the "Secret of Life" was discovered.

PLUTONIA was written by Vladimir Obruchev in 1924.

Like Pellucidar, Plutonia exists on the inner surface of our hollow planet. It's a world of rivers, lakes, volcanoes, and strange vegetation, a world that has its own dying sun, "Pluto," and is inhabited by savage beasts and bestial savages. A team of Russian scientists penetrate Mother Earth through the Arctic polar opening. At first they find mammoths, but the further they travel, the older becomes the flora and fauna geologically. This evolutionary trip reminds one of Burroughs' THE LAND THAT TIME FORGOT.

All five of the best-known examples above were published prior to the first Pellucidar story in 1914. Burroughs was not the first but easily topped them all with his creation. His skill at world-building was unparalleled, and the world at the Earth's core was his best. Even those readers that prefer his Mars books will admit that Pellucidar is the most fascinating world.

Author Lee Strong takes us back to this wonderful place in an exciting new adventure with a young Russian who encounters challenges undreamt of. Strong's love for all things Burroughs is evident, and he's certainly clever enough to play in the Burroughs universe.

Strong's book takes place during the events of TANAR OF PELLUCIDAR, the third book of the original series. Burroughs fans will enjoy Strong's "Easter eggs" that refer to other Burroughs characters. Too, there are settings that may be recognized from hollow Earth fiction. Readers new to Pellucidar need not worry about what has gone before. This is an enjoyable self-contained story.

If this is your first time entering savage Pellucidar, I envy you. The world that's ahead is the very best there is. If you're a long-time fan, at last you have a new Earth's core novel, and you can become lost in Pellucidar again.

David Critchfield
Author, THE GILAK'S GUIDE TO PELLUCIDAR

# INVADERS OF PELLUCIDAR

*Chapter One*

## "We have passports for Pellucidar...."

Leningrad, USSR
February 1925

The streets of the former capital of Russia were piled high with winter snow. Grandmothers organized by some obscure arm of the Soviet bureaucracy were diligently plying shovels and brooms to clear the streets and sidewalks.

Inside a faceless government building, the temperature was scarcely warmer as two foreign scientists demanded action on their entry permits. The frustrated clerk was about to deny their requests for the tenth time when he spotted his superior approaching. Gratefully, he yielded to the impressive figure.

"Who are you and why do you wish to visit Zarovitch Island?" the latter demanded.

Neither of the scientists quailed as expected. "Good day, sir. I am—" began one.

The mountainous official interrupted, "Do not say 'sir.' People's Revolution has abolished titles of knighthood. I am Comrade Commissar P.I. Visclosky."

Both scientists stared at the truculent figure for a moment. The speaker resumed, "Very well, Comrade Commissar Visclosky. This *gentleman* is Dr. Freidrich von der Tann of the International Astronomic Society and I am Dr. Gordon Warrington of the London Zoological Institute. We have passports for Pellucidar via the Romanov Island Scientific—"

"Do not say 'Pellucidar.' Is now *Novy Mir*, 'New World'

1

in English. And 'Romanov Island' is now Zarovitch Island in
honor of 19th Century revolutionary explorer Vera Zarovitch."
As the scientists digested this revisionism, the glacial Visclosky
turned to the one who had not yet spoken. "Why does German
astronomer wish to visit inside world lacking in stars and
planets?"

The second scientist cleared his throat. "I am Luthanian
actually, not German. As an astronomer, I wish to study the
pendant moon that orbits Pellucidar above the land of Thoria.
My colleague wishes to study the Cenozoic and Mesozoic fauna
of the Inner World. We both have the necessary passports,
special permits, and letters of introduction from our home
institutions and various distinguished authorities such as
Emperor David I, Viscount Greystoke, Colonel Fawcett, Mr.
Bowen Tyler, Jr., Mr. Burroughs..."

"Stop!" barked Visclosky, his face mottled in rage. "Do
you mean Mister E.R. Burroughs of Richmond, Virginia,
USA?"

Von der Tann was a scientist but he had fought in the War
of 1914-18. A war that the Soviets had lost before the Western
Allies rescued them. "Yes, Commissar. That Edgar Rice
Burroughs—a generous patron of the Society and an honorary
Russian citizen if I recall correctly. He saved the Czar's life—"

"Silence!" thundered Visclosky. "Guards!" Two soldiers,
previously impassive against the wall, sprang to attention, guns
upright. "Take these spies away! Any friends of E.R. Burroughs
are no friends of the Soviet People!"

Rifle butts quickly silenced the scientists' protests.

*Chapter Two*

## THE INNER WORLD

**P**ellucidar, Russian NOVY MIR (New World), a vast hollow or subworld within the planet Earth with a diameter of 7,000 miles and a superficial area of 165,480,000 square miles. "Pellucidar" is also used as the general name for the inner surface of the sphere.

*The land.* The surface of Pellucidar is divided into continental and oceanic areas similar to the divisions of Earth's surface. In general, Pellucidarian landmasses correspond to Earthly oceanic areas and vice versa. There are a number of exceptions. The International Geographic Society has named the landmasses for their principal explorers and adopted native names for the oceans. Thus, Perryland, also known as the Great Peninsula, lies under the Arctic and northern North Atlantic Oceans and Innesland lies under the central Atlantic Ocean. The Sojar Ocean lies below North America and the Korsar Ocean lies below Eurasia.

Soviet geographers attempted to apply the names of Communist political figures to the various features but these proposals have been generally rejected by the scientific community as not honoring explorers or natives. Soviet proposals include Leninska (Lenin Land) for northern Perryland and the Karl-Marx Ocean for the Korsar Ocean.

*Climate.* The climate of Pellucidar is tropical throughout most of the subworld. Arctic, sub-Arctic and temperate conditions are found near the North Polar Opening where chill polar winds enter the Inner World.

*Animal and plant life.* The animals and plants of Pellucidar

3

are generally considered to be "prehistoric" compared to those of Earth's surface. Dinosaurs and Pliocene/Pleistocene mammalian mega fauna dominate the tropical central regions while the sub-Arctic regions are dominated by avians and mammals....

*The people.* A wide variety of sentient beings inhabit Pellucidar including gilaks (humans), Mahars, Sagoths, and various hominids.... The cultural level of most Pellucidarian races is generally Paleolithic, or Old Stone Age, with the more advanced Mahars being the primary exception....

*Administrative and social conditions.* The Paleolithic tribe is the basis for most Pellucidarian cultures. In the period 1903-1918, American explorers David Innes and Abner Perry established a united federation of tribes known as the Empire of Pellucidar. Emperor David I and Prime Minister Perry are engaged in a systematic effort to introduce 20th Century technology to their subjects and elevate their overall cultural, social and economic level.

*History.* The history of the subworld prior to 1903 is poorly understood. Most scientists believe that humans entered the Inner World through the North Polar Opening during relatively recent interglacial warming periods. This theory is supported by the existence of a single human language throughout the subworld. A number of authors have written accounts of pre-1903 expeditions but there is little agreement on the validity of these early records....

The modern history of Pellucidar is generally accepted to have begun in 1913 when American science writer Edgar Rice Burroughs published *At the Earth's Core*, a popular account of David Innes' early adventures. An Imperial Russian attempt to colonize Stolypin Land in northern Perryland followed but was interrupted by the outbreak of the World War of 1914-1918. Subsequent colonization attempts were made by Theodore Roosevelt (1915), the Soviet Union (1924), ....—*The Universal Encyclopedia*, 1974 Edition, s.v. "Pellucidar."

## Coreless Planets
*Definition.*

A coreless planet is a type of terrestrial planet that has no metallic core, i.e., the planet is a hollow sphere composed of a rocky mantle. Examples of coreless planets and satellites include Earth, The Moon, Mars and Venus. Mercury is believed to be coreless but this has not been confirmed as of 2018.

*General Characteristics.*

Gravitational attraction within coreless planets is noticeably less than on the surface due to the pull of mass above the observer. The exact degree of difference depends on the composition and thickness of the mantle. Coreless planets' magnetic fields arise in the metallic layers of the mantles. Openings between the inner and outer surfaces may exist depending on the composition and structure of the mantle. Satellite observations confirm the existence of openings in the Earthly and Martian polar regions and in various locations on The Moon. Openings have not been observed on Venus or Mercury.

*History of the concept.*

Edmond Halley proposed the idea that the Earth was composed of nested hollow spheres in the 18th Century to explain the existence of the aurora borealis. Nineteenth Century scientists proposed the nebular hypothesis to explain coreless planets, i.e., all planets formed corelessly as the result of the proto-planetary masses reaching equilibriums between gravitational and centrifugal forces during the condensation of stars and other bodies from primordial galactic nebulas.

A 2008 paper by Linda Elkins-Tanton and Sara Seagar proposed two possible mechanisms for the formation of coreless planets. The first alternative suggested that a planet accretes from chrondritic fully oxidized water rich material where all of the metallic iron present is bound into silicate mineral crystals. Such planets may form in cooler regions relatively far from the central star and migrate inward. The second alternative suggests that the planet accretes from both iron-metal-rich and water-rich material. The iron reacts with water to form iron oxide and releases hydrogen before differentiation of a metal core has taken place. The predicted result is that sufficiently well mixed and small iron droplets will oxidize and become trapped in a mantle structure without forming a core.—*E*cyclopedia*, 11/23/2015, s.v. "Coreless planets."

**Zarovitch Island**, Russian POLUOSTROV ZAROV-ITCH, *Plutonia* autonomous *okrug* (area), Pellucidarian Polar Sea; it is separated from the northern Perryland mainland by the shallow Innokente Strait.

*The land.* The seas around the island are cold but seldom frozen. The climate is sub-Arctic dominated by mixed rain and snow throughout the year. Vegetation is low, dense and shrubby in a barren landscape; white grass and tripwire dominate the plant associations. There are no longer any land mammals indigenous to the island. A Russian scientific research establishment occupies most of the island.

*History.* The island was originally named for the Romanov Imperial dynasty of Russia. Professor Nikolai Innokentevic Trukanov discovered the island in 1914 and established a scientific outpost as a base for exploring the Plutonian region of the northern Perryland continent. During the period 1916-20, it was also used as a transit point for Russian peasants colonizing Stolypin Land. The Soviets established themselves there in 1924 and renamed the island and establishment in honor of revolutionary explorer Vera Zarovitch. Present Soviet writings claim Russian knowledge of the Inner World since 1881. The Novy Mir Military District was declared in April 1924 and all access to the island or the adjacent mainland is currently forbidden.—*The Universal Encyclopedia*, 1929 Edition, s.v. "Zarovitch Island."

Zarovitch Island, Zarovitch Scientific Research Area,
Plutonia, USSR
March 1924

Company Commander Wrangell found his leader, Regiment Commander Kandinsky, and the latter's staff officers seated in a small office in one of the Research Area's laboratories. The establishment's main administrative offices had been destroyed when the monarchists and their tame scientists had burned their files and specimens. This office's windows did have a fine view of the nearby mainland. A samovar brewed hot water for tea in the far corner.

Wrangell saluted and reported. "Comrade Regiment Commander, we have secured the island, the causeway and a security zone on the mainland. We have completed a preliminary search of the buildings but found no one except fighters whom we have either destroyed or captured. All of the monarchists here and in the town of Stolypin are either dead, captured or fled into the hinterlands."

He paused and added, "We captured very few of them. Those we did find have been turned over to Comrade Commissar Lvov." The latter nodded slightly in acknowledgement. Wrangell's face betrayed nothing. During the Civil War, very few prisoners had survived the attentions of the zampolit (political officer) and his brutes.

"What about the women and children?" asked Deputy Regiment Commander Drobanin. "The Whites had a sizable settlement here—" He gestured towards the town. "—and evacuated several thousand civilians from northern Siberia. What happened to them?" In 1920, the Whites had evacuated 150,000 soldiers and civilians from Crimea. The thought of an unconquered White army preparing to attack the Soviet Union caused many sleepless nights in Moscow and elsewhere.

"Gone, Comrade. We believe that the monarchists moved their entire civilian population somewhere deeper into the Inner World. The garrison that we fought was a relatively small rear guard intended to delay our pursuit. One fighter said that they hoped to find sanctuary in the 'Empire' of Pellucidar. They apparently began the migration soon after they lost the Revolution."

"That was 1920," interpolated Drobanin. "They've had almost four years to organize and move their people." He cursed. "According to the adventurer Burroughs, it only required fifteen years for Innes to construct his entire empire. The refugees are well and truly gone by now."

Wrangell stiffened to attention again. "Comrade Regiment Commander."

"Yes, Comrade Company Commander?" inquired the commander mildly.

"According to the fighter that we captured, Burroughs himself is with the monarchists. He was part of the rear guard and led the last fighters into the interior just ahead of our capture of the island and the town."

All of the seated Soviets leaped to their feet cursing like pirates. The office air blued with profanity.

Kandinsky recovered himself first and sat down heavily. The others imitated his example.

"Comrade Regiment Commander, do you have any orders?" asked Drobanin hesitantly.

Kandinsky sighed loudly. "Yes," he growled. "Get the men organized, fed and prepared to fight again. Assign one battalion to secure the research establishment and the town, conduct a more thorough search for survivors and information about the monarchists' plans, and establish a permanent base here. Make contact with Moscow as soon as possible and notify me when contact is made.

"The other battalions will prepare to march on Comrade Trotsky's orders. When he hears that Burroughs and the surviving monarchists have escaped, I am sure he will order us to invade Pellucidar." He glared out the window at the strange landscape rising before him.

Behind his back, the other Soviets shivered.

*Chapter Three*

## INVASION

Plutonia *okrug* (area), *Novy Mir* Military District,
Northern Perryland, Northern Pellucidar
April 1924

C ompany Commander Wrangell signaled his unit to
rest and his men eagerly complied. Noncommissioned
officers shouted at "volunteers" to stand guard while
the Company Commander, his platoon commanders and spe-
cialists walked up a low ridge. One squad began chopping up
scrubby bushes for firewood. Overhead, Pellucidar's tiny sun
hung at the zenith but provided little heat to these latitudes.
A nice fire would supply that oversight.

Wrangell took out his binoculars and surveyed the strange
yet beautiful landscape carefully. Ahead, a plain stretched
onward and upward from the base of the ridge until details
blurred into the distance. Numerous herds of animals grazed
on the scanty grasses and pale flowers. Off to his right, a river
snaked across the land. Wrangell guessed that it would eventually flow into the vast Ocean below Siberia. Further to the
right, he guessed that a series of smudges marked a mountain
range. Much closer on his left, two companies of Soviet infantry plodded forward to hunt down and destroy the monarchists. No good Soviet officer could ever forget the counter-
revolutionary threats surrounding the Soviet Union like wolves
surrounding an isolated farmhouse.

As Wrangell watched, the nearer company of men marched
up the gentle ridge bound for a ruined fort. The monarchists

had built a chain of forts reaching into the interior when they had controlled Mother Russia and the Motherland's scientific resources. When they retreated before the Red Army, they had burned the forts to deny the victors shelter. Kandinsky's infantry regiment included attached engineers to rebuild the forts and roads. Until that rebuilding was complete....

"Comrade Kandinsky has ordered that we stop here 'for the night.' His staff and troops will occupy the site of the monarchists' fort. Marakov's company will bivouac beyond them on the regimental left flank. We will occupy this ridge. Grenov, move your platoon up to the military crest and dig in. The scouts are out ahead of you; make sure your men don't shoot them by mistake. Schakowsky, move up behind Grenov. Make sure that you are both linked with the central column." He paused to look to his right where a clump of evergreens stood about one hundred meters away. "Borski, you're our right flank. Those trees will make a nice windbreak so they can be your headquarters."

The platoon commanders repeated the orders to their runners who started off to inform the *starshinas* (sergeants). "Just a minute, Kirov." Borski's runner halted and returned.

Mikhail Kirov was a tall, slender but well muscled young man drafted out of a University for his expertise in dinosaurs and other prehistoric creatures. His black hair, brown eyes and clear skin were typical of the Leningrad area. Borski had chosen him as runner for his endurance and intelligent cooperation with others.

Wrangell resumed scanning the landscape through his binoculars. "Comrade Specialist Kirov, so far the New World looks very much like the Old One. This could be Siberia rather than 'Pellucidar.' The wind here is as cold as it is at home. Those animals down on the plain look very much like reindeer, musk oxen and antelopes, not tyrannosaurs and brontosaurs. And those trees smell like pines, not palm trees."

"Yes, Comrade Company Commander. The northern portion of Perryland—"

"Leninska."

"—is subarctic…. Pardon me, Comrade Commander." The young man's face was puzzled but alert.

Wrangell clarified. "The Central Committee has decreed that this continent below the Arctic Ocean shall be known as Leninska in honor of the founder of the Soviet Union. The oceans under Eurasia and North America shall be known as the Karl-Marx and Friedrich-Engels Oceans. Regardless of what the capitalists and their tame scientists might say."

Kirov nodded. He had been born in the city originally known as Saint Petersburg and renamed twice within his lifetime.

"I understand, Comrade Company Commander. The continent of Leninska is subarctic in climate and vegetation, not tropical. Cold air from the Outer Arctic Ocean enters through the Zarovitch Opening and cools the entire region. So those animals are likely to be similar to reindeer and musk oxen but they may also be mammoths and other creatures that no longer exist on the outer crust. As we move further south, the climate will change rapidly. And the animals and vegetation will change as well."

"Another question: are we likely to encounter the adventurer Innes and his so-called 'empire' in this region of Leninska?"

"No, Comrade. The so-called 'Empire of Pellucidar' lies diagonally under New England, North America—well over seven thousand kilometers from here." The young specialist seemed sure of himself, or, at least, of his facts.

"Very good, Comrade. I for one will be very happy to discard this heavy clothing and bask in the eternal sunshine. Until then, you run along and tell your comrades to occupy those trees and provide us with plenty of firewood 'for the night.'"

Kirov saluted and ran off to inform Platoon Commander Borski's senior *starshina*.

WHILE THE OFFICERS continued discussing weighty matters with Company Commander Wrangell, Senior Starshina Voitinuik bawled orders at Borski's platoon. Whether because of him or despite him, the men soon had a small city of tents erected under the evergreens. As Wrangell had surmised, the trees did provide a buffer against the cold air rushing into Novy Mir. With the tents up, Voitinuik detailed a party to chop down a pine or two for firewood.

The Senior Starshina was in an expansive mood and he seemed to think that Kirov had put the bright idea of occupying the small forest into Wrangell's head. As a result, he was talking to the specialist rather than shouting at him. "So, what is a smart young fellow like you doing in the Red Army? Eager to liberate Pellucidar and all of the scantily clad women? Eh, Mikhail Kirillivitch?"

Kirov blushed. "I was a student of paleontology and languages at the University of Leningrad. When Comrade Stalin announced the liberation of the New World, I was drafted—"

The discussion was interrupted by a sudden shout. Kirov and Voitinuik jerked their heads toward a woodcutter jumping back from a tree in horror. Gouts of red blood spurted from the tree trunk, spraying the woodcutter and his comrades. As the men watched in shock, the tree trunk folded upward, lifting into the lower foliage, splattering more blood onto the ground. A golden anvil fell from above, crushing the woodcutter's skull. A monstrous screech drowned out human shouts of terror. The men scattered as the trees came to life around them.

Kirov froze in place. *Moving trees?* His mind gibbered. None of the adventurer Perry's reports had mentioned *moving trees!*

Senior Starshina Voitinuik had no such qualms. He leapt forward, bawling orders for Borski's men to fall back, to leave the woods, to get their rifles off their cursed backs! Now! Now! Now! The men were too panic-stricken to obey as more golden anvils appeared from the tops of the trees to smash into Soviet skulls. Other tree limbs flailed against the sky.

Standing twenty meters back from the nearest monster, Kirov suddenly realized what he was seeing. *They're not trees; they're birds! Giant birds!* The "foliage" was really green feathers on giant triangular bodies. The golden "anvils" were the birds' heads and beaks. And the tree "trunks" and "roots" were the birds' great legs and feet. *No wonder the first one screamed when the woodcutter tried to sever its leg!*

The birds were murdering Borski's men. Beaks split heads, backs and chests in fountains of blood. Great feet kicked humans into the air, shattering bones and mutilating flesh. The tents were ripped to shreds in a matter of seconds.

Behind Kirov, rifles began to crackle, feebly at first, but with mounting fury. The young student belatedly pulled his own Mosin Nagant off his shoulder and aimed at the nearest monster. He fired too hurriedly. The rifle's recoil bruised his shoulder painfully.

Shamefaced, Kirov flexed his arms to ease the pain and reseat the rifle properly. His eyes took in a scene of horror.

With one exception, the birds had annihilated Borski's platoon. Only Voitinuik fought on, dodging wildly as the monsters raked the ground around him with claws and beaks. He cursed wildly, condemning the avians to all manner of impossible acts. And all the while, his rifle barked, savaging his enemies at the closest of ranges.

Kirov's brutal military training took hold. He dropped to one knee, aiming carefully and bracing himself against the recoil of the gun. He began firing steadily into the knot of gyrating monsters. He couldn't tell if he was *hitting* anything but at least he was *fighting*. Until now, he hadn't been certain that he *could* fight.

The bloodthirsty roar of a Madsen machine gun howled from behind Kirov. The heavy weapons were coming into action. One giant collapsed, thudding to the ground, crushing Voitinuik flat. Others screamed defiance at the merely human weapon. One monster hopped forward, advancing on Company

Commander Wrangell's position. The Madsen lashed at it without apparent effect.

Kirov ran out of bullets. He reached into his greatcoat pockets for more ammunition. He bent over as he fumbled, not seeing the mad avian eye fastened on him. He didn't realize that, kneeling as he was, he was still the tallest, most conspicuous human within many meters of the birds.

Another giant smashed to the ground as Schakowsky's machine gunners found the range to their target. Rifle fire from a dozen directions stung the strange creatures. Maddened with rage, one monster hopped forward. It's free claw slashed through the air....

Kirov was still searching when a hammer smote his back, knocking him to the ground. Then he was yanked into the air, arms and legs flailing wildly. His rifle cartwheeled through the air to crash somewhere below him. The bloody ridge and the carcasses that had been men five minutes before receded rapidly. The dark green avians began to flee the fray. Soon, they were mere blurs in the distance, leaving the bloody ruin behind.

He looked up wildly. The great green body stretched above him and beyond that was the clear blue Pellucidarian sky. Giant wings flapped steadily, carrying him away, a thousand meters above the pallid landscape. The young man fought nausea and lost.

COMPANY COMMANDER WRANGELL charged the site of the battle as the last of the avians collapsed in a thunder of machine gun bullets. His staff followed and the starshinas yanked their Madsens' muzzles upright to avoid hitting them. In a wide arc around them, prone riflemen rose to their feet.

Wrangell and his staff slammed to a halt just short of the giant green bodies. They oozed red blood, not sap. He looked around wildly.

"Borski! What are those *things?*" shouted the company commander.

*Kirov... was yanked into the air, arms and legs flailing wildly... Giant wings flapped steadily, carrying him away, a thousand meters above the pallid landscape.*

His lieutenant gaped helplessly. Five minutes before, he had commanded thirty-one men. Now, he was the sole survivor of his entire platoon. Wrangell shouted again. Finally, military discipline took hold of Borski's mind and he responded to the question.

"Comrade Company Commander, I don't know. Kirov might have known but he's gone. He was our expert in these accursed monsters," Borski added needlessly.

He pointed towards the distant mountains. A speck was just visible in the distance—the flying monster and its victim's body.

OTHER EYES WATCHED the bird winging its way in the distance briefly and then swung back to the disorganized Soviets swarming around the avian carcasses. Those eyes were getting on in years but the brain behind them was as sharp as the day its owner had warned George Armstrong Custer not to underestimate the Sioux. The body that housed that brain was dressed in grey-green hunting clothes sold in a chain of general stores headquartered in Richmond, Virginia, USA.

"Well, Pardan, the Soviets were not as ready for Pellucidar as they thought they were. Will we be ready for them?" The speaker grinned savagely.

The person addressed was dressed in furs dyed the color of the grasses around him. He carried a stone hand axe on his belt and a Springfield rifle on his back. He answered, "Yes, Mister Burroughs, we will be ready for them." He grinned as well.

*Chapter Four*

## HOME FOR DINNER

Kirov stopped flailing. The giant bird carrying him across the weirdly beautiful Pellucidarian landscape was a thousand meters in the air. If he struggled free of the creature's claws now, he would encounter that landscape suddenly and fatally.

The strange land passed swiftly beneath him. This portion of Pellucidar's concave surface was a vast plain, not unlike parts of Siberia. Grasses and unknown but beautiful flowers covered it. Herds of animals cropped the vegetation short. In spite of himself, Kirov recognized mammoths and baluchiteria, long extinct in the Outer World but thriving in the Inner World, as well as antelope and musk oxen. Other beasts were less recognizable.

He tried to orient himself. His own body blocked his view to the rear, where—presumably—his comrades were planning his rescue. To his sides, the rolling plain stretched onward and upward blurring into the distance. Was there a glint of a vast body of water to his right? The Karl-Marx Ocean? Or some other body of water? Ahead of him, mountains began to loom into the sky, reaching towards the mighty avian and its unwilling burden.

The bird relaxed its beating wings, gliding downward towards the mountains. Granite claws thrust into the crisp, blue Pellucidarian sky at least two thousand meters over Kirov's spinning head. The bird navigated the twisting canyons between the peaks with a surety of purpose that the human could only admire. Naked rock surrounded them as the bird sped through the mountains.

Suddenly, the bird banked and twisted in midair. Kirov saw an isolated finger of rock thrusting upward in the chill canyon air in front of him. On the tip of the finger was a jumble of logs—a gigantic nest fit for an avian monster. In it, Kirov could see three smaller editions of the fearsome creature.

A bellowing squawk split the sky. Kirov's captor had announced its arrival. The younger birds looked up and began cheeping like a hundred high-pitched bullfrogs croaking in unison.

Thoughts flashed through the man's brain. *Home for dinner! And I am the dinner!*

Without warning, the great bird released its prey, sending its victim hurling through the air towards the nest. Kirov flapped his arms, attempting to fly like the Firebird's Mate of legend. Unfortunately, he had no magic feather to enable him to fly.

Instead, his greatcoat caught the wind rushing through the canyon. It slowed him just enough… He crashed heavily into a massive log built into the side of the nest. A hammer blow smashed him unconscious.

TWO SCOUTS CAUTIOUSLY raised themselves from the ground of the Pellucidarian plain a kilometer in advance of Wrangell's company of Kandinsky's regiment. When gunfire had erupted behind them, they had instantly sought cover among the pale green grasses. From their hasty blind, they had watched the battle between Borski's platoon and the monster birds. Now that the birds were dead or flown, they conferred briefly and decided to resume their advance. Whatever had happened on the ridge didn't look good from their angle. As Soviet soldiers, they knew that the higher ups were going to find someone other than themselves to blame. Therefore, it would be much, much better for a couple of brave scouts to be somewhere else when blame was assigned.

They eased forward, keeping their eyes and ears on the curious animals that grazed the plain ahead of them and resolutely ignoring the diminishing gunfire behind them. Thus, they missed the simultaneous rifle flashes low in the grass between them and Wrangell's company. When their lifeless bodies were discovered, the harassed Company Commander concluded that they were the accidental victims of "friendly fire" when Borski's men fired wildly at the gyrating monster birds. If Wrangell had ordered an autopsy, he would have discovered that the fatal bullets came from American Springfield rifles rather than Soviet Mosin Nagants.

KIROV WAS SHAKEN AWAKE. Dull pain tortured half his body, confusing his thoughts. The shaking must be Senior Starshina Voitinuik trying to wake him. A sharper pain jabbed his buttocks.

Kirov came wildly awake. Voitinuik might apply his boot to someone's fundament, but not his knife. *What?* The young draftee stared about him wildly.

The three young giant birds—only the size of large dogs—were pecking at him. Fortunately, most of their blows had landed on his battered backpack or his thick greatcoat. Above them, the mother avian perched on the edge of her nest, preening her great tree-like body distractedly. The piney scent of the birds assailed Kirov's nostrils.

The nearest monster pecked again, hoping for a nice human drumstick. Again, Kirov's military training took hold and he kicked frantically at the avians. Thoughts of Voitinuik's versatile knife drove his hand to his belt sheath. He whipped the bayonet to his now vanished rifle upward into a defensive posture.

The baby monsters were nonplussed by their dinner's obstinacy. They were accustomed to meat stunned into unconsciousness by its impact with the nest. Food this lively was something new.

The monster to Kirov's right edged closer. The soldier

waved his left hand at it. As it turned to focus on the motion, Kirov stabbed his bayonet savagely into the side of its head. The creature convulsed and collapsed.

The other birdlings gawped at their brother's corpse. Kirov froze in place, trying to translate immobility into invisibility. The ploy worked. The baby monsters pecked at the body, tentatively at first, then with increasing vigor. They tore bloody strips from the corpse. Their dining habits were—messy.

Kirov edged backward carefully. His heel caught on the uneven footing of the giant nest. He fell heavily, slamming his injured back once more. He choked off a bitter cry.

Too late.

The mother monster heard the strangled cry and looked down to see two of her young shredding their brother while their intended dinner painfully crawled away. She screamed and slammed her yellow head downward to crush the murderer of her young. A living anvil smashed into Kirov's body as he twisted, attempting to escape....

Providence (that all good Soviets denied) smiled on the young paleontologist. The monster's beak crashed into the remains of his backpack, cutting it loose from Kirov's body and carrying it upward. The gigantic bird shook the backpack savagely. The remains of valuable State property scattered in the air, arcing briefly and then falling into the nest or into depths of the canyon far below.

Kirov scrambled frantically across the interlocked logs that formed the titan's nest. They seemed cemented into place, not allowing any bolt holes for escaping soldiers. The younglings eyed him curiously but continued to dine.

The living anvil descended again. The powerful jaws seized the soldier. Once again, Kirov was yanked into the air. This time he was shaken savagely back and forth. Pain and fear lashed him into alertness. A corner of his brain guessed that the mother monster was still trying to tenderize her children's food. *Two can play that game!*

Kirov's arm flashed to the attack, plunging his bayonet

deep into the monster's eye. The creature screamed. The slender blade had pierced its brain.

Dying, the giant bird whipped its neck, releasing Kirov to fly through the air high above the canyon floor. He soared through a short arc and hung momentarily suspended by the interplay of gravity and momentum. His body cartwheeled slowly in the cold air.

All around him flashed the wind-sculpted stone of the canyon and mountain walls. A thousand meters below him, the canyon floor waited. He could see green vegetation and a blue river. He was surrounded by more giant birds circling the nest. Apparently, the monster had a large family.

His brief truce with gravity was over. Kirov began to fall towards the distant canyon floor. He was out of tricks and feints. The young Russian resigned himself to exploring the Great Unknown.

But before he could fall below the level of the giant bird's nest, he was seized by more claws. *Not again!* Another bird, this one a dull black color, had snatched him out of the air.

To Kirov's surprise, he heard a human voice. He looked away from his captor to see another great black bird flying beside him. On its back was a man clad in feathers and carrying weapons on leather belts. He was seated in a leather saddle, attached by bird-sized belts to the avian torso.

The birdrider gestured towards the bird carrying Kirov away from the monster's nest and shouted something in an alien language. Kirov looked up and saw a beautiful brown-haired woman peering at him between wing beats.

It was all too much. Kirov fainted.

*Chapter Five*

## THE ROOST OF THE BLACK BIRDRIDERS

Again, Kirov awoke to pain. This time, at least, he was lying on something soft and the noises in his head were human voices and birdsongs. He breathed deeply, eyes closed, enjoying the sensation of being back in the barracks at Zarovitch Island.

*Birdsongs?* Fear of another monster avian lanced into his brain. Kirov jerked fully awake and looked around wildly.

He was lying on a bed in a cage-like enclosure made of wooden slats. A few simple furnishings suggested that it was someone's room rather than a jail cell. He cautiously sat up.

His motion aroused the attention of a young woman seated near a doorway. She arose and spoke to him in a language full of monosyllables. When he didn't respond, she shook her head and stepped through the doorway.

As his head cleared, Kirov realized that he knew the language. It was Pellucidarian. He'd studied it, Capronan and English at the University of Leningrad as part of his training as a paleontologist. Since the American adventurer Burroughs had reported the existence of living dinosaurs, all serious paleontologists learned Pellucidarian and Capronan in order to communicate with the humans of those lands. And English to read Burroughs' accounts in the original.

The young woman returned, escorting another woman. The first young lady was pretty; the second was beautiful. Both were slender, athletic brunettes. The first was clad in a simple shift-like garment of brown feathers. The second wore a cling-ing dress of glossy black feathers ornamented with white feathers on her bodice and in her hair. A chunk of raw gold was suspended from her shapely neck.

The second woman eyed Kirov carefully for a moment and then gestured to her escort. "He does not look dangerous to me, Flana. You may leave."

"Yes, Ala." Flana bowed and left.

Ala resumed appraising the young Russian.

Kirov attempted to frame a flowery greeting but was balked by the simplicity of the Pellucidarian language. He settled for saying, "Great woman, I thank you for rescuing me from the great green birds. I am Mikhail Kirillivitch Kirov of the Red War Party." Pellucidarian had no word for *Army*.

Ala eyed Kirov curiously. "Where are the hunting grounds of the Red War Party? Why have you come to the Mountains of the Birds and the territory of the Black Birdriders?"

Kirov replied, "The Red War Party guards the lands of the Soviet Tribe in Pellucidar and far beyond. We hunt for enemies of the Soviet People including an evil war chief, Edgar Rice Burroughs. When we find them, we will take them to our great chief Josef Stalin for trial. I am here because a great green bird captured me and brought me to her nest to feed her young. I come to the land of the Black Birdriders in peace."

Ala's beautiful brow furrowed as Kirov spoke. "Will the Red War Party invade the Mountains of the Birds?" Her breathing quickened.

Kirov thought a moment before answering. Soviet leaders seldom included ordinary soldiers in their plans. Until now, he had no idea that the Mountains of the Birds existed, or where they were, much less Comrade Stalin's plans for them. Better to play it safe and declare peaceful intentions. "No. The Red War Party is far away hunting for our enemies. We will never invade the Mountains of the Birds." He showed his most diplomatic smile.

"Good," pronounced Ala. "Since the Red War Party cannot protect you, you are my slave."

## Chapter Six

## I WILL NOT BE A SLAVE!

Once Kirov recovered from wounds, he was put to work in Tralsi, the village of the Black Birdriders. His first set of wounds was a series of deep cuts and batterings inflicted by the *skals*, as he learned the giant green, treelike birds were called. His second set had been inflicted by Ala's thugs when he protested her decision.

No Russian was afraid of work and, in some ways, it was easier than working in his father's shop before he had entered the University. Pellucidar's sun hung eternally overhead, making time meaningless. The Black Birdriders and their slaves ate, slept and woke when their bodies told them to do so or when Ala needed their services. As long as the slaves obeyed orders and got their work done, the guards were inclined to allow them to work at their own pace. From time to time, Ala's elite guards would inspect the work and it was best to labor especially diligently. When they moved on, life returned to normal.

The Black Birdriders numbered several hundred warriors, and their families. They were the elite of Pellucidarian life and frequently told each other and their slaves exactly that. The men trained their giant black birds known as *trals*, manufactured weapons from parts made by the slaves, and hunted beasts and other humans, capturing some and killing many. The women prepared food gathered from the Plain of Grazers below Tralsi, made clothes, supervised their homes, and raised the children. Both sexes gave orders to the thousand or so slaves.

The slaves did all the heavy work apart from hunting game. They cleaned houses, carried loads, and manufactured many of the simple wood, stone and leather tools that the Black Birdriders used. No slave was armed. Ala's thugs had confiscated Kirov's boot knife. They had allowed him his warm Soviet Red Army uniform and spare bullets. The young Russian sardonically told his captors that the metal cylinders were good luck charms. One of the guards thought himself a wit and noted that they hadn't done Kirov any good. But the birdrider allowed the new slave to keep his "charms."

Kirov noted that the fleeing monarchists had obviously never penetrated this far into Pellucidar. Wherever "this far" was....

Tralsi itself stood on a proud promontory jutting outward from Val Kan (Bold Beak), one of the Mountains of the Birds. The village was a natural fortress overlooking the endless Plain of Grazers forty meters below. Like all Pellucidarian landscapes, the plain curved onward and upward until it faded into the misty distance.

Whenever he could take time from his chores, Kirov gazed outward searching for a rescue party from Kandinsky's regiment (or any other Soviet unit). Animals of various types grazed the pale green grass and oddly beautiful flowers and drank from the tiny streams threading the land. From his vantage point, Kirov recognized antelope, mammoths, mastodons, and many other species extinct for thousands of years in the Outer World. They lived, moved, fought and died in Nature's endless circle of life, passing to and fro before Kirov's searching eyes. But no Soviet feet crossed the landscape. No Red Banners shouted rescue. Kirov glumly returned to his work.

A slave could be called on to perform any task any Black Birdrider wanted done. As a newcomer, Kirov was assigned to the least pleasant tasks including carrying away the community's trash and hauling crudely cut logs to and fro. The Black Birdriders lived in wooden houses, not caves, as Senior Starshina Viotinuik had thought, and used wooden tools. They used enough timber that Kirov was kept busy.

The bare mountain rock that supported Tralsi allowed no

trees to take root. When the birdriders needed wood, they mounted a specialized hunting party to a small forest growing on the plain far below their town. A work party of slaves was assembled. The trals, or great black birds from which the tribe took its name, were brought forth and harnessed. The giant avians seemed tame enough under their handlers' hands but when a slave got too close, savage beaks pecked at him. He skittered back, dropping a load of tackle as he did. Ala's male war-chief, Ulu, barked an order and a guard's fist smashed the slave's face in punishment. The other slaves grumbled but dared nothing under Ulu's eyes. The struck slave glared at the guards darkly, his face reddening, but said nothing. He picked up the tackle and resumed his place.

The birdriders saddled their own birds, checking their lashings carefully, and mounted up. They had the same élan as pilots in the Red Air Force. Ulu shouted directions. One "wing" of five birds took off for the forest to scout for enemies. Another wing followed with baskets made of leather ropes and filled with tools. Finally it was the slaves' turn. Muttering all the time, they carried giant baskets to the edge of the plateau, then climbed into the baskets and crouched down, two per basket. Slender Kirov was paired with an amiable giant named Dyryth. The trals hopped to the edge of the cliff and dived off. Wings beating fiercely, they flew down and then up, circling around over Tralsi. As they passed low over the town, their pilots guided them with piercing voices and handslaps on their necks and heads. One by one, the trals passed over the baskets and snatched them off the cliff.

Burdened by the weight of three men, the trals glided rather than flew to the forest. Their pilots guided them expertly. Just before the slaves' baskets would have crashed into the loamy soil, the great pinions beat frantically and the slaves arrived on the outskirts of the small forest more or less intact.

One of Ulu's lieutenants formed the slaves up in a compact mass with armed birdrider infantry on all four sides. They

walked together until they reached the trees selected for timber-
ing.

Kirov and the other slaves were issued stone axes and directed to cut enough timber to satisfy Ala's requirements. A
thin cordon of birdrider guards screened the workers, facing
alternately inward and outward. Several times, trals came and
went carrying food and water for the workers and their guards.

On this occasion, Ala seemed to need a great deal of timber.
The slaves slept twice and ate four times before Ulu was satisfied with the number of trees cut down and then trimmed into
logs of more or less uniform length. The guards and slaves used
some of the smaller branches as firewood to burn their food
into greater palatability or to make simple huts to shield themselves from the constant glare of the tiny sun and the frequent
gusts of chill air entering Pellucidar from the North Polar
Opening.

Once Ulu was satisfied they had enough, he directed the
slaves to haul a log away from the pile to an open space on the
plain where the trals could reach it. Many leather ropes or
straps were attached to it and the slaves directed to stand back.
An entire squadron of trals descended to the plain near the log
and seized leather ropes in their claws. On a signal, the flock
rose in unison and beat slowly upward, carrying the log back
to Tralsi.

While the trals were imitating cranes, the slaves were
marched back to the pile and ordered to move another log to
the landing area. The trals were still somewhere out of sight,
presumably in Tralsi. Ulu allowed the slaves to rest until the
birds returned.

Dyryth flopped down in place and appeared to go to sleep.
Kirov sat wearily down on the log. He glanced at the placid
giant.

"Dyryth, why are you a slave?" asked the Russian.

The giant opened a sleepy eye. "Birdriders capture Dyryth
on Plain of Grazers." He gestured vaguely at the plain sur-

rounding the forest. "Dyryth not able to escape from birdrid-ers."

"Why can't you escape from the birdriders?" asked Kirov softly. His head bowed but his eyes took in his surroundings carefully. He had not become a prize student at the University based on family connections.

"They always watching," mumbled Dyryth sleepily. He rolled over.

Kirov cautiously raised his head. The slaves seemed to be sleeping or resting while the guards were watching for the trals to return from Tralsi. *I will not be a slave*, he thought. He looked around, hefted his stone axe, and rose to his feet. He quietly walked towards the pile of cut timber, his casual manner suggesting that nothing was unusual. Once past the pile, he bolted for the forest. Only the soft calls of Pellucidar's strange birds and animals marked his escape.

THE FOREST WAS NOT very large, only a few hundred meters across, but it provided concealment for the escaping Russian. The trees seemed to be evergreens of some sort. They smelled like pine trees as well as looking like them. Vividly recalling the slaughter of Borski's platoon by the skals, Kirov was cautious about approaching any supposed tree too closely. He zigzagged through the woods, avoiding stepping on roots or obvious twigs. Either might be skal feet. He stopped at the far edge of the wood.

He studied the Plain of Grazers quickly but carefully. He was tired but the prospect of freedom spurred him on. Black Bird Roost was behind him; before him were the limitless possibilities of the Inner World. American adventurers had flocked here for fame and fortune. Even their cowboy President Roosevelt had established a colony out there somewhere. Kirov had long planned to come himself (although as a distinguished scientist rather than a fugitive slave). He plunged forward, into freedom.

*Chapter Seven*

## A DEADLY GAME OF TAG

The Soviet advance into Novy Mir had temporarily halted on the ridge that the soldiers had privately labeled Borski's Blunder. Regiment Commander Kandinsky had relieved the unfortunate platoon commander and dispatched him back to Siberia and the tender mercies of higher command. More men were already on their way. But a stop would give the riflemen a rest and the engineers a chance to build a fortified position on the site of the former monarchist fort and make other improvements. The position was now called Fort Alinsky after some obscure Revolutionary hero.

Inside the packed earth ramparts, Kandinsky was unhappy with his intelligence officer. He sighed audibly.

"Comrade Battalion Commander Garman. Do you have any idea where the monarchists have disappeared to? They moved several thousands of people from Siberia into Novy Mir. Yet all we have found are burned forts and wagon tracks. Surely you and the scouts have found some trace of the enemy forces."

Ivan Garman was a plain-faced man from the Finnish border region whose ordinary appearance belied the brain inside. "No, Comrade. We have not yet located them. Their wagon tracks continue further south, apparently across the plain. The scouts explored three days march ahead and then returned to base for rest. The tracks still led onward to the south."

He continued, "Have we been supplied with horses? Or even reconnaissance balloons?"

Kandinsky grunted. "No. We have been promised further

supplies but for the moment we are dependent on what men can carry."

Garman nodded. "Then I propose that we equip a special scouting party to press as far forward as they can along the wagon trail and make contact with the fleeing monarchists."

Kandinsky grunted again. "Yes. Prepare your party. We must find the enemies of the State as soon as possible and kill or capture them. We cannot allow our enemies to wander around Novy Mir plotting trouble."

There was a brief silence broken by Deputy Regiment Commander Drobanin asking, "Comrade, do we have orders concerning the other enemies of the State, the Americans in their foolish 'New America' to our east?" He gestured in what he thought was the right direction.

Kandinsky paused before answering. "They will be dealt with when the time comes," he said blandly. The other Soviets knew what he meant.

THE LEFT FLANK of Kandinsky's spearhead into Pellucidar was directed by Company Commander E. Marakov. His company was camped between Fort Alinsky proper and a forest sloping upward towards a distant plateau. When he learned that Borski's platoon had been destroyed by giant birds disguised as trees, he ordered his men to use the nearest trees as target practice. Not only was it good training but it prevented any giant "treebirds" from sneaking up on his company. Marakov was well pleased with himself.

Deep in the forest being fired upon by Marakov's men, Edgar Rice Burroughs of Richmond, Virginia, grinned. The racket the Soviets were making covered up a multitude of things. Pardan and he had located a giant cave bear's lair in the caves pocking the plateau that the Soviets hadn't yet investigated. Waiting until the bear was well outside his home, they had taken turns shooting him. Both crack shots, either Pardan or he could have killed the prehistoric giant with one carefully aimed bullet. If their Springfields didn't do the job, Burroughs packed an express rifle for Pellucidar's truly large game.

But the two men weren't hunting cave bears. They were hunting Soviets. Their carefully aimed shots stung the bear, enraging it, while the noise of their rifles attracted its attention. Maddened, it lumbered to attack.

For all its size, the cave bear of northern Pellucidar moved with the speed of a charging bull. Normally, it would have overhauled any two humans and made a short meal of the interlopers. But Burroughs was of the opinion that the cave bear was the most dangerous predator in the entire Inner World, even more so than the dinosaurs of southern Perryland. So, he ran for a previously hung rope ladder and scurried up into a tree too big for the bear to climb, push over or tear apart. When the bruin stopped to concentrate on how to get its intended meal out of the tree, the younger man trotted to a new position deeper in the forest. From there, he fired, stinging the bear's flank. Again the bruin charged…. The human fled, boldly luring the animal closer to Fort Alinsky and Marakov's company. When he heard the ursinoid getting close, he went up a second tree like his simian relatives.

The deadly game of tag ended when the bruin came close enough to the Soviets to hear their gunfire and decide that he had finally run his tormentors to ground. He charged out of the forest….

Burroughs and Pardan watched the epic battle of bear and men from the relative safety of the woods. They left before the battered Soviets learned that cave bears have families. Large, vengeful families.

*Chapter Eight*

## KA-GODA?

**K**irov jogged across the vast plain, every step leaving Ulu's Forest— a name that he had just invented—and Black Bird Roost further behind him. His heart sang with joy. Even so, he watched carefully as he ran. The adventurers Innes and Perry had vividly described Pellucidar's multitude of dangers in their reports. Fortunately, the wild life in this part of the Inner World seemed to be limited to field mice and specimens of *eohippus*, ancestors of the modern horse but no bigger than fox terriers. They scampered away from the fleeing human, glad of their tiny lives.

The young Russian continued running away from Tralsi and Ulu's Forest as long as he could. The weariness caused by long hours cutting wood seemed to have vanished with the prospect of freedom. Finally, he came to a creek cutting through the rolling plain and stopped to rest. He flopped down in the tall grass and lapped up water like a dog. He didn't realize that fierce eyes rested on his form.

Satiated, replete with water, Kirov rolled over on his back to rest. Lightning shot through his brain. High in the sapphire sky, a flock of ebony trals sailed in his direction.

Energy suddenly restored, Kirov leaped to his feet and bolted to his right, seeking sanctuary somewhere, anywhere, on the open plain. As he pounded across the landscape, he clutched his stolen stone axe. If he had to make a last stand.... Heroic thoughts of Alexander Nevsky and other defenders of Old Russia rose in his mind.

Running desperately up a slight rise in the ground, he tried to look behind himself to see if the Black Birdriders were closing in. As he crested the rise, he hit something soft and tripped, spilling his abused body across the obstacle and the Pellucidarian landscape.

Frantically, he twisted himself into an upright sitting position. The obstacle was a young woman and a saddled giant brown bird. She had been seated on the animal, crouched down, hidden in the tall grass. Kirov had apparently taken her by surprise and knocked her off the avian's back. She was attempting to untangle herself from the Russian's legs. The bird clucked and similar clucks sounded from the concealing grass around them.

He thought quickly, *The birdriders ambushed me! One wing flew overhead to herd me into the trap while a second wing waited for me!*

Determined not to be retaken easily, he lashed out, kicking the birdrider's pretty chin. She grunted and fell backwards against her clucking mount. She slid into a prone position and lay still.

Kirov's first impulse was to help his fallen foe but he quickly decided that escape was more important than chivalry. He staggered to a half-standing position and threw his leg over the bird's saddle. He slapped the bird's neck as he had seen Ulu's men do.

The bird didn't seem inclined to take orders. It squawked loudly and lurched upright. It shrieked again even more loudly as Kirov slid off its back and fell heavily to the ground. Pellucidarian saddles had no saddle horns or stirrups. Unless your feet and body were strapped to the saddle, you were dependent on your sense of balance.

The bird pecked at Kirov, who dodged wildly. He'd had enough of that mistreatment in the *skal's* nest. He gathered himself, twisted into a fighting posture, and waved his axe in a circle, trying to keep the belligerent bird from pecking him to death.

A sudden pain stabbed through Kirov's brain followed by blackness.

When he came to, he was lying face down, his hands bound behind him. The back of his skull ached mightily. He looked up to see a rough circle of Pellucidarians dressed in brown feathers surrounding him and the young woman that he had knocked down. Two guards were watching him. Both faces were contorted in anger. Another man was speaking urgently to the young woman. Her face and the faces of the others were anxiously scanning the sky.

Kirov saw a tral cruise overhead. He recognized the bird-rider in the jet black feathers as Ala. Above him, more trals circled, their riders holding spears ready.

"Ka-goda?!" shouted the queen of Tralsi. *Do you surrender?* in Pellucidarian.

"We must," whispered the young woman in obvious agony.

"No!" stormed a man, like the woman, clad in brown feathers.

"We must," she repeated. She gestured vaguely towards Kirov's prone body as she studied the sky. "He found us and led them to us. There are too many flying birdriders to fight."

She looked upward at the circling trals. "Ka-goda!" she shouted and dropped her spear. *We surrender.* Her warriors angrily stabbed their spears into the earth.

In a thunder of wings, the Black Birdriders descended on the scene, spear tips glinting in the sun. The black clad warriors formed a circle surrounding their captives.

Eyes gleaming, Ala slipped from her saddle with the dignity of the semi-legendary warrior Empress Catherine the Great. She surveyed the scene, taking in the surrendered warriors and their captive lying on the ground. She first addressed herself to the brown clad woman.

"Well, Lal, I have you at last." Ala's smile was more poisonous than ten vipers. Her captive returned a tightlipped silence, shoulders slumped in despair.

The triumphant queen turned to the bound Kirov. "Well done, slave. I will punish you for attempting to escape. However, it will be a light punishment because you led us to my most dangerous enemy, the chief of the Dyal Riders."

*Chapter Nine*

## THE WIZARD OF PELLUCIDAR

Ala was true to her word. Kirov's punishment for attempting to escape was relatively light—only one guard beat him brutally instead of many. He withstood it as manfully as he could. He had already learned that open resistance merely brought further punishment.

What was worse was the attitude of Lal's warriors. They blamed him for their captivity and, more importantly, for Lal's. One sleep period, he awoke suddenly and painfully to find many fists pounding on him. In timeless Pellucidar there was no way to tell how long he was dead to the world but when he awoke he was ravenously hungry. He guessed that days had gone by while his brutalized body had slowly healed. His dreams had been full of pain, sometimes caused by men's fists, sometimes caused by skals' beaks.

He also found that Ulu had promoted him to toolmaker and given Lal's men his former assignments as trash haulers and lumbermen. All of Lal's men had black and blue faces. Kirov didn't ask how that had happened. Instead he concentrated on his new job. Only Dyryth dropped by his new workspace to chat at odd moments and relay news of the other slaves.

The American adventurers Innes and Perry had described most Pellucidarians as Stone Age cavemen. Kirov's academic classes in anthropology had taught him the fallacy of assuming that "stone age" meant that every tool was made of stone and nothing but stone. The Black Birdriders used wood, bone and leather tools extensively. Their black-feathered costumes were glued to leather undergarments. They lived in log cabins built directly on the naked rock of the mountain promontory jutting outward from Val Kan mountain. Thick walls and constant fires protected them from the cold air rushing into the Inner World through the North Polar Opening.

Shortly before Ala's birdriders had captured Kirov, fire had destroyed several homes in their village. Kirov's first job upon recovering was to help trim logs to build cabins including carefully notching them so that they would fit solidly together. As he sweated to shape logs with stone axes and then move them into position, the young Russian began to study his captors.

The notched logs fitted together poorly. The Black Birdriders had never invented daubing to fill in the resulting gaps in their walls. So hearth fires needed to burn constantly, requiring a great deal of wood and therefore a great many slaves to maintain the comfort of the master class. Once the first new cabin was erected and roofed with logs, Kirov was drafted to move furniture to suit the opinions of the lady of the house. As he did so, he observed the man of the house pile small branches on the naked rock and lit them with a brand borrowed from a neighbor. The fire caught and burned merrily in a natural hollow in the center of the room, the smoke rising to leave the cabin through a hole in the roof. Around the fire pit, sawdust covered the floor in place of the rugs that the Birdriders had never invented.

When Kirov returned to his workplace, he rounded up all the stones that he could find and built a walled fire pit for his own hearth. When a slave delivered more wood, the Russian noticed that the slave unloaded it sloppily only a pace or so away from the flames. Many Russians did no more work than strictly necessary. Kirov told the slave to stack the wood in the corner of the room away from the fire pit.

"Why?" asked the slave. Kirov recalled that his name was Rell. "More work to fetch wood from corner to fire."

"But safer," rejoined Kirov. "Fire can't escape from a fire pit. Fire can't burn down the house if it can't reach any other wood."

Rell was puzzled by the thought but complied.

Thus began the career of Pellucidar's Wizard of Oz.

Like L. Frank Baum's Wizard, Kirov was really importing ideas created elsewhere, not truly inventing new things. But, like Baum's Ozians, the natives couldn't tell the difference.

Once Kirov began thinking in terms of more than simple survival, ideas occurred faster and faster.

The use of primitive tools to cut and shape wood left a great deal of sawdust and other debris lying around Tralsi, especially in the houses and workplaces. Most Black Birdriders and their slaves simply walked on the sawdust and kicked the chips out of the way. A fire hazard even if the humans didn't build their fires *on* the sawdust and debris. Kirov tied some tral feathers to a conveniently sized branch and invented the broom.

At first he fed the wood chips into the fire but a cold gust of air inspired him to begin chinking shut the gaps in his workshop walls. He hunted up more wood chips in his off time despite the hoots of laughter from the other slaves.

Rell was the first person to notice that Kirov's workplace was warmer than the other buildings and began loitering when he delivered firewood. The slave toolmakers were assigned individual cabins to work in, perhaps because Ala had realized that separating the slaves from each other made conspiracies against the masters more difficult. A slave master named Oyo made rounds constantly to ensure that the slaves worked diligently and stole no weapon parts. Since Kirov was always busy, even during his allowed rest periods, Oyo spent very little time inspecting the young Russian and more time shouting at the apparent slackers among the other slaves. Rell's firewood deliveries took long enough for him to realize the difference between Kirov's cabin and the others.

"Why is your work place warm when other houses are cold?" asked the puzzled slave. "Your fire is no bigger than others."

Kirov smiled and put down the ax heads he was chipping. His academic training had proved surprisingly useful. "I closed the holes in the walls. Heat stays inside better." He grinned with pride.

Rell studied the chinked walls carefully. "Why does heat stay with you but not stay with Rell or others?"

"Heat wants to be free," Kirov paraphrased his secondary school physics to suit the Pellucidarian vocabulary. "All walls trap heat and make heat escape slowly. My walls trap heat better. Heat escapes very slowly from here."

Rell nodded his head in agreement. He might not understand thermodynamic insulation efficiency but he understood the concept of hunting and trapping better than another man. He studied Kirov's workplace, especially the walls, until Oyo found him apparently idle and shouted that lazy slaves would be beaten.

Kirov was already busy inventing the wheel.

Of course, the man from the Outer World already knew what a wheel was. The challenges were, first, building a true wheel with the primitive tools at hand and, second, finding a use for one. Both processes were delayed by Kirov's assignment to produce ax heads and other, more traditional tools but he persevered.

Kirov settled on chipping a cross section of a log into a relatively thin slice and then cutting a hole through the middle. His progress was impeded by the fact that no Pellucidarian had invented a drill and no Black Birdrider trusted a slave with a knife. Finally he chipped and sanded his way to success. He spent some time just rolling it back and forth across the floor of his workplace in celebration.

What to do with his "invention" was suggested by Rell. Each waking period, the slave trudged around Tralsi carrying firewood for the voracious hearths of the Black Birdriders and their slaves.

Kirov started with one of the boxy containers that the birdriders' slaves used to carry water and loose items. He placed it on its side and set Tralsi's first wheel next to it. Then he began the long task for chipping handles and supports out of branches. When he had shaped them as well as he could, he tied the results together with wet rawhide ropes. When the rawhide finished drying, the construction was as solid as the young inventor could make it with the technology at hand. He tested it by moving loads of firewood and hand axes around his workplace. He had to rebuild the handles and wheel supports several times before he was satisfied. The ungreased wheel squealed like a wounded pig but Pellucidar's first wheelbarrow was born.

When the slave toolmakers finished five of anything, they were supposed to carry the resulting production to a central storehouse guarded by a guard detail of Black Birdriders. Once Kirov was satisfied that the wheelbarrow would do its job, he loaded his regular production of ax heads and other tools into his new invention and wheeled over to the relatively large building that he thought of as the Arsenal.

"What is that thing?" demanded one of the guards, eying it curiously.

"A *wheelbarrow*," responded the young Wizard airily. He used the Russian term since Pellucidarian had no words for *wheel* or *barrow*. "It's like a carrying box only better."

"I have never seen a 'wheelbarrow' before." The native eyed the contraption suspiciously.

"Of course, not. This is the first wheelbarrow in all of Pellucidar," proclaimed Kirov breezily. He suspected that the American adventurer Innes had introduced wheelbarrows in the latter's Empire of Pellucidar but that nation was at least seven thousand kilometers away. No Black Birdrider was likely to challenge his declaration. Or want to challenge it. "Only the Black Birdriders have a wheelbarrow to make work easier."

The guards were typical of the master class of Tralsi. They swelled with pride at the recognition of their national superiority. "Yes, only the Black Birdriders have a 'wheelbarrow'," agreed the guard. He mangled the pronunciation but Kirov simply nodded in agreement with the birdrider's sagacity. As the old Russian saying had it, *Flattery will get you anything*.

Slaves didn't enter the Arsenal freely. The proud guard signaled Kirov to enter and followed him in. Ala's lieutenant in charge of the central tool store also challenged the ungainly invention. The guard answered before Kirov could speak. "This is a wheelbarrow. It is the greatest wheelbarrow in all of Pellucidar. Only the Black Birdriders have one." The guard's attitude suggested that he had invented it personally.

The lieutenant eyed the contraption warily but its resemblance to an ordinary box of things allayed suspicions.

"Very good. You, unload the axes." He gestured at Kirov. The latter obeyed quickly. He smiled as he worked. The differences between the humans of the Inner and Outer Worlds were less than many people imagined.

On the way back to his workplace, Kirov encountered Rell making his rounds with an armload of firewood.

"Rell," announced the ebullient Russian. "This is a *wheelbarrow*. It can make your work *much* easier."

The tired slave gave his full attention to Pellucidar's first wheelbarrow salesman.

The Great Wheelbarrow Revolution was underway before any member of Tralsi's master class realized it.

Rell had already seen that Kirov could trap heat and live more comfortably than other slaves could. He was therefore receptive to Kirov's salesmanship about the wheelbarrow. He tried moving loads of firewood using the strange contraption. Soon enough, Rell was an advocate. Other slaves asked about it and Rell explained that the device helped him accomplish his assigned work more quickly and easily. Once his work had been accomplished, he had more time to himself. Rell was proud to loan it out and to instruct others in the mysteries of its use. The original wheelbarrow was soon in constant use. Slaves began dropping by Kirov's workplace to ask if they could have warm walls and more wheelbarrows. Like human beings everywhere, they gossiped about many things as well as work.

Oyo noticed the sudden popularity of Kirov's place and intervened. The crowd dispersed at his shouting. He demanded, "Why are the slaves hanging around your workplace?"

"They wish to work easier and live better. They want more wheelbarrows. With wheelbarrows, the slaves can move firewood, tools, trash and other things more easily. Only the Black Birdriders have wheelbarrows," replied the young salesman. "And they enjoy the warmth in my workplace." His tone was very bland.

Oyo was not convinced about the mysterious devices and ordered the young Wizard back to producing more conventional tools. But he also began checking up on the slaves' use of the wheelbarrows that Kirov had already produced. And his attention had been drawn to the fact that Kirov's workplace was warmer than those of the other slave toolmakers.

A few sleeps later, Oyo brought word that Ala's war-chief, Ulu, wanted to see Kirov.

Now.

As Kirov began walking towards the building that he called the "Palace", he grinned at the comparison with the Czar's Winter Palace in Leningrad. Ala's royal residence was simply a large log cabin, twice as wide and long as the average Tralsi building and twice as tall. The upper story had small windows cut into the logs to allow spears to be thrown at attacking monsters or uprising slaves. Heavy logs formed the roof and overhung the sides. But the building was a true palace: it projected a confident air of strength, security and command. For all of their arrogance, the Black Birdriders had genuine accomplishments in building and fortification to boost of. No human enemy had ever stormed Tralsi and, if Ala had anything to say about it, none ever would.

Kirov approached the royal fortress, where he saw Ulu outside the building, scowling at him.

Danger waited ahead of him.

And above him.

As he approached, Kirov heard a scream followed by thunderous squawking. His head jerked upward as shadows eclipsed the eternal Pellucidarian sun. Skals—the great green birds of his nightmares—were attacking Tralsi.

*Chapter Ten*

## A NIGHTMARE IN BROAD DAYLIGHT

The Black Birdriders trusted no slave with weapons and Kirov had no thought of fighting the aerial monsters with his bare hands. He dove for cover in the angle formed between a log cabin and the bare stone on which Tralsi stood. Landing suddenly on hard mountain rock reminded him painfully of the abuse that he had already suffered.

The deadly skals swooped down from high above, hurtling through the streets of Tralsi. Great claws snatched up human and avian prey alike. The trals were big enough and strong enough to put up good fights against the larger predators, but the smaller humans were easier prey. Often a skal would grab two humans before sweeping upward, en route to nests in the Mountains of Birds. Whole families of skals would shortly dine well.

Kirov looked upward. He tried to watch in five or six directions at once lest a skal attack him from behind. Fortunately, none of the ungainly monsters seemed interested in forcing its great green body into the confined space next to the building. Not when fleeing slaves and overconfident masters could be snatched up from open areas so much more easily.

As the young Russian watched, he realized that trals carrying Black Birdriders were appearing from a point high up on Val Kan mountain. The great birds leapt outward from the mountain, circled and descended to counterattack the raiders.

Revelation struck Kirov like lightning. *That was how the Black Birdriders spotted his attempted escape! And the advance of Lal's Dyal Riders across the Plain of Grazers! A hidden observation post and outwork!* The upward curvature of Pellucidar's landscape would only make spying on those below all the easier. Ala's military security skills were better than he had thought.

Encouraged by Ulu's shouted orders, the warriors of Tralsi rallied. Spears and stone axes flashed upward, seeking skal vitals. Many weapons fell back to earth harmlessly, unable to reach the huge targets circling above the mountain town. Other spears, cast from above, missed as well. One spear crashed to ground centimeters from Kirov's nose. Startled, he grabbed it and jerked back deeper into the shadow of the log cabin. Other spears passed over the edges of the ledge on which Tralsi stood, clattering down to the Plain of the Grazers far below. The airborne cavalry were scoring some hits on the great green monsters but not many. The skals' ability to withstand damage was frightening.

Ulu screamed more orders, underlining them with waves of his spear. A dozen or more Black Birdriders raced for the Arsenal to snatch up more weapons. Slaves raced towards the Palace to reach relative safety behind its impressive walls. Kirov suddenly realized why the Birdriders went to the trouble of building log cabins rather than the woven grass huts described by the American adventurer Perry. Timbered walls and roofs protected the inhabitants better than flimsy grass mats.

A vast shadow swept low over the plaza. A green colossus landed there clumsily, its vast wings flailing the timbered roofs of the surrounding log cabins. The golden anvil of its head dipped towards Ala's lieutenant, doubly conspicuous by his upright stance and wigwagging arms.

Ulu stabbed upward with his spear. The colossal avian's jaws closed on the wooden stick and yanked it from his hands. Pulled forward, Ulu fell to the ground as if worshiping some colossal demon god. The bird's head reared upward, its jaws splintering the spear's shaft. It spat out matchsticks. The skal's head rotated, again seeking more palatable prey. Its eye fell upon the prostrate Ulu.

The Birdrider staggered to his feet, his hand unsteadily

pulling his knife from its thong. From his vantage point behind the skal, Kirov saw fear in Ulu's eyes....

Just then, a female clad in the brown feathers of slavery raced across the plaza, near the royal wall, frantically seeking the hoped for safety of the regal doorway. The avian head jerked sideways, its eye attracted by the motion.

Ulu saw the skal's attention shift. His eyes narrowed. Before the woman could pass behind him and enter the palace, he whirled and seized her with his free hand. Brutally, he pushed her in front of him, a human sacrifice for the giant's appetite. The golden anvil descended, jaws gaping....

Kirov took in the tableau within a heartbeat. Without thinking, he was on his feet, spear in hand. No one would mistake the slender young paleontologist for a heroic warrior, such as Alexander Nevsky or Peter Romanov, but he had been raised on stories of Russian chivalry and valor. He was compelled to act. He thrust the spear deep into the skal's bowels.

Deeply stung by the unexpected stabbing blow, the colossal avian screamed like wounded thunder. Its head jerked upward, venting its rage against the amethyst sky. It turned quickly, surprisingly so for its mighty size. The movement yanked the spear from Kirov's hands, and savagely twisted the weapon inside its own body. The writhing monster smashed the young Russian into the wall that he had been crouching beside. It spun its gigantic head around, seeking its tormentor and finding Kirov lying crumpled in a heap, stunned and helpless.

*Without thinking, he was on his feet, spear in hand... He was compelled to act. He thrust the spear deep into the skal's bowels.*

*Chapter Eleven*

## GOOD RUSSIAN STEEL

C omrade Senior Starshina, another flight of *birnam* birds is coming towards us," stated the lookout calmly. He didn't lower his binoculars as he reported. "From the mountains again."

"Very good, Alexsei. We'll show these slow learners what good Russian steel and powder can do," grinned Senior Starshina Voitinuik. He took a quick look at the dots winging their way toward the Soviet position from the nameless mountains to their east. Then he bellowed at the various gunners dug in along what was now called Russian Ridge. (The enlisted men still called it Borski's Blunder when the officers weren't present.) As a formality, he notified the Company Commander commanding the defenses.

The latest battle between the Soviet forces and the great emerald skals was short and brutal. Engineers had been improving the fortified position surrounding the old monarchist fort since Kandinsky's regiment had occupied it. A graveled road capable of bearing heavy traffic ran northward to what was now called Bogrov Town—the Soviet beachhead in the Inner World. Trucks and mule trains brought in more equipment and supplies constantly.

The former monarchist fort had been built up into a major installation overlooking the rolling Plutonian Plain before it. Artillery commanded all the approaches and any attacker would have to penetrate rings of barbed wire, machine gun nests and rifle pits.

Overhead, great green "treebirds" intended to dine on good

46

Russian flesh. Some scholar on Kandinsky's staff, ignorant of the Pellucidarian name, had labeled them birnam birds in honor of the moving trees of Shakespeare's *Macbeth*. No matter what they were called, this time the Soviets were prepared to meet them.

Antiaircraft guns thundered, flinging steel jacketed death upward to greet the avian monsters. Most of the skals died in the first minutes, flayed into bloody gibbets. A few managed to penetrate the curtain of shrapnel only to meet a hail of machine gun and rifle bullets. Red blood sprayed against the cerulean sky and giant bodies crashed to the ground, well outside the rings of barbed wire. Waiting rifle grenades were not needed.

Some skals survived.

Any flock of birds has some in front and some in back. Those fortunate skals in the rear witnessed their fellows dying amid fire and thunder. They screamed, wheeled and retreated, winging their way back to the mountain chain that the Soviets had not yet named. There must be easier prey elsewhere; perhaps on the far side of the Mountains of the Birds, where guns were unknown.

Senior Starshina Voitinuik waited until he was sure that the birnam birds had retreated back to the nameless mountains. Then he reported to Company Commander I.D. Grenov. "Sir—I mean, Comrade Company Commander, the flying monsters have been driven off once again. I estimate that we killed sixteen creatures. We suffered no losses ourselves. I will send parties out to recover the bodies for our cooks."

Grenov nodded as he gazed eastward. "Very good, Comrade Senior Starshina. I am sure that the Second and Third Battalions will appreciate some bird stew for a change." He smirked at the mountains looming in the distance. Dinosaurs or giant birds alike, Soviet power would defeat any threat. "I would like your assessment, Senior Starshina. Are the birnams likely to attack us again?"

"Company Commander, I would guess not. Since the

engineers have delivered these fine guns, we have shown these monsters what good Russian steel will do. Each attack has fewer monsters in it. I think that they have learned that Russians are not such easy prey as they once thought. I cannot be sure but I think that they will stay away from now on." He grinned.

Grenov looked at his senior enlisted man. "What about *you*, Starshina? A birnam *fell* on you in our first battle with them. Have you fully recovered?"

Voitinuik snorted and made a dismissive gesture. "Of course, I am, Company Commander. Bonaparte couldn't kill me at Borodino; the British couldn't kill me at Sevastopol; the Americans couldn't kill me at Murmansk; and no giant chicken will kill me in Pellucidar—I mean, *Novy Mir*." He thumped his massive chest proudly. Grenov nodded sagely.

OFF TO THE WEST of Fort Alinsky, working parties were chopping down the trees of the Bear Woods, so named for its former inhabitants, now hunted out by strong parties of heavily armed riflemen. Not only did the trees provide plenty of timber for fires and buildings, but the clearing process improved the fields of fire that any attacker would have to cross to reach the fortress. By dint of constant labor, the Soviets were improving their grip on the vast resources of the Inner World.

Their grip was still being contested, though. One hunting party had penetrated completely through the Bear Woods to discover a cave-pocked plateau above them. Cautiously, they began investigating the caves. They quickly discovered ample proof that the bears attacking the right flank of Kandinsky's pioneers had been living there. Fierce fusillades eliminated the young cave bears that had been left behind.

When the triumphant riflemen emerged from the caves, they were startled by the sound of thunder above them. Rocks catapulted outward from the top of the cliff and rumbled downhill at freight train speed. The startled hunters froze for a moment and then bolted in all directions. Most of them were too late to escape the avalanche. Those that did fled for their lives, leaping and bounding across the rocky terrain. They were cut down by the bullets of Springfield rifles fired from the cliff above.

When the sounds of death faded into the quiet of prehistoric Pellucidar, two men carefully stood up atop the cliff.

The shorter man grinned. "Much fun. Let us find more Soviets and ambush them." He gestured towards the Bear Woods.

The taller man shook his head. "No, Pardan. These tricks only work one time each. We killed a patrol. Soon an entire company will be here to investigate. We can't fight that many by ourselves." He looked outward and southward. The cliff top gave him an excellent vantage point to survey the seemingly endless Pellucidarian plain rolling onward beyond Fort Alinsky.

"It's time for us to rejoin the retreating Imperial Russian Army."


Kandinsky took Company Commander Grenov's report on the latest Soviet victory. "I agree with your assessment, Comrade. The birnams no longer present a significant threat to the Soviet occupation of Novy Mir."

He dismissed the Company Commander and turned to his senior staff. "Comrades, our current position in the Plutonian region of Novy Mir is secure. We have been amply reinforced. We already control lands equal in size to Poland or Scandinavia. We will now press forward to capture the fleeing monarchists and to add the lands between here and the Karl-Marx Ocean to the Soviet Union."

The members of his staff nodded in agreement.

*Chapter Twelve*

## AFTERMATH

Again, Kirov awoke to pain. This time at least he was lying on something soft and the noises in his head were human voices and birdsongs. He shook his head groggily. He'd had this dream before.

He opened his eyes. It wasn't a dream. He was back in Ala's palace, once again lying on a bed rather than a slave's grass pallet. Once again, the slave Flana was seated nearby, carefully watching him. When she realized that he was awake, she put her soft fingers over his lips and looked around cautiously. She had a huge bruise on her face.

"Be quiet," she whispered. Her musical voice was quiet but urgent. "I am supposed to call Ala when you awaken but I wanted to warn you about Ulu first. He says that he saved your life and my life from the skal. If Ala asks, tell her that."

Genuinely stupid people didn't survive long in the Worker's Paradise officially known as the Soviet Union. "I understand. Thank you for warning me."

Flana relaxed and smiled. "You saved me from the skal when Ulu tried to feed me to it. You are a brave man and a cunning hunter. Ulu says that he is the greatest hunter in all of Pellucidar but he is a liar. If his men had not attacked the skal from behind as it reached for you, we would all be dead. You attacked the great bird by yourself and wounded it deeply. Ulu did not wound the bird at all but claimed your spear as his own when his men asked. When I said that you had wounded the skal first, he hit me." She indicated her bruise. "When Ala asks, tell her that Ulu is a brave warrior."

"I will." Kirov relaxed, the party line firmly planted in his head. He closed his eyes and was asleep in seconds.

Flana smiled and turned to go. She paused and looked at the handsome young hero lying peacefully before her.

She smiled mysteriously as she rose to summon Ala.

WHEN ALA QUESTIONED Kirov about the skal raid, he stuck to the party line. He had witnessed Ulu fending off the monster with his spear until it was distracted by something or someone on the other side of its great green body. No, Kirov didn't know what had distracted the bird. Ulu had stabbed it and Kirov had been knocked out when its head swept around apparently seeking its tormentor. Yes, Kirov had seen a slave woman bump into Ulu when she attempted to escape the monster. Ulu had grabbed her to prevent her from falling into the monster's reach. No, Kirov had not seen the arrival of any other Black Birdriders; he assumed that Ulu had slain the skal by himself. Yes, Kirov thought that Ulu was a brave warrior.

Ala looked at Kirov coolly, but then nodded in apparent satisfaction. Before she disappeared on her royal rounds, she gave Flana orders that Kirov might stay in the palace for five regal sleeps. Flana paused to silently smile at him before she followed her queen out. Her smile was as lovely as the rest of her.

KIROV'S SUBSEQUENT INTERVIEW with Ulu was less pleasant. The war chief obviously knew the truth about the fight and probed deeply but the young Russian blandly repeated the party line. Ulu nodded in satisfaction and changed the subject.

"Oyo says that you are making the slaves lazy with your warm walls and wheelbarrows." He mangled the Russian word that Kirov had grafted onto Pellucidarian but the latter realized what he meant.

"Oyo is mistaken," protested Kirov. "I am making the slaves work better. That helps the Black Birdriders." He repeated his various arguments. This led into a discussion of Russian science and technological achievements. The conversation took a long time because of the frequent need to translate Russian terms into their closest Pellucidarian equivalent. Many words had no equivalent and Kirov's translations concealed as much as they revealed. Ulu picked up the word for "guns" but Kirov wasn't sure if the war chief really understood the concept.

Ulu was clearly suspicious but he did seem to accept the general concept of improved tools. He didn't understand 20th Century industrial engineering but he did know about hunting effectiveness and the idea of learning new tricks. He changed the subject back to the fight with the skals. After a new round of questioning, he concluded the interview with a warning not to listen to liars or to repeat lies.

Kirov solemnly agreed that lying was a bad idea.

KIROV NATURALLY TOOK the greatest advantage possible of Ala's regal hospitality. He was in genuine pain from his most recent battering and wanted to recover. His nurse, Flana, was pleasant to talk to. And he had a lot to think about.

Five sleeps later, Kirov thanked Flana on behalf of Ala and returned to the slave barracks and his workshop. Behind his back, the pretty slave girl wiped away tears.

TRALSI WAS A DIFFERENT community than it had been before the skal raid. The emerald giants had killed or carried off dozens of humans and trals. Fires caused by smashed timber falling into open hearths had destroyed several buildings. Slaves, including the elite toolmakers, labored to haul away debris and rebuild the ruined dwellings. Formerly generous free time was reduced to rare breaks. Kirov soon became aware that the numbers of Black Birdriders patrolling the streets of the community had doubled. He kept his ears and eyes open as he worked.

Another change was the attitude of the slaves. Previously,

they had tended to separate into cliques based on their tribal loyalties. Amiable fellows such as Dyryth were the exception. Lal's warriors had been particularly hostile since they blamed Kirov for their capture. Now all factions greeted his return cheerfully. Even Lal's Dyal Riders were gingerly friendly.

Cautiously, Kirov asked Rell and Dyryth about the change. Dyryth responded simply, "You good man. Other slaves not understand this before. Not understand man of *Soviet Red Tribe*. You showed them that you are a great hunter and fighter and that you help everyone. You still strange but good." He pointed to Kirov's Soviet Army greatcoat, so different from the woven feathers worn by the Birdriders and their slaves.

Rell nodded, pointing to a wheelbarrow and the slave pushing it towards the town trash dump. "Black Birdriders make everyone work extra hard after skal raid. Wheel-barrows make work easier. And warm walls make rest better."

A powerful slave standing behind Kirov coughed to attract his attention. A set of healed claw marks disfigured his otherwise handsome face. "I am Pol, deputy chief of the Dyal Riders. Kirov, you are a brave man. When Ala captured the war party of Lal, I thought that you were Ala's riding bird. I was wrong. Ala's riding bird would not have rescued Flana from the skal or protected her from Ulu. You are a man."

Kirov stood and said simply, "And so are you." He held out his hand, ready to shake hands in the European manner.

Pol clasped the startled young paleontologist turned inventor in both arms. Pellucidarians had not invented handshaking. Other Dyal Riders joined in and then slaves from other tribes.

Eventually, Oyo and two guards came along to break up the gathering. Oyo shouted a warning that lazy slaves would be beaten. Once the crowd dispersed, the Black Birdrider stayed to lecture Kirov on the need to work hard and not cause trouble. He had his eye on every slave, especially troublemakers, and *especially* troublemakers from the Soviet Red War Party Tribe. Kirov listened stoically and agreed with Oyo's logic at

the appropriate pauses.  Eventually Oyo and his guards left to
hector other slaves.

Kirov stared after the slave master.  Intuition nagged at
him: the Black Birdriders were worried about something and
he doubted it was really the slaves' work habits.

*Chapter Thirteen*

## ALA COMMANDS

A few sleeps later, Kirov realized what was worrying the Black Birdriders. The skals returned for more tasty human and tral food.

Once again, the unarmed slaves hid as best they could while the proud master class fought the great flesh eating birds with spears and stone axes. When the flying monsters had departed, clutching struggling humans and birds in their gigantic claws, people crept out of hiding.

Another log cabin was in flames as the result of monsters crashing into it and knocking logs into the ever present fires. Pellucidarian firefighting consisted of trying to rescue as many people and property from the flames as possible. There wasn't sufficient water or dirt on the barren rock of Tralsi to throw either on the fire. One woman ran screaming from the burning building, her hair on fire. Kirov knocked her to the ground and smothered the fire with his greatcoat. The skin on her head was scorched but only lightly so. Kirov thought that she would recover and handed her over to the Birdrider elder who seemed to be the community nurse. Even Oyo was thoughtful when he required Kirov to return to the endless work of repair and rebuilding.

Ala's lieutenants conducted a census of trals, Birdriders and slaves. They didn't share their findings with Kirov but the young inventor could count as well as if not better than any Birdrider. In their continuing search for food, the voracious monsters were destroying the Black Birdriders' community.

Each skal foray fell particularly hard on the Black Birdrider master class, especially the male warriors, and their tral mounts. Pride would not allow most of them to avoid battle and, vastly overmatched, they became skal food. The slaves had outnumbered the masters when Kirov had arrived in Tralsi. That was even truer now. The masters were obviously worried that the slaves would notice and revolt.

The human losses were compounded by the losses of trals. The masters needed war birds to fight the skals, to overawe the slaves, and to transport the necessities of Pellucidarian life to the barren rock that they lived on. The rocky promontory of Val Kan mountain was a natural fortress high above most dangers of Pellucidarian life. But it required endless flights to transport food, water, timber and other things to the site. Each tral lost to skal appetites was a triple blow to the Black Bird-rider way of life.

While Kirov was wondering how the Black Birdriders would solve the problem of the skal raids, he was once again summoned to the Palace. This time, the command came from Ala herself.

THIS WAS THE first time that Kirov had been in the throne room of the Palace. It was a large wooden chamber well lit with torches. Animal heads and hides intermingled with bunched spears decorated the walls. A number of spear-men stood about the chamber: an obvious royal guard. The young Wizard noticed that the floor was thickly paved with flammable sawdust. Royalty had its privileges, even at the price of dangerous fire hazards. One of those privileges was a soft floor covering to comfort the regal feet.

The queen of the Black Birdriders was even more beautiful than the last time that Kirov saw her. Apparently, the challenges of war agreed with her. She sat on her royal stool like the semi-legendary Empress Catherine the Great surrounded by her barbaric courtiers and guards. Two attractive female slaves knelt beside her, faces downward. Ulu and other warriors were close at hand. Kirov automatically bowed before the queen of Tralsi.

Ala acknowledged his bow by inclining her head. Firelight glinted off the raw gold at her throat accentuating her brunette hair and her dress of woven black feathers. Her dress emphasized rather than hid her superb figure.

"Toolmaker Kirov, can you make *guns* for me?" She had obviously absorbed and applied the idea of firearms. Her beauty was not limited to her body.

"No, great woman. I do not have the proper materials." Pellucidarian did not have a native word for *queen*. The American adventurers Innes and Perry had grafted a number of English words onto Pellucidarian but their Empire and language were far distant from Tralsi.

Her eyes flashed. "We must have better weapons or the skals will destroy us all!"

One of Ala's female slaves looked cautiously up at Kirov. It was Flana. Her face pleaded with him silently.

The other slave continued to study the floor although the Wizard noticed that her head turned slightly as the royal conversation shifted back and forth.

Electricity moved along Kirov's spine. He could not allow Flana or the other slaves to die without making an effort even if it strengthened the Black Birdrider master class for the moment. "Great woman, I cannot make guns for you but I can make spear throwers and other weapons. In addition, I can make other things to make work easier and life better in Tralsi."

"What other things?" demanded Ala.

"Rugs," replied the young inventor. The word was necessarily Russian. A long discussion ensued about the dangers of fire hazards caused by torches and hearth fires burning so close to layers of sawdust.

Ala was not convinced. "Make me spear throwers and other weapons first. We can talk about *rugs* another time. Go now and make weapons or the skals will eat us all!"

Kirov bowed again.

He did not realize that three women smiled after him as he left the Throne Room.

*Chapter Fourteen*

## "WE'VE FOUND THE MONARCHIST ARMY."

Intelligence Officer Ivan Garman paused to glare at Pellucidar's eternal sun, hanging serenely overhead but providing relatively little heat to these latitudes. Novy Mir was supposed to be a tropical paradise. So far, it had turned out to be little different from portions of Siberia—a mere eight hundred kilometers beneath his feet. Garman didn't like thinking about *that*. Even many of the animals looked much like antelopes, wolves and wild dogs. Of course, *most* of the animals resembled things out of nightmares but at least they moved away when Garman's scouts advanced towards them. The intelligence officer found that suspicious.

Ivan Garman found almost everything suspicious. That was why he was an intelligence officer in the Red Army.

Ahead of him, two scouts looked around and gestured for Garman to come to them. He advanced quickly, but warily.

Ivan Garman did everything warily. That was why he was in Novy Mir rather than Moscow where Comrades Trotsky and Stalin were having an uncomradely discussion over Soviet policy.

When he reached them, the senior scout pointed to a collection of bones amid the tall grass and curious flowers dotting the rolling Pellucidarian plain.

"What am I looking at, Comrade?" snapped the intelligence officer as he bent over to examine the scene.

"An animal skeleton with a bullet hole in the skull, Comrade," responded the senior scout. His partner kept watch on the various animals slowly moving away from the humans, cropping the pallid grass as they went.

Garman nodded. "How fresh?"

"Very fresh, Comrade. I would guess that whoever shot the animal did so within the last few hours. We were attracted to the scene by vultures—or something like vultures—flying away. When we arrived, rats and other small predators were still cleaning the bones."

Garman examined the wound. "The hole is consistent with a Mosin Nagant bullet. This situation is consistent with a monarchist rifleman in the area. That would explain why the large animals move away when they detect us. This rifleman hunts them for food and they have learned to be wary of humans."

"Could the rifleman be the American adventurer E.R. Burroughs?" hazarded the scout.

Garman shook his head. "We don't have evidence of that yet. We must continue to look."

So saying, he stood up and surveyed the endless plain, sloping gently upward as it receded into the distance. To the east was a chain of nameless mountains, gaunt with naked rock rising from the fertile lowlands. Savage birnam birds lived there but abundant firepower had taught them to leave the Soviets alone. To the west were forested plateaus that the men of Kandinsky's regiment had named the Bear Hills after their frightful denizens. Ahead of the scouts, more kilometers of grass and occasional copses of trees stretched southward to the Karl-Marx Ocean. Out there somewhere the fleeing monarchists would be run to ground.

"Let's go," ordered Garman. He and the scouts oriented themselves on a thin picket line of engineers' flags marking the wheel-rutted road originally laid down by the monarchists attempting to colonize Novy Mir. The Soviets had continued that practice with surveyors' stakes, flags, maps, compasses, clocks, and many other large and small devices of 20th Century civilization painstakingly imported into the Inner World. The

scouts saluted and began trudging onward, parallel to the road.
Garman returned to the road where his small command staff
waited.

"Comrade Radioman, report to Comrade Kandinsky that
we have found signs of monarchist activity in this area. We
have not found either monarchists or natives but we anticipate
contact soon."

No sooner were the words out of Garman's mouth than a
rifle shot echoed across the plain. Heads jerked southward to
stare at a copse of trees standing on a lonely hillock.

The heads of the scouts ahead of Garman were visible
momentarily above the grass but disappeared as they went to
cover. More gunshots were heard, followed by an ominous
silence. The grass around the copse rippled as scouts wormed
their way forward.

"Report this!" barked Garman at the radioman. "Come!"
he ordered his guards. He began running up the rough road
towards the trees. He bent low, obscuring any enemy's view
of his valuable self.

As he ran, there was a new fusillade of gunfire from the
copse. One insufficiently cautious scout jerked frantically,
sprayed blood across the pale grass, and then collapsed. Screams
rent the endless noontime stillness. Garman couldn't tell who
was crying out.

Garman slowed and entered the small clutch of trees wary
of any ambush. His face showed no relief when he heard
Russian voices calling out "Clear!" The copse no longer sheltered
any dangerous enemies. His guards caught up with him as he
moved through the trees. "Report!" he barked.

"Here, Comrade Battalion Commander." The intelligence
officer advanced cautiously toward the voice.

Garman found three scouts looking down at a man dressed
in a blood soaked Imperial Russian off white uniform. Beyond
was another, similar man, now quite dead. The first man
wouldn't last long. His head lolled and blood poured out of
his mouth. He whispered something and then his breath

stopped. His eyes stared upward into the eternal Pellucidarian sun peering through the trees.

"What did he say?" snapped the intelligence officer.

The scout thus addressed paused, uncertain of the Soviet officer's reaction, but answered. "He said, 'God Bless the Czar and Holy Mother Russia.'"

Garman grimaced. There were no longer doubts in his mind. "Where's the radioman? We must report this to Comrade Kandinsky at once. We've found the rear guard of the fleeing monarchist army. The main army and the monarchist civilian population can't be too far away now.

"And when we find the enemy army, we will find E.R. Burroughs. Comrades Trotsky and Stalin will reward us handsomely when we deliver the American warlord to Soviet justice." He smiled at the thought. After a moment, so did his men.

*Chapter Fifteen*

## INVENTIONS

Ala wanted Kirov to build guns for her army. What he started building were Central American atlatls, European long spears, and Zulu assegais. A guard working for Oyo watched him carefully but didn't interfere as long as the young inventor worked diligently on his new assignment. The slave master himself also checked in from time to time. A quiet, thoughtful Oyo worried Kirov more than the more usual shouting Oyo. Kirov's friends Dyryth and Rell spoke to him when they fetched materials. They assured him that the master recovered his temper and voice completely when he left Kirov's workshop.

When Kirov had completed a sample of his new weapons, he tested them (under guard) against the walls of a partially burned out log cabin. The atlatl, or spear thrower, worked perfectly. The young inventor placed a regular spear in a wooden trough and whipped it through the air, effectively extending the length of his arm. The spear sailed far further than Kirov could manage without mechanical aid. The long spear and the assegai didn't work as well in the thrower. The guard made some crudely humorous comments that Kirov took in stride. As arrogant as many Black Birdriders, the guard didn't notice the young inventor's secret smile and paid no attention when the latter left the long spear and assegai in his workspace.

When Kirov demonstrated the spear thrower for Ulu, no one noticed Rell diligently wheeling his barrow of firewood around Tralsi. He brought a load of wood to the young inventor's workshop, stacked half of it carefully away from the fire, added the assegai and long spear to his load, and then wheeled away. He smiled as he worked.

Ulu liked the added distance and penetrating power of the spear thrower and ordered ten tens of them for his warriors. The young Wizard agreed but taught another toolmaker how to carve spear throwers rather than working on them himself.

Instead, the inventor of Tralsi began working on carts, ropes and pulleys.

ONE OF THE ADVANTAGES to living on a bare mountain rock was that garbage disposal was easy. Slaves gathered up the community's trash and tossed it over a particularly steep edge of the rock. The midden forty meters below Tralsi on the Plain of Grazers attracted all sorts of scavengers but the resulting fights were both entertainment to the unsophisticated Pellucidarians and a constant reminder to the slaves of the dangers of escape. One particularly vicious fight between a pack of dog-like *jaloks* and a sounder of pig-like *golloks* lasted almost an entire waking period.

Everyone and everything had to be transported from Plain to Tralsi and return on tral-back. With the constantly increasing menace of skal raids, there weren't enough trals to provide aerial cavalry and truck service both.

Kirov broke the problem down into pieces. Normally, Black Birdriders hunted game on the Plains of Grazers and brought the food back to Tralsi. On the strength of his spear throwers, the young inventor persuaded Ulu to order slaves to transport the meat, always guarded by a Birdrider or two, to the base of Tralsi's promontory rather than using *trals*. That freed up war birds for defense. One slave tried to escape but he was hunted down and executed. The other slaves glared at their guard but could do nothing about the Birdrider soaring above them. The slaves were diligent enough when someone was watching them.

Once meat arrived at the base of Tralsi, Kirov introduced his pulley, rope and cart system to move the food up the mountain. Two four-wheeled carts ran up and down the smoothest, gentlest slope connected by a leather cable running through pulleys fastened to rocks at the top of the slope. The weight of one cart counterbalanced the other, thereby reducing the work of the sweating slaves who provided the energy to get the food to the community's doorstep. That freed up even more trals.

When the skals next raided Tralsi, they were met with volleys of hard flung spears. The Black Birdriders still suffered but less than before. Ulu ordered his entire war band armed with spear throwers and asked if Kirov had any other ideas. The latter explained about catapults and similar weapons. Ulu enthusiastically ordered ten of each. Kirov smiled and got to work.

The next time the skals returned, a "battery" of simple catapults guarded the Arsenal and Palace. Five green monsters attacked the warriors standing apparently foolishly in the plaza. Four skals succumbed to flying rocks and heavy spears. One escaped with its life. The Black Birdriders celebrated long and loudly that waking period, feasting and boasting of their prowess.

The next step was a bold one. Lal's tribe, the Dyal Riders, were birdriders as well as the Black Birdriders, using large flightless birds as avian horses. Like the *phororhacos* of the Outer World, the *dyal* was a powerful creature about two and a half meters tall. Kirov proposed that the tral-riders authorize use of dyals as draft animals to transport food and other necessities across the Plain of Grazers and even within Tralsi. Under guard by flying Black Birdriders, of course. That concept required a great deal of argument. The more conservative tral-riders proudly proclaimed the dyals to be a mere food animal. But the necessities of life on Tralsi's rock combined with Kirov's new prestige won the argument.

The former Dyal Riders were put to work rounding up and training their two legged "horses." Under guard by flying Black Birdriders, of course. Soon, flocks of dyals were penned in a light stockade below Tralsi and each waking period saw teams of dyals carrying provisions to feed the community.

Finally, even the most conservative of the master race approved the introduction of cart-pulling dyals in Tralsi itself. The pro-dyal faction pointed with pride at "their" clever idea. Those Black Birdriders charged with guarding the squadrons of working birds and birdboys began to lord it over their dyal-less fellows. Kirov noted the latter development with quiet approval.

With fewer and less deadly skal attacks and with dyals providing additional muscle power to the community, Tralsi changed again, becoming more relaxed than it had recently been. The master class prided itself on its courageous defeat of the avian monsters. The slaves were busy but quiet with dyal power replacing human muscles. Everyone seemed to have enough to eat and enough leisure time to enjoy life.

No one asked the dyals' opinions.

One development that would have startled any professional anthropologist studying the still primitive community was the sudden eruption of *fashion*. With more free time and resources at their disposal, first the slaves and then the masters began adopting brooms and then rugs as status symbols. At first, most rugs were merely scraps of leather but they quickly progressed through shaped sheets of leather to tanned animal furs. Such luxuries were so much softer and more comfortable than layers of sawdust.

Oyo personally brought Kirov the latest and most auspicious news.

Ala, queen of the Black Birdriders, announced that *inventor* Kirov—another Russian word grafted onto Pellucidarian—would soon receive the supreme honor for his many contributions to the community of Tralsi. She would take him for her mate.

*Chapter Sixteen*

## CIVIL WAR

**K**irov presented himself at the Palace with Oyo in tow. This time, the Throne Room was packed with Black Birdrider warriors divided up on either side of the royal stool. Again, Ala sat in regal if barbaric splendor flanked by her two female slaves and dozen or so lieutenants. This time, her beautiful face was flushed red and twisted in anger. She glared at Ulu who returned the disfavor. When Ala noticed Kirov, her expression changed completely, becoming enchanting, inviting, beguiling…. The young inventor's blood stirred. In contrast, Ulu's face hardened further as he noticed Kirov's presence.

Ala spoke, "*Inventor* Kirov, I have decided to take you as my mate. Do you accept?" Kirov instantly realized that the question was a token one. Ala had decided and, naturally, he would agree.

Around her, the roomful of warriors tensed. White knuckled hands gripped spears held in the vertical guard, or parade rest, position.

Kirov paused, noting the barely controlled tensions. His eyes wandered. Both female slaves cautiously looked up at him. One was Flana. Her pretty face quivered, shaking slightly from side to side. The other slave was an even more beautiful young woman. Kirov had seen her somewhere before but couldn't remember exactly where. Her resolute face nodded, signaling approval. He *was* tempted…. Ala was *very* beautiful and life as a prince consort was surely easier than slavery.

He looked again at Flana's sad eyes.

He bowed to the queen of the Black Birdriders. "Great woman, I am not worthy of your attention. I am merely a toolmaker and *inventor*. A great warrior would be a better mate for…."

Ulu's shout interrupted Kirov's attempt at diplomatic evasion. "Aha! You see! The slave knows his place! Even he says that I am your true mate!" His face flushed with triumph as he exulted. Almost half of the warriors shouted a victory cry in unison.

Ala's face twisted through a dozen emotions, none of them pretty. "You dare…!" she hissed. Kirov couldn't tell if she meant Ulu or himself. Possibly both of them.

She snapped at the young inventor. "You! Return to your workplace! At once! I will deal with you when I am ready!" The queen turned away from her slave, obviously assuming obedience. Perhaps life as Ala's prince consort would not be so different from life as her slave…!

Kirov was glad to escape Ala's immediate attention but curious to see the outcome of Ulu's suit for his queen's hand. Clearly, a simmering conflict was breaking out into the open. The young inventor began slowly moving away from the Throne, his eyes taking in everything while he analyzed.

Ala's attention was fully on her chief lieutenant now, her slave momentarily dismissed from her mind. She spat out harsh words, "Ulu. I am the chief of the Black Birdriders. I will mate with whomever I please. You are a deputy chief and you will take orders from me. Is That Understood?"

A birdrider standing behind Ala shouted, "Ala is our chief!" The other half of the warriors in the room chanted their queen's name in unison. Everyone still held his spear vertically. No one had raised his spear to a fighting position… yet.

Ulu shouted at his queen. "I am the greatest warrior in Tralsi! When the skals attacked, I slew one before your dwelling and placed its head before your doorway! No one else has done this! I am fit to be your mate!" He thumped his chest in pride.

Ala sneered. "Kirov's tools have slain many skals! And done the work of many slaves! He is fit to be my mate! I will mate with...." She paused in fury and continued, "with the man I choose!"

"Kirov is a slave!" rejoined the chief lieutenant. He suddenly became conscious of the female slaves kneeling beside their mistress. "You! Slaves! Depart! Slaves have no business in the councils of the Black Birdriders!"

Both female slaves rose, turned quickly away and left the Throne Room through a side doorway. Kirov decided that it was time for him to leave as well. He turned to go....

And bumped into one of Ulu's partisans. The latter lashed out with his spear butt, knocking the young inventor to the ground. The warrior repeated his leader's words, "Depart! Slaves have no business here!" He waved his spear threateningly.

The disturbance attracted the attention of the squabbling leaders. As Kirov rose to his feet, Ulu shouted, "Look! Ala! He has defied your orders! He is spying upon us! You! Igi! Kill the spy!"

Igi lowered his spear to the stabbing position....

Kirov stepped forward, inside the warrior's reach, and hit him in the solar plexus. Hard. The arrogant representative of the master class whuffed, collapsing on the soft rug that now covered the royal floor. He held onto his spear as he went down.

There was a moment of silence. Kirov loudly said, "I go to my workplace in obedience to the orders of Ala, great chief of the Black Birdriders!" He backed up towards the doorway, scanning the room in all directions for further death threats.

Ulu's shout "Kill him!" and Ala's countermand "No! Let him live!" were almost simultaneous. The warriors stirred, some spears coming up into the throwing position, others lowering into the stabbing position. Some stepped a pace forward, ready to kill.

Igi came to his knees, his arm bending back into the spear throwing position, murder in his eyes.

Kirov reached his left hand towards a torch while his right hand dug into his greatcoat's pocket. Seeing Kirov leaning left towards a weapon, Igi shifted his aim…

And hurled his spear towards Kirov's center of mass.

The young inventor was watching the birdrider's spear arm muscles. When they started to move, he jerked to his right. The spear cut the cloth of his greatcoat but missed the lean body inside. He thumped into the wall and fell. Quickly, he pushed himself into an upright position.

Kirov shouted, "Ulu is defying Ala's orders! He is a traitor to the Black Birdriders! His riding bird is murdering slaves who are loyal to the Black Birdriders! Ulu is a traitor! Ulu is a traitor!"

As he chanted, he waved his left hand over his head to attract attention. Meanwhile, his right hand plucked a handful of Mosin Nagant rifle bullets from his pocket and flung them into a fire pit.

Ala's warriors picked up the chant. Most of Ulu's partisans turned their attention to Ala's supporters. Some started chanting "Ulu is a great warrior!" One supporter shouted "Ulu should be chief!"

As Kirov edged out of the Throne Room, he saw Ulu seize Ala's arm, yanking her aloft in triumph. Her other arm flashed, burying something in Ulu's gut. His eyes glazed in shock, his hand going slack.

Ala dropped out of his grasp and straightened up, every centimeter a warrior queen. "Ulu was a traitor! And now he is dead by my own hand! Rally to me, my loyal warriors!"

For an instant, the fate of the Black Birdriders hung in the balance. Then the bullets cooked off (as an American might say). Their propellant charges exploded in the fire pit, sending the metallic bits of death hurtling in all directions. Pellucidarian feathers offered scant protection against the tiny messengers of civilized destruction.

Frightened by the unexpected noise and wounded by the bullets themselves, Ulu's partisans surged away from the fire pit of death. Their surge took them towards Ala's supporters. To the queen's men, the movement looked like a charge. Spears flashed, cutting, stabbing, killing....

The civil war was on.

KIROV HAD ALREADY escaped the Palace. Outside, in the plaza, he found Rell speaking to Ala's female slaves in an agitated manner.

The unknown slave from the throne room commanded, "The Dyal Riders must find weapons and attack the Black Birdriders! We must be free! Why do you resist my orders, Rell?"

"Great Lal," protested Rell, speaking to the unknown. "Kirov has a better plan. We have been working on it for many waking periods. We have weapons. Strange weapons but ones that work well. His plan is better!"

Kirov was thunderstruck to realize that Ala's second personal slave was the mysterious Lal, chief of the Dyal Riders. He had never seen her face clearly—not even when he kicked her while trying to escape from Ulu many sleeps ago.

Lal looked at Kirov coldly. "What is your plan, man of the Soviet Red War Party tribe?" She mangled the word *Soviet* but Kirov understood her.

"Revolution," answered the man from the Outer World.

*Chapter Seventeen*

## FORWARD! FOR THE GREATER GLORY OF THE SOVIET UNION!

Kandinsky's regiment, now reinforced to its full three battalion strength, was on the march. Leaving a small guard behind in Fort Alinsky, it flowed down onto the Plutonian Plain south of the fortress. Officers ordered, starshinas bawled, and enlisted men complained as it has always been in armies from the Inner World to beyond the farthest star. The long columns of riflemen marched forward to conquer Pellucidar for the greater glory of the Soviet Union.

Regiment Commander Kandinsky himself commanded the second wave, which was composed of the fresh Second Battalion. Behind him, the battered First Battalion brought up the rear. Ahead of him, his executive officer, Deputy Regiment Commander Drobanin, commanded the leading Third Battalion. And ahead of them, vast herds of strange animals moved slowly away from the well-armed soldiers, grazing as they went. Creatures that moved too slowly were slaughtered for the greater glory of Soviet stomachs.

And far ahead of the masses of both men and animals, the advance guard scouted forward. The recent skirmish with the monarchist rear guard had everyone on alert for possible ambushes, outposts, battles, or simply more evidence of the fleeing White Russian population. None were more alert than the advance guard.

Senior Starshina Voitinuik strode easily forward, following the dirt road rutted by monarchist wagons. Those wagons couldn't have passed too long ago: the grass had not yet reclaimed the road. Around him stalked a screen of the most advanced scouts, the very tip of the spear as Alexander Nevsky had said to Voitinuik on the banks of the Neva River. They were good fellows. They would find the Czar's last defenders. Voitinuik started up a slight ridge....

Ahead of him, a scout reached the top of the ridge, stared southward for a moment, and dropped to the ground. Voitinuik reacted briskly. "Down!" he commanded in a voice calculated to carry to his men but not to a nearby enemy. The scouts disappeared into the tall grass covering the endless Pellucidarian plain. Grass and curious but beautiful star-tipped flowers wavered as men crept towards the military crest of the ridge. Voitinuik obeyed his own command as soon as he saw the scouts vanish. He bent over and bear-walked rapidly forward.

The lead scout crawled backwards, keeping his head out of sight of any enemies to the Soviet front. He rolled over and opened his mouth to call Senior Starshina Voitinuik forward. He gaped for a second and closed his mouth when he realized that Voitinuik was already beside him.

"Report," demanded the latter.

"A wagon convoy stopped on a ridge ahead of us, Comrade Senior Starshina," answered the scout. "A great many wagons in laager formation. We've found the monarchists!"

Voitinuik sniffed in professional caution. "We'll see if we have found the monarchists, Leonid. Let's have a look."

Both men crawled a meter or two forward, their eyes cautiously clearing the ridgeline....

Young Leonid was right. Voitinuik saw a shallow grassy valley ahead of them and then a new rocky ridgeline a short distance away. Parked along the further ridge were several dozen wagons circled for the night (if night ever came to timeless Pellucidar). An American might think of them as Conestoga weapons. Voitinuik carefully lifted binoculars that he had "liberated" from an inattentive officer and surveyed the sight. He saw a few sentries staring listlessly in his general direction. Behind them, other figures moved to and fro among the wagons. He nodded slightly to himself.

Other scouts began reporting in confirming what Voitinuik had seen. He took the reports and ordered them to halt here, concealed by the grass and the slight rise of the ground. Other Soviet riflemen approached from the rear. He gestured for them to take cover. When a junior starshina arrived, Voitinuik left him in charge of the line and crawled back to report to Battalion Commander Garman, the officer in charge of the advance guard.

GARMAN QUERIED VOITINUIK carefully, his round face pinched in thought. Then he ordered the radioman to report to Regiment Commander Kandinsky, now not too far in their rear. Swiftly an order came back to investigate the wagon convoy further. If possible, the scouts should determine the strength and disposition of the enemy. The leading Battalion would arrive in force shortly.

"Comrade Senior Starshina, take your best scouts and infiltrate their position. Learn as much as you can. Don't fire on them unless necessary." Voitinuik grunted. Garman took the noise as an acknowledgement. "Report back when you have thoroughly scouted their position. I will be at the point where the road crosses the nearer ridge."

"Yes, sir… I mean, yes, Comrade Battalion Commander." Voitinuik carefully saluted and returned to his men.

BACK ON THE NEARER RIDGE, Voitinuik quietly assembled his best squad of scouts to the right of the road. Garman came forward and took command of the line of Soviets along the gentle rise. After a few more words, Voitinuik led his squad forward, slithering through the pale green grass and white crowned flowers towards the enemies of the Soviet Union.

Moving carefully, they maneuvered to the right of the circled wagons. Stealthily, Voitinuik reached a point just below the further ridgeline and several meters from the nearest white uniformed sentry. He tapped a scout on the shoulder, made a cutting gesture across his own throat and pointed to the stolid sentinel. The scout nodded, quietly laid down his rifle and drew his knife. He wormed his way towards the oblivious guard.

Satisfied that the sentry would present no problem, Voitinuik cautiously peered over the further ridge....

He froze in place, unable to immediately comprehend what he was seeing.

There was no circle of wagons or camp of monarchist refugees. Instead, the wagons formed a line along the ridge. Beyond was an area denuded of grass by sheep-like animals grazing the barren ground. Apes—or something like African gorillas—moved excitedly back and forth in this area, pausing to snatch up biscuit-like disks or gourds from tables placed behind the wagons. They applied both biscuits and gourds to their gaping mouths. The apes resembled nothing so much as a gang of drunken nobles capering at some pre-Revolutionary party...!

Strange odors assailed Voitinuik's nose. He quickly recognized the scent of alcohol. *The apes were drunk! But why...?!*

Just then, the puzzled Soviet heard a hissing sound. He turned to see his knifeman holding a scarecrow dressed in an Imperial Russian off-white uniform, a puzzled look on the scout's face. Strings led from the dummy to the apes. As they danced, the scarecrow made small, lifelike movements. He caught a whiff of naphtha.... *Then, the sentry... this whole situation is....*

"It's a trap!" screamed Voitinuik at the top of his lungs.

*Chapter Eighteen*

## REVOLUTION

The Pellucidarian language had no word for *revolution* but the slaves of the Black Birdriders had learned to trust the strange ideas of the man from the Outer World. With Lal's backing and Pol and Rell as his lieutenants, Kirov set his plan into motion.

Several slaves ran from house to house in Tralsi, alerting all of the warriors not already in the Palace to report there at once. Half of the master class was told that Ulu had tried to kill Ala who needed their assistance to crush his revolt. The other half was told that Ala had killed Ulu and was now killing all of his supporters. The civil war grew rapidly.

Meanwhile, the remaining slaves congregated away from the palace, staying undercover as much as possible to conceal their movements from the outpost high up Val Kan mountain. They armed themselves with assegais and longspears that Kirov had designed while inventing spear throwers for the master class. Since the Black Birdriders used spears approximately two meters long, the slave masters hadn't realized the significance of sticks either shorter or longer.

With the Black Birdrider males killing each other in and around the palace, groups of slaves raided the homes of the master class, carrying off food, water, weapons, and rugs. They hauled their loot to the site of Kirov's primitive tramway, which was already lowering women and children to the Plain of Grazers.

Meanwhile, Pol led more slaves to attack the tral aviaries, assegais and longspears in hand. The Birdrider guards hurled their standard spears and watched in shock as the slaves deflected the incoming shafts with leather rugs converted into simple shields. A typical Pellucidarian enemy would hurl spears back. Each side would pick up the other tribe's spears and reuse them against their foes. This would continue until one side admitted defeat and fled. Instead, the slaves charged with assegais and began stabbing their erstwhile masters to death. Escaping Birdriders were cut off by another team carefully positioned by Kirov. Shaka Zulu (and Kirov's instructors in history) would be proud.

Inside the aviaries, the giant trals proved to be at least as dangerous as their human masters. One enthusiastic Dyal Rider tried to capture and saddle one of the great black birds. It pecked him to death while he was trying to fasten the saddle to its back. Pol's men thrust longspears and hurled standard spears past tral beaks, slaughtering the great creatures in their nests. Without their namesake aerial mounts, the Black Birdriders were just another tribe, one among Pellucidar's many isolated communities. Pol's men jogged back to the tramway with tral feathers in their hair, whooping in triumph.

Once on the plain, Lal's tribesmen, the Dyal Riders, led their fellow slaves to the great pens where dyals were held to provide bird power for Tralsi's economy. Rugs were slapped across bird backs and tied underneath bird bellies, becoming saddles in the process. Women, small children and the elderly mounted up and began riding away.

Lal and Rell led the way, running across the Plain of Grazers towards Ulu's Forest. Their fellow escapees ran beside the laden dyals, to guide and protect them. Herbivores and even many of the smaller carnivores scattered with the advance of the new freedmen and freedwomen. Crushed flowers released sweet scents into the air.

*Chapter Nineteen*

## FREEDOM

The former slaves reached Ulu's Forest where they came to a stop. Lal and Pol shouted orders and the escapees entered the pine forest where any flying enemies would have trouble seeing them much less reaching them.

A sleeping period later, they began to disperse. Without their common enemy to hold them together, tribal loyalties reasserted themselves. Lal's Dyal Riders were the largest group of the former slaves and the core of the fragile alliance. They wished to ride outward in a straight line away from Tralsi. But tribesmen from Bari wished to march to the left, along the foothills of the Mountains of the Birds, to reach their cavernous homes. Others wished to march to the right to reach an island in a river snaking across the Plain of Grazers. Lal pleaded with everyone to accompany her to Dyalsi (Dyal Town) before separating to maintain their common strength but only a few outsiders accepted. Kirov, Flana and Dyryth were three who did.

The former slaves lost a waking period arguing. In the end, Lal decided that she would not hold the others by force. The Cave Dwellers, the River People and the others took their shares of food and water and departed. Some tried to take dyal workhorses with them but the avians refused, sometimes bloodily, before Lal could restore peace. Before they left, all of the departing communities thanked Kirov and invited him to their homes. He declined the offers as diplomatically as he could.

THE DYAL RIDERS and their new recruits spent a few

waking periods organizing themselves, hunting for game, and cutting the stolen rugs into better saddles and shields. Layers of "rugs" mounted on a wooden frame would stop or deflect most spear thrusts. Finally, they advanced cautiously onto the Plain of Grazers, guided by the mysterious Pellucidarian homing instinct.

A waking period later, they were attacked by the Black Birdriders.

KIROV HAD HOPED that the civil war in Tralsi would keep the master class occupied indefinitely. When a scout spotted the wing of tral-riders headed for the escapees, the young inventor sighed loudly in disappointment. Some Black Birdrider had gained control of Tralsi and called out the reserve war birds normally stabled at the outpost above the community. Still, the reserves were only a fraction of the flock that had protected Tralsi before the civil war. Lal and Pol began directing the Dyal Riders into a circular formation with teams of warriors surrounding groups of women and children. The adult women cooed to the riding birds and the avian workhorses knelt to the ground, making themselves and their small burdens more difficult targets.

The tral-riders circled overhead and some warrior that Kirov didn't recognize shouted "Ka-goda?!"

"No!" shouted the trapped queen. "I am Lal of the Dyal Riders and I defy your puny numbers! We are armed by Kirov the inventor! Fly away and live! Land among us like men and die!" She waved her assegai defiantly at the giant black birds overhead.

"Hah!" sneered the Black Birdrider. "We need not land. Your little sticks cannot reach us. Surrender or die!" Indeed, the trals were circling above the range of a normal spear cast.

Before Lal and the warrior could exchange further pleasantries, Kirov interrupted, whispering to the queen of the Dyal Riders. She smiled with savage glee and nodded agreement. Kirov gestured to Dyryth.

The amiable giant was carrying a longspear—an ungainly weapon for a normal-sized gilak but completely natural in his oversized hands. Seemingly without effort, he hurled it aloft, piercing the neck of the spokesman's tral. The war bird attempted to squawk, spraying a red mist across the plain, and heeled over. It spiraled into the ground, crashing with a dull thud, followed by its rider.

Flana dragged another longspear to Dyryth while the Dyal Riders cheered.

The Black Birdriders' organization was efficient enough. Another warrior took command and trals gained altitude to escape the reach of Dyryth and Kirov-designed spear throwers. A few Birdriders, slow to adapt to the new ways of war, felt the shock of spears hammering home. They joined the first spokesman smashing into the Plain.

Once they had gained enough height to feel secure, the Black Birdriders began hurtling their spears groundward, targeting the enemy warriors. A few weapons hit their targets, slashing into Dyal Rider flesh. Blood colored the pale green grass and curious flowers. But most spears were deflected by layered leather shields and then captured for reuse. Soon enough, the arrogant Black Birdriders had exhausted their quivers of spears, having done frustratingly little damage to the escapees.

One angry Birdrider dove his tral towards Lal, trying to snatch the enemy queen off the ground. He and his mount died in a thicket of longspears.

After that, the Black Birdriders circled for a while and peeled off, heading back to Tralsi. They were followed by Dyal Rider cheers.

Pol frowned and pointed at one avian monster flying towards them rather than away. "That is no tral. That is a skal! Someone is riding a skal and guiding it to us!"

Lal breathed, "A skal-rider? That can only be—"

"Ho! *Traitor* Kirov!" came Ala's commanding voice, melodious even in angry triumph. "You have destroyed Tralsi and killed my trals! But my *pet* will devour you and your women!" The warrior queen guided her gigantic skal forward almost casually.

The great green monster descended towards the escapees, its golden beak gaping, hungry for flesh and blood.

"Ho! Traitor Kirov!" came Ala's commanding voice, melodious even in angry triumph.
"You have destroyed Tralsi and killed my trals! But my pet will devour you and your
women!"

## Chapter Twenty

## "IT'S A TRAP!"

I t's a trap!" bellowed Senior Starshina Voitinuik just as
bullets began hitting the deceptive wagons parked along
the further ridge. He lurched forward, rising to a bear
walk and launching himself into the area shorn of grass by the
sheep-like animals. A bullet struck him in the leg and he
grunted savagely as he collided with the ground. He lay still.
Feigning death had saved him more than once during a long
lifetime of war.

A hail of bullets raked the wagons, smashing lamps deliberately set dangerously close to the wagons' cargos. Flaming
oil spilled onto a mixture of explosives and incendiaries....

The wagons erupted in volcanic fury. A blast like a giant's
fist smashed the Soviet scouts (and apes and sheep) into unconsciousness. Fire fountained into the azure sky. For a
moment, a curtain of flame blotted out the view of the entire
further ridge, then collapsed to the earth, setting the dry grass
alight. How long had the grass been drying under the eternal
Pellucidarian sun? Who can say in the timeless Inner World?
The wall of flame engulfed the ridge, and began marching
northward—toward the Soviet troops.

In the barren area south of the trap, Voitinuik, the apes
and the sheep lay on the ground, stunned but otherwise largely
unhurt. The fiery blast had angled away from them and the
lack of grass in this shallow valley prevented any backfires from
killing them or the Imperial Russian riflemen hiding behind a
rampart of rocks.

The scouts north of the trap were not so lucky. They fled

as fast as they could but the tall grass impeded their movements. The fire burned through the grass faster than they could run.

IVAN GARMAN had been waiting on the dirt road on the back of the nearer ridge. He frantically pressed himself into the packed earth as the flames raced through the grass on either side of him.

DROBANIN'S ADVANCE BATTALION pressed forward, anticipating a battle with the escaped monarchists. Their initially broad front narrowed as they closed in on the site of the wagons reported by Garman.

Their advance halted when brilliant light flared before and above them on Pellucidar's inward curving surface. Thunder echoed across the plain. They saw the fire beginning to spread across the landscape....

Spreading towards *them*.

And masses of animals that had been fleeing *from* their column suddenly turned around and charged back *toward* them, frantic to escape the oncoming wall of flame.

Momentarily, the Soviets were awed by the sight of thousands upon thousands of strange animals—antelopes, mammoths, baluchitheria, brontops, qirqirns, sloths, and things that no Outer World scientist had ever named—streaming forward in an avalanche of flesh; behind them, a wall of towering flames.

Military training reasserted itself. Starshinas and officers bawled orders. Slowly—all too slowly—engineers began hacking at the grass and ground, trying to create firebreaks. One team started a backfire. Animals crashed into the frantic humans knocking them down, injuring them and impeding the already desperately slow work. The sheer number of beasts smothered the backfire. Soviet gunners began firing into the stampede, trying to defend themselves and, perhaps, to create firebreaks of animal flesh....

Thousands of animals fell to Soviet bullets and rifle grenades.

But there was not enough ammunition in all of Russia to halt the panic.

The creatures leapt the wall of the dead and dying to trample the proud invaders of the Inner World into the rich soil.

And after them, the cremation....

A SHOCKED KANDINSKY surveyed the blood-soaked, fire-cooked plain. Human and animal bodies carpeted the landscape as far as he could see.

In the distance, he spotted two human figures standing on a rock. He couldn't make out their faces but their body language was unmistakable. They were surveying the destruction. The eternal Pellucidarian sunlight glinted off binoculars sweeping the battlefield and coming to rest on *him!*

Kandinsky snatched up his pistol and emptied it futilely at the distant figures. The taller one waved gaily back. The shorter one raised a rifle to his shoulder and fired back. The first bullet ripped through the Soviet's sleeve. He didn't wait for the shorter figure to correct his aim. Kandinsky ran behind a mammoth's corpse seconds before a second bullet smacked into the giant body.

He would live to explain this disaster to Commissar Trotsky. And after that? He hoped that he would merely be shot for his failure.

On the rock, Pardan grunted in frustration. He swept the Springfield back and forth, hunting for the escaped commander. After a minute, he concluded that his target was unlikely to show himself.

"Shall we pursue?" asked the native.

"No," replied his chief, still surveying the scene. He remembered a time when a troop of US Army soldiers were similarly "attacked" by buffaloes. "I'd like to make a clean sweep but it's too dangerous. The stampede didn't kill all of them. And there are bound to be more soldiers out there somewhere. Too many for us to fight here and now."

"How many more?" questioned Pardan eagerly. His eyes still hunted for Kandinsky.

Burroughs lowered his binoculars and mused. "Hundreds of thousands if Commissar Trotsky pours the entire Red Army into Pellucidar. He won't send that many men, of course. A few thousand modern soldiers are more than a match for any tribe in Pellucidar. Except for the Empire, of course. Still, I'd love to see Trotsky's face when he hears about this." He turned to face his companion directly and said, "Don't worry, Pardan. You'll get your share." He bared his teeth in his knowing smile. "Let's go and rest. We need to tell our friends what happened." He climbed down from the rock, grinning broadly.

Pardan followed his chief, already thinking about the fighting yet to come.

*Chapter Twenty-One*

## DAVID AND GOLIATH

Stand back, slaves!" commanded Ala, more beautiful than ever, and magnificent in her boldness. Alone except for her terrible giant, she defied a hundred threatening weapons as if she were defended by ten thousand warriors. "I will have the life of the traitor Kirov. Stand back and I will spare your lives!"

Many Dyal Riders quailed at the immense power of the great green monster confronting them and the élan of the warrior queen who had tamed it.

Lal bristled in defiance. She shouted, "Dyal Riders! Stand ready! Aim...!"

Kirov interrupted. "Wait, Lal. It's me she wants. There's no need to risk your men. I'll fight her alone."

Behind them, Dyryth and Rell each took a step forward. Flana strangled a cry.

After a moment, Lal nodded her head in fierce approval as if she expected nothing less.

Kirov shouted his challenge upward to Ala, circling out of range of any spear throwers. With a joyous laugh, the warrior queen of the Black Birdriders accepted.

Kirov took an assegai and a longspear from Lal's warriors and walked away from the circle protecting the noncombatants. Tiny animals scampered from his path—a reminder of the sweetness of life in the Inner World.

He walked about a hundred meters, stopped, and looked around. Ala watched from above, the skal's vast wings easily sustaining it and her. Kirov stabbed his weapons into the ground and unbuttoned his tattered grey Soviet Red Army greatcoat so that it hung loosely across his shoulders. He looked up and waved to his foe, almost cheerfully.

She waved back and slapped her giant mount on its neck. The great green monster circled to position itself and dived at Kirov, razor sharp claws outstretched.

The young inventor snatched up his longspear, braced it against a rock and aimed it at one oncoming scythe.

The skal's own vast body obstructed its view of its prey. It was expecting to feel a meaty thump and close its claws on a tasty gilak. Instead, a sharp lance of pain stabbed into one claw. It screamed and jerked itself upward, frantically trying to escape its wound. Surprised, its mistress frantically slapped its neck, trying to regain control.

Kirov's longspear had done its job but the monstrous impact had shattered the wooden shaft. Once again, the young inventor's body went flying through the air before crashing to the rich loam of the Inner World. This time, his flight was relatively short. He rolled upward, shaking his head in pain, trying to focus his eyes.

A few dozen meters away, the giant skal was hopping around on one foot, the other foot waving in the air, a broken stick protruding from it. Atop its mighty shoulders, Ala was slapping frantically. Finally, the colossal avian settled down and seized the offending shaft in its golden beak. Jaws that could swallow a cow closed and yanked the weapon out of the wound. The skal spat out giant matchsticks.

The great avian's wild eyes surveyed the plain, hunting for its tormentor.

It spotted the brown clad Dyal Riders standing quietly eighty or ninety meters away and hopped towards them. Ala stopped it with more slapping. She began looking around for her foe....

The skal screamed as Kirov stabbed its bowels as deeply as his assegai would reach. The avian monster jerked forward, releasing itself from the stick held firmly in the young inventor's hands, but not from the maddening pain. The mighty bird, savagely stung by a foe beneath its contempt, hopped forward another dozen meters, stopped and looked backward. Red blood watered the grass. On its shoulders, Ala hung on grimly.

The colossal avian saw a grey human target standing on the plain, half of it standing still, half of it waving fiercely. Its mad eyes focused on the movement. It hopped around in a circle and then sprang forward. The golden anvil of its head descended in a swift arc, smashing through the fragile tissue of its target and into the earth of the Plain of Grazers.

The impact tore Ala loose from her saddle. She flew head over heels and landed with a thump on the soft soil.

As the skal's head smashed into the ground, Kirov whipped his hands from the greatcoat that he had used as a bullfighter's distracting cloak and seized his assegai. The skal's mighty beak had ripped the greatcoat into shreds—but missed the fragile human being waving it. The colossal avian's last sight was Kirov driving his stick through its eye and into its brain. Trapped by its own beak buried in the ground, the skal convulsed and died.

Covered in blood, Kirov panted, frantically drawing the fresh, cool air of northern Pellucidar into his lungs. He was dizzy with adrenaline and afire with pain. When his head cleared, he walked over to where Ala was moving feebly. "Ka-goda?" he asked, quietly but firmly.

"Ka-goda," she whispered.

He collapsed onto the grass beside her.

A handful of Dyal Riders ran to the battle site. Lal waved her men to a stop. She and Flana walked quickly to Kirov as he sat panting. Flana carried a gourd of water, which she began applying to the young victor's throat and wounds. Lal stood guard beside her champion, one warrior protecting another.

Ala groaned and looked up. She saw Lal standing proudly beside the young inventor and then Flana kneeling possessively next to him. She addressed her conqueror, "Will you take me as your third mate?" Her commanding voice was subdued, bitter, but also conveying an emotion that Kirov could not decipher.

"No," pronounced Kirov. "Since the Black Birdriders cannot protect you, you are my slave." He paused to catch his breath. Behind him, the other Pellucidarians nodded in grim agreement. "However, I give you, my slave, to Lal of the Dyal Riders."

All three women looked at Kirov in shock.

He continued. "Lal, teach Ala what it is like to be a slave. When she has served you as long as the Dyal Riders served her, I will ask you to free her. Perhaps then, she can truly be a great woman."

Ala rolled over, hiding her face in the grass. Lal nodded in agreement, slowly at first and then more vigorously. Flana glowed as she gazed at the Solomon of the Inner World in awe and admiration.

Lal drew herself fully upright.

"Come, slave," she commanded with immense authority. "When Kirov is ready to go to the nest of the Dyal Riders, you will come as well, willingly or not. This waking period, we will all rest. But next waking period, the Dyal Riders old and new will celebrate our freedom."

The thick grass did not hide Ala's moan of despair.

KIROV AND FLANA stood quietly together gazing across the endless Plain of Grazers. Behind them, wild dancing in celebration of freedom went on and on and on.

The young girl's face was troubled. She quietly asked, "What will you do now? Will you return to the lands of the Russian tribe?"

Kirov *was* tempted. Russia had so many things that Pellucidar lacked: beautiful women to picnic with, stalwart men to drink with, sleigh rides in winter, canals, art museums, great universities, libraries, laboratories, scientists respected by their peers, professional societies, personal achievements and honors....

No, that wasn't entirely true : Pellucidar had at least one scientist, one respected by his community and with a lifetime of research and achievement ahead of him: Kirov the inventor.

"No," he answered gently. "I would like to stay here—in Pellucidar—with you."

Her face turned upward towards his, glowing with joy like the eternal sun of the Inner World.

# KIROV SKALKILLER

## *Chapter One*

## "HOW COULD SHE RETURN FROM THE DEAD WORLD?"

Zuul, acting chief of the Dyal Riders, was sunning himself lazily when the thunderbolt struck.

"Thunderbolt" was a metaphor. Pellucidar's clear skies did not turn black with clouds. Lightning did not flash downward to strike any of the many trees sheltering Dyalsi (Dyal Town). But life in the settlement of the Dyal Riders would never be the same from then on.

Zuul stretched himself contentedly in the rays of Pellucidar's eternal noontime. The cold winds that chilled this portion of the Inner World were still and the tiny Sun baked the acting chief on his throne like an expert chef.

Of course, Zuul's throne was really a wooden stool and the royal palace that he dozed in front of was really an elaborate thatched grass hut. An American might call it a shack. He had neither by right. Zuul was only a deputy chief, temporarily empowered by the absence of his queen, Lal, and her senior lieutenants, Pol and Rell.

But Lal had been gone for a very long time and showed no sign of returning from her foolish reconnaissance of the lair of the Black Birdriders. Soon enough, Zuul would sadly proclaim her to be long dead and himself to be the chief of their people. When? Who can say for sure in timeless Pellucidar?

In the meantime, the life of Dyalsi went on. Many men had disappeared in the war between the Black Birdriders and the Dyal Riders. The remaining hunters had to work twice as hard to feed the community. They saddled their great war birds and prepared to hunt game with spears, axes and clubs. Women attempted to control their children and prepared to gather edible nuts, tubers and seeds from Dyalsi's grove of trees and the surrounding grasslands. Older women continued the endless job of repairing the thick grass matting of the huts to keep the cold winds at bay.

A group of young women walked by, carrying skin bags en route to the spring that watered Dyalsi and its trees. When they passed in front of the royal palace, they swerved away from Zuul's less than regal presence. Their gaily chattering voices dropped and they watched the acting chief as they moved.

Zuul opened an eye and hailed one of the women. She jerked to a halt and then turned to face the deputy chief.

"Hail, Zuul. Please excuse us but we must fetch water for our families."

"Yes, yes, Bel. But after you have finished that, come to m... the house of the chief." He indicated the great hut behind him with a motion of his head. "It needs cleaning and it is your turn. To clean the house." His mouth described a smile such as the Serpent must have made when he invited Eve to partake of the apple.

Bel's face clouded. "Are you sure it is not the turn of some other maiden? I cleaned Lal's house a few sleeps ago."

Zuul's face darkened at Lal's name. He sat upright. His voice sharpened. "I am chief of the Dyal Riders. I decide when it is your turn to clean the house of the chief. When you have taken your water skin to your mother's house, come here."

Bel looked around for support but her fellow water carriers had vanished. She breathed deeply and straightened her back. "Mighty Zuul, Lal is still chief of our tribe. I will clean her house for her when I return.... With my sisters and cousins. Many hands will make the tasks easy." She smiled knowingly and departed while Zuul was still analyzing her strategy.

He sniffed and then spoke softly if fiercely to her disappearing back. "Well, Bel, you are rightly called the Clever One. You think that there is safety in numbers. You will not always have your sisters and cousins around to protect you. And I *am* the chief of the Dyal Riders and you *will* be my mate!"

The words of Zuul's unchivalrous oath had no sooner departed his mouth when he heard the thumping of running footsteps approaching. He swung his attention away from the now distant sight of Bel's shapely figure to the business at hand.

A young man burst into the clearing in front of the royal palace. "Zuul! Zuul!" He shouted. "Lal returns from the mountains of the Black Birdriders! She has rescued our people who were slaves! And she brings Ala, the chief of the Black Birdriders, as her prisoner!" The runner collapsed in front of the suddenly demoted *deputy* chief, gasping for air.

"What?" screeched Zuul. "Lal has been dead for many sleeps!" The lie that he had been saving for the right moment popped out without his thinking about it. "How could she return from the Dead World?"

The runner answered, "She has returned due to the power of a strange man, Kirov the Skal Killer."

*Chapter Two*

## HOMECOMING

Mikhail Kirillivitch Kirov, formerly Specialist Kirov of the Soviet Red Army and now Kirov Skalkiller of the Dyal Riders tribe of Pellucidar, marched into Dyalsi.

Ahead of him marched Lal, the queen of Kirov's newfound tribe, her chief lieutenant Pol, her prisoner Ala, and Ala's guard, the amiable giant Dyryth. Behind him came more than five hundred Dyal Riders, the men walking, the women and children riding on the fearsome flightless birds from which the tribe drew its name. Far behind him, Lal's second lieutenant Rell chivvied the stragglers to keep together.

And beside him was Flana.

The returnees were very tired from their hurried journey across the Plain of Grazers but elated to reach the freedom and security of their home.

HOMECOMING WAS A happy time. Many families torn apart by the Black Birdriders' slave raids were reunited with tears of joy. Even families that had not lost loved ones rejoiced at the return of friends or the simple pleasure of knowing that the tribe was once more together. Men and women brought food and drink. A wild gyrating dance of celebration began and continued for a long time.

Lal was as happy as any of her people. But she had work to do and she needed rest. She hunted up Zuul, who was still standing in front of her father's hut. She frowned as they met; she had expected him to greet her at the entrance to Dyalsi.

"Hail, Zuul. I have returned from Tralsi, the roost of the Black Birdriders. You know Pol. These people are Kirov Skalkiller, Flana of the Seashore People, and Dyryth the Quiet One. They are now Dyal Riders." She gestured to her companions.

Zuul looked at the newcomers. Kirov was a lean young man wearing a strange grey featherless garment. To the suspicious deputy chief, he seemed cunning, dangerous and generally untrustworthy. Flana was an attractive brunette clad like most Dyal Riders in brown feathers glued onto a leather undergarment. Her pretty face had a slightly foolish expression on it. Not as attractive as Bel or Lal certainly but worthy of a chief's attention. *Perhaps when he was tired of Bel....* Dyryth was truly a giant of a man with a taunting smile on his face. Zuul could easily understand how this newcomer had become named for the giant ground sloth he resembled. He escorted a stunningly beautiful woman clad in black feathers and covered with bruises. Zuul stared at her until his chief coughed to attract his attention.

"Hail, Lal. We had heard that you were dead. I am glad to see that you are alive. I have kept the Dyal Riders safe until your return." The lies came easily to Zuul's lips.

Lal nodded diplomatically. The unknown woman snorted. Even her sound of disgust seemed charming.

"Very well. I go to my house. Flana will come with me as my guest. My handmaidens will guard Ala while I sleep. Pol, take Kirov and Dyryth to the men's quarters. We will find suitable houses for them when I wake."

Zuul coughed. "Pardon, Lal, but m... your handmaidens have returned to their families. There are none in the house of the chief."

Lal frowned. "Why did this happen? The maidens of Dyalsi take turns assisting the family of the chief."

The former acting chief stammered and said, "Your handmaidens became unruly and disobedient in your absence. They said that I was not the chief and that my mate could clean your house as well as ours." From Zuul's point of view, that was the truth. The maidens of Dyalsi would have told a different version of the story.

The returned chief and her captive snorted in unison. Lal pronounced, "Very well. This matter can wait until I wake again. Zuul, take Ala to the house of your sisters. They will guard her until I make other plans. I go to my house."

The men saluted the departing queen by raising their right hands, palms outward, Zuul grudgingly, the others sincerely. Pol led Kirov and Dyryth to the bachelor men's quarters.

Ala's eyes flickered from Zuul to Lal and back again. When Lal entered her home, the beautiful queen of the Black Birdriders caught the deputy chief's eye. She smiled deeply, brightly, beguilingly. She dropped her head in seeming modesty before his admiring gaze. Zuul flushed and his pulse raced. He stepped forward and took her by the hand.

Ala's new campaign to conquer the Dyal Riders had begun. Already, she had her first conquest.

*Chapter Three*

## LIFE WAS WONDERFUL!

Kirov had only been a boy in 1913 when Pellucidar had exploded into the consciousness of the Outer World. The idea that the Earth was actually hollow had been theorized by scientists as far back as Edmund Halley. An obscure pre-Soviet revolutionary Russian Vera Zarovitch had explored part of the Inner World in 1865-80. (Owing to monarchist censorship, her account had been published in a little known American newspaper rather than the scientific journal that her discovery deserved.) Professor Nikolai Trukanov had explored another portion in 1914.

But it was E.R. Burroughs' accounts of the 1903~1913 adventures of David Innes and Abner Perry that had dramatically confirmed what many had long suspected. A youngster in Saint Petersburg at the time, Kirov had eagerly devoured both *At the Earth's Core* and *Pellucidar* and resolved that, one day, he, too, would enter the Inner World to study its dinosaurs and Pleistocene mammals for the glories of Russian science and the honor of his family.

And now, here he was in the land of his dreams with a lifetime of happiness and accomplishments ahead of him. He had freed a community from slavery, "invented" things undreamed of in an entire world, and had discovered strange new species unknown to the paleontologists of the Outer World. And—he smiled foolishly—he was engaged to marry Flana.

Life was wonderful!

Once Lal had reinstalled herself as chief of the Dyal Riders, she had adopted Flana as her sister. Kirov had become an adopted brother to Rell, the deputy chief that he had met as a hewer of wood in Tralsi. Lal proclaimed that the skal Kirov had slain on the Plain of Grazers met the Pellucidarian requirement for a hunter to slay a beast and lay its head before the door of his intended's hut. In five more wakes, Kirov and Flana would become mates. Only five more wakes…!

Indeed, life was wonderful.

In the meantime, Pol and Rell started him on his new career as *inventor* and *military advisor* for Dyalsi. The two natives had seen his "inventions"—actually copies of things invented long ago by various Outer World Neolithic peoples— among the Black Birdriders and were enthusiastic for him to recreate them for his new tribe. Kirov had had long talks with Pol and the other community leaders about the wonders of Outer World science. The native Pellucidarians had trouble understanding most of the things that Kirov described. But they had gradually worked out a plan to equip the Dyal Riders with life-changing advances over their existing saddles, straps, spears and axes, that Kirov called "stirrups", "bows and arrows" and "catapults."

Even as he mused about life as Flana's mate, he was carefully cutting a piece of leather into a saddle with stirrups. Stirrups had made Scythian and Mongol cavalry the terrors of their respective ages. Potentially, they would do as much for the Dyal Riders.

Truly, life was wonderful.

He was jolted out of his reverie by a runner shouting his name. Lal wanted to see him at her palace.

Immediately.

There was no time for new inventions.

War again threatened the Dyal Riders.

*Chapter Four*

# THE WAR COUNCIL

The messenger ushered Kirov into the war council in Lal's "palace." He recognized her deputy chiefs, Pol, Rell and Zuul. The young inventor repressed a grimace at the sight of the last. His first impression of the older man had not been good. Two strangers were present with them.

First things first. "Hail, Lal. I am here at your command."

"Hail, Kirov Skalkiller," replied the chief of the Dyal Riders respectfully. Here in her own throne room, clean and rested, Lal was more beautiful than ever. "I present Hortul Paddle-maker of the River People and Chirp of the Lodge Builders. They come as friends." In savage Pellucidar, such an introduction was necessary. One did not casually assume that a stranger was anything but a potential enemy.

Kirov greeted them politely. He had briefly met Hortul before, when they were both slaves in Tralsi, the town of the Black Birdriders. Now he was dressed in a curious garment of reeds woven together and glued to a leather undercoat. The Dyal Riders' tribal costume was somewhat similar but with brown feathers rather than reeds. Hortul greeted his liberator warmly. Chirp was a bulky fellow dressed in a luscious looking fur coat—much more like the Outer World's stereotype of a "caveman." He returned Kirov's welcome more cautiously.

The two newcomers illustrated the wide variety of tribal cultures within the "primitive" Inner World. If the restrained Chirp was the standard "caveman", then the Dyal Riders were the cowboys of Pellucidar while their allies the River People were the Volga Boatmen.

99

Lal came to the point. "Kirov, the River People and the Lodge Builders are allies of the Dyal Riders. Chirp has come to ask our help against a new threat from beyond the hills where the Lodge People roost."

Chirp took up the story. "The Wava Hills are twenty waking periods' march in that direction." Guided by the unerring homing instinct of native Pellucidarians, he pointed to his homeland—directly away from the Mountains of the Birds. "Even there, we, the brothers of the wava, have suffered from the raids of the Black Birdriders and we also have heard of the great deeds of Kirov Skalkiller. Now a great tribe of enemies advances towards our lodges and the lodges of the River People and Dyal Riders. We therefore ask for your help in defeating them and driving them back across the Plain of Grazers." He turned to face Lal. "We, the brothers of the wava, ask that you send the great Skalkiller to our lodges to aid us."

Before Kirov could respond, Rell enthused, "Kirov the *Inventor* can do anything. Many wakes ago, he was a simple slave of Ala Skal-rider. Despite her keen eyes, he organized the slaves of many tribes and freed us all. He *invented* long and short spears, spear throwers and rock casters. He slew many skals himself and led us in killing the trals that made the Black Birdriders feared." His pronunciation of the Russian words that Kirov had grafted into Pellucidarian was less than expert but the war council understood who and what he meant.

Chirp and Hortul nodded sagely. Chirp agreed, "We have heard these things and therefore believe that Kirov Skalkiller can defeat the Pulka Horde."

Hortul chimed in, "We told these things to the River People, the Marsh Dwellers, the Snake Eaters, and other tribes as well. We, too, say that Kirov Skalkiller can defeat the Horde."

Kirov was tremendously flattered by the description of his prowess and by the confidence shown by his new tribal allies. But, he was still wary about tackling the Inner World's equivalent of the Mongol Horde.

"Great Chirp, I thank you for your words. But I wish to

know more about this Horde. How many warriors does the Horde have? How are they armed? And what is their *strategy*?" The last word was in Russian and the council paused while Kirov translated it into Pellucidarian as best he could.

Chirp informed the council. "The Horde has many tens of ten tens of warriors as well as their women and children." Kirov rendered that as 'many thousands' of soldiers plus at least as many dependents. "They are armed with stabbing spears, throwing spears, and clubs. They ride on pulkas—strange beasts similar to the riding birds of Dyalsi but smaller. They also have other strange beasts from the Plain of Grazers with them. When they attack, they advance and hurl spears. Then they retreat beyond our reach. So far, they have done only little damage to our lodges but they have killed our brothers. They say that they will return and take our brothers and us captive. Then they will capture all of the tribes of the Plain of Grazers as far as the Mountains of the Birds."

The Pulka were sounding more and more like the Mongols. Pellucidar's scattered tribes were small by comparison with the great nations of the Outer World. If the Pulka Horde really had multiple thousands of warriors, it could easily conquer every settlement on the Plain of Grazers.

Kirov realized that a reputation as a wonder worker meant that you were expected to produce miracles on demand. He asked more questions, probing for more insight into the threatening enemy, as he stalled for time, trying to formulate a strategy. Chirp answered each question patiently, providing what information he had.

Zuul interrupted, a beatific smile on his face. "Great Lal, great Chirp, I, too, believe that Kirov *Skalkiller* can defeat the oncoming Horde." He gave the sobriquet a sneering intonation. "Did he not defeat many skals personally? Did he not invent great weapons under the very eyes of Ala of the Black Birdriders? Surely he can do the same for our fellow hunters, the Lodge Builders." Had butter existed in primitive Pellucidar, it would not have melted in Zuul's mouth.

Rell enthused. "Zuul is right. Kirov can do anything. Let him ride to the Wava Hills where he will defeat the Horde with the help of the Lodge Builders. If any escape, the war bands of the Dyal Riders and River People will destroy them!"

Pol was more judicious than Rell but agreed. Kirov was increasingly uncomfortable about his reputation as the Alexander Nevsky of the Inner World, but Lal decreed that he would leave for Wava, escorted by a small war band of Dyal Riders. The full allied war bands would follow behind them.

Kirov raised a final objection. "Great Lal, in five waking periods, I am to take Flana as my mate—"

The queen of the Dyal Riders cut him off. "War threatens us all. You must postpone your mating." A glacier crushing Dyalsi into rubble might have changed her mind but nothing less than that.

*Chapter Five*

## A WAVA AND A RYTH

Fifteen wakes later, a very much unmarried Kirov and his party arrived in the hill country claimed by the Lodge Builders. Three waking periods had been consumed learning how to ride and more-or-less control the fierce dyals that Lal's people had more-or-less tamed. Unlike the Black Birdriders who controlled their aerial mounts by slapping hands, the Dyal Riders cooed to direct their steeds. Kirov had never been a singer and cooing almost defeated him. Eventually, though, he learned enough of the right signals and the small war band set out with Rell as leader and Chirp as guide.

The Mountains of the Birds receded behind them, fading into mere smudges on Pellucidar's upward curving surface. A waking period's ride from Dyalsi, the war band crossed the impressive Coldwater River in small boats provided by Hortul's clansmen with a stopover at River Town Island on the way. Another waking period was consumed with a feast celebrating Kirov's previous freeing of the River People from the Black Birdriders. The young scientist had never realized that fish could be prepared as many ways as the River People did.

Once across the river, Kirov and party pounded onward, always guided by Chirp's homing instinct.

En route, the young scientist observed the flora and fauna of the vast undulating land. Beautiful flowers reared star like heads above the endless pale green grasses. Sweet scents caressed the nostrils of man and bird alike. Great herds of creatures, some startlingly similar to those inhabiting Siberia only eight hundred kilometers beneath their feet, some extinct on Earth's

103

outer surface for thousands of years, some totally unknown, grazed and hunted across the wilderness barely scratched by humanity. Kirov recognized saber toothed *Smilodons*, bison-like *Crassicornis*, armadillo-like *Boriostracons*, *Brontops*, *qirqirns*, and several species of giant ground sloths. Overhead, the *Teratornis*, ancestor to the Outer World's condors, cruised by on patrol. The entire party watched for menacing trals and skals but none appeared. In contrast, families of antelopes, sheep, deer, tapirs, musk oxen, mammoths and mastodons were almost old friends.

A waking period later, the war band spooked a herd of antelopes. Lurking codons—Canis dirus (dire wolves) to Outer World paleontologists—had been stalking the herbivores and decided to dine on gilaks (humans) instead. The powerful dyals escaped the wolves but not without a long roundabout chase. When birds and men were rested, Chirp again patiently headed them towards the Wava Hills.

As the party grew closer to their guide's homeland, the terrain became rougher. Minor ridges grew into hills. Rocky outcroppings forced the dyals to swerve around them, complicating the journey. Small streams laced the land and one rest period the party dined on what the American adventurer David Innes had described as small freshwater whales. The occasional trees and small copses dotting the vast Plain multiplied and gathered into forests. Evergreens and hardy nut bearing trees predominated.

Eventually, the forest parted, revealing a large park-like meadow with a sparkling lake in the center. Streams and other waterways stretched from the lake into the woods. Black mounds dotted the lake's surface and dark bodies moved quietly through the waters.

"Behold our homes!" proclaimed Chirp proudly. "This is the Lake of Lodges. In the center are the lodges of our brothers, the wava. On the far shore are the lodges of the gilaks. Ourselves." He thumped himself on the chest.

The war band rode slowly forward, beginning to circle the lake. They stopped at a waterway cutting across their path.

Unlike natural rivers and streams, the waterway ran as straight as an arrow into a grove of birch trees. It appeared to be of uniform width and depth as well—too wide and deep to cross easily.

The young scientist asked, "Did men make this stream?"

Chirp smiled. "No. Our brothers, the wava, dug it to fetch trees to their dam and lodges. One comes now." He pointed toward the birch grove.

A huge log moved silently along the canal. Behind it, pushing it, was a huge dark brown creature, easily the size of an adult Siberian brown bear. Its front paws rested on the trailing end of the log as its rear feet paddled vigorously.

"A beaver! A Pleistocene *Castorides*!" exclaimed Kirov softly. The words were necessarily in Russian and scientific Latin.

The Dyal Riders watched in amazement as Chirp greeted the huge mammal by slapping his hands lightly together and making chittering sounds. The creature looked up and paused in its paddling to chitter back. The log drifted to a halt.

After a few moments' palaver, Chirp grandly announced. "We can cross the canal on this log." He urged his dyal forward. The riding bird balked at first but responded to repeated urgings. It strode forward to the edge of the canal, jumped onto the substantial piece of timber, and then down on the far side of the waterway. Chirp turned to face his allies, face expectant.

Kirov realized that the Lodge Builder's fur coat made him look very much like a beaver himself. Had the humans of his tribe adopted other habits of their totemic animals?

The Dyal Riders muttered among themselves. They were brave enough in their own setting but the strange situation upset them. A long tiring ride, the strange creature, and its musky smell—all these were disconcerting. A bold young tribesman gallantly urged his dyal forward but misjudged the jump. Bird and man landed on the log but it rotated under them and dumped them into the water. Sputtering, he swam ashore on the near side of the canal, climbed out, and turned to help his squawking mount to safety.

Kirov concealed a smile. "Rell, Chirp, can we ride around the canal?" He pointed to the birch grove.

Chirp gravely agreed. He clucked at his dyal, which took a few steps towards the woods. The wava looked at the Lodge Builder, who chattered at him. The great beaver resumed paddling and the huge creature was soon in the lake heading into the distance.

The Dyal Riders needed no further suggestions. They turned their fierce riding birds and headed across the meadow. Chirp paced them on the far side of the canal. As Kirov suspected, the waterway ended a short distance into the birch grove. The wava had dug its canal only as far as was necessary to transport freshly cut trees and no further.

Kirov began to ride around the canal's end. The dyal picked its way carefully through the stumps of felled trees.

As the riding bird moved, another wava appeared out of the trees. Kirov glanced at it and imitated Chirp's friendly chittering as best he could. He turned around the canal end, facing his guide.

Chirp's face was white with fear.

"Kirov! That is no wava! It's a ryth!" he shouted.

The ryth—the giant cave bear of the Pleistocene and the most ferocious predator in Pellucidar—reared upright. Its massive claws struck at Kirov's unprotected back.

*Chapter Six*

## THE CONQUEST OF DEATH ITSELF

The ryth—*Ursus spelaeus* to the paleontologists of the Outer World—reared upright. Two paws full of claws smashed into Kirov and his dyal before either could react. One claw swept Kirov off his steed, his feet ripping out of his stirrups. He flew brutally sideways, landing in the mud and water of the wava's canal. Fire wracked his side.

The other claw slashed into the dyal's thick body. Feathers flew and muscles shredded under the giant cave bear's attack.

Dying, the dyal kicked backward. Its own powerful clawed feet smashed into its attacker's guts.

The Dyal Riders shouted in unison. Their war birds lurched forward. Stone-tipped spears stabbed into the giant bear's side. The great carnivore's claws were entangled in the body of Kirov's dyal. It screamed in pain. Rell leaned forward, hammering the bear's skull with his ax.

The ryth turned, shaking the dying dyal off its claws. It faced the puny gilaks who dared contest its rule over the Wava Hills. Five spears were embedded in its hide but its colossal vitality was undiminished. It roared its challenge. The leaves on the trees shook in fear.

The ryth swatted Rell contemptuously. The brave Pellucidarian grunted. Ursine claws had missed his flesh but not the anvil-like paw. Unlike Kirov the Inventor, Rell was strapped to his dyal's saddle. The force of the blow crumpled up the deputy chief of the Dyal Riders and knocked his fierce war bird off its feet. Both slumped to the ground. The other Dyal Riders

paused, appalled by the giant carnivore's power. Traditional
axes and newly introduced assegais waved weakly.

Kirov shook himself off, spraying water and mud like a
dog, and lurched upright. The water had cushioned his landing.
He pulled his assegai from his belt and ran forward. The ryth
was facing the Dyal Riders beside the canal end. Kirov struck
home, spearing the animal in the back.

The Pleistocene monster screamed again in pain. It looked
around for its tormentor. Momentarily, it overlooked the inventor standing in the wava's canal. Its claws glittered in the
eternal noonday Sun of the Inner World.

Heartened by Kirov's example, the Dyal Riders cooed and
their war birds surged forward. Assegais stabbed into the
distracted monster's massive body while axes smashed down
on forearms and skull.

Savagely hurt, the ryth flailed about. Whether by instinct
or cunning, it hit two more Dyal Riders. Men and birds collapsed, knocked off their feet. For a moment, the battle seemed
an insane dance as gilaks and dyals maneuvered to find the
ryth's weak spots without succumbing to its flashing claws.

Kirov slogged out of the canal's shallow waters to Rell's
still body. The giant bear was dangerously close but the young
inventor needed weapons more powerful than his remaining
flint knife. He cut Rell's back up ax and spear from their bind-
ings.

He pointed Rell's spear at the ryth and braced the butt into
the soggy ground as best he could. He shouted and waved one
arm to attract the bear's attention.

Whether because the bear understood Kirov's Russian
insults or simply because the young man was relatively station-
ary and close at hand while the mounted Dyal Riders bobbed
and weaved out of reach, the great Pleistocene mammal focused
on Kirov. It brought itself more fully upright and roared to
intimidate Kirov who crouched and waved at it. Then it sham-
bled forward, a terrible parody of a hungry man striding towards
his dinner table, but moving more swiftly than a man could

run. Its powerful body smashed down onto the young inventor....

.... Impaling itself on the spear that Kirov had aimed at the advancing monster's abdomen. The creature's own momentum forced the stone-tipped spearhead deep into its vitals.

The ryth screamed again, shaking the forest with its pain and rage.

No cowards, the Dyal Riders still quailed at its brute energy as it struggled upright, ready to kill again. They circled, looking for openings.

As the monster moved, Kirov's spear dug deeper through its body. The stone spearhead savaged the great creature's internal organs. Red fluid poured from a dozen wounds, baptizing Kirov and Rell in blood.

Battered and bleeding, the ryth swayed and then collapsed. A half ton of bone and muscle smashed Kirov and Rell into the ground. Blood soaked the ground and crimsoned the canal's waters.

The Dyal Riders rallied. Axes and clubs crushed the ryth's skull. Spears levered the ursine bulk off the men's' bodies.

Freed from the ryth's smothering weight, Kirov lay on the marshy ground, panting, sucking in air that had never seemed so sweet. Even his own sweat and the bear's stink seemed like rare perfumes.

A Dyal Rider examined Rell's fallen body and shook his head. "Rell the Brave One has gone to the Dead World," he declared sadly. "When he fell, I hoped that he was merely sleeping but he breathes no more."

Another Dyal Rider added, "The Dead will honor him for his scouting of the roost of the Black Birdriders, for his battle with the ryth, and for other brave deeds."

Chirp quietly agreed. "And for coming to the aid of the Lodge Builders against the Pulka Horde."

Kirov had originally come to Pellucidar as a draftee in the Soviet Red Army and all Soviet soldiers were taught basic first aid. "Let me see him," the young man said between pants. "Let me try chest compression."

WHEN THE WARRIORS of the Lodge Builders arrived to investigate the ryth's screams, they found Chirp, Rell and the Dyal Riders in awe of Kirov for his conquest of Death itself.

## Chapter Seven

## CONTACT WITH THE ENEMY

Rell pointed to a barely visible smudge moving across the grass green background, hazy with distance. "The Horde approaches."

Kirov grunted agreement as he gazed across the Plain of Grazers from his vantage point in an oak-like tree in the Wava Hills. Pellucidar's upward sloping landscape made scouting and spying out distant objects easy compared to the downward sloping curve of Earth's outer surface. Kirov supposed that a powerful enough telescope could see across the vast void inside the hollow Earth and look down on the Empire of Pellucidar more than seven thousand kilometers distant. An amusing thought: spying on the American Emperor and his Stone Age court from overhead! However, until the young inventor could introduce glassblowing and telescope making to the Inner World, he would have to observe potential threats with his own eyes.

Far out across the Plain, three groups of black dots resolved themselves out of the blur of distance. A thick vee led the way, a large rectangle occupied the middle position, and a small square followed. The three groups moved as a unit, pointing straight at the Wava Hills where Kirov and his allies waited. The young inventor easily recognized the units as advance guard, main body and rear guard. Multitudes of strange Pellucidarian creatures grazing or hunting on the Plain scattered before them.

Rell noted admiringly, "They are coming exactly as you

said." The oncoming Horde was indeed advancing directly toward Kirov's men.

The hero worship in Rell's voice annoyed and frustrated the young inventor. The deputy chief of the Dyal Riders had been Kirov's friend, colleague and blood brother. Since Kirov had saved his life, he had become a worshipper. As had many other Dyal Riders and their allies, the Lodge Builders.

Kirov sighed sadly. Rell didn't notice the unspoken emotion.

The former Soviet Red Army Specialist regurgitated some of his military training. "The slope of the ground in front of us forms a natural ramp into the Wava Hills. Those small hills on either side will encourage the Hordesmen to ride here rather than over those rocks. Dyals don't like running over rocks."

Rell frowned. "I don't think those beasts are dyals." He pointed at the rapidly approaching creatures.

Kirov squinted his eyes against the eternal noonday Sun. Rell was right. Chirp had said that the Pulka Hordesmen rode creatures like the Dyal Riders' flightless war birds, the *Phororhacos* of Outer World science. But the oncoming creatures were quadrupeds, more like horses than birds....

Suddenly, the aspiring paleontologist's training smote him. "*Gigantocamelus!*" gasped Kirov.

The advancing creatures were indeed the Pleistocene progenitors of the common Arabian dromedary. Camels in the Leningrad Zoo stood two meters high at the hump. These monsters were at least three meters high at the hump and four meters high at the head, and proportionately shaped and muscled.

Like their Arabian cousins, these giant camels carried men. At least they were normal sized. The camel riders were typical Pellucidarian Stone Age warriors clad in khaki skins—camel hides, Kirov guessed—and armed with spears. Kirov noted that those spears were longer than the common two-meter spear that many tribes used. The spearmen would need the extra length to reach enemies on the ground.

As Kirov watched from his vantage point, the first camel

reached the trap prepared by the inventor and manned by Lodge Builder spearmen.

Reached it—and ignored it!

The allied warriors had spent a great deal of work cutting sharpened stakes and pounding them into the ground across the expected approach of the Horde. Kirov's plan was that the enemy dyals or dyal-like creatures would run onto the stakes and be impaled. Then the Lodge Builders and Dyal Riders could easily spear the immobilized attackers.

The great camels had indeed advanced exactly where pre-dicted. But their eyes, mounted high above the ground, had obviously detected the line of stakes hidden in the tall grass. Contemptuously, the tall mammals simply stepped over the barrier!

Kirov longed for the catapults that he had "invented" to defend Tralsi from the attacks of the great skals but he had not had time to build even one since he came to the Wava Woods.

The Lodge Builders were also hidden in the grass. One of them lay flat directly in the path of an oncoming giant. A hoof the size of a samovar or tea kettle came down on the spearman's back. The snap of bones echoed loudly.

Perhaps that Lodge Builder was fortunate.

The other camels balked as they spotted the hidden men. Lodge Builders gallantly rose, attempting to spear the great beasts. The camels lurched backward, evading the first, awkward blows with intelligence.

High above the land of hidden men, the camel riders were not slow to respond. As their mounts balked, they spied out the reasons. Long spears stabbed downward into the bodies of rising Lodge Builders. Cries of pain echoed across the Plain.

Kirov shouted orders at the Dyal Rider cavalry hidden in the tree line below him. His tribesmen cooed and their fierce war birds leaped forward. The gilaks mounted on their savage war birds raised their spears like Cossack lancers.

Dyal Riders and camel riders clashed furiously. Kirov's tribesmen drove their charge home. The great camels had stopped to deal with the Lodge Builders. Their giant bodies made excellent targets. Dyal Rider spears thudded home in camel breasts and beaks shredded flesh. The huge quadrupeds screamed in pain and reared upward, trying to escape the vicious bipedal attacks. Camel riders spilled to the ground. Freed from control, maddened by deadly pain and the scent of blood, the giant camels fought to escape. Some attacked the agile dyals with teeth and hooves but most tried to turn and leave the sudden battlefield. As they did, they trampled their fallen masters into the soft soil. The allied tribesmen cheered the fleeing giants' backs in sudden victory.

Rell smiled savagely. "We are victorious, mighty Kirov! Your plan worked—"

Kirov shook his head and pointed. One group of camel riders had been defeated. But from behind them came hundreds more.

*Chapter Eight*

## A BATTLE IN THE WAVA WOODS

The oncoming line of camel riders halted as their retreating fellows plunged into their ranks. Shrill shouts—battle cries and orders—echoed across the outskirts of the Wava Hills. Gradually, the camel riders brought their giant mounts under control. Savage eyes examined the allied defense line and the Wava Woods behind it.

Lodge Builder infantry and Dyal Rider cavalry warriors peered back.

Kirov could see a charge forming up, one with more than enough power to smash the thin line of allies opposing it. He shouted for his fellows to retreat into the woods.

Slowly, the allied tribesmen began to withdraw. Pellucidarian warriors valued bravery, not unquestioning obedience to orders. Kirov's almost godlike prestige and the obvious mismatch in numbers caused them to obey. Kirov and Rell started down their arboreal command post to join the retreat.

Some horde leader bellowed. The camel riders charged, their long spears aimed at the backs of their retreating enemies.

The allies raced into the tree line.

The camel riders' pause to reorganize had cost them precious time. The allies reached the woods and vanished into the leafy maze.

Giant camels pulled up short at the threat of low hanging tree limbs. Their necks bobbed and weaved. Their riders shouted commands and thumped their sides. Camels protested but moved forward, this time at a walking pace as they avoided thick branches. Riders, too, had to duck. The charge dwindled to a walking advance.

THE RETREATING ALLIES burst into the great clearing surrounding the Lodge Builders' lake. Strange animals ran with them. The wild withdrawal from the planned battle-field had spooked deer, antelopes and less identifiable creatures out of the wood. The animals instinctively skirted the water-walled fortress, heading for the woods on the opposite side of the clearing.

The lodges from which the tribe took its name were built on the shores of a woodland lake inhabited by a large colony of *wava*—giant Pleistocene beavers the size of Siberian brown bears. Like the smaller beavers of the Outer World, the wava cut down trees, eating the tender bark and using the stripped timber to build and maintain their dams and homes. As the forest retreated from the shores of the lake, the wava had dug canals across the meadowland to ease the transportation of timber to the sites of their homes and dams.

Some time in the past, a tribe of *gilaks* (humans) had be-friended the wava and settled down beside them, adopting many of the beavers' traits in the process. The Lodge Builders built shoreside homes in imitation of their totemic animals' lodges and improved the canals into a series of defensive ditches. The result was a strange but effective fortress from which gilaks and wava alike could defy the constant threats of Pellucidarian life.

Lodge Builders shouted at their fellows to take cover. Women dropped baskets of bark and other food, seized children, and ran over log bridges to take shelter in their thick wooden lodges. The older and younger men—Kirov would have called them the Home Guard—seized spears and shovels and ran to defensive positions. The retreating Lodge Builders fell into beside them, panting with exertion.

Chirp, the war chief of the tribe, clapped his hands loudly

and chattered at the wava. They slapped the water with their tails and disappeared.

The Dyal Riders had been moving at a walking pace to protect their slower moving allies. Once out in the clearing, they collected in a knot, trying to assess the situation and plan their strategy. Their savage war birds danced about nervously.

It was then that the warriors realized that both Kirov and Rell had disappeared.

*Chapter Nine*

## THREATS

The White House, Lincoln (city), Seward (state),
Republic of New America
Northern Perryland, northern Pellucidar
(diagonally under the Territory of Alaska)

E dgar Rice Burroughs tapped the window gently. He
shook his head in wonder.

"Something wrong with the window, Ed?" came
a squeaky yet powerful voice from behind him.

Burroughs turned around to face his host who was offering
him a drink. He took it as he answered. "No, Theodore. Just
amazed and amused to see a window made out of glass here in
Pellucidar. You really have created a New America just as you
promised." He took a sip of the Outer World drinking whiskey.
Another sign that civilization was coming to the Inner World.

"My New Americans have. Their work and ingenuity have
created a bully new nation with all the promise of the United
States and none of the vices." Ed's host was an orator among
other things.

That host stepped over to the wide window and waved
grandly at the outside landscape lit by the eternal noonday Sun
of the Inner World. A small city stretched down the hill on
which the house sat. House and city might have been snatched
up from the Kansas prairie of sixty years ago by one of L. Frank
Baum's super-tornados and deposited intact in the Pellucidar
of today. Neat streets—only dirt at the moment—formed a
grid, defining spaces for houses, hotels, shops, schools, church-

es, saloons and other buildings. Energetic people clad in warm American frontier clothing strode or rode through the streets as mammoths pulled wagons and baulks of timber to and fro. Beyond them, farms filled the valley below the city. In the distance, a cloud of dust marked the location of a huge coal mine. A moving pillar of smoke marked the railroad delivering cargos of coal and other minerals north to the port of Lexington in the Arctic Ocean to heat the homes and feed the factories of Alaska and Canada.

"Twelve years ago, this was nothing but rolling grassland," declaimed the host. "A hill with a view here; a river valley down there; rolling plains stretching for miles in every direction. Nothing but antelopes, mammoths, furry herbivorous dinosaurs and the carnivores that fed on them. Not even your famous cavemen in this part of the world. Now, look at it!

"What do you see?" he asked rhetorically. Burroughs sipped his whiskey.

"I'll tell you what you see! Civilization! Civilization coming to savage Pellucidar! The best that American civilization has to offer to the people of our New America." The host gestured grandly again.

"And it's people that made it happen, Ed. People. Thousands of poor Americans looking for a fresh start. Tailors and bricklayers from New York; ranchers and farmers from the Dakotas; miners and lumbermen from California. Thousands of Americans who couldn't make a go of things Outside but took up land and built a new nation.

"A *great* nation, Ed. We learned from our mistakes Outside. We didn't push the original Pellucidarians aside the way that Andrew Jackson pushed the American native tribes aside. Instead, we purchased rights to the land with trade goods. If they didn't want to sell, we respected their decisions and their tribal lands. And those who want to be citizens *are* citizens with all the rights and privileges. They're still learning how republican government works but they *are* learning. We have no hyphenated New Americans here. Just New Americans."

The orator paused and then added, "Including your refugee Russians."

Burroughs had been patiently waiting for his friend of many years to take a breath. "I'm glad to hear that. Most of *our* Russians are royalists, loyal to the memory of Czar Nicholas. Many of them wanted to fight to the death in Stolypin Land instead of coming to New America. I'm glad that they're adjusting to life in your postage stamp republic." He grinned as he described his host's pride and joy.

His host took the bait. "'Postage stamp?' 'Postage stamp?!' Old man, I'll have you know that we now have five whole states laid out! Five! A population of almost 40,000 people! More than 5,000 here in the city of Lincoln alone! Thousands of acres in cultivation! Mineral production doubled in the last year! A thousand miles of railroad! Steamboats on the Longview River trading with a dozen tribes! This isn't some dinky little principality that Rand McNally won't give a distinctive color to! This is the Republic of New America!" He flourished his glass triumphantly. Amber liquid leaped through the air to splash onto the ryth-skin rug. He appeared not to notice.

Burroughs ignored his friend's well deserved boasting. "You mentioned your railroad. Have you connected to the Empire of Pellucidar yet?" His face was serious.

His host came back down to Earth. "No. Not yet. And maybe not for a long time to come." He kicked back the remains of his drink with a single gulp before continuing. He gestured to a pair of comfortable chairs and they sat down before the great window.

"Pellucidar is a huge place, Ed. The Soviets call it a New World and, for once, they're right. I have a hundred scouts out day and night." He paused and snorted in self depreciation at his unconscious use of an Outer World phrase. "Well, I have them out waking period and sleeping period. But we haven't actually reached the Empire by land yet. Or Maharland. We've found things that even you wouldn't believe but we don't yet *know* for sure where the Empire is!"

"I thought the Mahar maps that Abner got from Phutra showed that New America and the Empire are on the same coast of the same continent," interjected Burroughs. He made a mental note: *Ask Theodore about these "things that even I won't believe" later. The other ERB is always looking for new stories to publish.*

"The maps show that," confirmed his host, "but we haven't confirmed those maps yet. A Mahar flies over things and maps them differently compared to a human walking or riding across the ground. In the meantime, we're driving the Lexington, Lincoln & Sari Railroad east and southeastward—along the shores of the Sojar Ocean—to where we *think* the Empire is. And a branch line across Alaska. Until we connect up, contact with the Empire is telegrams relayed through Old America plus David's occasional visits to the Outside. David and I have met in New York and Hartford but never in Lincoln or Sari."

Burroughs sighed. "I was hoping that you would have linked up with David and Abner by now. Pardan and the Russian royalist rear guard stopped the Soviet advance on the Plutonian Plain many sleeps ago but that was just a temporary check. The Soviets didn't actually retreat to Russia; they're just waiting for their leadership to sort things out and issue new orders. In the meantime, they're digging in. I estimate that they control a chunk of land the size of California if not more. And, each report the scouts bring back lists new roads and buildings. And guns. Big ones.

"Pellucidar makes a tempting target and cavemen can't fight Twentieth Century weapons with spears and axes," he concluded.

His host nodded glumly. "The British and French aren't letting any grass grow under their feet at the South Pole, either. Mussolini and Hitler are both talking about seizing living space in Pellucidar as well. Even some Japanese and Chinese have expressed interest in Pellucidarian territories. David's cousin says that the Japanese are interested in building their own mechanical prospectors. Officially for civil engineering purposes. In the meantime, they're buying up every cheap mechanical prospector knockoff that the French and Germans will sell them." He looked at his glass and seemed surprised to find it empty.

Burroughs shook his head. "A land rush in Pellucidar. It was inevitable once the Europeans finished dividing up Africa and Asia.

"Still, our immediate problem is the Soviets. They're only a few hundred miles from here. Once they start moving again, it won't take them long to reach your western border. And based on their record to date, it won't take them much longer before they provoke an incident and cross that border. You're a much tougher target than the Stone Age tribes are but your entire army is smaller than one Soviet division. David's industries and trained manpower would be a big help."

His host added grimly, "I guess you haven't heard the latest news. David has his own problems. The latest telegram says that the Mahars have reappeared in the northern Empire. Fortunately only in small, isolated groups. So far."

Burroughs winced. The great reptiles had made much of Pellucidar a land of terror for untold centuries. Breaking their iron-clawed grip had been David Innes' first and possibly greatest achievement. If they returned in numbers, the Empire would have to deal with them first. There could be no help for New America against the Soviets even if Theodore and David connected their respective railroads.

The two old friends were silent for a long time. They gazed out of the glass window, visualizing the future that they were trying to build crumbling under the Soviet heel. Both of them felt cold despite a fire burning merrily in the hearth behind them.

Ed's host coughed. "Well, when the Soviets bump up against New America, I guess we'll have to show them that we make good neighbors—and terrible enemies—even without David's help."

Burroughs considered the statement. "I guess we will."

There was another long silence.

"Mind a political question, Theodore?"

The host's hearty laughter filled the room. "Me? 'Mind a political question'? Never! Ask away!"

"Why didn't you return to the United States in 1916 or 1920? You could have had the Presidency again for the asking."

Theodore Roosevelt was silent for a second or two. He smiled infectiously. He leaned forward. His eyes gleamed.

Edgar Rice Burroughs leaned forward to hear his friend's confidence.

"Because Pellucidar keeps me young."

Fort Alinsky, Plutonia okrug (area), Interior Zone,<br>Novy Mir Military District<br>Leninska, Novy Mir

DURING THE BATTLES of the 1917-20 Russian Civil War, Edgar Rice Burroughs had found Soviet military music unspeakably pompous. But, apparently, the Soviet Red Army liked it. Cymbals crashed to a crescendo and the band fell silent. A senior officer barked a series of commands. The troops of Fort Alinsky came to attention, saluted their new commander, and began marching to their barracks.

Brigade Commander E. Varan descended the reviewing stand and entered the rambling log building that was the command post of the Soviet beachhead in Novy Mir. His staff followed him. He seated himself in the commander's chair. In contrast to the well fed Kandinsky, Varan was a tall handsome blond with classical features. There was a rumor that he had a Mongol grandmother but wise soldiers kept their opinions to themselves. Officially, the Soviet Union was committed to the equality of all races. Unofficially? The white Great Russians ruled and other nationalities obeyed.

Varan opened the staff meeting briskly.

"Comrades, thank you for welcoming me to Novy Mir. Before we begin the regular staff meeting, I have important news from Moscow." The officers, neatly clad in their best winter field grey uniforms, leaned forward in anticipation. The disaster on the Plutonian Plain several months previously had brought things in Moscow to a head. Comrade Trotsky had been forced to resign as People's Commissar of Army and Fleet Affairs and as Chairman of the Revolutionary Council. Several officers too closely associated with the fallen leader had committed suicide rather than face Soviet justice. All of the survivors wanted to know what would happen next.

"Comrade Secretary General Stalin has reviewed the events of the Plutonian Plain battle." Another man might have paused for dramatic effect but Varan plowed ahead. "He has determined that our unfortunate reverse was the result of Regiment Commander E. Kandinsky's lack of foresight. Kandinsky has been remanded to a court martial for negligence. In addition, former Intelligence Officer I. Garman has been reassigned to new duties. No other personnel actions are to be taken at this time." There was a noticeable breeze in the closed room as the assembled officers simultaneously let out their breaths. Varan pretended not to notice.

"In addition, Comrade Stalin has directed that we continue the liberation of Novy Mir for the greater glory of the Soviet Union. The resources of the New World will enable us to break the capitalist encirclement of our nation. Our strategic advance will first be south to the shores of the Karl-Marx Ocean. The ocean forms a natural defensive boundary for the expanding Interior Zone. Upon completion of that operation, we will expand to the east and west.

"That expansion will include establishing control of *all* Russian territory as far as the border of the so called Republic of New America. Any persons found in the Interior Zone will either acknowledge Soviet rule or be eliminated. That includes primitive humans, humanoids, hominids and nonhumans, revanchist monarchists, and capitalist mercenaries. Once we have consolidated our position sufficiently, we will receive new orders. In the interim, we will establish diplomatic relations with New America and convince them of our peaceful intentions."

Everyone present understood the hidden message and nodded in agreement.

Imperial Palace, Sari, The Empire of Pellucidar
Southern Perryland, Pellucidar Temperate Zone

DAVID INNES LOOKED at his returned general in disbelief.

Not that Vakar the Tall One would have seemed like a general to someone of the Outer World. He was clad in loincloth and sandals. His hair was a windblown bird's nest. The only outward sign that civilization had touched him was his weapons belt. It carried holsters for steel pistol and sword and stone knife and ax. During military operations, he would add a musket and bandoleer of ammunition. The belt buckle was ornamented with the insignia of Empire and generalship. For the people of the Inner World, that was uniform enough.

One of Innes' counselors spoke up. "Vakar says that the Mahars wish peace with gilaks. That is hard to believe." There was a murmur of agreement. Most of the chiefs present remembered the not too distant past when the great reptiles had tithed their human subjects for food and labor. To the men of the Inner World, *gilak* meant "human being"; to the Mahars, it meant "cattle."

In 1903, David and his close friend Abner Perry had ridden the Mark I mechanical prospector from Connecticut to Pellucidar. Despite the fantastic dangers of the savage world at the Earth's Core, both men had fallen in love with the strange new land and its uncivilized but striving peoples. In particular, David had fallen in love with Dian, the Beautiful One, princess of Sari. Together, they had overthrown the rule of the vicious reptilian rulers and established the Empire as a vehicle for introducing the best of Outer World civilization to the humans—and other beings—of Pellucidar. The Mahars had fled—and the Empire seemed to have peace, and a chance to grow into a full member of the community of nations. Now, however, all seemed threatened.

Fash, chief of the kingdom of Suvi, and Oose, chief of the kingdom of Kali, emerged as the spokesmen for two groups of opinion. Suvi was on the northern border of the Empire, close to the Mahar menace. Fash wanted a powerful army to push the reptiles as far away as possible. If the reported sea raiders killed Mahars, so much the better. Kali was on the coast of Pellucidar's great ocean, the Sojar Az, and therefore closer to the corsair threat. Oose was willing to attempt peace with the Mahars who now seemed a lesser problem.

After each of the Imperial chiefs had given his advice, David decided in favor of peace. "I did not think that I would ever sympathize with the Mahars but I pity an intelligent race in danger of extermination by a ruthless enemy. If the Mahars will have peace with us, we will have peace with them."

Further arguments from Fash were cut off when a breathless messenger arrived from Thoria, the Land of the Awful Shadow.

The dreaded Korsars had arrived in Thoria and had surprised and killed or captured some hunters. Goork, the king of Thoria, frantically implored his Emperor for help. The counselors erupted in an excited hubbub.

David I's imperial voice cut through the confusion. The federated tribes were to mobilize their armies. He, David, would lead one division against the invaders. Ghak of Sari would command his tribe's regiment. Other regiments would join them en route. Tanar the Fleet One, son of Ghak, would immediately depart for Thoria to locate the invaders and offer an honorable peace. Meanwhile, Vakar was to return to the Mahar camp and offer peace if the reptiles submitted to Imperial rule and promised peace with all gilaks. And David's wife, Dian, would rule the Empire in his absence.

As the war council broke up to deal with the Korsars threat, Abner Perry's report on extending the Imperial Railroad to the north was forgotten.

*Chapter Ten*

## BEHIND ENEMY LINES

**K**irov and Rell started to climb down the oak-like tree where they had been observing the oncoming camel riders. As the latter advanced, they stopped. The enemy was too close. Concealed in the tree's abundant leaves, they had a chance to hide.

The camel-rider advance thundered past. Behind the advance guard came the main body—a rough rectangle of warriors with women, children and massive bundles inside—all mounted on the great *Gigantocamelus* precursors to the camels of the Outer World.

Kirov thought that the camel riders should have stopped their main body and pitched camp while their warriors fought it out with the Lodge Builders and Dyal Riders. To his surprise, the horde moved forward, into the Wava Woods. Fierce cavalrymen, shouting women, screaming children, all passed below the tree where their enemies crouched and watched. The earth shook under the impact of great hooves. The air trembled with the bellowing (and the smells) of the ugly beasts.

Finally, the main body had entered the woods. The rear guard reined in their great beasts just outside the tree line. Keen eyes scanned the rear. Camel riders shouted questions, asking if "they" were in sight.

Kirov was puzzled about the camel riders. Chirp had said that the Pulka Horde rode beasts like the Dyal Riders' great war birds. Instead, the hordesmen had domesticated the giant four legged *Gigantocamelus*. And their numbers were much smaller than Kirov had been led to believe. Chirp had implied that the Pulka had thousands of warriors — far more than the usual Pellucidarian tribe. Instead, their numbers were a more typical few hundred.

Kirov shook his head. A few hundred was still many more than the Lodge Builders or his Dyal Rider contingent could face alone. His long absent military instructor Senior Starshinka Voitinuik always said that you had to deal with the situation you found rather than what you imagined it to be. He peered in all directions, probing for possibilities.

The rear guard paused to kill the wounded camels. A handful of warriors stood watch while another handful butchered the beasts roughly. Apparently, the giant camels were food to their riders as well as beasts of burden. That, too, was typical of Pellucidar.

Rell gestured to the low hills beyond the rear guard. Animal heads appeared from behind rocks and in the tall grass. The horde had been followed by packs of hunters. Kirov recognized hyena-dog jaloks, pig-like golloks, codons and *stolons*. The aspiring paleontologist classified the latter two as the *Canis dirus* (dire wolf) and *Amphicyon* (giant dog) of the Outer World. The packs maintained wide spaces between each other and glanced suspiciously at the other animals as they crept forward. But, clearly, all were united by their hunger.

Kirov decided to help them.

He whispered a few words to Rell. Both braced themselves on the tree limbs that they were standing on. Kirov sat down to give himself better stability and withdrew his spear and atlatl from his backpack.

A camel-rider guard, nervously eying the circle of carnivores edging towards him and his fellows, heard a giant camel's bellow behind him. He turned in time to see the huge beast charging forward.... Towards him! He leaped to the side as its hooves flashed over his body. Out of the corner of his eye, he saw a small spear hanging in the camel's rump.

He hit the soft earth of the Wava Hills and rolled over. The small herd of rear guard camels had broken loose from their handlers and stampeded. He could see more spears in rumps. And camel riders smashed into the ground by their own panicked creatures.

He stood up and surveyed the scene. Giant camels had stampeded away from the woods that his tribe had entered. Some of them had crashed directly into packs of oncoming carnivores. The golloks had scattered, allowing "their" camels to escape, but the canine predators had counterattacked savagely. One camel was already down, hamstrung by flashing codon teeth. The great beast's screams echoed across the vast Plain of Grazers.

Far away, numerous creatures grazing the endless grasslands looked up, eyes scanning for danger. Most returned to feeding. If the screams came closer, they would flee. Until then….

Life was cheap in the Inner World.

The surviving camel-rider decided that discretion was the better part of valor. None of his tribesmen were moving and the unfed carnivores had resumed their advance. He gathered his weapons and began jogging into the Wava Woods.

As he passed under a giant oak-like tree, a sudden weight smashed him to the ground. Once again, he tasted the rich soil of primeval Pellucidar.

Stunned, he felt hands ripping his great spear and knives from his body and then rolling him over. He looked up to see two fierce warriors dressed in brown feathers.

"Ka-goda?" barked one belligerently. Sharp knives menaced his throat.

"Ka-goda!" answered the camel-rider.

The warriors withdrew their knives to their own belts and pulled him upright. The belligerent one introduced his companion and himself. "This is Kirov Skalkiller, and I am Rell. We are Dyal Riders, who are allies of the Lodge Builders and many other tribes. We will defeat the Pulka Horde."

"I am Hurn, called the Lucky One," replied the captive. "No one can defeat the Pulka Horde. When the Horde advances, all must flee or submit." He spoke calmly and simply as if he was describing the flow of a stream or the taste of a fruit.

Rell swelled up with confidence. He brushed over the earlier skirmish, saying, "The Pulka Horde has not yet fought the Dyal Riders. Or faced the powerful weapons of Kirov the *Inventor*." The last word was Russian imported into Pellucidarian. Hurn furrowed his brow at the unknown term but Rell plunged on. "We will defeat the Horde as we defeated the Black Birdriders of Ala Skal-rider and...."

Kirov coughed. "Hurn, you are the slave of Rell the Brave One but we will not kill you if you do our bidding. Do you agree?"

Hurn thought the proposition over for a few seconds. "Yes, I will do your bidding. What would you have me do?"

"Fetch food to your people," said the inventor simply. He looked past Hurn at the carcasses of the giant camels still lying on the ground. Most of the circling carnivores were occupied with other bodies, brought down by their own powerful jaws. Occasionally, a diner would look up to be sure that a competing predator didn't hijack its meal. The golloks had reassembled and were advancing on the original corpses.

Hurn gaped at the inventor in astonishment. He didn't see Rell's face. The latter stared briefly but then smiled. The Brave One had experienced many of Kirov's strange ideas before.

Kirov amplified. "Hurn, you see that one of your tribe hacked a large haunch of meat from that beast. Go, pick it up and carry it to your tribe in the Wava Woods as quickly as you can. Rell the Brave One will protect you from the golloks and other creatures. When you have done this, you will be free and your people will reward you for the food. I will hunt for more food and bring it to your tribe."

Hurn turned to look at the partially butchered giant camels. Rell quickly hid his smile and solemnly nodded agreement with Kirov's directions.

The captive paused, clearly trying to see a trap in the simple instructions. Finding none, he nodded. "I go."

He breathed deeply and began jogging towards the camel carcasses. Rell waved a salute to Kirov and followed Hurn, weapons in hand.

Kirov watched them for a moment and turned to trot into the woods. His path took him in a wide arc past the Lake of Lodges.

HURN'S PEOPLE HAD surrounded the community of the Lodge Builders. Their giant camels swiftly bore their human masters in an arc around the community of beaver-like lodges. The open meadowland around the lake made movement easier than in the Wava Woods surrounding the clearing. But further advances were balked by the complex network of canals radiating outward from the lake. Even the giant camels could not easily step over waterways two meters or more wide. The invaders hunted for access to the community from the lake shore. They found none. The wava had done their work well.

Lodge Builder warriors crouched behind their watery barricades, spears pointing outward, ready to repel any creature that attempted to jump the barriers. Squads of Dyal Rider cavalry circled slowly; warily keeping an eye on their foes, ready to counterattack any breaches.

Camel-rider chiefs conferred. Eyes turned towards a point where the water barrier seemed relatively shallow....

Screams echoed from the mass of their tribesmen behind them. Attention jerked to the temporary camp under the trees where their women and children rested from their flight. A warrior, Hurn the Lucky One, burst out of the trees, carrying a great haunch of meat on his shoulders. Blood trailed on the grass behind him.

A chief barked an order. Another warrior enforced it, swinging a great club in an arc towards Hurn's feet. The runner was knocked to the ground. The chief barked a question.

Panting, Hurn gasped, "The camp is under attack by golloks and other meat eaters! They hunger for our people!" Screams

and shouts underlined his warning. Women and older children
fled out of the forest, carrying smaller children with them.

Stunned, the chief bellowed orders. Many of his warriors
were scattered around the long perimeter, probing for an entrance to the Lodge Builder town. Few of them heard him.
Those that did urged their ungainly beasts in circles, facing
towards the sudden threat. They breasted the crowd of tribesmen escaping from the threatening woods.

The ugly noises—screaming, shouting, bellowing, and
snorting—that emanated from the forest grew louder.

The camel riders plunged forward, seeking their enemies.
In the wooden cathedral of the forest, giant camels milled about,
masterless. Great piles of gear—tents, clothes, cooking pots,
firewood, dried food, spare weapons, and a hundred and one
other things—littered the ground where the women had been
setting up camp and now impeded movement.

The center of the confusion was yet another giant camel,
screaming as a sounder of golloks savagely attacked it. A spear
hung from its chest, the wound spraying blood over the battle,
exciting the vicious prehistoric pigs. Some swine were already
investigating the camp.

And behind the golloks stalked a milling crowd of still
hungry codons, stolons and jaloks. If a few camels were good
eating, more would be better!

Focused on the threatening animals, no rider noticed the
blood trail that had led the creatures to their camp, or the
amused eyes hidden in the high tree branches They forced their
great mounts through the labyrinthine woods. Plains dwellers,
both riders and mounts, were slow and uncomfortable within
the tight proximity of the trees. Accustomed to the endless
sunlight of Pellucidar's Inner Sun, the arboreal gloom confused
them and robbed them of their normal courage. And stabbing
branches harried and harassed them, drawing blood as they
forced their way to their prey.

When the camel riders reached the savage golloks, they
thrust their spears at the giant pigs, their blows hampered by

the tightness of their quarters. The trees seemed to shield the vicious omnivores from the long spears of the horde.

Some warriors struck their targets squarely, and shrill porcine squeals rent the already tortured air. Pigs began dodging camel hooves and spear points alike.

As the camp camels tried to escape the chaos, some blundered straight into the jaws of canine predators. Packs of ferocious dogs, wolves and hyenadons counter-attacked. The din increased. The blood fury mounted.

Other camels thundered into the meadowland of the Lake of Lodges where they collided with camel riders attempting to rally to their chief's orders. The siege of the Lodges dissolved into swirling confusion. Riderless camels milled about, seeking escape. Mounted beasts scarcely seemed more purposeful. Jostling camels slid and fell into the canals. The giant beasts honked frantically as the unfamiliar water closed over them.

The allied warriors gaped in awe as the seemingly invincible attack dissolved. Crouching Lodge Builders slowly uncoiled, standing upright as they stared at the milling mass, their ears deafened by pandemonium. Even the more aggressive Dyal Riders stood still, bemused by the sight and sounds.

Eventually, the camel-rider chief stopped fruitless shouting. He began riding through the chaos, slapping warriors on their shoulders with hands and, occasionally, long spear. Gradually, he began imposing order on his troops. By dint of personality and much pointing, he gathered a group of warriors around him. He dispatched messengers to gather in the camel riders still strung out along the lake and canals.

Suddenly, another man, this one dressed in brown feathers like the Dyal Riders, came running out of the woods at right angles to the bizarre battle. He ran furiously, feet flying. A sentry camel-rider noticed him and attracted the chief's attention.

At some unheard signal, the fleet figure stopped, waved his arms, and slammed a short spear into the soft ground at a sharp angle. He glanced behind him and waved again.

A ryth, perhaps the mate of the one at the canal, charged out of the woods behind him. Her powerful legs hurled her towards the waving figure as quickly as an Outer World race-horse.

The brown-clad figure took off again, obviously attempting to escape the gigantic cave bear. Her four feet quickly overhauled his two.

Focused on the tasty gilak before her, the ryth failed to notice the spear jammed in the ground in her path. Her own powerful legs slammed her huge body onto the spear. She screamed in sudden pain and momentarily halted. As she reared upright, the camel-rider sentry realized that she already had several other spears hanging from her furry chest.

The brown clad figure sprinted towards the apparent safety of the still distant knot of camel riders. All across the meadow of the Lodge Builders, human and bestial eyes turned to watch the foredoomed chase.

The maddened ryth resumed her pursuit. Again, her vast power overhauled her intended victim.

Did the brown clad man have another spear in his arsenal to buy more time?

No!

His backpack was empty. He was out of weapons.

He ran onward, determined to make the ryth work for her meal. He neared the camel riders gathered around their chief. He obviously hoped that they might save him.

The gigantic bear was almost upon the fleeing figure. He could hear her hot breath, loud in his ears. Her stride changed slightly so that she could bring a mighty paw smashing down onto her meal's shoulder.

A Dyal Rider shouted something and pointed to the doomed man....

The fleeing figure flung itself to the side, out of the bear's oncoming path!

Mighty muscles surged as the ryth flung herself forward—where she *expected* her prey to be!

The brown clad figure fell heavily to the ground. It blended into the rich loam of the Inner World.

Momentum carried the great creature forward....

Towards the camel riders!

The sentry camel-rider shouted a warning.

Too late!

Mesmerized by the chase, the camel riders had allowed their guard to relax, fatally so.

The mighty ryth crashed into the legs of the giant camels. Its powerful jaws quickly closed on one leg. The wounded animal went down, screaming, crippled and soon killed. Its rider catapulted through the air, his landing announced by the sound of breaking bones, a noise unheard by the guards as the roaring ryth continued her savage attack.

Unnoticed, the brown clad figure slowly raised itself to an upright posture. It was Kirov Skalkiller, who carefully moved to the waterway that barred the camel riders from the Lodge Builders' community.

The young inventor lowered his aching body into the water and swam across. Friendly hands pulled him from the moat. Behind him, the camel riders continued their fight with the savage creatures of the Inner World.

Kirov sat on the inner edge of the moat and gave orders. Any Soviet officer would have harshly criticized him for lacking a "command voice." The allied Pellucidarians didn't care. Anyone who could lure a ryth into attacking their enemies could do no wrong.

When the decimated chief's guard finally killed the ryth, they discovered that they were surrounded. Lodge Builders had swum the moat and captured many dismounted camel riders trying to escape the other carnivores. Dyal Rider cavalry had crossed on logs positioned by wava and circled behind the invaders. A small knot of camel riders attempted to break out. Dyal Riders cooed and their savage war birds counter-charged....

WHEN LAL AND the main army of Dyal Riders reached

the Lake of Lodges in accordance with the allies' earlier agreement, there was little to do.  Many giant camels had fled and
their erstwhile masters had surrendered.  Dozens of warriors
were dead.  The survivors and their women and children were
captives.  Many camel-rider women were already at work under
the supervision of Lodge Builder women gathering nuts and
berries from the once again peaceful Wava Woods or render-
ing the dead camels into steaks and chops.

THE VICTORY DANCES consumed an entire waking
period, stately Lodge Builder wheels alternating with wild Dyal
Rider gyrations.

Rell swelled with pride.  "Hail mighty Kirov Skalkiller!
We have defeated the great Pulka Horde!"  He twirled his arms
in celebration.

Hurn looked at Rell in amazement.  "'The Pulka Horde'?"
he repeated.  "We are not part of the Pulka Horde.  We are
the Sojar Pah (Great Camel) Riders.  We *flee* the Pulka Horde
lest we become their slaves or meals.  They will be here in a
handful of sleeps (five days) or less.  Then you must fight a *great*
battle!"

*Chapter Eleven*

## THE HORDE APPROACHES

Several waking periods after the battle with the Great Camel Riders, Kirov was working in the village when a Dyal Rider messenger rode up on his vicious war bird. Around him, Lodge Builder craftsmen were cutting branches into piles of long and short shafts. Other craftsmen were knapping small flints and carefully trimming animal gut into strings.

"Kirov Skalkiller," he said respectfully. "The Pulka Horde approaches. Lal commands you to come to the line of spears."

The young inventor smiled as he handed the catapult parts he was chipping into existence to another craftsman and rose to his feet. A Soviet Red Army man would have said *the first defense line* but Pellucidarian military vocabulary was more limited than Russian. Perhaps, if the Soviet Army completed the conquest of the Inner World, Pellucidarians would understand such ideas. Until then, he and the allied tribes translated concepts as best they could.

"I come, Bol," he said to the messenger. He gave parting instructions to the craftsmen as he walked to where his dyal was resting. "Is Lal sure that the *Pulka* Horde approaches?"

The messenger nodded. "Yes, great Kirov. Lal sent scouts across the Plain of Grazers. They report that *small* camel riders approach."

Kirov nodded as he cooed orders at his dyal. The savage war bird grumbled.... Actually, it squawked but Kirov was now familiar enough with dyal sounds to interpret the noise as a grumble. The young inventor threw his new saddle over the

dyal's back, cinched it into place, and mounted up. The powerful bird arose and the two Dyal Riders headed for Lal's position.

Bol commented, "Your new saddle is easier to make ready
than our old ones. I wish one."

Kirov promised, "You shall have one." He paused and
added, "If we have enough time to make them."

The messenger nodded in understanding. Their dyals trotted
quickly from the village, across a simple log bridge over the
moat, and across the surrounding meadow. They passed Dyal
Riders trying to master riding the giant camels that the Great
Camel Riders had brought with them in their flight from the
Pulka Horde. Many camel riders had accepted slavery to Kirov's
people and their allies in return for their lives. They were trying
to teach their masters to control the great beasts with some
success.

Kirov and the messenger entered the woods, passing women
gathering edible nuts, berries and roots for the village. Powerful dyal legs carried the men swiftly through the forest.

A few minutes later, the men burst out of the far side of
the woods and paused under the oak-like tree from which Kirov
had commanded the first skirmish against the camel riders.
Lal had established her command post under its boughs, shaded
from the eternal noonday sun of Pellucidar and overlooking
the first defense line.

The Dyal Rider warrior queen and war leader of the allied
tribes wasted little time in greetings. She pointed far across
the Plain of Grazers. Kirov recognized the area where the
Great Camel Riders had first appeared a handful or more of
sleeps ago (about five days previously). A line of black dots,
barely visible in the distance, stood across the Plain filling its
breadth.

"Our scouts have seen those riders at a hand of spear casts
distance (close range). They ride small camels, not dyals. I
believe we are looking at the true Pulka Horde."

Kirov nodded. Previously, he had planned a defense line

that should have stopped a dyal riding force only to have his opponents' giant camels simply step over the line of spears. So, the inventor had insisted that Lal's scouts confirm critical details. If the Pulka rode small equines, the line of spears and pits should stop them and check their advance. Then Lodge Builder infantry supported by Dyal Rider cavalry should be able to fight the Horde on even terms.

Unless....

Far across the Plain, the enemy line thickened as more and more black dots appeared. Kirov could see the vast herds of strange Pellucidarian animals drifting away from the threat as they fed, grazers upon the lush grasses and strangely beautiful flowers of Pellucidar's northern latitudes, and carnivores upon unwary grazers.

Kirov's face moved from side to side, surveying the yet distant Horde, assessing, calculating.... His brow furrowed.

Rell noticed his concentration. "Mighty Kirov, do you see danger? The Horde aims itself at this spot as did the Great Camel Riders.

"But that line is very wide," said Kirov, "If they advance in formation rather than concentrating here, they will *outflank* us. We can't fight in every direction at once."

"Surely the Pulka Horde will come to this place as did the Great Camel Riders," Rell said. His confidence in Kirov's plans still strong. "The slope of the ground to this place has not changed."

Lal alternated watching Kirov and the Plain before her.

Kirov ignored both of them.

The Horde had begun to move.

Distant noises sounded across the Plain. The thick line of enemy cavalry moved forward as a unit, maintaining an easy riding pace. For a moment, Kirov wondered if he was hearing bugles. He estimated that the allied tribes were facing at least a thousand warriors advancing in a block about five ranks deep but two hundred files wide. A devastating overlap and double flank attack was no longer a possibility; it was a certainty.

And the center of the defense line was soon hit by hundreds of animals fleeing the Horde. When the Great Camel Riders had advanced across the Plain, their entire formation was only a hundred meters wide or so. Disturbed herbivores had merely moved out of their line of advance until that tribe had passed, followed by the ever-vigilant carnivores. In contrast, the Pulka Horde's formation was several thousand meters wide. Antelope, deer, musk oxen, brontops, tapirs and stranger creatures looked up, saw the Horde approach and began moving away—slowly at first and then more quickly. And soon the Horde began to make a loud sound driving the beasts forward. Since other advancing Hordesmen blocked the sides, the herds and packs became the Horde's advance guard.

The rising ground in front of the Wava Hills forced the fleeing creatures into pseudo-military columns with fiendish precision, one aimed at the allied position.

The native Pellucidarians gaped at the waves of animal flesh thundering towards them. Again, loud strange piping noises from the Horde echoed across the Plain.

"Lal!" shouted Kirov. "Those animals will cover the line of spears! We must withdraw to the woods! The trees will shield our men from the charging beasts!"

Lal took precious seconds to absorb the idea. When she did, the waves of fleeing creatures were very near. She ordered, "Dyal Riders! Lodge Builders! Retreat to the trees! *NOW!*"

Her commanding voice broke the hypnotic spell cast by the awe-inspiring sight of the onrushing creatures. The warriors began moving back towards the trees. Several Dyal Riders, carried by their powerful war birds, reached safety, vanishing behind stout trees. Most cavalrymen, however, spun their steeds around, cooing wildly. Their birds returned to the line of fleeing infantry spearmen, almost entirely Lodge Builders. Dyal Rider arms clasped Lodge Builders arms, pulling them onto their mounts. The agile war birds pivoted again, and fled into the trees.

Kirov sought out the relative safety of his now familiar

vantage post. He leaped from saddle to the lower branches and scrambled upward. Behind him, Dyal Riders, strapped to their own birds' backs, noted the ease and mobility of the new invention Kirov called *stirrups*.

Behind the allied warriors, the first wave of beasts blundered into the defense line. Antelope crashed into concealed pits; deer smashed into the spears rammed into the earth; and tapirs discovered the *punji sticks* of the Outer World. Animal cries rent the air as hundreds of creatures died in and on the products of Kirov's ingenuity.

But behind those victims were thousands more beasts. They filled the pits and smothered the spears and sticks with their bodies.

The first defense line was broken.

A herd of mammoths strode through the chaos, crushing lesser beasts into jelly. Behind them came other creatures, following the path that the great elephants had smashed through the maelstrom. Kirov saw one mammoth calf with a white patch on its left jowl gamely charging along in the wake of its massive mother. The beasts entered the Wava Woods, streaming past the men huddled behind trees mighty enough to turn even the great pachyderms of the Inner World. An armadillo-like *Boriostracons* shuffled along in their rear and disappeared among the trees, grunting fearfully.

Once he saw that his tribesmen and their allies were as safe as the situation allowed, Kirov turned his attention to the Horde. As he had expected, they had advanced, calmly and deliberately, behind the herds that had destroyed the first defense line.

Kirov ignored the chaos below him, studying the foe, now at comparatively close range. His scientist's mind observed, made notes, and compared the ongoing enemy with known things....

Astonishingly, the dreaded Pulka Hordesmen were midgets! Or pygmies![*]

---

[*] *Dr. Augustus Starkweather of the College of William & Mary has suggested that the Pulka Hordesmen are similar if not identical to the Homo floresiensis species of hominids*

The average Hordesman appeared to be no more than 100-125 centimeters (three to four feet) tall in the saddle. They were well-proportioned men but *small!*

Their steeds were proportionately small—the pony sized *Merychippus* or *Mesohippus* of the Pliocene era. They seemed almost dainty as they leaped over carcass after carcass, moving quickly over the blood-soaked morass that was supposed to be a battlefield.

The tsunami of animals had passed the first defense line, moving into the woods. Who knew what chaos they might cause when they reached the meadow of the Lake of Lodges?

In the meantime, the Pulka Horde advanced. Kirov could distinguish chiefs and lieutenants directing their men. The Horde was much better organized than most Pellucidarian tribes. With their numbers—vast by comparison with almost any other tribe—they would need to be. Kirov wondered briefly about their history…. Later!

The Hordesmen were well armed with short spears and *atlatls*! Kirov cursed. He had laboriously introduced atlatls to the Dyal Riders and here another tribe had had them for who knew how long! It wasn't fair!

Again, he shook his head to remind himself that he had to deal with the situation that he found, not the situation that he would like to have.

As the Hordesmen began to enter the Wava Woods, Lal counterattacked. Dyal Riders swarmed out from behind trees, men and birds screaming battle cries in unison. Behind them, Lodge Builder spearmen charged, spears held in one hand as they slapped their thighs in their strange variant of a war cry. As they closed with their enemies, the slapping stopped so that they could thrust their spears with the power of both hands.

A grand melee erupted along the wood line. Lal had judged

---

*whose remains were discovered on the island of Flores in Indonesia in the late 20th Century. Since Mikhail Kirov entered Pellucidar almost 70 years prior to that discovery, he would not be aware of that possibility and therefore referred to the Pulka tribesmen as "pygmies." Also see Abner Perry, "A Survey of Pellucidarian Hominids," The Journal of Pellucidarian Anthropology, August 2010.*

the moment well. Dyal Rider and Lodge Builder spears cut the first line of horse riders into ribbons. Powerful dyal beaks hacked into horses' necks. Horses screamed and died. Blood again watered the grasses and mosses along the forest edge.

But the Horde scarcely paused.

More waves of horse riders pushed forward over the corpse-laden ground. The allied warriors were clearly outnumbered.

But not outfought.

Dyal Riders and Pulka Hordesmen began hurling short spears at the opposing ranks. Meanwhile, the front lines fought with more conventional weapons—spears and clubs. Brawny Dyal Rider muscles had the advantage in contests of strength with their diminutive opponents. Horde skulls split open and horse riders rolled to the hellish field. The air was thick with death.

Less skilled than their aggressive allies, the Lodge Builders jabbed and poked where they could. There was no monopoly on courage. Hordesmen continued to press forward, smaller weapons flying and taking a surprisingly heavy toll on their larger foes.

Kirov sat down on a convenient tree limb and unslung his latest invention. He fitted an arrow to his bow, sighted at a Pulka chief directing the battle, and fired. The chief went to join his ancestors in the Dead World.

A few arrows later and an alert Pulka discovered the source of swiftly flying death. He pointed Kirov out to some Horde lieutenant who was now acting as chief. Voices shrilled. New Hordesmen came forward, shrike-like birds resting on their arms.

*Falconers?* wondered Kirov. *Falconers!*

The falconers pointed and unleashed their birds. Powerful wings flapped, carrying the living weapons towards Kirov. He caught one with an arrow before they were upon him.

Beaks stabbed and claws slashed. Kirov fought back with his knife. Birds died. Kirov's blood dripped from a dozen wounds, rolling down his body and onto the tree branch.  He twisted in position once too often....

He slipped and plummeted towards the earth.

Arms flailing, weapons flying, Kirov grasped desperately for a new handhold among the tree limbs.

He failed.

He smashed into the ground.

Warriors clashed over his body and trampled it underfoot.

*Chapter Twelve*

## "WE TAUGHT THEM TO FEAR OUR SPEARS."

Cold water splashed into Kirov's face. He woke, coughing and spitting. He was in flame-lit darkness. For a moment, he thought that he had gone to the Dead World.

Lal's beautiful face hove into view. She was smeared with dirt and blood and hammered by exhaustion. She had seldom looked so beautiful.

"Kirov Skalkiller," she began. Somewhere, a trumpet should have sounded. "You were right. The Horde surrounded us on both sides and overwhelmed us. The Dyal Riders—and the Lodge Builders—have been defeated."

Kirov sucked in damp air. It seemed as though experts had been beating him for hours. He rose painfully to a sitting position. "Where are we now?"

"The lodge of Chirp. All of our survivors retreated to the village of Lodges. For the moment, the enemy is watching us from the woods." Her voice shifted in tone. Her mouth quirked in a thin smile. "We taught them to fear our spears."

She paused and continued, "However, they must soon attack the village. They can cut down trees as easily as we can to cross the canals. You will lead our women and children to safety at the Coldwater River."

Kirov sighed deeply.

The warrior queen continued, "The wounded warriors will go with you to protect our people. When you arrive, tell Pol, Hortul, and the other war chiefs that the Pulka Horde will

soon arrive at the River and attack the River Tribes. They must
name a new war chief and defeat the Horde. I think that Pol
would be the best leader."

Kirov coughed. The Coldwater was a twelve wakes' ride
on fast war birds. Leading a mob of panicky women and
children on an emergency evacuation...!

He took a deep breath. "I go. I ask that Rell go with me
as deputy leader of the movement to the River." Pellucidarian
had no word for *evacuation*.

Lal shook her head. She spoke softly. "Rell the Brave One
has gone to the Dead World. When your body fell from the
tree, he rescued you and insisted that you would triumph over
Death once again. As you have. But a black spear struck him
in the arm and he died. You were sleeping and unable to rescue
him. His face turned black, he coughed blood and he went to
the Dead World."

"'The Dead will honor him'," quoted Kirov. "There are
other brave Dyal Riders who can guide us to the River and
safety. What will you do?" He suspected that he knew the
answer but had to ask. He made a mental note to find out
more about the "black spear."

"We will fight the Horde here. It is a strange fortress but
a true fortress. It is better to fight them and their small camels
here than in the open plains. We will teach them to fear our
spears once again." The smile on her lovely features would have
given His Infernal Majesty pause.

The lodge was silent for a long moment.

Then Kirov repeated, "I go."

*Chapter Thirteen*

# "YOU ARE A DEMON THAT MUST BE KILLED."

A young man dressed in the brown feathers of the Dyal Riders sat his war bird on a slight ridge and surveyed the Plain of Grazers intently. Behind him the Coldwater River Valley began its gentle slope to its namesake river. The concave landscape of the Inner World stretched outward and upward before him like the inside of a tora (tortoise) shell. In the distance, he could see a dirty smudge moving across the rolling plains. As it approached, it resolved into a more or less tidy mob of people walking slowly across the plain. They were guarded by a handful of dyal riders. He smiled and rode to greet them.

KIROV APPROACHED THE SCOUT. "Hail, tribesman. I am Kirov of Dyalsi. This band is the women and children of our allies the Lodge Builders and Great Camel Riders. We go to the Coldwater River at the order of Lal, chief of the Dyal Riders."

The scout gulped and then nodded. "Hail, Kirov. The river is less than a half wake's ride from here." He pointed behind him.

Kirov nodded weakly but gladly. The journey from the Wava Woods to this point had been a nightmare of fear, exhaustion, thirst and starvation. But, now, they were almost at the river where the allied tribes would shelter the survivors and mobilize a new army to defeat the Pulka Horde and rescue the defenders of the village of Lodges. He would report to deputy chief Pol, see Flana, take a short rest, and then....

The scout coughed. "Great Kirov, there is news from Dyalsi. Zuul the Old has declared that Lal, Pol and you are dead and that he is now chief of the Dyal Riders. He has also declared if you, Kirov, return from the Dead World, then you are a demon from the Molop Az (the Sea of Fire) that must be killed until you return no more."

The young inventor swayed and collapsed slowly to the ground. His knees folded and hit the soft soil of Pellucidar. For a moment, his still upright body knelt before the bearer of ill tidings. An accusation of demonhood was simply one stress too many. His weary mind closed down.

The scout gawped for a moment. Then he drew his spear. He had his orders from the chief of his tribe. He raised the grim Pellucidarian weapon to the overhead position to stab down into Kirov's unresisting body. He thrust....

Kirov's upright body collapsed further. His knees and hip joints folded again, and his body sat down onto his lower legs. The spear cut the air over his head harmlessly.

Startled, the scout recovered. He paused to look at the semi-conscious man who had evaded death once again. An experienced hunter, the scout had missed his prey often enough but never at such close range. A simple accident or some demonic power? Well, he would not miss a second time. He aimed carefully at his unresisting target....

A rock slammed into his chest, knocking him off balance. He flailed wildly and his savage war bird danced frantically, both of them trying to recover their stance. When they had steadied, the scout looked at the refugees.

Women had come up beside the silent Kirov. They had rocks in their hands and anger on their faces. Behind them were tens of tens of more women, children and a few wounded men.

One woman screamed, "Who threatens Kirov Skalkiller?

We kill!" Her light brown hair matched her strange khaki furs. The scout had never seen any animal with such fur.

Astonished, the scout clucked and his dyal danced backward. "Who are you?" he challenged.

"I am Fama of the Great Camel Riders. I am deputy chief of the Women's Band of the allied tribes. I will kill whoever threatens Kirov the Dyal Rider and champion of the Women's Band." Her arm wavered in mid air, clearly ready to hurl another stone at a fully armed warrior and war bird.

"And I," echoed another woman dressed in thick wava furs. The scout had never seen a wava. To him, the savage beauty looked (and acted) very much like a small ryth. Behind the leaders, many more women and children were coming forward. They were exhausted by great exertion but hurrying as quickly as they could. More of them stooped, hunting for stones.

The scout rallied.

"I am Yawl the Swift One of the Dyal Riders. Zuul the Old, chief of the Dyal Riders, has commanded that this... this demon from the Sea of Fire be killed! I obey!" He waved his spear overhead, threatening his challengers but not actually attacking their superior numbers.

The women cocked their arms, ready to throw their stones, but not actually attacking the trained warrior.

The stalemate was broken when another Dyal Rider appeared, riding around the mob of women and children. His war bird was thin and he was even thinner. One arm was bound to his body by grass ropes. But his spear was ready. He looked willing to attack a hunting tarag* by himself.

"Hold, tribesman! I am Gul, lieutenant of the Women's Band. Kirov Skalkiller is no hand-sized demon from the Sea of Fire. He fought the Great Camel Riders at the Lake of Lodges and made them our allies by his courage and kindness and recognition of their honor and their need." Fama nodded.

---

\* *The savage saber-tooth cat of Pellucidar. Tarags are not only physically powerful and armed with fearsome natural weapons but highly intelligent and capable of coordinating bands of its fellows in hunting vast numbers of lesser animals including men. – Ed.*

Gul continued, "He fought the Pulka Horde until they surrounded our war band. When Lal commanded him to bring
the women, the children and the wounded warriors of the three
tribes to safety, he marched for thirty sleeps and brought us
here despite the attacks of codons and jaloks. He walked when
he could have ridden. He ate little and gave his food to feed
the children.

"I have seen Zuul the *deputy* chief, who was once called
the Hunter, eating well when better men brought the meat of
thags* to Dyalsi. But I have not seen him in battle or on the
march. Nor have I seen the judgment of Lal, *chief* of the Dyal
Riders and war chief of the allied tribes, naming Zuul anything
but *third deputy chief.* Therefore, return to Zuul and say that I,
Gul, demand proper judgment according to the customs of the
Dyal Riders." He closed his mouth and stared at the scout.

The latter individual looked at Gul, at the fierce women
now forming a protective screen around Kirov, and at the
accused himself. He blushed. Perhaps the thought of fighting
women armed with rocks did not appeal to him. Perhaps the
justice of Gul's claim did. In either event, his decision was not
long in coming.

"Hail, Gul. You have spoken well. A chief must sit in
judgment upon an accused one. I go to Dyalsi to demand
justice for Kirov known as the Skalkiller." He raised his spear
in a casual salute to Gul. He clucked and his dyal danced
backward, turned, and sped away.

Fama collapsed to the ground in nervous relief.

---

*    *A cervine animal similar to a bull or elk. Considered a great delicacy by most Pellucidarian tribes. – Ed.*

*Chapter Fourteen*

## "KIROV COMES TO
## SURRENDER TO ZUUL."

O nce again, Kirov recovered consciousness with a beautiful female face above him. This time, he did not recognize her. Behind her oval face was a background of reeds waving in the cool breezes of northern Pellucidar.

"Who are you and where are we?" he asked.

"Hail, mighty Kirov," greeted the woman in a soft voice. "I am Bel, a Dyal Rider, and sister to Bol the Messenger. We are in a place of the River People on the Coldwater River. We are on the far shore beyond River Town Island."

Kirov sat up. His rested mind was functioning again. He looked around. The River People lived on an island in the great Coldwater River, the Volga River of northern Pellucidar. They also maintained small outposts on either bank. The Women's Band had arrived at the outpost while he was unconscious and occupied the huts of the outpost. A few River People moved back and forth directing traffic and trying to find places for the Band in the overcrowded facilities. Canoes shuttled back and forth between island and outpost carrying people in both directions. The tang of frying fish spoke of meals being prepared.

He was lying on the soft ground near the primitive piers on the river. Around him were Fama, Gul, Bel and three other men. He recognized one but not the other two.

"Hail, Bol Messenger," he greeted. "Why are you here?" He had last seen Bol before the battle with the Pulka Horde.

With him close at hand, the resemblance between brother and sister was obvious.

The young messenger sighed. "Hail, mighty Kirov. The Pulka Horde has defeated the war bands of the Dyal Riders, Lodge Builders and Great Camel Riders. Some have been captured and enslaved. The Horde will come to the great River when they have rested."

The little circle sighed in unison. Of the strange men, one's face was impassive. The other was obviously shaken although he maintained a stoic silence.

Bol continued, "We fought them for many wakes and sleeps. We slew chiefs and lieutenants as well as mighty champions and valiant warriors. They feared our spears. And they feared the *bows and arrows* that you created." A shadow of a smile raced across his face. "But there were too many Pulka for us to kill them all. Their bodies filled in the straight rivers (canals) of the village of Lodges. Their strange small camels leaped over individual carcasses and advanced over the mounds of the dead without fear. Their hunting birds attacked us from the air. Their weapons are smaller than ours but many of their spears are black. When a black spear struck a victim, he would turn black, spit blood, and die—"

"Poison," grunted the impassive stranger.

"Evil magic," agreed Bol.

"*Science*," corrected Kirov. The word was necessarily Russian but one that he had taught the Dyal Riders as being the source of his numerous "inventions."

"I do not know the Soviet Red War Party Tribe words but the black spear 'poison' slew many brave warriors," said Bol judiciously. "Some warriors surrendered to the Horde rather than face it." He grimaced. The Pellucidarian ideal was heroic courage even in the face of death. The reality was that Pellucidarians were subject to the same weaknesses of all men and women.

"What of Lal?" asked Kirov quietly. She was the heart and soul of the alliance. Without her, the allied tribes had little chance of resisting the Horde's sheer numbers and advanced weapons.

Bol paused. "When I last saw her, she was alive. Lal and the few remaining warriors retreated to a wava dwelling in the middle of the Lake of Lodges. The Horde dared not swim across the lake. The wava are not fighters but they will seize an enemy swimmer and drown him." Bol smiled thinly. "But the Hordesmen were tearing down the dwellings of the Lodge Builders when I escaped. I think that they will build rafts or bridges and cross to Lal's fortress."

The messenger shook himself and continued. "That was ten sleeps ago. When the Hordesmen cross the Lake to Lal's fortress, she will slay them until the Lake is red with blood. But they will kill or capture her in the end. Even Lal the Fierce One cannot slay tens of tens of men with only a handful at her side.

"She knew this," Bol commented simply.

He reached into his backpack and extracted an assegai. "Before she retreated to the Lake, she gave me her short spear and commanded me to find you, Kirov Skalkiller. She appointed you second deputy chief of the Dyal Riders in place of Rell the Brave One. Here is her short spear in token of your appointment." He handed the assegai to Kirov who recognized the royal insignia carved in the middle of the shaft: the head of a gilak with a forest of dyal feathers in his hair. Only Lal or her now dead father had owned weapons with this carving.

Bol was not finished speaking. "Kirov, Lal sends a message by my mouth. She says that you must save the Dyal Riders and the allied tribes. Use your strange magic and *invent* a solution to the Pulka Horde."

Kirov turned the royal assegai over and over in his hands. His mind raced, seeking a way out of the trap. Then the tumult of images in his head cleared and the face of his intended mate, Flana, appeared. Kirov spoke.

"I will."

KIROV WAS PICKING his way along the banks of the great river when Tsassal the Snake Eater approached. He had wanted some time alone to think things through but his walk was proving anything but relaxing. The marshy shoreline wanted to suck his sandals, feet and legs into the mire. In contrast, the Snake Eater seemed completely unconcerned about the softness of the ground.

"Hail, sure footed Tsassal," greeted Kirov. "How do you walk so easily in this marsh?"

The normally impassive tribesman's face twitched into a ghost of a smile. "Hail, Kirov Skalkiller. I place my feet on the handfuls of grass rather than in the mud." He pointed to the ground. His own sandaled feet were indeed planted on tufts of grass while Kirov's were centimeters deep in muck.

The young inventor quickly copied the Snake Eater and thanked him. "Why have you come to me, Tsassal?"

"Will you slay Zuul the foolish one with weapons or with magic?"

"*Science*," corrected Kirov again. Something tickled his mind. The native Pellucidarians consistently took *science* to be *magic*. The implications....

"I do not care what the name of the magic is in the language of your homeland. But the magic must be powerful to slay a chief, especially if you remain on the shores of the Coldwater River and he remains in the nest of the Dyal Riders." He pointed in the direction of distant Dyalsi, invisible in the direction of the Mountains of Birds.

Kirov frowned, and swung around to face his ally more directly. Tsassal's face seemed carved from stone and his voice utterly sincere.

"Do you believe that I, Kirov the *Inventor*, am a magician?"

"Of course. How else could you create the strange weapons that you used to defeat the evil Black Birdriders and the Pulka Horde? How else could you kill a monster skal with two spears and a garment? How else could you summon tribes of monsters to attack the Great Camel Riders including a she-ryth whose mate you had previously slain?" He fell silent. There was not the slightest hint of irony in his description.

The cold winds of northern Pellucidar ruffled the hairs of both men. They were warm enough in their heavy clothes, Kirov in a leather undergarment with brown feathers glued to it, Tsassal in a multihued garment of thick hide. Along the great river, birds and creeping animals called, hunted, fed, hid, and lived their small lives.

Kirov asked, "Do you advise me to go to Dyalsi to confront Zuul?"

"Of course. Mighty champions go to the lairs of their enemies to destroy them. You went to the nests of the Black Birdriders and to the village of Lodges to fight your enemies. I do not see Zuul the Old here fighting you." Did his level voice hide a sneer?

Kirov smiled thinly.

"Will you go with me to Dyalsi to fight Zuul?"

"Of course."

"Why?"

"My father and the fathers of Lal the Fierce and Hortul Paddlemaker pledged that our tribes would fight side by side against all dangers. Zuul would break this pact and hide behind the great river, hoping that the Pulka will not discover boats. He must die. You have the spear of Lal the Fierce. The Snake Eaters will march on Dyalsi when you bid us come."

Kirov looked down at Lal's assegai in his hand. In savage Pellucidar, even scientists—or magicians—out for peaceful walks to clear their minds needed to carry weapons for safety. For a moment, he was struck by the resemblance of the assegai to a stage magician's wand.

He looked into Tsassal's calm face again.

"Will you fight the Pulka Horde with me?"

"Of course."

"They have poison on their spears."

Tsassal snorted. "Snake Eaters know poison and how to handle it. We do not fear it." He tapped himself on the chest.

Kirov looked at his ally's thick, scaly garment.

"Do you truly eat snakes?"

"Of course."

"And make their hides into your clothes?"

"Of course."

Kirov nodded sagely. "The Snake Eaters have great power." The Pellucidarian language had no word for *mana*, the magical power that many primitive peoples believed underlay all things. Eating one's enemies to gain their power was another primitive belief. Kirov was suddenly glad for his college anthropology courses. "The Dyal Riders and the other tribes are glad that your people are our allies."

"Of course."

There was another pause. Kirov sighed deeply and shook his head. He seemed deep in thought. Tsassal waited for his strange leader to express himself. When the young inventor turned to look across the Coldwater River, Tsassal spoke.

"What will you do now?"

Kirov turned to face his ally.

"I will go to Dyalsi to confront Zuul the Evil One in his lair and free the Dyal Riders from his spell. I *ask* that you and the other loyal war chiefs go with me."

The phlegmatic Snake Eater grunted approval and said, "Of course, I will go with you. We will slay Zuul's band to the last man."

"That will not be necessary. We will slay no gilaks."

Tsassal's eyebrow quirked upward.

Kirov smiled and said, "Come, my friend. We will return to the River outpost. I need to convert my bow and arrows into a *fire drill*."

"What is a 'fire drill'?" The phrase had been Russian.

"Magic," responded Kirov.

ZUUL THE OLD ONE, self proclaimed chief of the Dyal Riders, was on the throne of his tribal kingdom when the demon's messenger rode into Dyalsi. The latter was quickly escorted to the presence of the man who would be king.

Bol the Messenger rode to the plaza in front of the "palace" where Lal and her family had lived for generations. He looked at Zuul with contempt but saluted with his upraised hand. Zuul's guards had confiscated all of his weapons at the entrance to the town lest a raised spear turn into an assassination.

Despite this precaution, fear washed over Zuul's face when he gazed upon Bel's brother. Bel's abrupt departure from Dyalsi might be misunderstood by Bol—or anyone else who respected women. Zuul summoned his nerve and beckoned the messenger forward. Behind his back, a guard flushed at Zuul's failure to return Bol's salute.

Bol cooed to his dyal. The hard-ridden war bird crouched down. The messenger unstrapped himself from his pre-Kirov saddle and stood tall before the chief and his guards. Bol grimaced at the sight of warriors surrounding the pasty-faced chief. Neither Lal nor her father had ever needed guards against other Dyal Riders. He began to speak.

"Hail, Zuul, deputy chief—"

"*Chief* of the Dyal Riders!" snapped the Old One. His withered face flushed with sudden anger. His voice was still strong.

Bol glared at the interruption. He breathed deeply to calm himself and began again. "Hail, Zuul, chief of Dyalsi—"

Zuul opened his mouth but closed it again, letting the distinction pass.

"— Kirov Skalkiller, deputy chief of the Dyal Riders, sends a message by my mouth. He comes to Dyalsi with the war chiefs of the allied tribes. He will be here in three waking periods."

Zuul paled. His voice quavered. "For what p-p-purpose does the demon Kirov come to Dyalsi?"

Bol paused, choked with emotion. Finally, he spat out his message.

"Kirov Skalkiller comes to surrender to Zuul."

*Chapter Fifteen*

## "I PRESENT THE SPEAR OF LAL, WHICH DESTROYS THE ENEMIES OF THE DYAL RIDERS."

Three waking periods later, Kirov approached Dyalsi as promised. He rode a well-groomed dyal like a king.

With him came the war chiefs of the allied tribes who lived in the great shallow valley of the Coldwater River and the Women's Band of refugees from the battles of the Wava Woods. In numbers, they were a formidable host. In fighting power, much less so.

His followers could not see into Kirov's mind and he was grateful for that inability. He had trained much of his life to become a scientist. He had never been a magician before now.

The allied "forces" approached Dyalsi, the primitive city of the Dyal Riders, and primary meeting place of the allied tribes. The site was a grove of oak-like trees watered by springs and small streams threading the Plain of Grazers. The Dyal Riders had built their thick-walled huts under the trees to protect themselves from the aerial menace of the Black Birdriders, now decimated by a civil war triggered by Kirov many sleeps ago. The city was surrounded by a palisade of wooden stakes to prevent the great carnivores of the Plain—or even a stampeding herd of herbivores—from overrunning its homes. Beyond the wall was the endless sea of grasses and beautiful flowers that cloaked the plain and fed the grazers from which it drew its name. Strange perfumes arose as the feet of the allied forces crushed flowers.

Based on various descriptions, Kirov guessed that the plain

was at least twice the size of Germany and Poland combined. Many tribes inhabited the expanse. Many of them had attacked the allied tribes. But, Dyalsi had never been captured by an enemy.

Zuul's "home guard" was drawn up to defend their city—and its chief. Zuul himself sat on his royal stool outside the main entrance to the city with guards thickly packed around him. Every able-bodied Dyal Rider male clogged the entrance, weapons in hand. Dyal Rider children and females peered out from the stakes of the town wall. Puzzled faces revealed inner turmoil. A sensitive nose might detect the scent of fear.

As agreed to by a volley of messengers riding back and forth, Kirov's forces stopped two spear throws outside the wall. The allied war chiefs rode forward half the distance to the entrance, halted their dyals and dismounted. The refugees behind them were silent, intent on the impending confrontation. Even the cold winds that chilled northern Pellucidar were quiet.

Kirov stepped forward from the knot of chiefs, accompanied only by Bol, Fama, and Tsassal. They walked half a spear's throw towards Zuul and stopped.

Kirov was armed only with the assegai of Lal the Fierce, the absent—and possibly dead—chief of the Dyal Riders and heart of the allied tribes. Bol and Tsassal carried the spears, knives and hatchets of pre-Kirov warriors. Fama carried several water skins.

No one moved.

There was a long silence.

Finally, Bol shouted, "Hail, Zuul, Old One. Kirov Skalkiller has approached for judgment. It was agreed that you would come forth and meet him as one chief to another."

Faces glanced back and forth.

Kirov did his best to project an air of complete confidence tinged with irritation at the man's obvious stalling.

Eyes turned to Zuul, who sat frozen on his throne, sweat beading on his forehead. Finally, he stuttered, "The-the d-d-demon K-kirov is no chief of the Dyal Riders. He must approach me-me for *my* judgment."

A furious expression darkened Bol's face. His fellows remained impassive. "Lal the Fierce appointed Kirov Skalkiller *second* deputy chief of the Dyal Riders in place of Rell the Brave One who fell in battle at Lodges. He holds her short spear in token of his appointment." He gestured and Kirov held the assegai aloft in both hands, displaying it for the Dyalsi crowd. The latter saw many heads nodding in agreement. His own followers had seen it several times before. After a moment, he lowered his arms.

Bol continued, "Therefore, *third* deputy chief Zuul should meet with *second* deputy chief Kirov as equals. As Zuul agreed by the mouth of his messenger Yawl the Swift One!"

Yawl himself stood beside Zuul along with Ala, the former queen of the Black Birdriders, and several Dyal Riders that Kirov knew only slightly. One lanky Dyal Rider seemed familiar for some reason. Had that man been at the battles in the Wava Woods? The familiar face looked away when he saw Kirov studying him. Two faces that Kirov hoped to see—Pol Taragkiller and Dyryth—were both absent. Pol was the first deputy chief of the Dyal Riders and Lal's designated heir. Dyryth was an amiable giant and friend to Kirov. Neither would accept Zuul's pretensions lightly. The other Dyal Riders, it seemed, had accepted Zuul's assumption of authority and accusations of demonhood....

Or were they merely loyally obeying the man who held the title of deputy chief of their tribe?

Yawl leaned over and whispered in Zuul's ear. The enthroned chief shook his head violently.

"No demon can be a chief of the Dyal Riders! Therefore, the demon Kirov must approach and receive judgment!"

Bol raised his voice further. "Zuul speaks foolishly! The little demons of the Molop Az are one hand tall! Kirov is 18 hands tall—a man among men! The little demons live in the

ground!  Kirov lives on the ground among men as men live!
The little demons carry pieces of the dead to the Molop Az!*
Kirov is a great warrior, skillful (statesmanlike) chief, and
cunning *inventor*!  He makes good weapons and tools for the
Dyal Riders and the allied tribes!  He is no demon!"

Murmurs of agreement broke out in the two crowds.  Zuul
heard snatches of conversation recalling Kirov's previous feats,
including his freeing of the slaves taken from the allied tribes
by Ala's Black Birdriders.  Kirov noticed Ala's eyes darting
across both crowds and back to Zuul.  Captivity had not dulled
her intelligence.

Zuul rose from his royal stool, shouting for order.  "Kirov
the Stranger is indeed a demon from the Molop Az!  Demons
are able to move through the ground with pieces of the dead!
Therefore, they are able to disguise themselves as gilaks as Kirov
has!  How can a gilak create strange weapons except by magic
from the Molop Az?!

He continued, growing louder and more strident as he
shouted.  "Has Kirov the Stranger not told us that he comes
from a strange world deep under our feet?!  A world of alternating light and darkness?!  A world with a great fire called *The
Sun*?!  A world of powerful magics called *science* and *socialism*?!
Has he not told us these things himself?!  What can his homeland be except the Molop Az, which is a sea of fire beneath our
feet?!!"

There was another moment of silence followed by more
murmuring.  Now the Dyalsi crowd's reaction supported Zuul's
analysis.  Faces turned towards Kirov in wonder—and horror.

He suspected that many among his supporters were waver-
ing in their allegiance as well.

Kirov was awestruck by Zuul's malign brilliance.  He *had*
said those things to anyone and everyone who would listen.

---

* *The most common Pellucidarian explanation for the normal process of decay.  Most Pel-*
*lucidarian tribes believe that their world is a limitless plain of solid rock floating on a sea*
*of molten rock, the Molop Az, or Sea of Fire.  Volcanic eruptions provide evidence that the*
*Molop Az is capable of breaking through into the material world.  In addition, the Molop*
*Az is the home of small demons who pick corpses apart and transport the remains to their*
*homes in the Sea of Fire. – Ed.*

Those things were the honest truth: a straightforward description of the major features of the Outer World eight hundred
kilometers below the concave surface of the Inner World.

What Kirov had *not* considered is how a Pellucidarian—
especially a hostile one—would interpret or misinterpret his
statements. In retrospect, it was obvious that Pellucidarians
would tend to interpret his statements in light of their own
cosmology. Even brilliant scientists, trained in analysis and
dedicated to discovering truth, were inclined to resist overthrow-
ing established theories and practices when confronted with
new evidence. Were Pellucidarians more revolutionary than
the men of the Outer World?

And so the eight hundred kilometer thickness of Earth's
crust became the *depth* to a great cavern *below* the Inner World,
a great cavern filled with a Sea of Fire called The Sun.

And so Mikhail Kirillivitch Kirov became a demon in the
eyes of many whom he had rescued from the tyranny of the
Black Birdriders....

In the common Pellucidarian language the word for *stranger* also meant *enemy*.

Kirov sighed deeply in regret. He held himself erect, apparently unmoved, and commanding. He inhaled deeply of
the sweet air of savage Pellucidar.

He stepped forward, still carrying Lal's assegai in both
hands. He released the left end of the short spear so that he
could gesture with it very much as a stage magician would
gesture with his wand.

"Zuul the False One lies!!" shouted Kirov. He pointed the
assegai directly at his opponent. The latter flinched. "He says
that he is chief of the Dyal Riders rather than Lal or Pol. In
saying this, he lies! He promised by the mouth of Yawl that
he would meet me as an equal and render fair judgment. In
saying this, he lies! He says that I am a demon and not a human.
In saying this, he lies!"

Kirov pivoted, facing all the assembled tribesmen in turn.
No one dared speak.

When he completed a circle and again faced Zuul, he resumed.

"I was a stranger but am now a Dyal Rider. I was a slave—as were many of you—but am now a free man—as are all of you. I was a messenger of the Soviet Tribe but am now a warrior of the allied tribes, a man who fought the Great Camel Riders and the Pulka Horde. I fought for you in the roost of the Black Birdriders and in the Wava Woods. I bled for you then as I bleed for you now."

His voice lowered, forcing everyone to strain to hear him. "As a man bleeds."

So saying, he adjusted his grip on Lal's assegai, holding it near the haft end with his right hand. Dramatically, he slashed the sharp tip across his left palm.

A line of blood welled up and began draining down his palm and wrist.

Kirov pivoted again so that all could see his red blood coloring his arm.

When he completed his circle, he gestured to Fama with the assegai. She splashed a skin bag full of water onto his left hand and arm. Kirov's blood washed away....

... and was replaced by more red fluid welling up. The wound had not had time to clot.

"I am a man among men," he said simply as he rotated again, once more showing the allied tribesmen his life's blood.

When he completed his third circle, Kirov looked directly at Zuul, his left palm clearly visible to his enemy and his enemy's guards.

"Zuul, am I not a man among men?"

There was another pause. Many among Zuul's followers were nodding in agreement, murmuring their support for the Skalkiller. Their soft words filled Zuul's ears.

The enemy chief leaped to his feet, panic driven anger chasing fear from his face. He screamed.

"No! Kirov the Stranger must be a demon from the Sea of Fire! Kill him!"

There was a ripple among his guards as some started to obey while others looked at Zuul in confusion.

"Stop!" shouted Kirov. The rippling effect halted. Zuul's guards looked back and forth at the two contending chieftains.

Kirov continued. "Let there be no war among the Dyal Riders or the allied tribes. The Pulka Horde will be here soon and there will be enough fighting for the greatest warrior. Instead, I will give the spear of Lal to Zuul and accept the judgment of the Dyal Riders and the allied tribes."

There was an audible sigh of relief among the crowds, especially Zuul's faction. Clearly there was little appetite for civil war among the defenders of Dyalsi, *especially* when reminded of the Horde's approach. None breathed more easily than their chief.

Behind his back, several of Zuul's guards frowned at him. Ideally, a Pellucidarian chieftain was braver than any ordinary warrior. The guards could not help but compare the courage of Lal and Kirov in confronting their foes with Zuul's obvious fear.

Kirov advanced towards his judge accompanied only by Fama. His face displayed a bland, submissive expression. Zuul had never lived in the Soviet Union and therefore did not know how readily a Soviet citizen could mask his emotions. In contrast, Bol's face was dark with anger while Tsassal's eyes narrowed as if mentally aiming a spear cast.

Zuul noted the strange woman walking beside the condemned. With her burden of water bags, she seemed nothing more than a man's mate. He pointed to her and addressed Kirov, demanding, "Why does that woman come before the chief of the Dyal Riders?"

Fama spoke for herself, "Hail, Zuul of the Dyal Riders. I am Fama of the Great Camel Riders. I am chief of the Women's Band and acting chief of my tribe. I come to unite the Women's Band and the Great Camel Riders to the allied tribes."

Zuul flushed with pride. Lal and her father had assembled the alliance of the Coldwater River Valley peoples to fight the

Black Birdriders. Adding another tribe to the alliance would add more fighting strength to protect his throne from the Horde and cement his authority as chief.

And! Fama was a very attractive woman…! And obedient, too! A powerful chief could not have too many women…!

Kirov and Fama stopped an arm's length from the conceited Zuul. The latter's guards had resumed their observant stances, ready to fight but relaxed now that the crisis had passed. A Soviet military commander would say that they were in their Rest positions, spears grounded, knives and hatchets thrust into their primitive thongs and belts.

Kirov raised Lal's assegai above his head, gripped in both hands again. He spoke loudly, not shouting but his voice carrying.

"I present the spear of Lal, which destroys the enemies of the Dyal Riders!"

Zuul reached forth his hand….

Kirov Skalkiller twisted the spear in midair and smashed its blunt tip into the chest of the man who would be king. Blood gushed forth, vividly coloring the royal torso.

Stunned by the sudden violence, Zuul staggered backward, blood dripping from his costume.

Caught off guard by Kirov's apparent submission, the guards gaped as their leader clapped his hand to his chest and brushed the blood aside.

"Behold the true demon!" shouted Kirov as he stabbed his finger at the impact point. "He does not die when killed! His wound has healed already!"

Fama splashed a water skin onto Zuul's chest.

The blood washed away.

Nothing replaced it.

Everyone stared at the miraculously unwounded chieftain.

Kirov thrust both hands into the cool Pellucidarian sky, his bare left hand still dripping blood, his right hand holding the spear of Lal aloft. "I bleed when cut but Zuul does not! He is the true demon! He lied to deceive us! He lied!"

A few heartbeats of time passed.

Ala closed her mouth and opened it again. "Zuul is the true demon! He lied about Kirov Skalkiller who unites our peoples! Death to the demon!"

Astonished, Zuul whirled to confront his suddenly rebellious captive, his face contorted in rage. He screamed, "You lied to me! You promised me…!"

Ala's fist cut off any further words. Zuul's head rocked backward.

The shock of physical violence broke an emotional dam. The Pellucidarians had been gripped by powerful emotions, teetering between alternatives. Kirov's revelation had swept one alternative away.

Yawl the Swift One lashed out, his fist rocking Zuul's head forwards. The lanky guard that Kirov had half recognized began chanting "Death to the demon!" He struck his erstwhile chieftain again and again.

Other Dyal Riders, furious at being deceived by the demon that had replaced their once respected deputy chief, closed in. The confined space prevented using spears or knives but fists driven by fear and anger were enough.

After many minutes, the mob drew back, panting. In the center of the resulting circle, the bloody ruin that had been Zuul the Old One lay on the ground.

Kirov gently parted the crowed and stepped forward.

In the exhausted silence, he intoned, "The spear of Lal destroys the enemies of the Dyal Riders."

He thrust the sharp tip of the assegai into the corpse and left it there.

"Fetch firewood," he commanded softly. "Fire will force the demon back to the Molop Az and prevent its return."

Glad to have clear orders, Dyal Riders ran off to gather the required materials. Soon, a pyre was complete. Kirov and Tsassal lifted the body, spear still thrust through it, onto the wood. A torch was applied.

Kirov watched as the fire consumed the mortal remains of

Zuul and the spear of Lal. Whether demon or man, Zuul would never return from the Dead World.

And no one other than tight-lipped Tsassal would ever know that Kirov had secretly converted the original spear into a stage magician's prop. Fama might suspect something but all she *knew* was Kirov's instructions to splash water at the appropriate moments.

The young *inventor* had worked alone preparing his "magic" while the phlegmatic Snake Eater guarded his privacy. First, Kirov had cut off one end of the spear and saved the resulting spear point. Then he had carefully drilled out a hollow tube down the length of the shaft. Next had come the trimming of the spear point so that it would slide freely in and out of the tube. Finally, the tube had been filled with watered animal blood and lightly closed with glue. Careful handling had prevented premature breakage.

But the painstaking work had paid off. When the prop smashed into Zuul's chest, the blunted spear point had been forced into the tube, breaking the glue dams and allowing the blood to spray the enemy chief's body. Kirov's pointing and shouting had focused attention on the "demon" rather than the spear.

And now the evidence was gone.

As the fire burned down to ashes, Kirov became aware of Ala standing demurely beside him. He looked at her, distracted by many thoughts.

"Hail, mighty Kirov, chief of the Dyal Riders and the Coldwater River Valley tribes. I, Ala, am your slave again." She looked modestly downward. "What do you wish me to do?" she cooed.

"I greet you, Ala." Kirov paused. "Where is Flana of the Seashore People?"

Ala swallowed and then answered without lifting her head. "Flana has returned to her People...."

"What?" barked Kirov. "When did she leave?" He took a

step closer to Ala, his body stiff with tension. He forced himself to relax, to hear the news in full.

Ala seemed to lose centimeters in height, becoming more vulnerable, more placating. Her voice softened. "A handful of sleeps ago, Zuul announced that he would take Flana as his mate."

Kirov sucked in his breath. He seemed to expand, gaining centimeters in height. And power. His face darkened before he remembered that Zuul was already gone far beyond any human vengeance.

Ala continued, her voice caressing Kirov's ears.

"Zuul announced that Lal and you were dead at the village of Lodges. Deputy chief Pol and Dyryth had gone to Bari to defeat some monster that threatened your... our allies, the Cave Dwellers. Flana was a stranger in Dyalsi. She fled to the Seashore tribe rather than submit to Zuul's wishes." Ala gracefully pointed in the direction that Kirov knew led downriver.

"What about Bel the Clever One?" demanded Kirov. "Or the other women of the Dyal Riders? Would not they protect her?"

Ala bowed more deeply. "Bel had already fled to find her brother beyond the River. And the other women respected Zuul's authority as chief of their tribe." Her tone sharpened. "It was easy for them to do since Zuul did not wish *them* for mates as he did Bel *and* Flana." She seemed on the verge of adding something more but held her tongue.

Kirov snorted. He looked across the Plain of Grazers in the direction of the seashore. He had never seen it but Flana had described its wonders many times.

Minutes went by. Around them, the Dyal Riders were resuming their normal lives. Ala could hear voices directing the Women's Band to safety inside Dyalsi. She peered at Kirov's thoughtful face. He was even more handsome than ever.

Finally, she asked, "What will you do?" She paused and added the word, "Master."

Kirov continued to gaze into the distance as he answered

crisply. "I will go to the seashore and hunt for Flana. If she is willing, she will be my mate."

Ala's eyes widened. "No! Master," she contradicted. There was still a pause before the word "master" but it was noticeably shorter than before.

Kirov's head jerked to face Ala again. His eyes blazed; his body tensed. "Do you dare defy me?" he snapped. He added, "Slave?"

Ala winced and knelt before him. She scarcely seemed to be the same woman who had enslaved Kirov many sleeps ago. "No, master. I speak to remind you that the Pulka Horde approaches the Coldwater River. You have become chief of the Dyal Riders and the allied tribes. You must defend your people. You do not have time to hunt for one woman." She paused and added, "A woman who must have gone to the Dead World."

Kirov was silent for a long time, his eyes closed, his face contorted in anguish.

Carefully, Ala repeated, "What will you do, master?"

Kirov had aged a thousand years in as many heartbeats. "I will defend my people from the Pulka Horde."

*Chapter Sixteen*

## THE COLDWATER RIVER RAN RED FOR MANY WAKING PERIODS.

The Horde approaches," announced Bol the Messenger as he pointed to a smudge, barely visible far across the upward curving green surface of the Plain of Grazers.

A sardonic smile flickered across Kirov's face. This was the third time that he had heard those words. In the old Russian saying, *The third time is charming*. The Horde had overrun the territory of the Lodge Builders and now invaded the heartland of the allied tribes.

"Yes," agreed Kirov. "The Horde approaches our trap." He spoke with confidence to impress his followers.

And himself.

A handful of messengers surrounded him, ready to mount dyals and take his words to the war chiefs of the allied tribes. Kirov knew that Soviet generals would be surrounded by a battalion of officers, political "advisors" and technical experts. In primitive Pellucidar, the chiefs and lieutenants of the various tribes were commanding their tribesmen. (And tribeswomen.) As war chief of the allied tribes, his staff was himself: a jumped-up college student who had become a king.

The inward curving surface of the Inner World stretched before him, much like the map tables beloved of Soviet military commanders.

The distant smudge began to resolve itself into smaller groupings. An irregular mass of brown was closest, a tiny brown blob next, and finally a box of black dots. Based on Kirov's observations at the Wava Woods, they were easy to identify as a wave of animals fleeing the oncoming Horde, thirty or so Dyal Riders scouting and harassing the enemy, and finally the Pulka Horde itself. The latter was aimed at the low hill on which Kirov and most of the allied war band waited.

Kirov estimated numbers.

Interesting....

The Horde was distinctly smaller than it had been at the Wava Woods. And their great boxlike formation was more ragged. The implications....

They still outnumbered the combined manpower of the allied tribes....

"Bol."

"Yes, mighty Kirov?" Did stout Bol's voice quaver?

"When you brought the last message from Lal the Fierce One, did you not say that the Dyal Riders and Lodge Builders had killed many Pulka tribesmen? Including chiefs, lieutenants and champions?"

"Yes, mighty Kirov."

The war chief smiled thinly. He suspected that Bol was repeating the word "mighty" to encourage himself as much as his leader.

"Good hunting. Your mighty blows have made them weaker and us stronger." He raised his voice so that the warriors assembled on the low lying Hill of Warriors could hear him. Some of them passed his words along to the Snake Eaters moving around on the Plain of Grazers at the foot of the hill facing the oncoming Horde. Others passed the words to the boatloads of River People hugging the shore behind him.

Bol glowed with pride. The allied tribesmen murmured. Kirov couldn't distinguish their words but the tone seemed hopeful.

The Horde advanced.

Far across the Plain of Grazers, the animals fleeing the Horde began slamming into a line of spears planted in the thick grasses. Faint cries of pain echoed in the clear air of the Inner

World. Rapidly, a wall of flesh developed in a vast white-brown chevron enclosing the allied warriors.

"Again, the animals have covered the line of spears," commented Bol softly.

"Yes," agreed Kirov. "As we have planned. The Horde leaders will think that we are fools who have repeated our mistakes."

"Yawl the Swift One goes to the right," observed Bol.

Across the Plain, the small band of Dyal Riders that had been retreating in front of the Horde, harassing them with spears and arrows, broke off the running battle and began a headlong rush to Kirov's right. They raced towards the outpost of the River People on this bank of the Coldwater. Kirov could see the front ranks of the Horde shifting to his right....

A lone Dyal Rider broke off from Yawl's band, turning at right angles and heading towards Kirov's left.

"Woel the Lean One plays his part," stated Kirov simply.

Bol shook his head. "I do not understand. Woel the Fearful One fled the battle at the village of Lodges without orders. He brought false news to Dyalsi and caused Zuul the Demon to proclaim you dead and himself chief. Yawl almost killed you. Yet you spared their lives. Why?"

"We need their spears," answered the war chief as he continued to study the advancing enemy. "And this time Woel's flight convinces the Horde that they have discovered our secret weakness. Look."

Still far off, Woel raced through a gap in the line of spears and then straight towards the rise called the Hill of Warriors.

Behind him, piping sounds cut the aire. The Horde's advance broke into columns. One continued to follow Yawl and his band. Another chased Woel into the gap. Trapped behind the wall of dead and dying animals caught on the planted spears and the living wall of the Horde, creatures panicked and ran in circles. They battered the corpses, each other, the Hordesmen.... The Horde's advance lost momentum as dozens of *Merychippi* riders turned to fight the fear-crazed animals. Other

Hordesmen—perhaps luckier than their fellows—streamed through the gap, forming a great puddle of obviously confused mounted warriors.

Kirov smiled. "It's working," he said softly.

He intended his words for himself but Bol and the other messengers heard him. They whispered among themselves as the vast Horde's advance broke down.

"Mighty Kirov, we do not understand your thoughts. How have you managed to slow down and confuse the Horde?"

Kirov paused to translate his thoughts into the limited vocabulary of the Pellucidarian language. A Soviet military analyst would say that the Horde had lost unit integrity and that their command and control network had broken down as a result of previous battle losses and a skillful deception operation. Not having centuries of experience with civilized warfare, Pellucidarian simply lacked those words.

"Men and women of the allied tribes, the Horde gains great power by fighting as a single band and by riding their small horses. By the magic of *history* and *psychology* (which I will teach you later) we have caused them to believe that they have discovered our weakness. They have foolishly divided their forces and no longer fight as a single band. Their horses are not as agile as our two-legged dyals. When they turned to pass through the gap, they lost speed. Now they are confused and must re-form."

Along the wall of flesh that had been the line of spears, the Horde had ground to a stop. The column chasing Yawl's "platoon" towards the outpost slowed and halted. Other "troops" of cavalry attempted to enter the gap but found the space too limited for their preferred maneuvers. Faintly, the allied warriors could hear irate shouting as the Horde leaders attempted to bring order out of chaos.

Woel rode up to the Snake Eaters below the Hill of Warriors, delivered a report, and began picking his way around the allied lines. He visibly preened as he headed toward the outpost where Yawl awaited him.

Finally, more piping noises came from the Horde. The faint shouting died away replaced by the thin voice of someone giving orders. The Hordesmen inside the great chevron of flesh began moving forward. Pygmy heads began appearing over the wall as the agile *Merychippi*—half the size of horses from the Outer World—climbed the mounds of dead animals and then jumped down inside the enclosure.

The advance of the victorious Pulka Horde resumed.

"Snake Eaters!" shouted Kirov. "Come back to the second line of spears!"

The stoic tribesmen thus addressed were the forward most defenders of the Hill of Warriors. They silently turned their backs on the enemy and walked carefully to the second defense line where the Marsh Dwellers and Women's Band awaited.

The allied leaders could hear Horde voices raised in excitement. This battle was unfolding as they, the Horde, would wish. It was common enough for humans, great and small, to repeat ideas even if they failed before. Now, the Horde's enemies had made the same blunders here as at the Wava Woods. Those enemies were retreating before the battle had truly begun. And behind their foes coursed the mighty Coldwater River, cutting off further escape.

Individual Hordesmen charged, eager to slaughter and enslave.

More and more horse riders became enflamed by the prospect of an easy victory. With rising excitement, they picked up speed. Soon the entire mass of the Pulka Horde was in movement, charging towards the Hill of Warriors. *Merychippus* feet—not yet evolved into true hooves—drummed across the Plain.

The distance between the forces closed rapidly.

As they charged, the pygmy horse soldiers' eyes widened. Their enemies were women! The so-called allied tribes must be desperate to place their women in the front line of battle!

The charge picked up more speed.

Hordesmen's eyes gleamed.

*More and more horse riders became enflamed by the prospect of an easy victory. With rising excitement, they picked up speed. Soon the entire mass of the Pulka Horde was in movement, charging towards the Hill of Warriors.*

Cruel snapping sounds followed by screams of equine pain pierced the thunder of myriad *Merychippus* feet.

Kirov's trap slammed shut.

The legendary warrior prince Alexander Nevsky would be proud of his distant student and his tactics.

The Hill of Warriors was an isolated swelling amid the marshy borders of the great river. All around it, firm dirt and rock gave way to sucking mud and muck concealed from Horde eyes by the abundant plants of northern Pellucidar and the picket lines of Snake Eaters. From long experience along the great river's margins, the Snake Eaters had learned how to walk apparently normally in muddy terrain. Seeing their enemies ostentatiously defending the Hill, the Hordesmen had *assumed* that the ground beneath the defenders' feet was solid....

*Merychippi* plunged into the mire, legs breaking, bodies shattering, and hearts failing. Their riders catapulted into the air, some landing in yielding ooze where they would be trampled by succeeding waves of their own tribesmen, others slamming into the spear wall of the Women's Band, solidly braced against unyielding rock and earth. Behind them, horse riders increasingly crashed into the chaos of death and dying.

Hordesmen who attempted to turn around ran into the spears and assegais of the Dyal Rider bands of Yawl and Gul closing in from the right and left rear. Those who went forward died on the spear wall. Poisoned arrows flew—and bounced off the snakeskin armor of the Snake Eaters and the leather shields of the Women's Band. Falconers launched their strike-like attack birds—only to lose them to volleys of arrows fired by River People archers concealed behind the front lines. When the birds were dead, the archers redirected their fire onto the struggling mass of horse riders.

The great assault ground to a halt.

Surviving Hordesmen and their gallant steeds floundered in the marshy ground.

Then the Snake Eaters and Marsh Dwellers strode forth, stabbing and hacking.

The great river ran red for many waking periods.

*Chapter Seventeen*

## DAWNING HOPE

Tsassal and Woel escorted a Hordesman to Kirov. Tsassal was impassive in victory. Woel's face suggested that he had defeated the entire Horde single handedly.

The diminutive Pulka was unsteady on his feet but he held himself upright. He saluted his conqueror. "Hail, mighty Kirov Skalkiller. I am Dolkon, acting chief of the Pulka Horde. Pulk the Great and his sons are dead. *Ka-goda.* I ask for the lives of my people."

There was a moment of silence as Kirov and the assembled representatives of the allied tribes studied their foe. To them, he was no bigger than a child. Yet, his people had proven a greater threat than the once feared Black Birdriders.

Kirov's eyes rested on a reed-impaled bag under Dolkon's arm. Bagpipes! he realized. *That was how the pygmies had managed to control an army that was huge by Pellucidarian standards. There was so much to learn about Pellucidar; so much that the various tribes could teach each other.*

He spoke.

"I greet you, Dolkon of the Pulka. You must surrender all of your peoples to us. We will spare your lives if you serve us well."

Dolkon grimaced but nodded. In savage Pellucidar, slavery was the merciful option.

Kirov pointed to Fama, who was leaning on her reddened spear. "Behold Fama of the Great Camel Rider Tribe. A double handful of sleeps ago, the Great Camel Riders fought the allied tribes. Now, they *are* allies. The Pulka Horde may become a free people again when you have served us for a time."

Dolkon stared at Fama for a moment, then nodded again.

"You must also surrender all humans to me. They will return to their tribes and families. Your people will serve them to repay the death that you have caused.

"And you must surrender the secrets of your magic—" Kirov pointed to the bagpipes "—to us. In return, we will teach you the secrets of our magic when you are ready to learn them."

Some of the assembled allies looked at Kirov askance but eventually all of them nodded their heads in agreement.

Dolkon looked up, hope dawning in his small face.

He knelt before his conqueror and embraced the latter's legs.

Allied eyes followed his movement—and thereby missed the look of astonishment that crossed Kirov's face.

*Chapter Eighteen*

## THE KING OF THE COLDWATER VALLEY

Kirov surveyed his kingdom. The slaves of the Small Horse Rider tribe—formerly the Pulka Horde—were laboring to cover the bodies of their fallen kinsmen and conquerors alike with earth. The numerous scavengers of the Inner World—prehistoric rats, wolves, jackals, and vultures—were circling the rapidly growing mound but they would retreat unfed. Instead, the little demons of the Molop Az would soon do their rightful job and consign the flesh of the bodies to the Sea of Fire far below Pellucidar while the spirits of the valiant dead would go to the Dead World.

Dyal Riders—a remnant of the once powerful tribe but proud defenders and victors nonetheless—escorted the Small Horse women and children to their new homes.

Kirov's knowledge of first aid would save many lives and limbs. Gul's broken arm was almost healed and he was loud in his praises of the tribes' new king.

He would rest.

Ala was waiting for him when he reached the River People's outpost. She smiled. "Hail mighty Kirov. You are again victorious. You have become the chief of all the allied tribes."

Kirov nodded simply. He murmured thanks.

Ala looked longingly into his face. She sighed, "Will you now take a mate, powerful Kirov?"

Kirov looked at her. "I will."

# FLANA'S STORY

I am Flana the Dyal Rider.

I am what my beloved Kirov Skalkiller would call a girl of Pellucidar, the vast hollow that exists inside the world of Earth.

I was once Flana of the Seashore People. I was born and lived what seemed like all of my life on the shores of the great Sea of Monsters.

Kirov says that the strange people of the Outer World have named the Sea the *Karl-Marx Ocean* to honor a founder of the Soviet Red War Party Tribe. If the Seashore People were to dig a hole that was as deep as *four hundred thousand* tall men are high, we might emerge in the Outer World where the cold waves of the *Arctic Ocean* break on the shores of *Siberia*.

All of these strange words are *Russian*—words that I learned from my beloved—because Pellucidarian has no words for these things. If a Pellucidarian wished to say *four hundred thousand*, he must say "four tens of hundreds of hundreds."

Truly the men of the Outer World are wiser and more powerful than we gilaks of Pellucidar. Is it any wonder that I should love such a man?

It was not always thus.

When I was a girl, I lived among the Seashore People in our homes of giant seashells.

Each shell is three to five times the height of a tall man and houses a family. When a family grows too large, the young men scavenge the beach until they find a shell cast off by the monsters of the Sea and drag it to our village where it is claimed

180

by the large family. The family then divides into two along with all of their possessions and occupies the new shell. When the monsters of the Plain of Grazers and the Coldwater Valley attack our village, they are defeated by the natural armor of our homes and the spears of our warriors.

Life seemed good. The women of the Seashore People gathered food, wove cloth from seaweeds, and raised our children. Our men hunted, fished, scavenged, and built canoes and weapons. The Seashore People were content.

But I was not content.

My brothers scavenged the beach for three sleeps' walk in either direction. They found many strange and useful things for our village. Once they found an oval shaped house or truly huge canoe that had been hurled onto the shore during one of Pellucidar's terrible black storms. In the house were the bodies of strange men dressed in weird, colorful clothing that was neither animal skins nor woven seaweed. We returned their bodies to the Sea and gave their beautiful but useless tools to uncle Gano, whose collection is the strangest in all of Pellucidar.

I wished to scavenge the beach and explore the world beyond our village with my brothers. I wished to paddle a canoe up the Coldwater River to the Frozen Sea that no Seashore Man or Woman has ever seen. Along the way I would pluck the starflowers from the Plain of Grazers and adorn my dark hair with their bright beauty. I wished to cross the Sea of Monsters and see the blocky shapes that are sometimes visible in the haze of distance. And from the sea I would scoop a hundred fish for my family and People.

I asked my parents for permission to do these things and they refused. My father said that the world beyond our village was too dangerous for a young woman. My mother said that I should be content to gather food and wait for a young man to place a beast's head before our shell in token of his desire to take me as his mate.

I asked my brothers if I might accompany them and they said yes—until Mother noticed and boxed our ears.

I asked my uncle Gano and he smiled his mysterious smile. He said that it was easier to ask forgiveness for a deed already done than to ask permission for a deed as yet undone. I smiled in understanding. Neither of us had said anything forbidden.

One waking period, my brothers assembled before our shell and left to scavenge the beach for three days march on one bank of the Coldwater River. I bid them farewell as I always do....

... and then followed them when the Seashore People returned to their common tasks.

My heart soared!

I saw great, voracious sharks cruising the waves, teeth flashing when packs of hunting azcodons, or *seawolves*, drew near. Beyond them, huge azdyryths and snake-headed tandorazes fought to the death, bloodying the waters for hundreds of hands around them. Mere fish swam for their lives, fleeing the battle of the titans.

Inland, rocks, molded into curious shapes by unending wave action, guarded the shore. My brothers moved stealthily among them, always watchful for the animals of the great Plain of Grazers: thags, tarags, qirqirns, sheep, antelopes, musk oxen, and tens of other types besides.

And overhead...!

Overhead flew danger.

I followed my brothers onto the open Plain, staying far enough back that they did not see me.

Suddenly one shouted and pointed upward.

Great black birds that I now know are called trals appeared in Pellucidar's clear blue sky. On the back of each bird was a leather saddle and in each saddle was a rider—the dread Black Birdriders of the village of Tralsi.

The trals swooped, ordered to capture slaves by their masters.

But my brothers were no antelope to be trapped by swift hunters! No!

They knelt in unison, making themselves smaller and therefore more difficult targets.   And they pointed their spears in every direction, each man guarding his brothers' backs.

The trals shied off, thwarted by the small forest—or *hedge-hog*—of spears aimed at their tender breasts.

They circled, seeking an unguarded approach to the hunters. They found none.

Instead they found me.

I was three hundred paces away from my brothers. There was no one to watch my back.

Suddenly I was lifted off the ground and high into the air.

I thrashed about, attempting to sink my knife into the breast of the evil creature.   But I was weak and I failed.

My beloved later said that I did not have the right *angle* to plunge my blade into the tral's chest.   He also said that such an event concealed good luck.   If I had injured the tral while it was soaring above the Plain of Grazers, I might have been killed when it fell to earth.

And more importantly, I thought, I would never have met my beloved.

And so I became a slave to Ala the Beautiful One, queen of the Black Birdriders.

I lost count of the number of sleeps that passed as Ala's body servant, house cleaner, and second pair of hands.   And the number of times that Ala struck me for being "lazy" or "slow" to do her bidding….

But there I met *Specialist* Mikhail Kirov of the *Soviet Red War Party* Tribe and fell in love with the great magician from the Outer World.

Kirov destroyed the community of the Black Birdriders and freed their slaves through strange magic.   He slew Ala's gigantic bird monster, the skal, with only two spears and his wits.   He made Ala the slave of Lal the Fierce, queen of the Dyal Riders, who had been Ala's slave for a time.   He guided the captives to Dyalsi, the village of the Dyal Riders.   And he promised to take me as his mate.

*He promised to take me as his mate!*

My heart glowed.  My body warmed.  My brain whirled.
I was content.

But then war threatened and Lal ordered Kirov away to
defeat the mysterious Pulka Horde.

My heart trembled.

Lal, who was a new sister to me, followed Kirov with the
main war band of the Dyal Riders and their allies.  Pol, her
deputy, who was a new uncle to me, left to fight another menace.

They left Dyalsi in the care of Zuul the Old.

A cold hand gripped my heart.

Zuul had been a great hunter many, many sleeps ago.  But
age had stolen away his heart and much of his brain.  He had
come to believe that all the women of the Dyal Riders were
his.

A messenger brought word that Kirov had gone to the
Dead World.

My heart died within my chest.

Zuul declared that Kirov was a demon from the Molop Az
far beneath Pellucidar.  He ordered me to his home....  He
said that I should be his handmaiden....

When he did so, his face betrayed his formerly secret
thoughts.  My heart fled from my body.

I sought help from the Dyal Riders but I had no family to
defend me.  The noble warriors had left for the wars.  Many
tribesmen had no wish to dispute their acting chief.  Others
concealed their fears with quibbling.  Surely, they said, you are
mistaken; being a handmaiden to the chief is an honorable duty
for unmarried women; surely Zuul means well....  They turned
their faces away when they said these things....

And so I fled from Dyalsi where Kirov and I had dreamt
of a new home.

I stole a dyal from the corral and guided it back to the
Seashore.  The great flightless riding bird of Pellucidar that
Kirov calls a *Phororhacos* ran for many thousands of breaths
along the Coldwater River before it collapsed in exhaustion.
We both slept for thousands of breaths more before hunger

woke us. After we both fed, we continued. Ten sleeps later, we arrived in Seashore Village.

We were lucky that the frightful monsters of the Coldwater Valley had not thought us a meal.

My heart leaped to see my family and clan again and their hearts leaped in unison with mine.

I should have been content but I was not.

Kirov was dead and so was my heart.

After many sleeps, the world changed.

My sisters and I were preparing a feast for the hunters when my cousin Hanu came racing into the village from the left of the River. He shouted that there was a great canoe upon the waters of the Sea of Monsters approaching the village.

The women, children and old men of the Seashore People gathered to see the great canoe.

To my surprise, I recognized the people of the great canoe from Kirov's previous descriptions. They were members of the Soviet Red War Party Tribe. No one else in all of Pellucidar wears gray clothing that is neither animal skins nor woven seaweed and no one else *flies* a red *flag* with a yellow star-flower design upon it.

They landed their huge canoe at our village. Chief Landu wished them to leave—in the language of Pellucidar there is but one word for both "stranger" and "enemy"—but they gestured with their strange magical weapons that Kirov calls *guns*. Seeing the guns, I spoke my few words of Russian to the Soviets to ask them for peace. Their mouths fell open but they lowered their guns.

For a time, it seemed as though there might be peace between the Seashore People and the Soviet Tribe. Landu ordered that the planned feast include the Soviet visitors as well as the hunters. All should have been content.

But a Soviet warrior followed several women when they went to bathe in the surf before the feast. When they removed their clothes, he became excited. He advanced upon them making strange noises that I could not translate. He seized my

cousin Kania. She screamed and struggled to be free. I shouted
for peace but the warrior ignored me. Landu rushed forth to
see what danger threatened his niece and his People. He seized
the Soviet warrior and tore the latter's hands from Kania's body.

The warrior swung around, aimed his gun, and fired. A
cave opened in Landu's chest, his lifeblood spewing outward
from his back.

Kania screamed again and began pounding on the warrior's
head and torso. He struck her with the thick end of his gun,
forcing her away from him. Then he aimed and fired again.
Kania screamed no more.

The old men of the Seashore People grasped their spears
and the women their knives. We advanced upon the invaders....

Soviet guns thundered death.

Seashells provided little protection against the guns of the
Outer World.

Some of us were lucky. A bullet grazed my head and I
collapsed. As I lay upon the corpse of uncle Landu, I heard
the Soviets *forming ranks* and firing again and again.

When it was over, the only living beings in the Seashore
Village were Soviets.

The few of us that survived crept away like mice escaping
from monsters.

Perhaps *ten thousand* paces from the destroyed village, we
collected ourselves into a pathetic band of two hands of People.
We had a single chance for survival.

We began our escape up the Coldwater River, hoping that
the Dyal Riders might aid us.

My heart quailed at the thought of returning to Zuul's
kingdom but slavery was better than death.

We were lucky.

The great river protected one flank and there were enough
of us to discourage many attackers. Still, only four of us survived
to be found by a Dyal Rider patrol as we approached Dyalsi.

The Dyal Rider patrol leader, a handsome man named Gul,
insisted that we borrow their riding birds for the remainder of

the journey. He and his warriors loped along beside us, guiding the fierce mounts and talking to us as fellow tribesmen.

My heart leaped upward. My body warmed. My brain spun around and around.

Gul said that Kirov was alive!

Kirov was alive!!

*My beloved was alive!!!*

Once again, my mighty magician had triumphed over death itself! He had come back from distant battles alive and saving many women and children in the process! He had revealed that Zuul the Old was actually a demon from the Molop Az and had defeated him in mortal combat! He had defeated the Pulka Horde and made them his slaves! Now he was the chief of the Dyal Riders and the Coldwater Valley alliance.

My heart expanded. It was as big as an elephantine tandor! No!! Bigger!!!

But then....

Gul continued talking.

He crushed my spirit.

Kirov thought that I had gone to the Dead World.

He had taken *Ala* as his mate.

They had a son.

His name, too, was Kirov.

I collapsed and knew nothing more until I awoke in the healing house of Dyalsi.

I learned that I had been asleep for many wakes.

I wanted to go to the Dead World. If I had been stronger, I would have destroyed my own life.

But I was weak and so I lived.

Gradually, I recovered....

Somewhat.

I was never truly content again.

Kirov visited me in the healing house.

Ala was by his side. Her eyes flickered from him to me and back again. And again. And again.

Ala the warrior queen was afraid...!

I told my story—or at least as much as I dared to share.

Kirov was intensely interested, especially when I described the Soviet invasion of the Seashore Village. I could see that my beloved wished to communicate with his original People once again.

He promised that the Dyal Riders would mount an expedition to Seashore Village and make an effort to locate and assist as many of my People as possible. If we wished, we would have new homes with the Dyal Riders or the other tribes of the Coldwater Valley alliance.

He was very, very kind.

But it was the dispassionate kindness of a great chief—not the love of a mate.

I sighed deeply.

A fish that falls into a fire is quickly reduced to a black rock. My heart was also a rock.

Kirov's eyes declared his love....

... and the fact that he would not betray his mate....

He would not betray Ala.

However much he might want to....

Is it any wonder that I should love such a man?

The worst thing of all was Ala's reaction....

Once she realized that Kirov would never betray her, she relaxed.

She smiled the beautiful smile of a great woman. A kind and loving woman.

*She wanted to be my friend...!*

I took her hand and squeezed it. I did my best to smile in return.

Later, I had time to think.

When I was done thinking, I asked the old woman who was the healer of the Dyal Riders for food and water.

I had to live.

When I recovered, I asked Ala if I might become a handmaiden of the chief of the Dyal Riders.

She hesitated for a moment but agreed.

After all, we were now friends.

You see, despite all the changes that we Dyal Riders have experienced, some things remain the same.

Ala has become a loving mate, a wonderful mother, a wise counselor, and an inspiring leader of our Peoples.

But she is still a warrior queen.

She still loves to hunt, to ride, to fight. And when she fights, she fights in the forefront of battle....

Where the danger is greatest....

Sooner or later, some enemy will drive a spear through her gut and all of Kirov's magic will not save her.

Sooner or later, Ala will go to the Dead World.

Kirov will grieve for her.

But life will go on.

And when it does, I will be there to comfort him.

# MAGICIANS OF PELLUCIDAR

*Chapter One*

## THE COMING STORM

**T**wo men trudged southward across the Plain of Grazers somewhere in northern Pellucidar.

Of course, they did not know that they were walking south. Few of the many tribes of humans living in the great world at the Earth's core had any conception of compasses, maps or similar methods of finding directions. Instead, they had evolved an uncanny homing sense that enabled every adult Pellucidarian to unerringly find his or her way home no matter where in the vast landscape of the inner world he or she started from. If someone had asked either of the travelers where they were going, they would merely say that they were returning to a village called Dyalsi, which was the birthplace of the smaller of the two men, Pol Taragkiller, the deputy chief of the Dyal Riders.

Both men were anxious to reach Dyalsi. Savage Pellucidar was a world of constant threat and only in the tiny communities that dotted the eerie landscape was there even a handful of safety.

Pol studied the way ahead. Myriads of dots were moving slowly across the green grasses. His mind automatically noted each and classified them according to the dangers that they presented. Most were grass eaters—dangerous only when attacked or stampeded. Others, mostly hidden from view in the grasses, were meat eaters intent on their next meals—meals that might well include Pol and Dyryth. None of the latter *appeared* to be dangerously close to the humans but Pol was too skilled a hunter to make assumptions.

He slowly scanned the plain. His head moved from left to right until…

Pol suddenly stopped scanning. His head froze in position. His eyes narrowed.

His right hand automatically grasped his spear more firmly.

His left hand touched Dyryth's shoulder. The latter quietly rumbled an agreement.

Neither of them had ever seen such a strange sight.

Five times the height of a tall man (about thirty feet) in front of the travelers a large flat-topped rock lay embedded in the plain. As Pol and Dyryth watched, a hand of (five) creatures emerged from the tall grasses beyond the rock and calmly mounted the natural observation post. One of them looked directly at the travelers.

His reaction to Pol and Dyryth's presence was typically Pellucidarian.

He produced a spear thrower aimed at the pair and shouted, "I kill!"

The two travelers quickly responded. They brought their spears to their own shoulders, preparing to launch an attack. Pol shouted, "We kill!"

The stranger was odd indeed in their eyes. He seemed to be a small man—well proportioned but only half the size of muscular Pol and a fraction of the giant Dyryth's mass. He was the height and weight of a child but conducted himself as the most ferocious of warriors.

His mounts were equally odd. Both Pol and Dyryth had seen *orthopi* many times before. According to their friend Kirov Skalkiller, the latter animals were the diminutive ancestors of the horses of Earth. No larger than fox terriers, orthopi hid among the lush grasses of Pellucidar's well watered plains and survived the myriad dangers of the land of terror by speed, dexterity and numbers. The stranger was riding a larger version of an orthopi and leading three others by a rope. Had Kirov been present, he would have quickly identified the four-legged beasts of burden as the pony sized *Merychippus* or *Mesohippus* of the Pliocene era. To Dyal Riders accustomed to their two-legged riding birds, the Pliocene proto-horses were odd indeed.

The small man was not intimidated by the size or numbers of the giants.

"Who comes to the lands of the Coldwater Valley Tribes?" he demanded.

Pol and Dyryth gaped at the sentinel. The Dyal Rider tribe was the heart of the Coldwater Valley alliance of tribes. This miniature sentry was blocking their return to their own home!

Pol waved his spear in what Kirov would have called a *threat gesture*. His voice boomed angrily. "We are Dyal Riders, little man! Stand aside that we might return to Dyalsi!"

The small man snorted derisively and ostentatiously looked around. "I see no dyals before me, loud giant! Be gone!" He dropped his horse rope into his lap and dismissively gestured in the direction from which the travelers had come.

Pol swelled up furiously. His spear gripping hand turned white from pressure. But he held his temper in check.

As he struggled, the genial Dyryth spoke up. "Our dyals were killed in battle with the Soviet Red War Party Tribe." He turned and pointed. "There—in the caves of Bari in the Mountains of the Birds."

The small man started violently when Dyryth named the Soviet Army by its Pellucidarian name and again when the latter named the cavern system that underlay the great mountain range to their west. His small horse danced nervously under him. He looked quickly at the jagged peaks as if to confirm their existence and returned his scrutiny to the travelers, peering carefully at them.

Pol noted the sentry's reaction and peered back.

The sentry broke the awkward silence. "Who are you and why were you in Bari?"

Pol named himself and Dyryth. He continued, "I am the first deputy chief of the Dyal Riders. We journeyed to Bari to assist the Cave Dwellers. They asked our aid against a new tribe that emerged from the mountains. They wished for the *inventor* Kirov Skalkiller to come but he had gone to the Lake of Lodges to defeat the Pulka Horde. So I went instead. Dyryth went to guard my back."

The small man laughed at Pol's report. Before Pol could take offense, the sentry amplified, "Kirov the Mighty defeated the Pulka Horde many sleeps ago. We are now the Small Horse Tribe of the Coldwater Valley Tribes." He gestured at his proto-horses with his free hand.

Pol goggled at the horseman.

The latter cleared his throat and declared, "I am Taddo of the Small Horse Tribe. I am a scout for the Coldwater Valley Tribes. We are fellow hunters (allies). The great chief Kirov has said that we scouts should watch for your return. He named you and your mission to Bari, and therefore I know that your words are true.

"Come. I will escort you to Dyalsi."

He paused and added, "I would offer you a horse to ride but you are too large for them."

Dyryth smiled amiably and even Pol had to grin at the thought of such large men attempting to ride the small horses.

The three allies paused to share a cold meal and to allow the Mesohippi to graze upon Pellucidar's lush grasses. When they were done, they turned their heads towards Dyalsi, home of the Dyal Riders and effective capital of the Coldwater Valley.

"WHAT NEWS DO you bring from Bari?" asked Taddo.

"Very bad news," responded Pol grimly. "The Soviet Red War Party Tribe has traveled through the Mountains of the Birds and conquered the Cave Dwellers of Bari. They journeyed through a canyon four fingers back from Dyalsi." Taddo nodded his head in understanding.* "The Soviet war chief demanded

---

* *The most common method of indicating direction in Pellucidar relies on the natural homing instinct and a primitive compass formed by using the outstretched fingers of both hands. The navigator points his left little finger in the direction of his birthplace and spreads his other fingers wide. He then duplicates the gesture with his right hand placing his right little finger atop his left little finger. The number of fingers named indicates the angle from the baseline course. By combining Pol's description with other information gleaned from the Soviet records, we learn that Bari is northwest of Dyalsi and the Soviets initially crossed the*

that the Cave Dwellers surrender to his tribe and be *sit-i-zens*
of the Soviet Yuun-yun—"

Taddo interrupted. "What are *sit-i-zens?*"

Dyryth spoke up, "Slaves."

Pol glanced at Dyryth in surprise. The gentle giant seldom
expressed opinions.

Dyryth understood Pol's look and clarified. "Kirov said
that life in the Soviet tribe is like a poisonous flower. It is
beautiful to smell but deadly to eat."

After a moment, both Pol and Taddo nodded in understanding.

Pol resumed his report. "When the chief of Bari refused
to crawl before the Soviets, the Red War Party fired their *guns*
and killed many Cave Dwellers. The survivors fled into the
caves but another Red War Band ambushed them there. They
had come through the caves as well as the canyons. The people
of Bari are now slaves."

Taddo was silent for a time as he rode along. Finally he
spoke.

"The Soviet tribe has many people if their chief can send
two war bands to surround Bari."

"I fear that they have more war bands beyond the Mountains," stated Pol. "And those war bands are crossing into the
Plain of Grazers. Soon they will attack Dyalsi and the other
tribes of the Coldwater Valley."

Taddo sighed in deep emotion.

Then he proclaimed, "Kirov the Mighty will defeat the
Soviet Red War Party with his magic."

Dyryth nodded in agreement.

Pol was less confident. "I wish this to be true. Did you
say that Kirov defeated the Pulka Horde?"

Taddo smiled thinly. "Yes. I was there at the Hill of
Warriors when mighty Kirov used the magic of *history* and

---

*Mountains of the Birds through the Middle Canyon north of Bari. Also see David
Critchfield, "System of Indicating Direction", The Gilak's Guide to Pellucidar, 2007.*

*psychology* to confuse and trap the Horde. There were thousands of us but he defeated and enslaved us all."

The small man paused for a long time and added, "And now he has freed us to be his allies." His voice was thick with awe. He repeated, "Kirov will defeat the Soviet Red War Bands."

The allies trudged or rode in silence for a timeless time.

Finally, Pol asked, "Taddo, why did your people come to the Coldwater Valley?"

The small man answered briskly. "We fled another tribe armed with *guns*. They called themselves Ah-mer-i-kans. They came to our lands near the Frozen Sea many, many sleeps journey in that direction." He pointed to the east. Pol and Dyryth looked but the Small Horse homeland was lost in the distant haze.

Taddo continued, "Pulk the Great wished to make them slaves but their weapons destroyed our warriors. So we fled.

Dyryth and Taddo moved on. After a moment, they realized that Pol no longer accompanied them. They turned and looked.

Pol was standing in place but his head looked to the west and the Mountains of the Birds, to the east where the Small Horse men had fled American thunder, to the south where Dyalsi had come into view nestled under its protective forest, to the west, to the east, to the south….

Dyryth and Taddo returned to the thoughtful chief. The giant Dyal Rider waited for his leader to speak but the Small Horseman was less patient.

"Mighty Pol, what is wrong?"

Pol took a deep breath and answered. "There is a great war coming. The Soviets advance from one direction while the Americans advance from the opposite direction.

"We will be crushed between them."

## Chapter Two

## DOCTRINE

Comrade Regiment Commander Kronstadt and Comrade Battalion Commander Kulongoski stood in the inner sanctum of Fort Alinsky briefing their commanding officer on Soviet plans to liberate the entire world of Pellucidar from its cavemen owners.

Soviet power had already liberated a portion of the northern continent of Leninska (Lenin Land) and bestowed the Russian name *Plutonia* on the resulting *okrug*, or area. The political capital of the okrug was the town of Bogrov, named for a Revolutionary assassin, on the coast of the frigid Polar Sea. But military operations, especially those intended to expand the Soviet foothold in Pellucidar, were commanded from the more centrally located Fort Alinsky.

Pellucidar, it seemed, was very hazardous for the careers of Soviet officers assigned to conquer it. Regiment Commander E. Kandinsky had been recalled and sentenced to a prison camp for allowing the American warlord Edgar Rice Burroughs to ambush and destroy an entire Soviet regiment at the disastrous "battle" of the Plutonian Plain.

Soviet military doctrine called for reinforcing success, not failure. The fate of Kandinsky would underline that doctrine and *encourage* other soldiers to do their best.

Varan was intently studying Kulongoski's maps of Plutonia and the adjacent regions of Leninska. Theoretically, his entire command staff should have been present to assist him but he had invited only his operations and intelligence officers to this

196

preliminary briefing. The latter devoted as much time as he could to analyzing his commander while the former spoke.

Varan tapped an almost blank region on the map to the east of Plutonia across an impressive chain of mountains called the Birnams after some analogy with a play by W. Shakespeare. The region was labeled "Unexplored" but colored pins and note cards indicated Soviet penetrations of the mountains on four axes of advance. The region's northern coast was washed by the Polar Sea. To the east, an unnamed strait connected the Polar Sea with the distant Friedrich-Engels Ocean under North America. On the far side of the strait an ugly green splotch was labeled the Republic of New America. To the south an isthmus connected the Unexplored Region with another land-mass named Beringia for its location under the Bering Sea. To the southeast, a huge blue smudge marked the largely unknown Karl-Marx Ocean.

With few exceptions, the capitalist dominated International Geographic Society had refused to accept the Soviet names but that was of no matter to the soldiers. Comrade Stalin had spoken and they would obey.

"I intend to push forward into this region and annex it. That will secure our eastern frontier and prevent the New American cowboys from threatening our position."

Again, Varan's juniors nodded in agreement. Before his recall, Kandinsky had sent probes forward into the unexplored region and they had reported manageable resistance from the prehistoric beings of the area.

"Kulongoski, the map shows an isthmus to the south. Have we confirmed its existence?"

"Yes, Comrade Brigade Commander. We sent two expeditions along the southern coast hoping to find a new sea route to New America but the isthmus (and natives) blocked our way. This map incorporates our latest findings."

Varan nodded in understanding.

"And the cowboys? Are they exploring this region?"

"Not at this time. They explored the eastern coasts of the

region about two years ago but did not penetrate very far inland or establish any permanent bases there. They encountered some trouble with the natives and withdrew after a sharp battle. I have a copy of their report and assessment if you wish to see it."

Varan sniffed suspiciously. "Why did they withdraw? Were the natives too numerous or fierce for them?"

"No, Comrade. The New Americans reported that the Pulka tribe was very large by native standards but they fled when confronted with gunfire. The New Americans simply did not consider it worthwhile to conquer them. Their overall policy is to consolidate their hold on the peninsula of New America and to expand to their southeast, eventually linking up with the Empire of Pellucidar. Their President T. Roosevelt decided not to tackle too many projects at once, especially since the strait separates the two zones."

Varan grunted.

He studied the map in silence for a moment.

Then he raised his head and began giving orders. "Kronstadt, begin planning a general offensive into this eastern region. Your expeditionary forces are currently advancing through these three canyon complexes plus this cavern system." He tapped the map at each location. A note card stated that the cavern system was called Bari. "Continue that broad advance but ensure that the four forces link up as this Middle Canyon force and Cavern System force have done. I do not wish any of our forces to be cut off and defeated in detail."

Kronstadt scratched notes rapidly.

Varan also tapped the map at a point between the Birnam Mountains and the southern coast. A note card indicated that only small Soviet scouting parties had explored this area. "Send a force to the south of the mountains as well. They will consolidate that territory and threaten the flank of any resistance east of the mountains."

Kronstadt nodded as he scribbled.

He looked up and asked, "How far should we plan on

advancing? Given the primitive terrain, we will be advancing on foot and the men will be carrying a great deal of their own supplies. At least until the engineers can provide roads and support services. Trucks, horses and mules are becoming available but most of those are committed to supplying Alinsky and the forts garrisoning Plutonia."

Varan frowned and leaned over the map again. "I would like our forces to advance to the isthmus where our new border will be relatively short."

Unseen by his commander, Kronstadt flinched. It was true that Comrade Stalin planned to *eventually* add the entirety of the vast Novy Mir to the Soviet Union but Comrade Varan was proposing a huge bite given the limited resources available.

"Yes, Comrade Brigade Commander. We will begin planning this operation at once." Did Kronstadt's voice quaver? If so, no one seemed to notice.

"Excuse me, Comrade Brigade Commander," interrupted Kulongoski. "At the present time, this new eastern region has no name. Do you wish to give it one?"

Varan nodded in approval. "A wise idea, Kulongoski. 'Stalin' or 'Stalinska' would be appropriate...."

"Excuse me, Comrade Brigadier General," repeated the intelligence officer. "That name has already been proposed for the Sub-Pacific Continent but not yet approved. May I suggest a more modest name—at least for the moment?"

"Such as?"

"Gori—in honor of Comrade Stalin's birthplace in Gruzhinia." For reasons that no Russian or Soviet understood, many Americans and Europeans called the latter republic "Georgia."

Varan nodded his head vigorously. "A very good idea, Kulongoski. I will propose the name 'Gori' for our new territory."

The intelligence officer smiled modestly and Kronstadt seconded the idea with enthusiasm.

MANY MILES NORTH of Fort Alinsky, the port of Bogrov squatted on the frozen shores of the Polar Sea. Ice crusted ships huddled beside their docks as human chains unloaded their cargos. Behind them, ice floes choked the Sea.

One worker glanced quickly at the seascape visible beyond the ships. Pellucidar's inward curving surface stretched upward and away into the distance. There was no horizon; distant sights simply faded into a grey blur. Just at the limits of the observer's vision, a dark circle dimpled the Sea surface. A crooked smile crossed his face. The circle was the North Polar Opening in the Earth's crust connecting the Northern Hemisphere of Earth with that of Pellucidar. That opening would never freeze; the heat escaping from the Inner Sun of Pellucidar saw to that. But on the outer surface, winter was closing in. The Arctic Ocean was freezing over and the ships now docked at Bogrov were the last cargo that Novy Mir would receive until the coming spring.

The observer worked diligently. If the brutal overseers thought that he was slacking, they might ask other questions as well.

Questions that he could not answer.

But, as he worked, he counted. And analyzed. And compiled.

The Soviet military buildup was well underway. A second division had arrived this year and now their equipment was pouring across the decks of the ice bound ships and into the interior.

Whatever "Uncle Joe" Stalin was planning, his local thugs would have the resources to carry it out.

The observer was already composing his report for New American Military Intelligence.

*Chapter Three*

## THE WAR CHIEF OF THE
## INNER WORLD

Kirov Skalkiller, war chief of the Coldwater Valley tribes, gazed outward and upward across the great Sea of Monsters. The ocean of the Inner World stretched upward like a gigantic wave about to crash onto the lands of the Seashore People. But it never fell. The illusion of height was one of the many strange sights of the vast lands and seas at the Earth's core. It was an awe-inspiring sight—and a symbol of the myriad mysteries of the Inner World.

Far out to sea—at the very limit of Kirov's vision—blocky shapes rose out of the surging waters. Curious, irregular sounds seemed to emanate from the colorful shapes.

As a scientist, Kirov was intrigued.

And frustrated.

None of his fellow tribesmen knew what those shapes were. The Seashore People might have known, but they had been slaughtered by a Soviet war party. A handful had escaped to Dyalsi, but none of them had any more idea than he did about the nature of the tantalizingly close objects.

Kirov shook his head, partly in frustration, partly to re-focus his thoughts on his mission. *Some other time—when he had settled the affairs of his tribes—and built the tools of Twentieth Century civilization—and founded a science academy.... Some other time he would investigate this latest mystery of Pellucidar...*

He looked around him. He saw his guards and the ruins of Seashore Village.

In contrast to most Pellucidarian tribesmen, the Seashore

People had lived in giant seashells cast up on the shore by the ceaseless waves. The thick natural armor had protected the villagers well against the claws and beaks of Pellucidar's native monsters.

But not against Soviet bullets and grenades.

The Seashore People were gone. Literally. The many scavengers of the Inner World had stripped the flesh from their shattered bones before Kirov's hunting party had reached the village. His men had gathered the pitiable remains of an entire tribe and buried them. The little demons of the Molop Az would have no flesh to carry away to the sea of fire that underlay Pellucidar in native legend. Kirov hoped that the souls of the murdered tribe had reached the Dead World where all men were brave and handsome and all women were wise and beautiful.

Kirov shook himself again and signaled to his guards. Silently, they returned to where their mounts, the savage dyals that gave his own tribe its name, were resting. To Kirov, trained as a paleontologist before he was drafted into the Soviet invasion of Pellucidar, they were *Phorushacidae*, the terror birds of late prehistory. To the Dyal Riders, they were mounts, beasts of burden, sources of clothing and even food.

The humans stepped into their saddles and cooed at their savage steeds. The powerful birds rose to their full height of two and a half meters. More cooing and the birds set off at a steady pace back in the direction of Dyalsi.

As they rode, the scientist turned magician was silent. He had much to think about.

Through the strange workings of fate, he was now the war chief of an alliance of primitive tribes and acclaimed as the greatest magician in all of Pellucidar. He had married Ala the Beautiful One and fathered a brawling young son, also named Kirov. He had defeated waves of enemies and made a start on bringing the science of the Outer World to his people....

The question that the young war chief was wrestling with was: Who were his people? Was he still a Soviet citizen? Did he wish to be one? Who was he? Mikhail Kirillivitch Kirov of the Soviet Union or Kirov Skalkiller, war chief of the Coldwater Valley?

His reveries were interrupted by the approach of a small band of Dyal Riders thundering across the Plain of Grazers from Dyalsi. The two parties halted and exchanged greetings. Kirov recognized his friend Bol the Messenger as the leader of the new party.

Bol's face was grim as he spoke to his chief.

"Hail mighty Kirov, killer of skals, trals and ryths. I bring fearsome news."

Kirov's face darkened. "Is Ala safe in Dyalsi?" His mate had a terrible tendency to ride willy-nilly around the Coldwater Valley. Kirov was constantly afraid that her seemingly endless luck would one day run out.

"No, mighty Kirov. Your mate is safe.

"The news is this: Pol Taragkiller has returned to Dyalsi. He says that he is the war chief of the Dyal Riders and of the Coldwater Valley Tribes. By my mouth, he commands that you come to Dyalsi, to surrender your chieftainship, and to become his advisor for the approaching war with the Soviet Union."

*Chapter Four*

## A COUNCIL OF WAR

**K**irov chuckled to himself. What war with the Soviet Union was approaching? As if the technologically backward tribes of Pellucidar could resist the powerful Soviet Red Army! And why was Pol claiming the leadership of the tribes in this crisis?

Kirov and his scouting party rode quickly home. As they passed through the outer defenses of Dyalsi, he smiled proudly as he noted the new trench and earthen wall built at his insistence. The palisade formerly implanted in the floor of the Plain of Grazers surrounding the town was now reestablished and thickened on top of the wall. By the prehistoric standards of savage Pellucidar, the large village was a fortress. Even so, work continued on improving its defenses. Kirov could hear banging and chipping sounds as craftsmen labored to finish a series of catapults. Except for captives, no enemy warrior had ever entered Dyalsi and none ever would.

Kirov's party rode slowly through the crude streets, greeting their fellow tribesmen, women and children as they moved. A scattering of other allied tribesmen was mixed in with the Dyal Riders: Small Horse Riders with their pony sized *Merychippus* steeds, proud Great Camel Riders—their *Gigantocamelus* mounts corralled outside town—Marsh Dwellers, Snake Eaters, and River People. The war chief saw no Cave Dwellers or Lodge Builders. He sighed quietly. The latter tribe had been almost wiped out in the Horde war and the former tribe....

He hoped that Pol had news of them.

As the old Russian saying had it, *Think of the Devil and he is bound to appear....!*

Kirov entered the small plaza in front of the Chief's House —his house!—and ordered his savage mount to halt.

He stared in surprise.

A ring of stools was assembled in front of the royal residence. Pol Taragkiller was seated on one, quietly discussing something with another seated tribal chieftain. Around the circle stood representatives of the other tribes in the alliance. Kirov recognized Hortul Paddlemaker, chief of the River People, and Taddo of the Small Horse Riders in attendance. Overhead, carefully cultivated trees shaded the scene.

He also recognized his mate, Ala the Beautiful One, standing in the doorway to their home. His heart fluttered at the sight.

And his heart quailed at her expression.

If the legendary Medusa were real, Ala would be she, and her basilisk gaze would have turned Pol to stone in a heartbeat!

"Hail, Pol Taragkiller!" greeted Kirov politely as he dismounted. He made the gesture of fellowship as soon as he alighted.

All eyes turned to Kirov.

Behind him, his scouts dismounted. The junior rider gathered up the reins and led the powerful war birds to their corrals for food, water and rest.

Pol began to rise....

Ala squealed girlishly—a curious trait for a woman of her dynamism. She bounded through the circle of stools and captured her mate in both arms. They kissed.

Pellucidarian women seldom displayed affection in public but Ala made her own rules.

After a timeless time, Ala relaxed her grip and stepped back a few centimeters.

"Hail mighty Kirov!" she breathed. After a pause, she defiantly added "War chief of the Coldwater Valley and chief of the Dyal Riders."

Kirov coughed and disengaged himself. "Hail Beautiful One," he responded.

He was still looking into her eyes when a thunderbolt struck his legs, almost knocking him over.

"Daddy!" shouted a stampede of dyals masquerading as a small boy. He clutched Kirov around both legs.

"Hail mighty Kirov, son of Kirov and Ala!" proclaimed the war chief. He leaned over and tousled his son's hair.

A cough interrupted the family reunion. Kirov returned his attention to the gathering of chieftains.

His handmaiden, Flana, formerly of the Seashore People, materialized and led the younger Kirov away.

The older Kirov's heart lurched at the sight of Flana. He resolutely put that thought away. He did not see Ala smiling with approval of his apparent indifference.

"Hail mighty Kirov, second deputy chief of the Dyal Rider Tribe!" greeted Pol formally.

"Hail Pol—" Kirov paused and added, "First deputy chief of the Dyal Rider Tribe."

"We must discuss the leadership of the Dyal Riders. Therefore, I have called this meeting of chieftains." Pol paused and added "And our allies."

He continued, "Come; seat yourself for council." He gestured at an empty stool.

Kirov noted that the "royal" stool of the tribal chief was absent.

He asked, "Where is the Seat of the Chief?" A Briton might have similarly inquired if the King of Great Britain had visited Parliament and found his throne missing.

Pol answered solemnly, "In the House of the Chief." He smiled, "Your mate would not allow me to touch it!" He recounted his repulse at Ala's hands with amusement—but also with an undercurrent of darker emotion.

Kirov barked a short laugh.

He was about to make some politic remark when Ala reappeared, this time with the stool in question in her hands. She carried it into the council circle, kicked the empty stool aside and replaced the displaced furniture with the simple throne of the Dyal Riders. She gestured grandly, saying "Mighty Kirov, *your* seat."

Pol's face darkened. "That is what we must discuss. Our former chief, Lal the Fierce, has gone to the Dead World. As first deputy chief of the Dyal Riders, I am now the chief. As the *second* deputy chief, you have led our tribes well in my absence but it is now time for you to yield the chieftainship to me." He crossed his arms over his powerful chest, obviously hoping to cut off further arguments.

An angry muttering broke out among the assembled chiefs and representatives. Pol's adherents were clearly in the minority.

Kirov paused to think. Despite his limited support, what Pol said was correct according to the Pellucidarians' laws of executive succession. Lal *had* appointed Pol, Kirov and Zuul the Old first, second and third deputy chiefs respectively. She had assumed that her trusted mentor Pol would survive his mission to Bari—as he obviously had—and would assume command of their tribe if she failed to survive—as she had. Kirov was a usurper. With the Pulka Horde bearing down on the Coldwater Valley, there had been no time to send for Pol and install him as war chief. The young scientist had simply assumed control....

Well, perhaps not so simply. Kirov had had to wage a duel of magical power with the third deputy chief Zuul to gain the throne....

Kirov sucked in his breath at a sudden memory.

Before the duel, Kirov had argued the succession with Zuul. He, Kirov, had claimed the leadership on the basis of his second deputy position outranking Zuul's third position...!

As the old Russian saying went, *Sauce for the goose is sauce for the gander.*

Kirov bowed his head. The weight of the world pressed down on his shoulders.

All around him, people were shouting and gesturing in anger and defiance. He heard none of their words.

He would not cheat his people. They might be Paleolithic tribesmen and –women but they had their traditions of government—their customs—their honor. If he was ever a Dyal Rider—much less their chief—then their honor must be his as well.

Kirov raised his head. He squared his shoulders.

Around him, the allied tribesmen fell silent.

The war chief of the Coldwater Valley, victor in three tribal wars and one coup d'etat, spoke. His words were not loud but they filled the plaza of Dyalsi.

"Ala, thank you for bringing forth the Seat of the Chiefs.

"Pol, the Seat is yours."

The screaming and shouting went on until the parliamentarians of Pellucidar dropped in exhaustion.

*Chapter Five*

## "I KILL!"

A strange cavalcade rode across the Plain of Grazers towards the caves of Bari under the Mountains of Birds. In the lead were Pol Taragkiller, chief of the Dyal Riders and war chief of the Coldwater Valley alliance, and his advisors Dolkon, chief of the Small Horse Riders, and Kirov Skalkiller, newly demoted *first* deputy chief of the Dyal Riders. Behind them were representatives of each tribe of the alliance. The Small Horse Riders and Great Camel Riders galloped across the Plain on their totemic animals. The other ambassadors rode dyals provided by their allies.

Around them, vast herds of strange animals were filling their bellies with the lush grasses of northern Pellucidar. Kirov recognized brontops and musk oxen among the grazers.

As the column of gilaks passed by, sentinel beasts observed them and honked warnings to their fellows. The herds parted so that no human came within a long spear's throw of the herbivores and then closed ranks behind the potential threats. They were more concerned with the giant Pliocene carnivores such as the bear-like *Agriotherium* or the dog-like *Amphicyon* lurking in the tall grasses than puny humans.

As they passed, the humans noted the plentitude of meat on the hoof provided by a generous Nature but each stifled thoughts of hunting and feasting. Dried meat in their saddlebags would nourish them until their mission was complete.

The men watched the Mountains of the Birds slowly begin to dominate the clear sky. From Dyalsi, the upward curving landscape made the tors seem like rocks pointing towards the

Plain. As they approached the foothills, the vast wind-sculpted peaks clawing the sky assumed their true awe-inspiring
forms.

Shortly after the beginning of the third waking period's
ride, scouts saw a grey smudge on the Plain, reminiscent of the
Pulka Horde's advance on the Coldwater River. The scouts
reined in their war birds and sent a messenger back to the main
body of Coldwater tribesmen. The remaining men moved
cautiously forward.

Before they could see the column clearly, it stopped in
place. Its neat rectangular dimensions were as out of place
among the natural contours of untamed Pellucidar as a battle-
ship magically positioned in a cathedral. The Inner World's
eternal sunlight glinted off dozens of bright surfaces, several of
which pointed directly at the scouts.

Bol the Messenger, the newly demoted *third* deputy chief
of the Dyal Riders, ordered his men to remain in place. He
clucked and his dyal strode forward. Bol raised his longspear
above his head with both hands.

He rode forward until he could clearly see the aggressors.

It was a column of men on foot. Each was clad in a long
gray coat that protected him from the chill winds of northern
Pellucidar. Each carried a large pack on his back. And each
carried a brightly shining weapon that resembled a pre-Kirov
spear. The men nearest Bol were pointing their weapons at
him. Above them cracked a red cloth with yellow markings
on a long pole.

Bol paused to study the strange men. He recognized them
from Kirov's descriptions.

They were the most dangerous predators in all of Pellucidar:
a *company* of warriors from the Soviet Red Army.

Bol cooed and his dyal began cautiously walking backward.
He smiled. Neither the great camels nor the small horses could
manage that trick! Was there any wonder that the Dyal Riders
were the most feared warriors in all of Pellucidar?

After the dyal had backed into the tall grasses, Bol heard

a sharp whistling sound. A star-shaped flower jumped into the air and drifted to earth, its stem cut. Behind the whistling sound came a banging noise. This, too, Bol recognized from Kirov's stories. He clucked loudly. His dyal turned and fled at its best speed.

There were more whistling sounds and bangs but none of the Soviet bullets struck the daring messenger.

THE GREY COLUMN continued to advance although more cautiously since its officers had observed natives watching. The Soviet leader questioned one of his command about the natives, and was apparently satisfied with the answer. The person questioned was quite different from the other troops. Among other things, he notably carried no bright shining weapon.

THE SOVIET COLUMN halted periodically for meals and the filling of canteens from the Plain's numerous creeks and rills.

As one break was coming to an end, a band of natives clad in brown feathers and riding small horses and giant birds and camels appeared. They carried a white rag fluttering from a long pole.

Soviet officers shouted commands and men lurched to their feet, still logy from their just finished lunch; a condition the approaching Pellucidarians depended on. Men with full stomachs are less alert and less aggressive than hungry men... However, the Soviet officers quickly got their men into a defensive formation with the majority of guns pointed directly towards the natives.

POL TARAGKILLER PAUSED to survey the Soviet position. His bitter experience fighting the Soviet Red War Party, as the limited Pellucidarian military vocabulary expressed it, in the caves of Bari inclined him towards caution. Still, he was the war chief of his people and he did not intend to crawl to the invaders.

He turned to his chief advisor.

"Kirov, are you sure the magic of the *white flag* will protect us from *So-vee-yet bullets*?"

The first deputy chief of the Dyal Riders replied, "It should. I can see their chiefs studying us with their *binoculars*. Our next step is to ride towards them with our spears aloft in the air as a sign of peace."

Pol agreed and gave the necessary commands. Most of his column remained in place. He, Kirov, Dolkon and two warriors—one bearing the white flag atop his longspear—rode slowly forward.

Perhaps thirty meters from the Soviet front line, the ambassadors of the Coldwater Valley halted. A wall of riflemen faced them.

"We come in peace," shouted Kirov in Russian.

Muttering broke out among the Soviet troops. A blonde officer pushed his way forward followed by another man clad in winter field gray.

Kirov looked intently at the second man. He spoke to Pol in Pellucidarian. "That yellow-haired warrior appears to be their war band chief. The other man is Nu of the Bari Cave Dwellers."

Pol nodded. Both he and Kirov had met Nu many, many sleeps ago when they escaped from the slave masters of the Black Birdrider tribe. He carried the proud name of an ancient hero.

The blonde officer shouted "Do you speak Russian?" in that language. Nu watched the officer alertly.

Kirov responded, "Yes, I do. I was…. I am Specialist Mikhail Kirillivitch Kirov of Task Force Kandinsky. I have been out of contact with Soviet forces for some time now."

The blonde officer started and his riflemen muttered louder. Starshinas bawled at their men to shut up.

Except for the wintery winds stirring the tall grasses and strange flowers, silence fell on the Plain of Grazers.

"Comrade Specialist Kirov," began the blonde officer.

"Welcome back to the Soviet Union! What are you doing here? And who are these savages?"

Kirov winced at the uncultured reference to the native Pellucidarians. He noticed that Nu briefly turned his head to stare oddly at the company commander. Nevertheless....

He pointed to Pol. "This man is the chief of the local tribes. He wishes to establish peaceful relations."

The blonde officer laughed. It was a brief, humorous laugh, but, again, Kirov found the implications unpleasant.

The Soviet commander shouted, "Very well. Ask him to come forward."

Kirov translated the invitation into Pellucidarian.

Pol nodded and cooed to his dyal. The powerful bird trotted a few steps forward.

He then shouted the standard greeting of the Inner World. "I kill!"

Kirov's tanned skin paled.

"Don't say that!" he commanded in Pellucidarian. "They won't understand what you mean."

Pol turned to his chief advisor, a questioning look on his face.

Before either could speak, Kirov heard the Soviet commander demand of Nu, "What did that fellow say?"

Nu paused, obviously uncertain of what to do.

The blonde officer slapped the man from Bari and repeated his question.

Nu translated it literally into Russian.

The officer's head jerked towards Pol who was arguing with Kirov. The Soviet screamed, "Fire! They're hostiles! Fire!"

A volley of gunfire decimated the ambassadors from Coldwater Valley. As their bodies fell to the soil of the Plain, the Soviets shifted their fire to Pol's followers.

## Chapter Six

## ANOTHER PROMOTION

Kirov forced his eyelids open. The eternal noontime sun smiled down on him. The sight gave him a splitting headache.

No. The headache came from some other cause. As he struggled back to consciousness, the pain settled in his forehead.

He felt his head gingerly. There was a nasty gash above his eyes but the wound was literally skin deep.

"You live," announced a voice from beside him.

"I live," agreed Kirov weakly.

He turned to look at the speaker.

"I am Nu of Bari," announced the man.

Kirov smiled at the irony. The Cave Dweller was crammed into a Soviet uniform with specialist's insignia very much like the one that Kirov had worn when traveling into the Inner World many years ago.

Nu smiled back, his face handsome beneath the streaks of dirt. His unruly black mane had been hacked into an approximation of a standard military haircut.

"What happened?" Kirov tried to look around him but the movement generated so much pain that he desisted. After a moment, he lay back down.

"The Soo-vee-yets killed most of your tribesmen as they killed most of mine. The Great Horses (Camels) were easy targets. The Dyal Riders and Small Horse Riders were very brave. They charged the Soviet lines. They died facing forward."

"Did any allied tribesmen survive?"

214

"A handful. Some dyals panicked and threw their riders off. They hid in the grass until the Soviets found them."

Kirov groaned.

He sucked in air and forced himself to sit up.

He was seated in a Soviet field camp on the Plain of Grazers. All around him were the homey sights of Russian soldiers resting after a battle. Coffee was brewing. Food was cooking. Men were pitching tents. All the comforts of home...!

At least as defined by the Soviet Red Army.

The Soviet invasion of the Inner World included much of the paraphernalia of 20th Century military civilization. For example, one civilized Soviet task force could slaughter as many natives in one battle as ten tribes of primitive locals could murder in ten lifetimes.

The blonde officer walked through the camp to Kirov. His gaunt face seemed permanently twisted into a death mask. Kirov suspected that he was frightened of something but hiding his fear as best he could.

"Are you Mikhail Kirillivitch Kirov?" he purred. The silky voice sounded odd from a Soviet officer but the question was clear enough.

"Yes, Comrade Company Commander, I am."

"Your men say that you are now the war chief of the local tribes."

This was news to the demoted leader but Nu nodded in affirmation. He amplified, "Comrade Company Commander Sem-ee-on Poe-vich interrogated your men while you were asleep. They said that your former leader Pol Taragkiller has gone to the Dead World. You are the new chief of the Dyal Riders."

Kirov managed a sickly smile despite the situation. Pellucidar, it seemed, was good for one's military career. Once again, he was the commander-in-chief of an intertribal army!

An army consisting of perhaps two thousand men and possibly twice as many adult women!

Hopefully, this time would work out better than his last one!

The newly promoted chief addressed Povich. "Yes, Company Commander, I...."

"Comrade Company Commander," reminded Povich.

"Yes, Comrade Company Commander. Please excuse me. I have been in Pellucidar for a long time and I have forgotten proper courtesy. I mean no insult by it."

Povich nodded. "When did you arrive in Novy Mir, which is now the proper Soviet name for Pellucidar?"

"March 1924. I was lost the same month that I entered Novy Mir."

"Humph. The date is 10 August 1926. Moscow time. You've been here for more than two years."

Kirov collapsed again. Fortunately the soil beneath his head was soft.

His mind whirled. Images swirled in a mad kaleidoscope: giant birds, endless mountains and plains, the unmoving sun constantly overhead, a paleontologist's dream of prehistoric animals alive again in Pellucidar, Flana's sweet smile, Ala's wild beauty, his son's infant energy, his people riding across the plains on their strange mounts....

His head cleared and he forced himself upright again.

He apologized to Povich who accepted his weakness with relatively good grace.

The Soviet commander looked Kirov squarely in the eye. "Comrade Specialist, I have a proposal for you...if you truly are the chief of the local tribes."

Kirov moved his head in a vague nod. Povich chose to accept that as agreement.

"The proposal is this, Comrade. If you subordinate your tribes to the Soviet Union, you can be governor of this land. Otherwise, you can face a firing squad for deserting your post two years ago. Which would you prefer?"

*Chapter Seven*

## GHOSTS

**K**irov took a deep breath. The sweet odors of grasses and flowers filled his nostrils. Life had never seemed so sweet.

"Obviously, Comrade Company Commander, I would prefer an appointment as governor of the Coldwater Valley region. However, most native Pellucidarians will not submit to Soviet rule. They value bravery to the point of suicidal behavior."

"It will be your job to make them submit." Povich paused and added, "Comrade Governor. Otherwise, we will simply liquidate the recalcitrant ones. The survivors will be much more tractable. Like Nu here."

The latter quickly hid his face. Kirov caught a flash of pure hatred. Regaining his composure, Nu returned his attention to Povich and Kirov.

The latter responded, "Yes, Comrade Company Commander. The Coldwater Valley alliance does not have a capital as Moscow is for Russia. However, the village known as Dyalsi is the effective capital. It is approximately two days ride from here. I will go and prepare my people for your arrival…."

"No, Comrade Specialist Kirov, you will remain with my column until we reach Dy-al-see."

"May I at least send messengers to prepare my people?"

Povich was reluctant but finally consented….

… provided Kirov gave his messages to his couriers in the presence of Nu and himself and provided that Nu's translations of the messages matched Kirov's.

217

The war chief pondered his options for a moment. As he pondered, he studied Nu's face. The native Pellucidarian nodded very slightly.

Kirov focused his attention on his new commander and accepted the post of interim governor of what Povich called the administrative region, or *okrug*, of Central Gori.

FOUR WAKING PERIODS LATER, the Soviet column came within sight of Dyalsi. The weary travelers paused on a slight rise to survey the scene. Kirov pointed out sights as enthusiastically as any docent in the Hermitage Museum in his native Leningrad.

The curving landscape created the impression of a vast valley floored in lush green. Povich guessed that the forest that sheltered Dyalsi was half an hour's walk ahead. Kirov had explained that the Dyal Riders made their homes in and under one of the small forests dotting the Plain of Grazers in order to protect themselves from aerial raids by the now defunct Black Birdriders.

Povich could see the great herds of animals moving from east to west in front of and behind the village. Closer to the village walls, the Soviet commander could see teams of women gathering edible seeds, roots and grasses from the Plain itself. Mounted hunting parties were returning with juicy carcasses slung across the backs of pack animals.

As he scanned the scene through his binoculars, mounted Dyal Rider scouts spotted the Soviet company. They waved in greeting. Then they turned and began shouting commands at the villagers. Povich couldn't hear the commands at this distance but Kirov had sent orders ahead for the villages to gather in the central plaza to meet their conquerors—Povich meant *liberators* of course—and to learn about their new rulers.

The liberator of Central Gori nodded his head in deep satisfaction.

The last Dyal Riders entered their village as their new masters resumed their march towards the wide-open gates.

The estimated thirty minute walk required twice as much

time as originally planned. The ground outside the village had proven surprisingly rugged.

But, at last, the conquering heroes of the Soviet Union marched into Dyalsi.

It was deserted.

And had been for some time.

The streets were empty of human and dyal life. The fluffy homes—heavily insulated against the cold temperatures of the northern latitudes—were quiet, leather doors and window shutters hanging open. Woven baskets lay here and there. Some still had food spilling out of them. Giant horned rodents that Kirov identified as *Epigaulus* feasted on the remains. Soviet trigger fingers twitched, shots rang out and the surviving rat-like creatures scattered.

Kirov was puzzled, then frightened, then horrified.

When the column reached the empty town plaza, he broke loose from his guards and ran about like a madman. He shouted a dozen names as he ran. Ala, Kirov and Flana were prominent among them.

Nu's eyes followed the distraught young governor with increasing horror.

Povich watched Kirov's fruitless search for long minutes. Finally he shook himself out of his bemusement and ordered the young governor be taken into custody again.

It took the guards several minutes to catch the madman racing around the long deserted village but they did. He struggled frantically. Eventually, one guard used his rifle butt as a tranquilizer. They hauled the unconscious man back to Povich and dropped him at the commander's feet.

The Company Commander was at a loss but Nu quietly suggested that the young paleontologist be taken to his own home, identified by a carving of a stylized beast called a *Triceratops*. Povich grunted his distracted approval. Nu and one guard carried Kirov home where the two Pellucidarians were confined indefinitely.

In the meantime, Povich turned his attention to the mystery of the missing villagers. He had *seen* the villagers as he approached. The figures in his telescopic view had been human beings, not dummies or illusions or nonhumans. They had acted intelligently greeting their liberators and otherwise following Kirov's orders. He had personally supervised Kirov's giving of those orders.

Where were they? How had they disappeared under the very eyes of himself and his company?

Povich ordered a comprehensive search made of the entire area. His lieutenants and starshinas began a systematic sweep of the entire forest and town. Soldiers ran through the village and established watch posts on the earthen walls. They surveyed the surrounding plain. They saw the expected peaceful herds of herbivores grazing their way from east to west but no fleeing humans.

Other soldiers ransacked the village. They tore through every building. They stabbed bayonets into walls and ceilings and other potential hiding places. They overturned baskets and wheelbarrows. They searched for hidden tunnels and found none. They climbed trees. They found no skulking humans.

Finally, Povich called off the search. The watch posts were to be manned but the other search teams were told to stand down. He ordered his senior lieutenant to assign places for his men to sleep. He himself confiscated the House of the Chief as his personal living quarters and official headquarters.

Then he sent messengers to bring Kirov and Nu to him for further questioning.

Five minutes after that, the messengers had not returned so he sent more to find them.

Another five minutes passed before the messengers and guards assembled in the central town plaza. They did not have either Kirov or Nu with them.

Povich spent at least another five minutes defaming their collective ancestries.

Eventually he got around to asking where the prisoners were.

No one knew.

Like the other Pellucidarians before them, Kirov and Nu had vanished.

*Chapter Eight*

## A VACATION IN PELLUCIDAR

While the Soviet Union was theoretically dedicated to world peace, in fact, it had been continuously at war for the last twelve years. First the October Revolution had overthrown the Provisional Government that had accepted the Czar's abdication. Then the Russian Civil War of 1917-21 had been necessary to crush the various White counterrevolutionaries led by Admiral A.V. Kolchak and the American warlord E.R. Burroughs. The European War of 1914-18 had been fought simultaneously until the Soviets had surrendered to the Kaiser's armies. (The Western Allies had rescued the Soviets from the consequences of their surrender but no Soviet mentioned that fact aloud.) Once the Civil War had been won, it was necessary to re-conquer unruly Central Asia. And then, in 1924, the leadership (including the no longer mentioned War Commissar Trotsky) had ordered the conquest of Wrangell Island in the Arctic Ocean and the Czarist Russian territories in the Inner World accessible through the great Zarovitch Opening in the Earth's northern crust.

Now, in the Common Era year of 1926, the Soviet Red Army continued to spread southward and eastward from its original beachhead now named Plutonia. Only Stone Age tribes offered ineffectual resistance to the Communist advance. Each waking period—a "day" by the clocks imported from Moscow—newly-promoted intelligence officer Battalion Commander T. Kulongoski reviewed reports from the advancing units and updated the maps in his sanctum within Fort Alinsky, the command center for the Soviet advance.

221

Each waking period, he smiled.

Today, however, he was not smiling. He looked at his map of Gori—the newly annexed region east of Plutonia. The unit assigned to Company Commander S. Povich had disappeared. Kulongoski had received no reports from Povich for some time now. He sighed heavily and summoned scouts to track down the missing company and find out what was happening in the uncharted lands of the Inner World.

SEVERAL WEEKS' MARCH east of Fort Alinsky, the missing company was enjoying a vacation.

No one called the period of idleness that aloud. Officially, they were garrisoning a liberated village and awaiting orders.

But it was a vacation in all but name.

The reason for the halt in place was their commander, Company Commander Povich. Every waking period he ordered yet *another* search of the village still called Dyalsi trying to locate the missing villagers.

Povich worried about even small things. But he had something *serious* to worry about…!

*He had to find the missing villagers!*

Repeated searches had turned up nothing. Scouts were deployed in all directions to no avail.

Povich could not explain the disappearances. But he knew that junior officers who could not explain mysterious events had a tendency to disappear themselves.

Permanently.

So, every day, Povich arose, his normally haggard face ever more desperate, and ordered a new search. He supervised most of the searches personally.

His men no longer cared. They went through the motions. When Povich was in their vicinity, they canvassed the long abandoned huts, chased away the curious giant horned rodents that infested the area, and poked into every corner.

When the Company Commander joined the scouts scouring other parts of his haunted kingdom, the men relaxed. A guard was posted to keep an eye out in case the commander backtracked but the others sat down and told each other tall tales until meal times when a few hunters would provide feasts of antelope, bison and less obvious creatures from the endless plains surrounding Dyalsi.

Compared to the blood, the starvation, and the mindless brutalities of the Civil War, Poland and Central Asia, Pellucidar—or at least central Gori—seemed to be a paradise.

Eventually, of course, a snake arrived in Eden in the form of messengers from Fort Alinsky. The vacation was over.

SEVERAL WAKING PERIODS' travel to the east of Dyalsi, Kirov Skalkiller stood on the Hill of Warriors surveying the landscape east of the Coldwater River with satisfaction. He smiled at the irony of once again standing on the Hill of Warriors. Some time ago, he had used the "magic" of *history* and *psychology* to defeat and then incorporate the Pulka Horde into his alliance. Now the Hill and the surrounding terrain was the staging area for an even greater feat of magic!

His most promising student of magic stood beside him, gazing into his handsome face with eyes of love.

This was natural enough since Kirov's most promising pupil was also his mate, Ala the Beautiful One. To Kirov, her most beautiful features were her mind and spirit.

"Mighty Kirov, you saved our tribe from the Soviet Red War Party invaders at Dyalsi. What will you do now?"

His smile deepened. "We are going to make our entire nation disappear."

"Will the Soviet Red War Party hunt for us?"

"No." Kirov smiled grimly. "They will be too busy fighting the greatest monsters in all of Pellucidar: Teodor Roosevelt and Edgar Rice Burroughs."

*Chapter Nine*

## THE SORCERER'S APPRENTICES

**M**essengers had arrived from distant Fort Alinsky with orders for Povich and his company to continue their advance. The Inner World would not be "liberated" from its primitive owners for the greater glory of the Soviet Union by "heroic" soldiers lying comfortably about the village of Dyalsi stuffing themselves with antelope and bison meat!

Company Commander Povich listened painfully to the messages from Battalion Commander Kulongoski reminding him of his duty. Kulongoski was soft spoken in person but his words could bite. Deeply. And these particular words wounded Povich very deeply indeed—for reasons that he could never openly admit.

Povich dealt with the messages in the manner typical of incompetent leaders since time immemorial: he claimed that the problem was not his fault, promised to improve his performance, and began screaming at his men. While they were running around Dyalsi getting themselves ready, he consulted his maps and notes.

A broad track led eastward from Dyalsi towards what Specialist M. Kirov had called the Coldwater River. It wasn't a road—more of a permanently beaten trail through the tall grasses of the Plain of Grazers. But it would do as a place to begin.

After an indeterminate time, Povich's company formed up and began marching eastward into the unknown.

They left the town ablaze behind them. Povich announced

that the fire would deny a potential supply base to an enemy. What he was really doing was trying to exorcise ghosts.

As usual, two scouts preceded the main body.

TWO "DAYS" LATER, the scouts crested a rise. They stopped to survey the landscape ahead of them.

They overlooked a wide but shallow river valley carpeted with sweet smelling grasses, strange trumpet-shaped flowers and copses of trees. Curious creatures grazed the grasses or stalked the grazers. The river itself was not as wide as the mighty Volga or Don but impressive enough. Perhaps three hours walk ahead a large island sat in midstream. The scouts could see primitive houses on the island and on both shores of the river. Human beings walked among the houses and paddled small boats on the river. Many of them appeared to be fishing.

One scout asked, "Is this 'River Town'?"

The other scout shaded his eyes from Pellucidar's eternal noonday sun. "It must be. It matches Comrade Kirov's description."

"How many hostiles do you think we're facing here?"

The second scout scanned the valley through his rifle's scope. He thought to himself that the upward curve of the Inner World's landscape made it easy enough to look across the land. But, the odd perspectives hid things surprisingly well. The fact that shadows were always beneath objects rather than stretching out beyond them removed an important visual clue to size and shape. Mountains, for example, first appeared as indistinct smudges and remained cryptic blurs until you were practically on top of them. Then they abruptly assumed their true pyramidal shapes. He had learned not to take things in Novy Mir for granted.

Thus it was that he missed his comrade's answer.

Through his scope, he had just discovered the greatest danger in all of Pellucidar.

"Look!"

His comrade noticed the movement and jerked his eyes

from gun sight to the indicated spot on the far hills. He saw a brown square on the opposite side of the valley. Tiny bits of color fluttered above it.

He cursed for a solid minute and then fell silent.

After another minute, he said softly. "This is too big for us. Let's return to the column and report to the Company Commander."

The first scout quickly agreed and they disappeared the way that they had come.

Distracted by thoughts of their discovery, neither scout noticed intelligent eyes watching them from the tall grasses.


ABOUT A DAY LATER, Company Commander Povich eased himself over the same rise. The senior scout was with him along with the company's second-in-command. The Company Commander and the second brought out their binoculars and surveyed the brown square. Povich cursed.

Silently, the second-in-command agreed but reminded himself of the demands of leadership. "Comrade Company Commander, what are your orders?"

Povich wanted to answer *Run back to Moscow, you colossal fool!* Instead, he remained silent while he considered his own orders. He hoped that his silence would be taken for judicious reflection rather than what it was.

He was already on Kulongoski's list of troublemakers. Despite the almost unthinkable dangers ahead of him, he could not refuse to investigate.

*After all,* Povich reminded himself, *the Soviet Union is at peace with the entire world!*

*And if I say this often enough, it will come true!*

He swallowed and said, "We will form up and advance to the enemy outworks on this side of the river. This will be a peaceful visit. We will advance with rifles and other weapons slung. We will convince them there is nothing to be concerned about."

There was a definite pause before his juniors acknowledged

but, for once, Povich did not notice. He was still trying to convince himself.

ABOUT FIVE HOURS LATER, the Soviet column reached the small collection of buildings on the bank of the Coldwater River. The buildings resembled American log cabins rather than the caves of Bari or the feather-insulated huts of Dyalsi.

*That's logical,* thought Povich sourly. *Given their political masters.*

A wooden sign carved in Russian and a language that the Company Commander guessed was English confirmed his worst fears. Large words read, "Welcome to Republic of New America. Teodor Roosevelt, President and Chief Commander." Smaller words added "River City, Territory of New Iowa."

Above it fluttered a red, white and blue tricolor flag. Povich had read somewhere that the flag was modeled on the flag of the American province of Georgia, which was the homeland of Roosevelt's mother.

Povich had been steeling himself for this moment ever since his scouts had reported their findings. The mental effort to appear confident and commanding in front of his men dissipated like steam on a summer day.

*The accursed imperialist American cowboys had gotten here first! They had colonized lands that were rightfully Soviet! And their leader is the eternally, infinitely accursed super-cowboy Teodor Roosevelt! The man who defeated the Spanish in 1898 when almost every military ministry in Europe had predicted an American defeat! The man who sent a huge White Fleet around the Outer World to proclaim "peace" when Russia was unable to defend its own eastern coast!*

Povich shivered despite his warm winter Soviet greatcoat and uniform. His normally haggard face did not change much. Human features can only express so much fear and Comrade Company Commander Semyon Povich had reached that limit long ago.

There were people standing in front of the buildings of River City staring at the intruders. Most of them were obviously natives in feathery brown garments. But two of the women were dressed in American frontier dresses made of leather to block the chill air of northern Novy Mir.

They stepped forward. Even Povich was stirred by their beauty.

One, a raven-haired stunner, raised her hand in greeting. A chunk of raw gold hung from a cord around her neck. It flashed in the constant sunlight with every breath she took. And reminded Povich of the endless riches of the Inner World.

"Hello. You must be Soviet soldiers. I am Alice Black and this is Flana Shore. Welcome to River City." Her Russian was a strange combination of a Leningrad lilt and one of America's barbarian dialects but it was understandable enough. She did not appear to notice anything wrong with Povich's contorted face.

There was a pause while Povich collected his nerve. Finally, he replied, "Greetings, Comrade Black. Yes, we are Soviet explorers visiting your city on a mission of peace. We wish to speak to the mayor and arrange lodging for the evening."

The black-haired beauty nodded in agreement and replied somewhat sadly.

"I'm sure that Mayor Hortul will be glad to see you. However, at the moment, he is up at Fort Grant discussing military matters with Colonel Burroughs."

She casually indicated the brown fortification topping the far hills about three hours walk behind her. Povich could see diminutive blue-clad figures pacing the ramparts.

"When he returns, he will arrange lodging or camping for you. Perhaps on the Old Battlefield."

She pointed to a gentle hill across the river. A large wooden cross loomed over the site.

Povich started to say something but his voice suddenly stopped working.

Alarm bells rang in his brain.

Loudly.

He jerked his head upward and stared at the solidly con-structed fortress visible over the woman's shoulder.

The Pellucidarian-New Americans looked at him in puzzle-ment.

Finally he squeaked, "'Colonel Burroughs'?"

The woman nodded and answered simply. She did not appear to notice anything peculiar about Povich's tone. "Yes, Colonel Edgar Rice Burroughs of the New American Army. He's the commander of Fort Grant and the New Iowa Na-tional Guard."

She turned to her companion and asked for confirmation.

The pretty brunette nodded and added, also in Russian, "They may be a while. They're planning placement of the new artillery pieces."

Povich turned pale white in shock.

The name of the warlord Edgar Rice Burroughs was the blackest of black curses from Leningrad to Vladivostok. The American cowboy was rumored to have *died* at the Battle of Little Big Horn and *come back to life!* It was a fact that he knew the secrets of Martian military science. It was a fact that he was married to a lady in waiting of the former Czar's decadent court. And it was a fact that he had nearly defeated the Soviets in the Civil War of 1917-1920.

If Admiral Kolchak, the commander of the White counter-revolutionary forces, had given Burroughs a free hand instead of micromanaging his army group....

If Burroughs had had a free hand then, Semyon Povich would be a prisoner in Siberia....

*Or a corpse moldering in some forgotten grave!*

The still living Comrade Company Commander Semyon Povich started backing up. He shook as he moved.

He bumped into something and jumped in fright.

He whirled and confronted a Soviet soldier. Both faces radiated confusion and fear.

All-consuming, mind-blasting fear.

Somewhere, someone was shouting something.

Eventually, the voice penetrated Povich's horror-crazed skull.

"Comrade Company Commander, what are your orders? What are your orders?"

Povich whirled about, trying to look everywhere at once.

Finally, he choked out, "Retreat! Retreat to our camp! Double time! About face, comrades, and double time back to our last camp!"

The Soviet column vanished over the slight rise west of the Coldwater River in less than two hours. Company Commander Semyon Povich led the way*.

Many hours later, he remembered to send scouts back to spy on River Town. When he sent other soldiers to relieve the scouts, all of them had disappeared.

ALA THE BEAUTIFUL ONE and Flana of the Dyal Riders continued gazing after the retreating Soviets until the invaders passed over the hill and out of sight. Ala barked commands in Pellucidarian and several scouts began jogging after the invaders.

"Again, mighty Kirov has saved us from the Soviet invaders," commented Ala softly. Her voice was filled with admiration and other, deeper emotions.

"True," agreed Flana simply. She shared Ala's feelings—but could not admit them aloud. "Although I do not understand how Kirov did this thing. Especially since he spoke through our mouths rather than speaking directly to the Soviets."

Ala gave her a predatory smile .

"Magic," she stated.

There was a moment of silence as the women watched the Pellucidarian scouts disappearing into the tall grasses on either side of the trail from River Town to Dyalsi. Soviet scouts were

---

* During the 1941 German invasion of Soviet Russia, many Red Army commanders panicked, abandoned their posts and their men, commandeered available transportation and fled the battlefront. The resulting chaos among the leaderless enlisted ranks contributed greatly to the initial German successes. — Ed.

good enough in the Outer World but they were *children* compared to men whose very lives depended on hunting and evading
creatures as much as ten times their own size and ferocity.

"Kirov used the magic of *psychology* to defeat the invaders,"
amplified Ala. "He studied the Soviets as a hunter studies a
beast and especially the Company Commander of that war
band. He walked with Sem-yon Po-vich for four waking periods
and learned his weaknesses. Po-vich is a coward who was made
Company Commander because he is a fellow hunter (political
supporter) of the Soviet War Chief Ee Varan. He is afraid of
*everything* in Pellucidar. Kirov pushed him over the edge of
the cliff and now he runs from two women—and the reputation
of the war chief Edgar Rice Burroughs."

Flana nodded. She wished to learn as much as possible
about "magic"—and about Kirov.

Ala continued, still staring after the vanishing Soviets. "If
Po-vich had been a brave man, Kirov would have found some
other weakness. But fear is a powerful weapon. Our chief sent
us messages to flee Dyalsi rather than die fighting Soviet *guns*.
Po-vich is a fool who thought that he controlled Kirov because
Nu of Bari said that Kirov's messages ordered us to crawl to
Po-vich. In truth, Nu hated the cruel Po-vich and lied to him
about Kirov's messages.

"When Po-vich's war band approached Dyalsi, they saw
what Kirov calls a *corporal's guard* remaining to deceive the
Soviets that the Dyal Riders were waiting to crawl before the
Red Army War Party. In truth almost all of us had already
moved to River Town. The Soviets could see beyond Dyalsi
when they were far away and so they assumed that no one could
escape in that direction. But, the town and forest hid the
corporal's guard walking out of the opposite side of the town
when the Soviets approached and entered. Kirov distracted
their attention by pretending to search wildly for us. By the
time that the Soviets posted warriors on the far side of Dyalsi,
the corporal's guard was walking quietly away hidden by the
grazers that pass the town. As long as the corporal's guard did

not attack the grazers, the grazers did not attack or flee them. So our entire tribe seemed to vanish.

"And so fear gripped the heart of the coward Po-vich because he could not understand what Kirov had done under his very eyes and ears."

Had Ala been a lesser person she might well have resented Kirov's practice of psychology and deception since he had used similar "magic" against her original tribe not long before. But her love for her former slave and now mate had changed her. She knew that Kirov would only use his awesome powers to protect her, their child, their new tribe and their new alliance. His brilliant (if strange) mind—and his growing legend—protected them more securely than a thousand warriors. Her mind blazed with fierce loyalty.

She continued, speaking as much to herself as to Flana.

"When Po-vich ordered Kirov imprisoned in our home, our chief removed his feathers and dressed himself in his former Soviet uniform. He and Nu (who was already dressed in a Soviet uniform) merely waited until their guards' attention was distracted, and walked away from our home apparently searching for *themselves*!

"The Soviets' fear grew as a lusty child."

Ala laughed heartily.

Flana quietly nodded again. Life in savage Pellucidar quickly weeded out the fearful. But, both women recognized the value of Kirov's alert and cunning mind and appreciated watching his plans in action. The two women watched the flight of their enemies with glee, and glowed with admiration for their hidden chieftain.

Ala resumed. "And when the great coward Po-vich came to River Town, the signs that Kirov created—including the make believe Fort Grant—made him think that the dread war chiefs Teodor Roosevelt and Edgar Rice Burroughs had already conquered this land and made us *Americans*.

"And so fear drove the coward forth.

"It will be many, many wakes before the Soviets return to

'River City.'" She sarcastically gave the village its American English name.

"And so we have time to help mighty Kirov with his next feat of magic...."

"Yes," agreed Flana, "making our entire nation disappear."

"Yes." Ala turned from the welcome sight of the Soviet retreat and faced her former slave and now friend. Her face glowed with a warm smile.

"But first, let's get out of these silly 'dresses' and into some sensible feathers."

*Chapter Ten*

## "IS ANYTHING IN
## PELLUCIDAR NORMAL?"

O nce again, Brigadier General E. Varan was huddled
with his two most valued staff members in his inner
sanctum in Fort Alinsky.

They were studying a map of Gori, the partially-explored,
partially-conquered region of Pellucidar east of the main So-
viet-controlled zone of Plutonia. The map had been drawn by
intelligence officer Kulongoski from numerous scouts' reports.
It showed Gori as a rough triangle pointing toward the body
of water beneath Alaska. An isthmus extended south into the
unknown regions of Pellucidar's temperate zone. The western
half of the triangle was mostly filled with various note cards
indicating the tribes that had joined the Soviet Union "voluntarily." So far, so good.

The flaw in the operation was a relatively small area in the
center. According to the latest reports by Comrade Company
Commander Povich, the accursed American warlord E.R.
Burroughs had established a huge fortress on the Coldwater
River in that area. Povich reported a garrison of at least a
thousand enemy soldiers. Burroughs had annexed half of Gori
to the cowboy Republic of New America and fortified it against
the ongoing Soviet advance.

Well…. The *formerly* ongoing advance….

As soon as Varan had learned of Burroughs' presence, he
had issued immediate orders to halt in place. The thought of
provoking the architect of the Soviet Union's near defeat in the
still recent Civil War was horrifying beyond words.

Even more terrifying was the fact that those orders had to travel across the strange landscape of Pellucidar by courier. That required time that Task Force Varan might not have! *Even now*, mused Varan, *Soviet soldiers might be in battle with American cowboys!* In spite of himself, the Brigade Commander shuddered at the thought.

Kulongoski and operations officer Kronstadt pretended not to notice. Their own thoughts paralleled their superior's fears. Calling the Americans names did not make them less dangerous enemies—as a half dozen defeated nations could attest.

Varan broke the silence. "Well, comrades, what are your recommendations? Comrade Kulongoski?"

The intelligence officer drew a long breath. "Comrade Brigade Commander, I believe we need more information about the threat. I propose that we send additional scouting parties at least as far as the Coldwater and determine the exact border of New America."

"We already have Comrade Company Commander Povich's report on the existence and location of E.R. Burroughs. Is that not sufficient information for action?" inquired Varan.

Kulongoski spoke gingerly. Povich was one of Varan's favorites and a frank discussion of failings was out of the question. "With the greatest of respect, Comrade Brigade Commander, Comrade Povich's report only covers one point on the map—this so-called 'River City.'" He tapped the location of the New American fortress near the center of Gori. "At the present time, we do not *know* if Burroughs or Roosevelt have fortified other locations along the Coldwater. The so-called river is a significant military obstacle and therefore a logical boundary. But we have no reports of *other* fortifications there."

Varan made a humming sound and then asked, "Comrade Kronstadt?"

The operations officer was tracing the reported course of the Coldwater River. He looked up. "Comrade Brigade Commander, I agree with Comrade Kulongoski. We need more information about our foes. And we need to tighten our hold on the tribes of Gori. At the moment, our conquests—"

"Our liberated areas," corrected Varan.

"Yes, Comrade Brigade Commander. Our liberated areas in Gori are tenuously held by small units that are widely scattered over an area almost the size of Poland. Communications are extremely poor and transportation is worse. With the exception of Comrade Po...."

Kronstadt coughed and started his sentence again. "With some exceptions, the liberated tribes have been sufficiently overwhelmed by Soviet firepower. For the moment. I would greatly prefer to increase our garrisons in all of the occupied settlements. Taking the time to scout out the Coldwater River frontier will also allow us time to reinforce our garrisons and to construct roads, buildings and so forth."

Varan grunted.

"I am concerned about both the time and manpower that additional scouting and infrastructure will require. This is now October 1926. I had hoped to liberate all of Gori down to the southern peninsula this year and to prepare for our inevitable conflict with the Republic of New America. And facing the cowboys along the Coldwater River instead of in their homeland will require a great deal more manpower than I had planned on using to control Gori."

He exhaled loudly. His face wrinkled in thought.

Kulongoski spoke softly but clearly. "Comrade Brigade Commander, I respectfully submit that expending the time and manpower in this manner is a vital necessity. We cannot afford to be further surprised by New Americans. We *must* have additional information." Kronstadt simply nodded in agreement.

Varan grunted again.

After a moment of silence, he agreed. "Very well, comrades. We must have additional information." He was again looking at the map and did not notice his officers' relief.

"Both of you plan a general advance to the Coldwater River.

Our goal is information, not battle. Have our reconnaissance
units report back daily so that we have the most current information possible. We must understand the situation in central
Gori better. We must determine the exact border between the
Soviet and New American zones as well as the extent and depth
of New American fortifications. The reconnaissance units are
authorized to contact New Americans if necessary and to determine their intent and knowledge about Gori and Novy Mir.
If possible, locate the missing tribe of 'Dyal Riders.' But avoid
battle unless the cowboys force the issue. We may be forced
to battle the New Americans on the Coldwater but we must
try to avoid that—at this time."

He paused and added, "If natives cause trouble, kill them
until they submit."

The two staff officers acknowledged their orders. Kronstadt
was furiously scribbling in his notebook. Kulongoski relied on
his excellent memory.

Varan also gave orders on a number of lesser issues before
he declared the staff meeting over.

Once outside the inner sanctum, the two officers adjourned
to Kulongoski's thickly walled and carefully locked office. There
were too many ears in the operations center for either man's
comfort.

Kulongoski began pulling maps out of file folders imported from Moscow and arranging them on a worktable. He
looked up to see the operations officer gazing intently at him.

"Is there something wrong?" inquired the intelligence officer
softly.

"No more wrong than usual. Teodor, thank you for your
suggestion to scout out the Coldwater River Valley more thoroughly. The sheer size of the territory is stretching my men to
the limit. We need this pause to consolidate and regroup more
than Varan seems to realize."

Kulongoski smiled thinly. "You're welcome. Perhaps you
can do me a favor sometime." He spoke softly, even casually.

Kronstadt understood the message. Favors were the real

currency in the Soviet Union including Novy Mir. He nodded silently but definitely.

He cleared his throat. "I need your latest information on what the men might face when they advance."

He paused and went on. "Let's start with why you called the Coldwater River a 'so-called river' a few minutes ago. Is there some reason why a river is not a river?"

Kulongoski paused before answering. "Possibly. The so-called river seems to flow uphill."

"What?" barked the operations officer. "That's impossible!"

The intelligence officer made a depreciating gesture. "That's what I thought until I studied the reports." He pointed to a map, tracing the river's southward course from the Polar Sea below the Zarovitch Opening, across Leninska, and into the Karl-Marx Ocean. "The river starts and ends at sea level after flowing up and over the intervening landmass. That would make sense if the Polar Sea were a lake at a higher elevation than that of the ocean but both bodies of water are at the same level. Yet water consistently flows southward from sea to ocean."

Kronstadt stared at the map as if its innocent seeming blue watercourse were a deadly serpent poised to strike him down. He seemed to be paralyzed.

Finally, his shoulders slumped followed by the rest of his body.

"Is *anything* in Pellucidar normal?"

## Chapter Eleven

## "JALOKS!"

Once again, Kirov Skalkiller rode a spirited dyal along the Coldwater River near the mighty Sea of Monsters. This time he was east of the river on the bank opposite the ruins of Seashore Village. He was leading a scouting party of Dyal Riders and Small Horse Riders in search of a new homeland far to the south of what Soviet geographers called Gori.

Logically, as war chief of the Coldwater Alliance, he should have been at some central location directing the overall operation. But Pellucidarians, being uncivilized beings, expected their leaders to lead from the front, not from some secure rear headquarters. Besides, it was a great relief to ride a powerful steed across the eternal but always new and interesting vistas of his adopted home.

In the near distance, the blue wall of the Sea curved upward like a tidal wave perpetually about to crash onto the heads of humans, dyals and horses alike. Closer at hand, the pale green grasses of the Plain of Grazers gave way to a mixture of scrubby pine trees and wind-beaten bushes. Patches of bright sand glinted underfoot.

He called a reminder for the scouts to be alert. The memory of the ambush by the powerful skals was still clear in his memory, though it happened two years ago.

No sooner had his caution echoed across the rolling plain but a dyal rider shouted, "Jaloks!" Kirov signaled his men to advance.

Sure enough, a group of powerful dog-like creatures the

size of Siberian brown bears crept out of the scraggly pines. Kirov's mind, trained in the science of paleontology, immediately classified them as Amphicyons—huge ancestors of modern dogs. The Pellucidarian language had a limited vocabulary compared to Russian or Latin; the natives used the same word for Amphicyons, *Hyenadons* and packs of other dog-like creatures.

The humans quickly formed a battle line facing the approaching hounds, spears forward. The Amphicyons mirrored the formation, fangs gleaming in Pellucidar's eternal sunlight. Both sides paused—ready for battle but unwilling to attack a prepared enemy.

"Hah!" sneered Taddo the Small Horseman. "They fear our spears!"

Barking laughter ran down the human line in agreement with Taddo's assessment.

Kirov did not share the condescending attitude. Another memory was tickling his mind.

Amphicyons were canines: much, much larger than true dogs, but definitely dog-like in appearance, ecological niche and....

And behavior!

Kirov twisted around in sudden horror.

Silently and efficiently, a larger pack of Amphicyons was creeping up on the unprotected rear of the distracted humans!

*Chapter Twelve*

## THE GODS OF THE HUNT SMILE

Silently and efficiently, a larger pack of Amphicyons was creeping up on the unprotected rear of the distracted human party! Savage and intelligent carnivores surrounded the tribesmen!

Kirov had never thought of himself as a military leader before he came to the Inner World, but unlike his fellow tribesmen, he had received professional military instruction and he had remembered it.

A rule pounded into his head by the long gone Senior Starshina Voitinuik flashed his mind: An adequate order when it is needed is better than a perfect order after the battle has been lost.

"Dyal Riders! Turn and kill! Small Horsemen! Forward and kill!" shouted the war chief.

The commander then followed his own directive. He cooed at his dyal, which turned toward the jaloks attacking the rear.

His fellow Dyal Riders were seconds ahead of him. Their riding birds wheeled and lunged at their designated enemy.

The rear Amphicyons were caught off guard. Longspears stabbed. Driven by the powerful muscles of the dyals, lances thudded home, passing through canine flesh and into the soft ground of the Plain of Grazers. Prehistoric dogs barked in pain—or relaxed in death.

The pack started to react. Their plan was ruined. Some leaped to attack the impudent—and tasty—humans; others broke and ran; still others dithered.

Another thing that Voitinuik had taught was the value of

having back-up weapons. The Dyal Riders released their grips on their longspears as soon as those lances had penetrated flesh or ground or both. Hands snatched stone knives and Zulu-styled assegai short spears out of sheathes. The dyals and their riders strode forward.

Amphicyons snapped at their prey with their powerful jaws. Dyals danced. Two-legged creatures were far more maneuverable than four-legged monsters. Once the canine lunges closed on air, dyal feet crashed down on furry heads and backs. Most of the attacking Amphicyons were trapped, dyal weight pushing canine heads into the soft soil.

Dyal beaks smashed downward like so many battleaxes.

Dogs died.

Like their descendants on the surface of the Earth, Amphicyons were pack animals. They hunted together and fought together. Few fled. Instead, they attacked more savagely than before, trying to rescue their brothers.

But the dyals were not just living war machines. They carried death on their backs as well.

Their riders thrust assegais into Amphicyon faces, leaning into their strikes. Humans thrusting downward and canines thrusting upward combined to force the short spears deep into canine flesh. Humans fended off teeth with knives and fists.

Amphicyons screamed in pain. More of them died.

The gods of the hunt smiled on one canine. No longspear had penetrated his flesh. No dyal beak had hammered his skull. No assegai had sought his heart.

He did not think of himself as brave. He was merely a dog. His brothers were being killed by the feathered two-legs and the hairy two-legs. He attacked.

His target was an unaware rider leaning forward, trying to dispatch a particularly tough opponent. He would not see the attack until it was too late.

With perfect timing, the dog leaped to the assault....

An assegai flashed through the air and thumped into the attacker's shaggy side.

*The Dyal Riders released their grips on their longspears as soon as those lances had*

The gods of the hunt laughed.

Startled by sudden pain, the Amphicyon twisted in mid-air. Bewildered, he sought the cause of his distress.

Distracted, he crashed into his target and his target's dyal.

But the perfect attack had been spoiled, transformed into clownish slapstick. The three prehistoric creatures—Amphicyon, dyal and man—tumbled together onto the Plain.

Kirov rode up. He cooed. His dyal's beak slashed into the giant canine's chest and destroyed the savage heart within it.

The great dog shuddered and lay still.

If animals can go to the Dead World of Pellucidar where all inhabitants are skillful and brave, this creature did.

The rescued rider's dyal rose to its feet. Its rider cooed and the terror bird turned to face the war chief. The man's face was filled with gratitude.

The Dyal Rider gestured respectfully with his knife. "Hail mighty Kirov, killer of skals and jaloks! I thank you for my life!"

Kirov responded with Pellucidarian courtesy. "Hail, Tol! We hunt together!"

Tol the Traveler gushed, "Truly you are the greatest magician in all of Pellucidar. You magically saw the jaloks hidden in the trees and grass and you warned us. You slew our enemies with spear and spell. You saved my life! Again, I thank you!"

Around him, other Dyal Riders were nodding in agreement.

Kirov was about to modestly describe his apparent magic as merely good hunting skills when he realized that he had not heard from the Small Horsemen attacking in the other direction.

He twisted around in his saddle. He gaped at the peaceful scene before him.

The Small Horsemen and their opponents had vanished without a trace!

*Chapter Thirteen*

## WITHOUT A TRACE

Where are the Small Horsemen?" shouted Kirov as he scanned the terrain. His eyes took in the line of scrubby pine trees that the Amphicyons had hidden in and the mixed patches of thin grasses and sand where the battle had been—should have been—fought. The only humans or steeds in sight were his Dyal Riders and their powerful war birds.

Each Dyal Rider glanced behind himself, hunting for their vanished allies. Automatically, they formed into a war party. Most of the primitive warriors faced about toward the line of concealing pine trees while some continued to guard their rear. Savage Pellucidar held many dangers and foolish warriors were soon meat for a lengthy list of carnivores. The Dyal Riders had not survived as long as they had by being fools.

No one caught sight of their allies or the horse-like Mery-chippus mounts that the diminutive warriors rode.

Cautiously, Kirov led his men through the line of pine trees and onto the white beach bordering the Sea of Monsters. On one side, the untiring waves splashed lazily against the shore. Giant seashells dotted the pristine sands. Out to sea, Kirov spotted a huge marine mammal that he quickly classified as a primitive whale, or *Zeuglodon*. The Sea of Monsters was well named. Inland, there was a small ridge crowned by pines and then the endless vistas of the Plain of Grazers. Again, there were no Small Horse Riders in sight.

The war chief split his party into two. One group, led by the worshipful Tol, raced west to the mouth of the great Coldwater River. Kirov led the other group east in the direction of the little known southern peninsula that had been the scouting party's original goal. Both parties followed the beaches until their dyals complained of the shifting sand beneath their claws. The Dyal Riders shifted to the ridgeline where the soft soil was more convenient for the riding birds.

After a time that Kirov guessed was several hours, Tol's party returned and rejoined the others. They had searched to the great river without success. The recombined party rode east for an entire waking period. When they had slept and recovered their strength, Kirov sadly ordered the scouts to return to River Town. Neither his warriors' hunting skills nor his own knowledge of science had uncovered a single clue to the mystery.

Their allies, Taddo and his Small Horse Riders, were gone.

*Chapter Fourteen*

## "WE ARE LEAVING THEM HERE TO DIE...."

A handful of waking periods later, Kirov and his unusually quiet scouts returned to River Town.

The River People's outpost on the eastern side of the Coldwater—away from the oncoming Soviet Army—had sprouted into a new city of tents and huts. The populations of Dyalsi and other tribes were congregating for Kirov's latest magic trick.

WHILE THE WAR CHIEF had been scouting the southern approaches to the allied tribes' territory, Hortul Paddlemaker, chief of the River People, and Kirov's wife and effective chief of staff Ala the Beautiful One, had summoned a meeting of the tribal chieftains.

As Kirov opened the council meeting, he thought that this occasion was quite different from one that his predecessor Lal the Fierce might have presided over three or four Outer World years ago. All the allied tribes had been decimated by brutal warfare. The Cave Dwellers of Bari and the Lodge Builders were ghosts of their former selves. Even the powerful Dyal Riders, River People, Snake Eaters, and Marsh Dwellers were greatly reduced in numbers. But, in partial compensation, the Great Camel Riders and Small Horse Riders had joined the alliance.

Kirov smiled as he surveyed the open-air gathering on the shore of River Town Island.

The men and women before him were barbarians by civilized

European standards. Many of them washed only when it rained. Their clothes were feathers, furs and skins rather than woven cloth. But they had their culture, their songs and stories, their simple governments, their painfully acquired proto-sciences....

Most of all, they had their families, their honor, and their ethics.

They were human beings in a world of monsters, and he was proud to lead them.

And now he must lead them into an unknown future.

The council meeting lasted the entire waking period and beyond. But the real business was conducted in the first half hour and the last five minutes.

"Fellow hunters," declared Kirov as an American President might say, "My fellow Americans...."

"The Soviet Red War Party Tribe has entered the lands of the Coldwater River Valley. They have attacked and destroyed the tribes of the Cave Dwellers of Bari and the Seashore People. Soon they will return and attack all of our tribes. They are equipped with powerful weapons. We cannot defeat them. I ask that all of the tribes of the Coldwater River Valley move to new lands far from the Soviet threat. These lands lie on the shores of the Sea of Monsters. The Soviets are moving into the lands from the Coldwater toward the Wava Hills and beyond. They will not enter our new lands."

No one asked how Kirov knew the Soviet plans. If the gilaks thought about the question, they assumed that their war chief's confident knowledge was the result of his magical powers. In fact, the arrogant coward Company Commander Semyon Povich had boasted of Soviet plans during the four waking periods that he and Kirov had spent together before they reached Dyalsi.

Kirov briefly thought that a European would have said that the new lands were southeast of River Town in a land beneath the Outer World's *Beringovo More*, or Bering Sea. No modern European or American had explored the area but Soviet geographers—working with stolen copies of American maps based on Mahar explorations—labeled the landmass as Beringia, in honor of the Danish navigator in Russian service who had explored the Sea in 1728.

Tsassal, phlegmatic chief of the fierce Snake Eaters and Kirov's staunch ally, cut to the heart of the matter. "Mighty Kirov, it is a hard thing to leave the lands of our tribe. Is there no way to defeat the Red War Party?"

Sopping, the tough minded chief of the Marsh Dwellers agreed with sentiment. "You defeated the Red War Band scouting party of Sem-mee-yon Poe-vich several sleeps ago. Why can you not defeat the Red War Band in the same way?"

The representatives of the Great Camel Riders and Small Horse Riders nodded in agreement. Kirov had defeated both of their tribes in the recent past.

"The Soviet Red War Party is too powerful for us," declared Kirov. "We deceived them with tricks. They will not be deceived again. They will kill us or enslave us. There will be no end to slavery."

The Great Camel Riders and Small Horse Riders grimaced in unison. While Kirov had enslaved them after their defeats, his un-Pellucidarian humane treatment and generous manumission had won them to the great alliance.

Konko, the acting chief of the Small Horse Riders in the absence of his leader Taddo, raised himself to his diminutive height and waved his hand for attention.

"Mighty Kirov speaks wisely," declared the small humanoid. "The Small Horse Rider tribe was driven from our lands by the *guns* of the New Americans when Pulk the Foolish attacked them. They were few in numbers compared to us but their guns killed many. Pulk decided that movement was better than death or enslavement. Now, if Kirov, who is the greatest magician in Pellucidar, declares that he is unable to defeat the Soviets, then we should not die but move to better lands."

There was a pause as the chiefs absorbed the thought. Fama, the chief of the Great Camel Riders, nodded in agreement with

Konko's analysis. Her former chief had made a similar decision when the Small Horse Riders had moved into their tribal lands.

Gradually, most of the tribal leaders came around to Kirov's proposal. Almost all valued bravery above most other virtues. But, tales of the Outer Worlders' weapons and Soviet brutality combined with the respect that they had for the Alliance's war chief convinced them. The Dyal Riders followed Kirov. Tsassal and Fama agreed for their tribes followed quickly by the Cave Dwellers, Seashore People, and Great Camel Riders. Hortul Paddlemaker opined that his tribe's fortress on an island in the great river might protect his people but quailed when Kirov described Soviet military bridge building technology. The new chief of the remote Lodge Builders held out for a time thinking that the distance to Lodge Town might save him but finally agreed to the plan.

At length, only Sopping refused to join the exodus. As their name suggested, the Marsh Dwellers' water-soaked lands were not the finest real estate in the Inner World, but they were the ancestral home of their tribe. They would not move without a fight.

Tempers flared; faces reddened; voices rose....

Kirov cut the conflict off.

"Fellow hunters!" he shouted. "No hunting party should include those unwilling to hunt. Our alliance is one of fellowship, not enemies. If the Marsh Dwellers do not wish to move, we will not compel them. Instead, we will wish them farewell and good fortune as brothers and sisters do when they part."

There was a moment of silence. Fama spoke sincerely, "Mighty Kirov speaks wisely. Mighty Sopping, the Great Camel Riders wish you good fortune." The other chiefs echoed her courtesy and the tension drained away.

Hortul spoke up. "Kirov, some River People will not wish to move to the new lands. I believe that this is true of the other tribes as well. I suggest that these bands remain here and choose Sopping as the new war chief of those who remain."

There was another moment of silence followed by murmurs of agreement.

Kirov spoke for the gathering. "Yes, Hortul has spoken wisely. Mighty Sopping, will you become the new war chief of those who remain? Will you protect those who remain as Lal the Fierce and her father protected all of the allied tribes before now?"

The stubborn Marsh Dweller was stunned by the turn of events. He flushed and bowed his head.

He rose to speak. His voice was free of the rancor with which he had defended his earlier decision.

"Fellow hunters, mighty Kirov and Hortul have spoken very wisely indeed. Let us part as brothers and sisters. I will be the war chief of the Coldwater River Valley. I pledge to protect all of those who remain. If any wish to join the Marsh Dweller tribe, they will be welcome as brothers and sisters. If not, you are still my cousins and I will defend you all."

He paused and added, "Mighty Kirov, when you find your new lands, send scouts back to us and tell us the trail to your lands. Then, your tribes and mine may come and go as cousins. When you visit us, we will feed you frogs and eels."

The two war chiefs embraced in front of the Seat of Chiefs as the council members pounded their feet on the floor in applause.

Much work remained to be done in order to plan the great exodus including the division of the peoples, but the tension was gone.

AS THE COUNCIL BROKE UP, Kirov remained seated, his handsome face furrowed in thought.

His handmaiden Flana approached. Her beautiful features looked a question. When her love did not volunteer his thoughts, she asked, "Mighty Kirov, what troubles you?"

The war chief of the allied tribes responded quietly, almost inaudibly.

"My heart aches for Sopping and all of those who remain. We are leaving them here to die."

*Chapter Fifteen*

## "A VERY UNUSUAL THING"

The great migration had begun. It was to become one of the epic tales of the Inner World—an entire people moving into the unknown in an attempt to avoid the blood-soaked claws of the Soviet Army.

Many "civilized" peoples of the Outer World had not shown such ability to understand unpleasant facts and adapt to them. Many of those who did not face facts died.

The Small Horse Riders and the Great Camel Riders came into their own. Both tribes had migrated into the Coldwater Valley sometime before. Now they shared their expertise in assimilating with the hundreds of new migrants. Quietly, confidence and self-esteem swelled.

The tribes moved in waves.

First, teams of scouts ranged outward, exploring the unknown lands along the shores of the Sea of Monsters. Hunting parties of mobile Dyal Riders, Small Horse Riders, and Giant Camel Riders led the way.

Each waking period, reports flowed in to Kirov. A Soviet army commander would have had dozens of staff officers to assist him. Kirov's staff was himself, Ala, and the tribal chiefs. (And Flana who kept his child in line.)

Fortunately, the dangers of life in savage Pellucidar had trained the tribes well. They needed coordination, not detailed directions. Soviet-style control would have produced endless revolts. Kirov's leadership produced results.

Expert builders followed behind the scouts. They listened to the scouts' reports and established fortified camps about a

252

waking period's march apart. When the women and children moved across the land of terror, they had strongholds waiting for them at the end of each march.

Bands of warriors alternated as the rear guard. Many of them watched nervously over their shoulders scanning the upward curving landscape for Soviet soldiers or other monsters.

But the invaders remained invisible.

The route curved to what Kirov thought of as east and then south. The Sea of Monsters' shoreline was an easy guide to follow.

Tribesmen walked determinately onward. Many women rode. Children seemed to stampede like herds of dyals, shrieking and shouting in glee.

Each mile revealed new wonders.

Few of the land-dwelling tribes had seen the sea before. The endless waves and curious creatures were fascinating. Children especially had to be restrained from running into the surf to study *azdyryths* and *tandarazes* and other leviathans first hand.

Kirov had worried about the perils of travel. Most of the creatures living on the Plain of Grazers were herbivores. But carnivores stalked the huge herds and few of them objected to a gilak steak! And the normally peaceful herbivores were quite capable of stampeding over a hundred warriors and women...!

But, as the former dictator of the Soviet Union V. Lenin had said, quantity has a quality all its own.

The allied tribes were small in numbers compared to any European nation but gigantic in comparison to other gilak tribes. Belligerent animals willing to attack a hunting party of a dozen puny humanoids shied away from threatening war parties twice or three times that size. Most of the refugees survived unharmed.

Gradually the climate changed as the tribes moved south into Beringia. The cold air entering Pellucidar through the North Polar Opening was increasingly warmed by the eternal sun. The plants changed from subarctic to temperate. And the animals changed as well.

Monstrous dyryths and related creatures drifted southward in parallel to the humans. Kirov's friend, named Dyryth for his size, received endless ribbing from primeval humorists who claimed to see resemblances between the oversized man and the ambling herbivores. Unlike the high-strung creatures, Dyryth merely smiled and agreed that the beasts were his handsome cousins.

The Giant Camel Riders were held up for an entire waking period by a migration of armored giants that Kirov classified as *Glyptodonts*—walking pillboxes trundling along encased in thick hides. The giant cousins to armadillos averaged two to three meters high and six or more meters long. Supremely confident that nothing could threaten them, the great creatures took their time crossing the path of the gilaks and their gigantic proto-camels.

One hothead attempted to spear a dinner for himself and his fellows. His lance glanced off the glyptodont's shell without the creature seeming to notice. Frustrated, the would-be diner charged in.... And went flying when the glyptodont's powerful tail knocked his camel off its legs with a bone-shattering crack!

The hothead thumped onto the soft soil of the Plain, unconscious but alive. His camel's legs were broken. With brutal practicality, the patrol put the injured beast out of its misery—and onto their menus.

When colossal baluchiteria approached, the patrol yielded the way to the gigantic proto-rhinoceri without a challenge. Kirov had realized the pride the Giant Camel Riders felt in controlling their huge beasts. Now, they were quiet for several waking periods following their encounters with even larger animals.

In contrast, the confident Dyal Riders were delighted to find flocks of *moas* striding across the Plain. The large flightless birds were extinct in the Outer World. (Kirov recalled an unconfirmed report that they had survived in New Zealand until the arrival of humans.) In Pellucidar, they still lived.

Whooping excitedly, Dyal Riders began rounding up moas. Generations of experience with their own savage war birds made corralling and controlling the newly discovered avians easy. Skilled hunters estimated the amount of meat that the tribes would need and cut moa flocks into segments. Some were steered into quiet valleys for slaughter while the others were allowed to escape. The tribes dined well for several waking periods.

As did the carrion-eating condor-like *Tetratornis* flocks that began to follow the migration scavenging for free meals.

Kirov was struck by the analogy with American cowboys. Change the dyals to horses and moas to cows....

After that, the tribesmen captured every moa they could. The migration swelled (and slowed) with the new flocks but the few complaints were stilled by fresh moa breasts and wings for dinner.

Kilometers rolled by. The weather warmed further. The Plain of Grazers curved around the eastern end of the Sea of Monsters where Leninska extended itself into the great isthmus of Beringia. Grasses thickened. The beautiful white tipped starflowers gave way to a yellow variety. Green tulips appeared. Deciduous trees now outnumbered the pine trees that dominated the Arctic continent. The tribes added apples to their diets.

Armadillo-like *Boriostrascons* and *Gomphotheria*—long trunked, heavy tusked relatives of the mastodons—paced the migration. Various species of fantastically horned prehistoric antelopes loped past. Herds of tiny orthopi scampered away.

Brightly colored *Archaeopteryxes* serenaded the movement with croaking birdsongs. And smaller birds flitted through the grasses to safety when powerful feet, hooves and claws crushed their humble homes.

Kirov strove to recall their many names. Most of his tribesmen didn't care. Moas had become *moals* to the Pellucidarians and the antelopes were simply "good eating."

Humans and beasts continued southward into the unknown.

A SCOUT CAME thundering into Kirov's forward camp.

Chief and scout greeted each other. Normally, the latter would have immediately reported on what he and his fellows had seen over the last waking period or so. This time, the man seemed to have trouble organizing his thoughts. Kirov waited patiently.

"Mighty Kirov, I have come to say that the hunting party of Tol has found something that is very unusual." He stopped speaking.

Kirov waited for the scout to continue. After a moment, he asked the man sharply, "What is this very unusual thing?"

The man's face contorted. He seemed bewildered by what he had seen.

Kirov attempted to coax the information out.

"Is this thing a gilak or gilak-like creature?"

"No, no, it is not."

"Is this thing an animal?"

"No, it is not."

"Is this thing a plant?"

"No."

Kirov sighed. "Is this thing a rock?"

The man paused. "I *think* that it is a rock."

"What makes a rock unusual?"

"It is hanging in the middle of the air. Above our heads."

Now Kirov was silent for a long moment.

The man continued, "The rock is large. It is shaped like a small mountain. It is about three or four man-heights in the air. There is nothing between the rock and the ground to hold the rock in the air. Yet it remains in the air."

Kirov sighed again.

"Get some food and a fresh dyal. I must see this thing myself."

A WAKING PERIOD LATER, Kirov cooed and his dyal came to a halt. He stared at the "very unusual thing" above and before him.

It was indeed shaped like a small mountain and hanging, unsupported, about twenty meters in the air.

Kirov focused his eyes on the space below the "very unusual thing" looking for hidden props, walls, and mounds of dirt, rocks, whatever....

There was nothing there.

The ground below it was covered with shiny black rock but nothing connected ground and.... Nothing connected the ordinary seeming ground and the astonishing sight hovering serenely overhead.

Silently, Tol approached his war chief. The latter scarcely noticed his presence. After a time, the scout leader cautiously spoke, "Mighty Kirov...?"

Kirov shook himself and looked at his tribesman and then back to the "very unusual thing." His words were distracted. "Hail, Tol, fellow hunter."

"Hail, Kirov Mighty Magician. Do you know what this thing is?"

The former Russian paused before answering.

"It appears to be what would be called a 'castle,' which is a very large fortified village for many people to live in. It is made of stone for protection against men and beasts." He pointed to various features of the triangular mass. "The outer walls keep men and beasts out. It has a large 'courtyard' where warriors live and the chief's tribe can be protected, and the inner 'castle keep' houses the chief and his family and deputy chiefs. It also gives his warriors a height from which they can fire weapons over the walls at enemies."

Tol transferred his gaze from his chief to the strange castle. His normally energetic voice was subdued.

"So there are many castles in Russia?" Most of the migrants knew that Kirov had come to the Coldwater River Valley from a land of wonders called Russia.

Kirov nodded his head without taking his eyes off the strange sight before him.

"Well, there are many castles in Russia but none of them floating in the air."

*Chapter Sixteen*

## MORE MAGIC

After a timeless time of merely staring in wonder, Kirov's scientific training reasserted itself. And that recalled him to his duties as war chief of the allied tribes.

"Tol," he snapped. Was his voice tenser than usual?

"Mighty Kirov?" asked the leader of the discovering patrol. Tol's voice was definitely subdued.

"There is a broad river about three waking periods' ride behind us. Most of our tribesmen should still be on the far side. Send a patrol to halt their movement. Keep them on the far side of the river. But tell Ala to send ten tens (100) of warriors here."

Tol acknowledged his orders with relief, transmitted them to his men, and the Dyal Riders thundered off to the north.

They happily fled the eerie sight of tons of rock hovering nonchalantly in midair.

Kirov asked Tol, "Has anyone walked below the castle?"

"No, mighty Kirov, we were afraid."

Kirov nodded. He appreciated Tol's honesty. Even many resolute scientists quailed when confronted with the unknown.

As the foremost scientist north of Innes' Empire of Pellucidar and leader of the mighty tribal alliance, Kirov sucked in a deep breath. He dismounted and cooed an order for his dyal to rest. The powerful war bird settled to the ground, unconcerned about castles and similar mysteries.

Kirov took his assegai and walked forward. After a moment, Tol followed. After another moment, his men followed as well.

The ground under the floating castle was dark with shadow.

258

Kirov could distinguish shiny black rocks projecting from the ground but no vegetation. He looked into the space between ground and castle. Beyond the shadowed area, the lush temperate grassland resumed. In the distance, he could see some antelope-like creatures grazing the greenery.

Was there some distortion in the air under the castle?

Kirov's scientific training asserted itself. He looked—and listened—for more evidence. He heard the usual wind rustling through the grasses and bushes. Various animal calls pierced the air—mostly the murmuring of antelopes and *Alticamelus,* occasionally the scream of a hunting cat. But no unusual noises or smells.

Kirov cautiously stepped forward, assegai probing the air in front of him.

Without warning, he fell down.

His assegai stabbed into the ground.

Kirov froze, partially in amazement, partially in response to his training. *What just happened? But don't jump to conclusions!*

His left leg was bent while his right one lay normally on the ground. His left ankle hurt.

He rolled around, scanning for information.

In a crescent formation behind him, his men stood stock still, eyes staring.

Specifically at his left foot.

Which was hanging in mid-air a few centimeters off the ground. Unsupported by anything that anyone could see.

Kirov rolled to his right. His left leg rotated through the air normally.

He continued his rotation and thumped normally onto his back, lying on the soft soil.

Kirov sat up and looked at his left ankle. There were two thin streaks of blood crossing his lower leg.

Long experience with the hazards of Pellucidarian life enabled him to see that the blood flows were not serious. He transferred his attention to the mysterious space that had tripped him.

There was nothing there.

No…!

There was a bare space on the ground surrounded by perfectly normal grasses. The bare space was depressed in a rectangular hole.

Was there some invisible something in the mysterious space?

Kirov cautiously probed the space with his assegai. The tip clunked into something unseen.

He continued feeling around the unknown thing. Whatever it was, it resembled a squared-off log about fifty centimeters long by ten wide and ten high. Looking closely, he could see tiny red lines hanging in the air. The blood from his wounds.

Kirov reached out his hand….

Tol interrupted.

"Mighty Kirov, a strange gilak comes from the castle." His voice was very high pitched.

Kirov turned around and gaped.

Striding confidently through the air, an angel approached the humans. His powerful frame was robed in white and his majestic face was framed in a halo of light gleaming in the sunlight. Kirov could see wings folded behind the being, tips moving playfully in the wind.

Tol squeaked, "So are there such beings in Russia?"

"No," replied Kirov. "Not in my lifetime."

*Chapter Seventeen*

## "HOW POWERFUL IS YOUR MAGIC?"

The angel advanced until he stood about seven meters away from Kirov—five meters horizontally distant and five meters above the ground. He crossed his arms and boomed a challenge. "I see strangers in the lands of the Avor. I kill strangers!"

His command of the language was clear and unaccented; his Pellucidarian manners were typical.

As Kirov confronted the strange being, he heard a sustained rustling-creaking sound from behind him and to either side.

Without taking his attention off the apparent angel, he ordered, "Dyal Riders. Return your assegais to your belts and ground your longspears."

There was a moment of silence followed by more creaking, rustling and the thumping of longspear butts hitting the ground.

Kirov noticed that the angel's forehead seemed suddenly shiny as the latter surveyed the crescent of tribesmen behind the war chief. Did angels sweat?

Hah! His long ago teacher Brother Grigori had stated the angels did not sweat. Kirov snorted at his own foolishness. Here he was, calling himself the greatest scientist in northern Pellucidar, and he was jumping to conclusions! He took a breath to settle his nerves and forced himself to think—exactly as Brother Grigori would have wished.

*The being appeared to be a typical gilak with typically human features. He had walked, not floated or flown. The robe was made of woven cloth but the wings.... The wings flapped idly in the gentle breeze. Hah! They were a cape fastened to the robe's neck.*

261

*An adjustable cape made a great deal of sense in a variable climate.
And the halo was really a necklace made of crystals. Therefore, the
supposed angel was really....*

"Hail, mighty man of the Avor. I am Kirov known as the
Skalkiller. I kill those who harm my tribes." Kirov's voice was
calm and commanding. The old Russian saying that *Knowledge
is Power* was true in Pellucidar as well as the Outer World.

The Avor refocused his attention. "Hail Kirov. You cannot
kill me or my kin. You cannot storm Avorsi which floats in
the air before you." He partially turned as he gestured upward.
"And how can your ah-see-gees and long spears harm our great
fortress if you could reach it?"

"Hah!" sneered Tol loudly. "Kirov Skalkiller is the greatest magician in all of Pellucidar! He slew many trals and skals
in the Mountains of Birds many, many sleeps ago! He defeated *two* invading hordes many sleeps ago and made them
his tribesmen! He caused the So-vee-yet Red War Party invaders to flee in terror some sleeps ago! And he has defeated ryths,
demons and other monsters as well! I, Tol, have seen these
things! If Mighty Kirov wishes, he will defeat you and make
your w... your kin his tribesmen! Defy him and taste his mighty
magic!!"

Kirov reflected that there were both advantages and dis-
advantages to having what Americans would call an overly
enthusiastic publicity agent. Fortunately, boasting was a
common Pellucidarian habit. The Avor seemed to be thoughtful rather than offended as he studied first Tol and then Kirov.

He drew himself up. "Your man claims that you have done
many great deeds. I ask you: How powerful is your magic?"

Kirov smiled to himself.

"That is a fair question. Behold."

With that, Kirov turned and took an exaggerated step
towards Tol and the line of warriors that had been behind him.
First one foot came to rest floating in the air a short distance
above the grassy plain and then the other.

Tol's eyes bugged out at the sight of his war chief standing in the air as did the eyes of the Avor. He paled....

Kirov smiled confidently. He turned so that he could address the Avor while still watching his troop leader.

"As you can see, O man of the Avor, Tol the Traveler does not lie. He has seen wonders and has told them to you so that you are wiser than you were."

His war chief's laudatory words caused Tol's fear to disappear. He swelled with pride. Smiles broke out on the faces of the other Dyal Riders as well

Once again, the magic of *psychology* had worked wonders. And on more than one being...!

Kirov rotated further so that he was facing the false angel directly. His eyes took in the being's troubled face, the no longer flashing halo, the wing-like cape....

"I, Kirov, who practice the magic known as *science*, say this: The allied tribes have come to this land in peace. If you will have peace with us, we will have peace with you, as we have with many tribes. But, if you attack us, we will climb the hill of invisible rocks that supports your nest, open it with our spears, and color it red with your blood, O man. I have spoken." He gestured dramatically.

The Dyal Riders raised their longspears and thumped them against the ground once all in unison.

The Avor flinched.

Kirov smiled serenely. He had discovered that uncivilized Pellucidarians found the discipline of Soviet units frightening. The unruly peoples of the Inner World did not understand how a single command could cause a multitude of individuals to dress alike, march alike, and fire weapons alike. It was as if professional army units were unearthly monsters with single minds and many bodies. The former Soviet Red Army specialist was no Peter the Great, but teaching the allied warriors a few simple maneuvers resulted in a significant advantage in battle.

Especially, *before* battle was joined...!

The Avor was silent for a long time.

Finally, he spoke up, his voice much quieter than before. "And how will you enter Avorsi now?"

Kirov smiled broadly and uttered one of the most powerful magic spells on Earth.

The Avor bowed his head. He said, "Come upward, mighty Kirov."

*Chapter Eighteen*

## NOVY MIR

Many, many kilometers distant from the perch of the Avor squatted Fort Alinsky, the military headquarters for the Soviet conquest of the Inner World.

Inside the fort's inner sanctum, Brigade Commander E. Varan was receiving a briefing from several of his staff officers. Varan's predecessor, like most Soviet commanders, enjoyed convening huge meetings with every staff department represented, even those with nothing to report. Unlike them, Varan preferred small conferences with only a few officers present. Intelligence officer Kulongoski silently noted that the lack of cross-fertilization meant that only Varan was fully informed on all issues. Hoarding information made the commander seem to be a genius to his men.

Varan faced operations officer Kronstadt. "Report on the liberation of Gori."

"Comrade Brigade Commander, we have now occupied the entire western half of Gori from the Birnam Mountains to the Coldwater River Valley. This area is approximately the size of Germany. We have established a line of small outposts along the River. Our scouts are probing the eastern half of the territory and expect to reach the strait connecting the Polar Sea and the Engels Ocean within three months."

Varan frowned and asked, "Why is it taking so long to cross the territory?"

"Comrade Brigade Commander, Gori is a completely uncivilized land. There are no roads or other infrastructure and so the men must walk the entire distance over difficult terrain.

We now have horses and mules but they must cross the wilderness areas to reach the frontier. The engineers are building roads, forts and so forth as fast as they can but they can only do so much with what they have. The draft labor corvees help but we really need equipment and trained construction workers, not ignorant barbarians. Not to mention mountains of supplies. Everything must funnel through the port of Bogrov and Fort Alinsky and then be carried east to the work fronts.

"In addition, the native inhabitants and ungo…." He coughed. "And the unearthly creatures are almost uniformly hostile. We are essentially fighting a continuous low intensity war as we go." He paused and added, "We are burning through weapons and ammunition at an alarming rate. If we are going to *liberate* New America in the near future, we will need more of everything including men, munitions…"

Varan cut Kronstadt off with a hand gesture. He then pointed to a logistics officer nicknamed Kopeck. His penny-pinching personality had caused his peers to call him by the name of a Soviet coin of little value. "Report on the labor program."

Kopeck resembled a trapped rat but mastered himself and answered. "Yes, Comrade Brigade Commander. The problem is that the natives are not yet ready for modern civilization. They do not understand work in the modern sense of the term. They do not read, nor have a written language so all instruction must be verbal. When they are drafted to provide industrial or housekeeping service in lieu of taxes, they must be trained to perform the simplest tasks. In addition, many of them attempt to escape into the wilderness rather than contribute to the New Soviet State." He paused and then added, "Further, we are experiencing a very high death rate in the new mines and building projects. The work gang leaders claim that the constant and unfamiliar labor is killing the men. I request your guidance, Comrade."

Varan spoke decisively. "The real problem is the anti-social attitude of the natives. They have a very indolent lifestyle—

eating, sleeping, hunting, fishing and gathering nuts and berries when they feel like it. That will stop. The solution is less whining and more discipline. Comrade, I want labor camps and model villages established where work is needed as has been done successfully in the Motherland. Having our new comrades concentrated in camps and villages will make guarding them easier and facilitate hostage taking if necessary. As soon as the first camps are ready, begin moving our new comrades where they are needed and where they can learn the Russian language, the Communist system and the value of work.

"Such training will, of course, refute the idea that hard work kills anyone. What kills people is shirking, desertion, rebellion and similar crimes against The People. Remind our new comrades of the penalties for those crimes. Do you understand, Comrade?"

Kopeck understood.

Varan returned his attention to Kronstadt. His face narrowed as he spoke, "Comrade, your men have explored approximately three-quarters of Gori. Have you contacted the New American cowboys there?"

Kronstadt took a deep breath.

"No, Comrade Brigade Commander. It appears that the reports that New America had extended its boundaries to the Coldwater River were incorrect."

Varan glared at the map and touched a delicate finger to a point near the center of Gori. His voice was professional enough but everyone present could hear an undercurrent of menace. "Comrade Company Commander Semyon Povich reported that the New Americans had established a Fort Grant and the city called River City here. He stated that the warlord Edgar Rice Burroughs was in the fort at that time. Was this report incorrect?"

There was a noticeable pause before the operations officer answered. Povich's report that the New Americans had annexed half of Gori had triggered an alarm as far distant as Moscow.

The fact that he had taken it upon himself to retreat all the way back to Fort Alinsky rather than sending a team of runners as Red Army protocol prescribed had triggered a desire on Kronstadt's part to beat the sniveling coward to death personally. A desire that the operations officer had prudently overcome....

Again, Kronstadt inhaled deeply. "Yes, Comrade Brigade Commander. Our scouts report that there is a group of native villages on an island at that point. The native name translates as 'River Town.' The inhabitants are unfavorably disposed towards annexation but not actively hostile. There were no signs of New American presence including the reported Fort Grant or the warlord Burroughs."

"And what is your conclusion about Comrade Povich's report, Comrade?"

The operations officer took another breath and answered cautiously, "Comrade Brigade Commander, I respectfully believe that Comrade Company Commander Povich was mistaken. I suspect that some statements were mistranslated and that led Comrade Povich to believe that Burroughs and other New Americans were present. Our most recent reports state that the local tribe has some knowledge of the New Americans but describe them as a distant tribe of magicians who have never visited River Town."

Kronstadt fell silent, stoically awaiting a career-ending thunderbolt.

The expected thunderbolt did not fall.

Everyone present could see the wheels turning in the commander's mind.

Presently, Varan spoke in a relatively mild voice. "Comrade, where is Comrade Company Commander Semyon Povich at this time?"

"Performing administrative duties in the Operations Center, Comrade Brigade Commander."

Varan nodded. "Very good; very good. Comrades, today's staff conference is concluded. Comrade Kronstadt, have Comrade Povich report to my office.

"Immediately!"

*Chapter Nineteen*

## AN UNEXPECTED QUESTION

Finally, the Avor spoke up, his voice much quieter than before. "And how will you enter Avorsi now?"

Kirov smiled broadly and said, "I *ask* that you allow me to enter your nest as a fellow hunter." In Pellucidarian, the term "fellow hunter" could mean several things. One of those definitions was "friend."

The Avor bowed his head. "Come upward, mighty Kirov. Enter the perch of the Avor as a fellow hunter."

Kirov nodded his agreement. He turned carefully around and spoke to Tol and the Dyal Riders. "Fellow hunters, await here and guard my back. I go into the house of the Avor to make peace between our peoples. If anything… bad… happens, report it to Ala the Beautiful One and listen to her commands."

The Dyal Riders shouted their agreement. Kirov suspected that many of them were secretly glad not to enter the castle of mystery.

He turned again and stepped off the invisible rock that he had been standing on. A few paces forward and his toe bumped into another invisible something. He took exaggerated steps forward and upward apparently planting his feet on nothing at all. He soon reached the point where the Avor stood in midair.

The latter turned and led the way upward. His black cloak flapped idly in the breeze. His necklace of glass shards flashed as his movements changed the angles at which the sunlight hit the ornament.

They climbed quickly. The invisible rocks sloped upward but the footing was firm. Soon the black basaltic rock of the castle was before them. A narrow entrance carved in the stone admitted them to a courtyard where the other Avor gathered.

Their faces showed a distinct family resemblance. All of them wore white robes and contrasting cloaks.

Kirov greeted them with a raised and empty hand. They responded with two outstretched arms. *Certainly a friendly gesture*, he thought. The Avor seemed to be quite unusual among the many mutually suspicious tribes of Pellucidar. Well, every rule in the universe seems to have its exceptions.

The first Avor spoke. "My kin, I, Sar, present Kirov Skalkiller. He comes to our perch in peace."

The other Avor chorused, "Peace," and smiled.

Sar and Kirov entered the main building. The castle in the air was an irregular triangular mass with stumpy towers groping for the distant Sun. Several of them had been shattered by brute force. The structures surrounding the central courtyard were carved from the stone, partially by nature, partially by the Avor. They had independently invented many elements of architecture from Europe's own castle building periods. Narrow windows provided weapons ports and natural lighting. The visitor glimpsed homes, armories, meeting and dining halls, kitchens, storerooms and other spaces familiar to historians.

With his attention on the castle keep itself, Kirov missed the excited whispering that broke out behind him.

THE TWO AMBASSADORS sat together in an inner chamber. Their tour of the Avor home had ended in a room with bright sunlight pouring in through a glass ceiling. A female Avor provided them with a light meal of vegetables, seeds and small fruits as well as a refreshing wine. The remaining tension dissolved.

Sar's face was relaxed. No longer was he the commanding ambassador defying potential enemies. Now, he was himself again. He was at peace with the world and some weighty decision.

They told each other their tribes' stories. In Kirov's case, the telling required much more time since the allied tribes had far more history than the family of the Avor did.

Sar shook his handsome head in wonder and admiration. He asked some shrewd questions about Kirov's part in recent history and listened carefully when the young war chief modestly admitted that Tol's brief history was largely true. He, Kirov, had added three new tribes to the alliance, including two former enemies.... He had defeated monsters and an alleged demon....

The Avor smiled and asked, "Well, then, mighty Kirov, will you please conquer my kin as well?"

Taken by surprise... *No! Shocked to his core*, the war chief sat bolt upright. His mind whirled. *No tribe in all of the Inner World had ever voluntarily...!*

He managed to choke out, "Why? Why do you wish to be conquered by strangers?"

Sar looked directly at Kirov. "There are monsters coming to attack and devour my kin. Our castle in the air cannot defend us. But you can."

*Chapter Twenty*

## THE DINOSAURS OF PELLUCIDAR
## SUDDENLY SEEMED TAME!

K irov breathed in deeply. His scientist's mind brought his turbulent emotions under control.

*Another war? It seemed as if life in Pellucidar was nothing but a series of battles against strange and hostile men and monsters. He had led his people east and south to escape the Soviet Red Army and here was yet another battle to be fought. When could he pause and enjoy life with F…. with Ala and their son? When could he be the scientist that he had so long wanted to be?*

*And yet….*

*And yet…. Scientist or war chief, he was a Pellucidarian. His brief time with the evil and cowardly Company Commander Povich had reminded him of the vast differences between the honest savagery of the Inner World and the calculated cruelties of the Outer World. Pellucidar was the primitive, savage, exciting world that it was. Did he really wish anything else? Anything less than Pellucidar?*

*He had become a Pellucidarian.*

*And he would fight to protect his mate, his son, and his people.*

Kirov focused his attention on the immediate issues. He would think about the future later. He spoke to the ambassador of the Avor.

"You wish to enter into the alliance formerly of the Coldwater River Valley. We are interested, but we must know much more about these monsters and why your castle does not protect you from them."

Sar had smiled when Kirov did not reject his request but

272

that smile faded at the renewed mention of the threatening monsters.

He sighed deeply.

"The monsters are great spiders. They resemble small spiders but their bodies are as thick as a man is tall and three times as wide in each direction. Their legs span a distance of six times the height of a man and support their bodies at least twice the height above the ground."

A strange expression contorted the young scientist's face. Was it surprise—or fear?

Great spiders indeed!

Spiders with bodies four to six times the size of the elephant in the Leningrad Zoo with legs spanning twelve meters in stride?

The dinosaurs of Pellucidar that he had once hoped to study suddenly seemed tame in comparison!

Kirov leaned forward intently.

"You said that they have legs. Eight legs? Do they have arms or hands?"

"Eight legs, yes. Hands, no, but they have small claws. Claws that are small for them. They batter things with their legs and seize things with their claws and mouths. And they can shoot threads of great size from their mouths that seize things and draw those things into their mouths. That is why our castle does not protect us. We hide within its walls but the great spiders' threads seize us and draw us out of our rooms." A storm of emotions crossed Sar's face including sorrow and fear.

"Are they poisonous? Many spiders of ordinary size are poisonous."

"We do not know if they are poisonous but their spittle changes the bodies of gilaks and animals to liquid that they then drink."

Kirov nodded.

"Some animals in my birth land Russia also change their prey to liquids. We call that *liquefaction*. And many spiders in Russia create *sticky webbing* that 'seizes' insects. The great spiders of this land seem to be simply huge versions of ordinary spiders." Kirov automatically translated the Russian terms into their nearest Pellucidarian equivalents.

Sar nodded. He did not express his thoughts but, clearly, he was again impressed by Kirov's knowledge and resolution.

Behind his own mask of command, Kirov's thoughts were simple. *My people have journeyed long to escape the Soviet Red Army and need rest. This is a good land and the Avor offer it to us on generous terms. We could conquer them as other tribes would do but then we would simply be smaller Soviets. And wherever we go, we will fight something or someone. Let us make our stand here.*

*Here—with new allies and a fortress to anchor our defenses....*

Aloud, he said, "The allied tribes will accept the people of the Avor into our alliance. But you must allow us to move into your lands and you must fight with us. You cannot hide in your castle while your allies fight."

Sar nodded. "We will fight beside you."

Kirov nodded in turn. "Do you know of a great shallow river about six waking periods' ride in the direction from which we approached Avorsi?"

Sar nodded. It was on the edge of Avor explored territory and had no special name. Kirov's fellows had already started calling it the Warmwater in contrast to their native Coldwater.

"Are there any gilak tribes living in the area from the river to Avorsi and as far in the same direction beyond your perch? And the same distance on the left and right hands from Avorsi?" A Russian might have said *Are there any other tribes within a hundred kilometer radius from Avorsi castle? Any competitors? Any allies?*

"No," responded Sar. "There were some gilaks living within the area that you have described but they have been eaten by the monsters or fled. There are many animals in this area but even they flee the monsters."

A thought struck Kirov. "Have the great spiders always lived in this land?"

"No, they appeared a hundred or two hundred sleeps ago following the herds of grass eaters."

Kirov nodded. Clearly the monster arachnids were apex predators following prey. Dire wolves and wild dogs displayed the same behavior in the Coldwater River Valley.

The young scientist wondered *Had something far to the north or northeast had driven the gigantic spiders into the lands of the Avor?* Violent contact with the New Americans had started the tribes of the Small Horse Riders and the Giant Camel Riders moving into the Coldwater River lands many sleeps ago.

He pushed the speculation aside. There were *so many* things about Pellucidar that he hoped to learn…!

And did not have time to learn…!

Not while his people needed his protection. He might be a college student snatched from his studies and hurled into adventure after adventure but he *was* the war chief of the allied tribes and he would not fail his people…!

Kirov spoke firmly. "I must ask the council of chiefs to accept the Avor as allies and I believe that they will do so. We will move to this side of the river we call Warmwater and claim all the lands within six waking periods' ride from Avorsi. This castle will always be the perch of your tribe but we will build a new town for all the tribes nearby." He smiled. "You will have many neighbors."

Sar returned the smile. "It will be good to have neighbors and fellow hunters. Our young people will especially appreciate having new neighbors."

The war chief's smile deepened. "So will ours."

*Chapter Twenty-One*

# "IT IS THE BEST THAT I CAN DO."

Company Commander Semyon Povich stood rigidly at attention before the desk of Brigade Commander Varan. As usual, his face was contorted in raw fear. The flickering of the kerosene lamps illuminating the inner sanctum lent an infernal hue to everything.

Varan sat behind his desk like Minos, the judge of the dead in pre-Soviet Russian myth. His voice was soft, almost monotone, but unmistakable. Long *association* with Varan enabled Povich to understand the emotions charging every word.

"We may speak freely in this room... Semyon. I inspected all adjacent rooms and searched this room for listening posts and microphones myself. People know that you are here to be disciplined but only you and I will know the truth."

Povich looked at his commander. His distorted features made it impossible for ordinary persons to read his emotions but Varan knew each of them.

"What will happen to me?" asked the terrified Company Commander.

Varan exhaled as if to expel unwelcome thoughts.

"Exile."

He paused and resumed. "I am assigning you to command Fort Chomsky. It is an outpost in the far southwestern corner of Plutonia overlooking the Karl-Marx Ocean. It is the best that I can do to protect you from the certain wrath of Comrade Secretary General Stalin."

Povich winced. More accurately, he further twisted his face into an expression that Varan knew to be a wince.

"Is there no alternative?"

"Death by firing squad," replied Varan in a repressed mono-tone. "Your report that the warlord Edgar Rice Burroughs was at River City on the Coldwater River went to Moscow. Given Comrade Stalin's all consuming hatred of Burroughs, I could not have withheld that information without jeopardizing my own position. The information that your report was false is on its way now. When Comrade Stalin learns of your... ah, mistake, he will order your death. Only the difficulties of communication between Novy Mir and Moscow have prevented me from receiving his order already. But that order will come. By assigning you to the most obscure corner of Plutonia, I hope to delay execution of that order until the correlation of forces changes.

"It is the best that I can do," finished the older man.

Povich digested the news. After a time, he timidly suggested, "Gori is more remote than Plutonia."

Varan shook his beautiful blonde head. "Every part of Gori is more dangerous than Fort Chomsky. Comrade Kronstadt is actively directing our advance there. I do not trust him not to order your assassination. In Gori, you will inevitably come to his *attention*. At Chomsky, you will be 'out of sight and out of mind' as the Americans say. It is the best that I can do."

Povich shook his head. "I understand. I will go. I want to live. All the things that I have done, I have done so that I can live."

"I understand. I have done the same things."

Povich closed his eyes. His shoulders slumped.

"I will go to Fort Chomsky as you command. You will report to Moscow that you have punished me in a way that makes use of me for the greater glory of the Soviet Union."

He paused and then continued softly and bitterly, "The Soviet Union: the *Great* People's Republic of Freedom and Equality."

Varan's previously impassive face darkened. "Be careful, Semyon. Do not allow anyone else to know your true feelings."

"Yes, yes, El...."

"Stop!" barked Varan savagely. "Even here you must never use my true name! Never! Otherwise you will forget yourself and use it in public!"

Povich hung his head. "Yes, yes, Comrade Brigade Commander. I understand."

He raised his head and looked at Varan.

"May I embrace you before I go? One last time?"

Varan was silent for a seeming eternity. He breathed his answer, "Yes, one last time. It is the best that I can do." He stood up and walked around his desk.

They clasped each other tightly.

After a time, they released each other. They helped each other straighten their clothes.

Their manner became strictly military. They had long practice in swiftly changing from the personal to the professional. They exchanged salutes.

Povich turned and left. He closed the door carefully behind him.

Varan sat down at his desk and buried his head in his hands. It was a long time before he sat up and turned his attention to his other duties.

One of those was the final conquest of Gori.

*Chapter Twenty-Two*

## "HE HAS GONE TO FEED
## THE GREAT SPIDERS."

A la the Beautiful One, Kirov's mate, arrived at the Avor castle with a guard of one hundred men and their mounts. She goggled at the great stone building hanging in the middle of the air. Normally as alert as anyone who hoped to survive in savage Pellucidar, she ignored the handful of Dyal Riders waiting for her. Their leader, Tol the Traveler, had to repeat his hail before Ala acknowledged him.

Ala tore her eyes from the astonishing sight and focused on her tribesman.

"Hail, daring Tol. Where is our chief Kirov?"

Tol pointed in a direction at a right angle to Ala's approach. Kirov would say that Tol's finger pointed *eastward*. "He has gone to feed the great spiders. He said...."

"*What?!*" screeched Ala. Her body tensed. Her dyal shifted uneasily beneath her. Then in a quieter voice, "*What* is my mate doing?!"

Tol's face reflected the limits of his own comprehension. Still, he strove to report his chief's actions as accurately as possible. "Mighty Kirov has gone to scout the movements of great spiders that live in that direction and come to feed on the Avor—" He pointed to the castle. "—every few waking periods. He said that he would drive animals to the mouths of the great spiders and see if they could be appeased by regular feedings."

Ala paused briefly to digest the news. She nodded decisively. Her beauty was not limited to her body.

"I understand," she commented. "What is that thing and

how does it float in the air?" She pointed to the stone mass hovering serenely above the level of her head.

Tol's manner changed subtly. "This is the *castle* or great dwelling of the Avor tribe. They wish to join the allied tribes of the Coldwater River Valley and Kirov has agreed provided that the council of chiefs agrees."

Ala nodded again.

"The castle is composed of a rock that Kirov calls *basalt*. It stands on a hill of invisible rocks called *glass*. Both basalt and glass are thrust out of the earth by fire mountains called *volcanoes*. The nature of glass is that light passes freely through it as light passes through air. If the *angle* of the glass changes, then the light bounces off the glass and flashes. Here...."

Tol dug a small piece of glass out of his pouch and waved it about. As it moved, it glittered in the constant sunlight.

"However, when the glass does not move, then the light passes quietly through the glass and it is hard to see."

Tol held the small glass still and the flashing ceased.

"The rocks beneath the castle do not move and therefore they are invisible."

Ala's face reflected her skepticism. She carefully held out her hand for the small glass and studied it thoughtfully.

"Kirov has told me these things," supplied Tol.

Ala nodded once again. If Kirov has said these things, then they must be true.

Even if she did not fully understand them.

As it was, Ala understood far more than many of her more conservative tribesmen did. She had previously learned the Russian words *basalt* and *volcanoes* directly from her mate. The new terms *castle*, *glass* and *angle* she gathered from Tol's explanation. She smiled to herself. She recognized Kirov's descriptions coming from Tol's mouth. Her mate's strange if brilliant mind contained many, many exotic concepts that he had to tortuously explain to his tribesmen. Unfortunately they often failed to understand.

It was characteristic of Kirov that, despite such setbacks,

he constantly sought to educate his followers so that they would be as brilliant as he was. And equally characteristic that he failed to realize the respect and awe that his efforts created.

"What else has Kirov told you?"

"He asks that four tens of men come to the castle and cover parts of the invisible rocks with dirt. He wishes the path from the castle to the ground to be visible for us to see when we come and go to the castle."

Ala nodded in understanding.

"He says that the dirt will frighten the great spiders away from the castle."

Ala's mouth fell open. She started to demand an explanation of the frightening powers of common dirt but stopped herself. Instead, she shook her head in bemused wonder.

Her own news would have to wait.

She began giving orders.

*Chapter Twenty-Three*

## A RENDEZVOUS WITH DEATH

Kirov's Dyal Riders rode slowly across the strange, upward curving landscape of the Inner World, yipping like genuine American cowboys.

The analogy was more exact than usual for the twenty-one primitive warriors were driving a herd of perhaps a hundred *Moeritheres* ahead of them much as Americans drive cattle.

Moeritheres were primitive ancestors of 20th Century elephants. They did not greatly resemble their distant cousins, being about the size of small modern-day tapirs. Herded by the Dyal Riders, their short strong legs heavily pounded the ground beneath them, carrying their relatively long bodies onward, in an attempt to escape the annoying humans. Their relatively long skulls had eyes set very far forward, short flexible proboscises, and powerfully developed front incisor teeth. The beasts had been peacefully feeding along the banks of a nameless river when the two-legged pests and their war birds had interrupted. They swiveled their long heads back and forth, attempting to discover any escape route. But the yipping riders were spread out in a wide crescent, cutting off all avenues but one. The moeritheres squealed in anger and frustration but marched onward towards their rendezvous with destiny.

Sweet smelling grasses and strangely beautiful tulip-like flowers were crushed underfoot as the dyals carried their human masters in pursuit of the proto-elephants.

Ahead of the beasts, Kirov spied other Dyal Riders approaching them swiftly. As the pachyderms came into sight, they swerved to go around the herd. He cooed and his own war bird turned to meet them.

"Hail, mighty Kirov!" shouted one scout. "The great spiders approach quickly!"

Even as the war chief acknowledged the report, the gigantic arachnids appeared out of the haze of distance.

Kirov sucked in his breath in astonishment. The other Dyal Riders showed similar expressions of surprise and repressed fear. Sar's description had not fully prepared them for the hideous appearance of the monsters.

Except for their colossal size, the spiders were duplicates of their tiny cousins common to Pellucidar and the Outer World. Their hairy bodies, unreadable blank faces pocked with multiple eyes, sword-like mandibles, and swiftly-moving legs created an overall impression of sheer horror.

Kirov swallowed and shouted, "Drive them to the great spiders!" His awestruck followers found their voices and began yipping more urgently.

The two forces drew together rapidly. Kirov counted four giant spiders but their size made each a match for all of the moeritheres and Dyal Riders combined.

With a sudden squeal of raw terror, a leading moerithere stopped in place. His head jerked back and forth swiveling to absorb and understand the terrifying sight before him. Despite the chivvying noises from behind them, the elephantine procession halted.

Behind them, the dyals automatically halted to avoid rear end collisions.

Kirov smiled sardonically. It was easy to understand what the herd was thinking. They had sighted the huge arachnids and were trying to decide which were more dangerous — spiders or noisemakers?

The war chief didn't allow the primitive elephants to take a vote on the subject. He had anticipated this possibility and shouted commands to his tribesmen.

Dyal Riders unstrapped longspears from their backs, gripped

them tightly, and crouched low on their powerful war birds. The humans cooed in unison and the dyals stepped forward. Sharp points pricked elephantine hides.

Moeritheres screamed in pain and lurched forward. Frantic to escape the spear points, they stumbled into a shambling run.

The two forces collided.

Hemmed in by Dyal Riders long accustomed to herding food animals, the primitive elephants thundered towards the gigantic spiders.

The arachnids paused, apparently assessing the oncoming meals.

Moeritheres, escaping the spear points, began to scatter. Some curved to the right, some to the left. One bold elephant charged directly under the nearest spider. The arachnid's immense body was suspended at least three meters off the ground and the tapir sized pachyderm fit easily into the gap.

Kirov had time to wish the inventive moerithere luck.

Others were not as fortunate.

Spider legs—gigantic pillars of muscle–flashed in Pellucidar's eternal sunlight. Columns of flesh crushed panicky elephants into mush.

Perhaps a third of the moeritheres escaped, fleeing wildly in all directions. A few braved the fence of spears behind them and routed back along their forced march. Dyals danced out of the way, saving themselves and their human masters from fatal collisions.

One spider seemed to focus on the Dyal Riders on Kirov's left. Was it simply seeking additional food to add to the mashed carcasses before it? Did it want a little variety on its menu? Or was it interested in creatures capable of organizing an elephantine cattle drive? *How intelligent were these monsters?*

It pattered forward, striding over a dozen dead elephantoids. Its flailing legs drove it swiftly across the grassy plain. Despite its colossal size, it was surprisingly quiet.

Too quiet and too swift for one Dyal Rider whose attention

was distracted by another spider beginning to feed a short distance away.

A gigantic leg whipped out. The inattentive Dyal Rider and his mount—powerful and speedy enough for most challenges—were smashed into goo instantly.

Kirov screamed orders.

The Dyal Riders cooed frantically. Their mounts wheeled in place and thundered away.

The inquisitive—and deadly—spider followed. Its eight legs moved with startling speed. It raced across the plain rapidly overhauling the escaping second course.

Kirov screamed more orders but they were unnecessary.

The dyals increased their pace.

As did the giant spider....

And behind the great arachnid, its fellow monsters began to follow.

There were only four great spiders pursuing twenty humans and as many dyals but their huge sizes made them seem like an avalanche of hostile flesh. Terrified, humans and war birds fled for their lives.

THE CHASE WAS a nightmare of fear, exhaustion and humiliation.

The Dyal Riders had tamed one of the swiftest creatures in all of Pellucidar. Their powerful war birds gave them speed and mobility unequaled throughout the northern reaches of the Inner World. Now, they fled—or tried to flee—from horrific monsters even faster than they.

One by one, Dyal Riders and their mounts were overtaken and smashed into paste.

Worse, the great spiders seemed to enjoy their new game!

Most predators would have stopped with the first kills to feed. Instead, the powerful arachnids forged onward, contemptuously slaughtering humans and avians apparently for the pure pleasure of the experience.

Despite the peril, Kirov attempted to force himself to think rather than merely flee and hope. The old Russian saying *If you maintain a cool head when all those about you are panicking, you clearly do not understand the situation* flashed through his mind. Resolutely, he forced the counsel of despair away and attempted to analyze the situation. He let the dyal have its head while he glanced around.

The Dyal Riders were fleeing in a straight line back towards their base at the foot of the castle of Avorsi.... And the spiders were following in a straight line....

"Scatter!" screamed Kirov at the top of his lungs. "Scatter! They can't follow all of us at once!" For a moment, he wished for a Small Horse Rider bagpipe to convey orders. But, neither he nor his Dyal Riders had had time to learn the relatively advanced instrument.

His voice penetrated terrorized minds. Dyal Riders cooed and their war birds began to peel away from their previous straight line retreat. The outermost dyals were soon racing at right angles to their pursuers.

The great spiders seemed puzzled by the changed tactics. They slowed, apparently considering their options. Dyal Riders gained a precious few meters....

The spiders on the right and left flanks turned and began chasing the outriders. But the humans and dyals had gained time....

The remaining pair of monsters continued their advance following Kirov and the other Dyal Riders.

One dyal collapsed in exhaustion and lay panting for air on the soft soil of the grassy plain. Its rider rolled with the fall and came to his feet. He had been holding his longspear in one hand. He braced one end against the ground.

Kirov remembered that he had done that very thing when he earned his sobriquet "Skal-killer." Would it work again?

No.

A powerful leg swooped and slammed into the sharp end of the longspear. The leg jerked back, reacting to the sudden pain. The weapon was yanked out of the Dyal Rider's hands. He let go and pulled his assegai from its straps.

But the gigantic arachnid had eight legs, not a skal's two.

A second pillar of muscle crashed into the human's body. He flew through the air, arms and legs flailing at unnatural angles.

His sacrifice was not in vain. The third spider was now distracted, trying to remove the galling longspear from its flesh without the benefit of true hands. Only one monster pursued the handful of survivors.

One Dyal Rider gasped "Avorsi!" to Kirov.

The war chief looked ahead. The nest of the castle dwellers had indeed come into view, emerging from the blur of distance and the odd perspectives of the Inner World. From this angle—looking across the curving surface of Pellucidar—Avorsi appeared to be a complex black blot. Kirov seemed to be peering into the castle from above. White dots highlighted against the black rock must be the Avors going about their "daily" lives.

Beside the black splotch of the castle was a brownish smudge that Kirov knew was a camp of allied tribesmen. He could not distinguish their dull feather-covered clothes against the dirt of the plain or their activities. A fervent wish that they were carrying out his previous orders flashed through his mind.

Another dyal collapsed, worn out by the fatal exertion of the long chase. Its rider cartwheeled across the plain and lay still.

Closer and closer came Avorsi. As the humans approached, their angle of vision changed. Now the castle was apparently hanging in the air above the ground.

Closer and closer came the remaining pursuer.

As Kirov approached, a new giant spider materialized. It was on the far side of the castle in the air but its appearance and ferocity were unmistakable.

Their retreat was cut off.

Kirov laughed.

## Chapter Twenty-Four

## A DANCE OF DEATH

Another Dyal Rider looked at his chief in horror. Laughter when they were trapped by unbelievable monsters? Only the insane would laugh at a time like this…!

*Or the most powerful magician in Pellucidar!* The Dyal Rider grinned instead.

The pursuing monster slowed. The humans and their exhausted war birds gained a few precious meters, then more, and more….

Kirov shouted for his fellows to ride to the camp at the foot of Avorsi's invisible hill. The troop bent its path to the side, aiming for the brown splotch of the camp.

Behind them, the great spider slowed further.

Kirov stole glances at the huge beast as his dyal raced towards the hoped for safety of the camp.

The young scientist could not tell definitely what the arachnid monster was looking at for sure. But its five eyes seemed to be oriented towards the invisible hill and the equally great creature beyond!

*Ah, hah! One hypothesis tentatively confirmed…!*

The Dyal Riders thundered into the camp. Their fellow tribesmen scattered at the hasty entrance. The riders halted their avian steeds as quickly as they safely could. They cooed and their dyals collapsed to the ground, gasping for air.

"Bring longspears!" shouted the war chief. "Now!!" he screamed. His tribesmen were gazing at the strange monster in bemused horror. His voice cut through their amazement. Hastily, they seized their four-meter long weapons.

288

Most Pellucidarians were unruly warriors whose basic military formation would best be described as a *mob*. Kirov's tribesmen were a long way from a classical Roman legion but their leader had taught them the value of fighting as a group rather than a collection of individuals. They formed two lines facing the great spider, grounded their longspears, and aimed the business ends at the monster. Behind them, Avors began exiting their castle, armed with spears contributed by their new allies.

They waited.

And wondered at the fantastic sight before their eyes...!

The monster was engaged in a strange dance perhaps a hundred meters from the base of Avorsi hill. It kept its eyes on the hill but moved its vast body back and forth, up and down, to one side and then the other.... To the former Russian, the result was eerily like a professional dancer performing his solo introduction before his partners arrived on stage....

"What is it doing?" asked a Dyal Rider in a quavering voice. His face echoed his fear. "Why is it not attacking us?" There was a murmur of agreement from his fellows.

Kirov did not answer immediately. He was studying his monstrous opponent. His head nodded up and down, apparently agreeing with something.

In the near silence, Tol the Traveler interjected, "Magic. Mighty Kirov has cast a spell on the beast."

"Ahhh," murmured the plaintive Dyal Rider, this time more positively. His face brightened. Again, his fellows agreed with his mood.

Kirov paused before commenting. "Tol, you and the others prepared the magic that has halted the great spider." Tol's body language shifted; he swelled up but also looked more thoughtful. Kirov continued, "When you placed dirt on the far side of the glass rocks, you changed them into a *mirror*—a thing much like the water that shows your face when you look into it. The spider sees itself in the hill and is puzzled."

Tol's face spoke a thousand questions that his voice did not articulate.

Kirov smiled. "Tol, turn and look behind you into the glass of the hill."

The tribesman did so. He started in astonishment.

He babbled, "Kirov speaks truly. There is another spider behind us."

Heads jerked around. Tribesmen gaped, staring alternately at the image behind them and the reality before them. The lines of spears wavered....

Kirov barked a command. The pitiful lines of the spear wall straightened up. Spearmen continued to sneak glances at the illusion behind them but they kept their weapons aimed at the dancing spider.

"What do we do next, mighty Kirov?" asked Tol, now confidently.

Kirov opened his mouth to speak but Fate intervened.

The Dyal Riders defending the base of Avorsi hill were looking east. A cacophony of noise erupted to the north.

Kirov whipped his head around.

Charging towards the base camp and the great spider alike came a line of Amphicyons — huge dog-like creatures the size of Siberian brown bears. They yowled plaintively as they ran.

And behind them came a line of Small Horse Riders, charging pell-mell in pursuit, yelling triumphantly as the prehistoric dogs fled.

To his astonishment, Kirov recognized their leader: Taddo, chief of the Small Horse tribe...!

Taddo—who had disappeared without a trace many, many waking periods ago...!

Taddo—whose noisy reappearance had just galvanized the great spider out of its reverie and into an attack!

## Chapter Twenty-Five

## "ADVANCE AND ATTACK!"

The giant monster rotated to face northward where Taddo's war band approached.

A human would have swiveled his neck. Instead, colossal arachnid legs beat the ground—surprisingly softly—and the creature's entire body rotated as a unit.

The spider took a gigantic step towards the newcomers.

Kirov leaped into action.

He did not stop to analyze what he was doing. If he had, he might have thought *I am the war chief of the tribes who have followed me hoping to find safety from the Soviet advance. As chief, I must lead them in war and peace. My people are threatened; therefore I kill!*

But he did not think that. He merely whipped his head around searching for a new dyal to replace his exhausted war steed.

Ala was immediately behind him, already mounted on her favorite dyal. Her eyes glittered with battle fever....

"Ala! Dismount! I need your dyal!" shouted her war chieftain.

Ala stiffened in defiance and then relented. Normally, she would do nothing meekly but this situation was certainly not normal.

She cooed and her war bird knelt. She stepped off, as gracefully as a dancer, and pulled her weapons from her belts. She offered them to Kirov.

Her mate nodded his thanks and seized her assegai and

longspear. Extra weapons were always useful. He vaulted onto the back of the powerful dyal and cooed orders.

The savage avian surged forward.

Kirov shouted orders. "The monster attacks our tribesmen! Advance and attack!"

He led the way.

The great spider loomed up before him, many stories tall and apparently unsatiated by its earlier kills.

Ahead, Taddo, his war band, and the Amphicyons had frantically skidded to halts as they realized what lay ahead of them. Their eyes seemed to budge out of their heads. The prehistoric dogs attempted to scatter.

The movement attracted the spider's attention.

Kirov nodded his head even as he charged. *Another hypothesis confirmed!*

The colossal rear legs of the titanic creature loomed up.

Behind him, he heard vague shouting. He hoped that the Dyal Riders and other tribesmen were mounting up and riding to the attack. What tiny chance for survival the humans had was increased if they attacked together. But he had no time to look.

Taddo had realized that the inhabitants of the base camp were his allies. He screamed orders for his fellow small horsemen to turn and ride for the camp.

The Small Horse Riders began their turning maneuver, attempting to cross diagonally in front of the vast beast. From Kirov's perspective, they were changing course to his left.

The gargantuan spider pivoted to face Taddo's war band.

Its huge legs swung…

Too late, Kirov saw that a pillar of flesh was swinging towards him…!

He attempted to spur his dyal forward. The colossal creature's belly was four meters or more in the air. There was more than adequate room for the two meter high bird and its rider to pass safely beneath it….

The dyal balked. Its present rider was unfamiliar to it. The normal trust that existed between rider and ridden was not present. It refused the inconceivably dangerous order.

Kirov's mount jerked to a halt—directly in the path of the pivoting leg!

The vast limb smashed into bird and rider carrying them high into the air.

A kaleidoscope of images whirled through Kirov's mind. Pictures of spider, landscape, a flying dyal, and a vision of Ala holding their son flashed by.

There was a mighty thump and Kirov's battered brain went black.

How long was the war chief of the allied tribes unconscious?

In timeless Pellucidar, who can say?

He awoke when something slammed into his aching body. He forced his eyes open.

He was lying on a vast carpet of grey ground among numerous black spiny trees. The ground was undulating rhythmically. The swaying motion had caused Ala's assegai to bounce against his ribcage. The jolting motion continued.

Kirov seized the short spear. His own were still belted to his body.

He levered himself upright using one of the springy black spines as a support. He looked around.

The grey ground was a circular patch apparently detached from the usual grasslands that formed the landscape of northern Pellucidar. Beyond the patch, vast columns pumped up and down.

He was near one end of the patch. As he looked around he saw the floating castle of the Avor receding in the near distance. He shook his head and looked again. The castle continued to recede but refused to disappear.

He turned his head. There were five mounds at the other end of the patch, also grey. Beyond them, he could see a gap and then the Small Horse Riders fleeing across the upward curving landscape of Pellucidar.

Kirov collapsed in shock.

*He was on the back of the gigantic spider! The swinging leg had knocked him—and Ala's dyal?—into the air and onto its own back!!*

Again, he forced himself upright and surveyed the situation.

His scientist's mind began to fill in the gaps in his understanding.

The pumping columns were the spider's legs. The spines were bristles, not trees. Normal-sized spiders felt hairy to humans because of their normal sized bristles....

*And the spider was chasing his tribesmen!*

A memory of a past battle flashed into Kirov's mind. He had earned the sobriquet of "Skal Killer" by plunging his assegai into the mad eye of the greatest avian monster in northern Pellucidar. And those mounds were the backs of the five eyes of the even greater arachnid monster...!

Unsteadily at first, the war chief lurched forward to attack a monster many times his size. He picked up speed and purpose as he moved. He charged.

The black spines impeded his progress but they were not that different from the tall grasses of the Plain of Grazers. He charged.

A war chief of the Dyal Riders should be riding a powerful war bird to give his thrust a deadly increment of killing power but he was not about to take the time to hunt up Ala's steed. If it even lived.... He charged.

He slammed Ala's assegai into the back of the rightmost eye. There was a brief resistance as if he had stabbed into a leather shield. Then the lance slid home into softer tissue.

The world convulsed.

The spider shook itself in sudden pain, trying to eject the splinter of death hanging in its rightmost eye.

Kirov hung on for his life.

And the lives of Flana, Ala and young Kirov.

His weight drove the weapon deeper into the gigantic eye.

As the world spun around him, Kirov caught a brief image of Taddo frozen on his diminutive *Merychippus* proto-horse

*He slammed Ala's assegai into the back of the rightmost eye. There was a brief resistance as if he had stabbed into a leather shield. Then the lance slid home into softer tissue.*

staring upward at the colossal arachnid that had been on the verge of swallowing him—horse and rider both—whole. The Small Horse Rider's face gaped wide in wonder.

Gradually, the frantic antics of the monster diminished.

The great legs gestured. They beat the air within yards of Kirov's head.

He crouched down. One hand held onto the embedded assegai. The other pulled his own assegai from his belt.

A boast from the long-vanished Senior Starshina Voitinuik came to him: *I have not won every fight that I have been in, but every fight that I have been in, the winner knew that he had been in a fight!*

The young scientist, drafted into the Soviet Red Army so many years ago and now the commander-in-chief of his own tiny nation, grinned.

After a timeless time that seemed an eternity long, he realized something....

The legs were not striking the spider's head area!

The articulation of the vast creature's limbs did not permit it to strike him!

It made sense. What were the chances that *any* creature could reach the spider's back and stab its eye? In all likelihood, he was the first creature in all of Pellucidar's unrecorded history to do so.

*Well, then...!*

Kirov's grin deepened into Satanic triumph.

The tiny human being straightened up.

He surveyed the futilely swinging legs to be sure that he understood their motions and their limitations.

He tugged on Ala's weapon. Stuck tightly, it resisted his pull.

No matter; he had another.

He turned to the second rightmost eye and charged.

Again, he struck.

Again, the spider convulsed in agony.

Again, his world shook.

This time, the short spear tore out of the giant eye. Kirov lost his footing and began sliding forward across the spider's face.

The war chief released his lance and seized the black bristles. He jerked to a halt on what might be called the monster's cheek. His assegai slid past him and passed out of his sight.

(The colossal arachnid had nothing that a human might call cheeks or a face but he had to call this portion of the creature's body *something!*)

Again, Kirov used the bristles to haul himself upright. Ahead of him, the vast cheek curved downward, out of sight. The Small Horse Riders had disappeared.

He turned around.

A colossal eye regarded him from a few feet away.

For an eternity or two, the titanic spider and the puny human studied each other.

Kirov had landed almost directly in front of the monster's central eye. It was at least a meter tall and equally wide. There was nothing human about it.

The young Pellucidarian shook himself.

He drew his stone knife from his belt and stepped forward.

He glared at the monstrous eyeball and shouted, "I kill!"

His arm came up to strike....

The spider lurched backward in an earthquake of flesh.

Kirov lost his balance. The slender bristle slipped through his hand. He fell.

As he fell, he saw the spider scurrying backward. Two eyes were red ruins.

But then the Earth reached up and smashed him into blackest night.

## Chapter Twenty-Six

## THE MAGIC OF PELLUCIDAR

Has mighty Kirov gone to the Dead World?" asked one voice.

"No," sang another. "He sleeps."

Some voice sucked in air. When words came, they were choked with emotion. "Mighty Kirov is so powerful that he dares sleep on a battlefield. He saved many lives and now sleeps protected by his magic."

There was a murmur of agreement. Many voices seemed to agree with the third voice but were too awestruck to actually speak words.

Kirov stirred.

The second voice sang, "He wakens!" An enchanting presence came near. Warm lips kissed his bruised forehead. In spite of the lips' gentleness, he winced with pain.

His eyes fluttered open.

Ala bent over him. Around and behind her, he saw a dozen allied tribesmen. He recognized Tol the Traveler and Taddo, chief of the Small Horse Riders, among them.

"Hail, fellow tribesmen," he croaked. "Where is the great spider?"

"Gone," answered Ala serenely. "It fled when you stared it in the eye. Taddo and other Small Horse Riders saw this thing and we know that it is true."

Kirov tried to nod but he was lying on the soft ground of the plain surrounding Avorsi castle. Nodding did not come easily.

"I am glad, my tribesmen, I am glad." His weary mind

298

suggested going back to sleep. He started to ask Ala to take him to their temporary home in the base camp.

Tol interrupted. "Will the great spiders return? We lost many brave warriors in this fight."

Kirov's mind was not asleep yet although he was fading fast.

"If they return, we will fight them and defeat them. We know their secrets now. Their eyes see motion and their mouths smell food. And when you are *very* close, they believe that you are a giant. We can distract them by driving food animals towards them while we remain still. We will surprise them and kill them."

Once more, he started to ask Ala to move him but, once more, he was interrupted.

Taddo asked, "Mighty Kirov, how did you come to this land before us? We chased the jaloks (the Amphicyons) around the Sea of Monsters for most of a waking period and yet you arrived here first. Even more, you brought thousands of our tribesmen with you. How did you do this great thing?" His normally authoritative voice was colored with amazement — and possibly fear.

Kirov was almost unconscious again. But he gave Taddo an honest answer. He was a paleontologist, not a physicist. He did not understand the strange laws governing the world at the Earth's Core. He knew that the American adventurers David Innes and Abner Perry had experienced similar situations in which time seemed to pass more slowly for one than for the other. It was yet another mystery of Pellucidar that had yet to be answered.

Someday, he would find the answer.

But for now, he said, "We did this with magic."

*Epilogue*

Kirov was seated on the Seat of Chiefs, hearing reports on the closing of the great migration. In this, the war chief of the allied tribes was not greatly different from imposing Russian leaders such as Alexander Nevsky or Peter Romanov.

Things were going well. The tribes had now all moved south of the Warmwater River and were building permanent homes. New fortifications along the River were progressing. The giant spider traps and catapults to the east were successes.

Finally, the business of governing the tribes was almost over. A single scout remained to report. He pointed in the direction that Kirov thought of as south and stated, "Ten waking periods ride in that direction we discovered strange animals. They are large like dyryths but have smooth hairless skins that are like those of snakes. We have not seen such creatures before."

Kirov's heart leaped. He blurted out, "Dinosaurs?" in Russian. His face glowed. Years ago, he had fallen in love with dinosaurs and yearned to study them. Ironically, in all his time in Pellucidar, he had never seen one. Now the tribes had come far enough south....

His sense of wonder was interrupted by another scout, this one riding his dyal hard from the north. The scout requested... no, *demanded* an audience.

Kirov came down from Cloud Nine and directed, "Speak. What have you seen?"

"Mighty Kirov," began the scout. His voice trembled. "I

300

have returned from our outpost where the Coldwater River meets the Sea of Monsters. The River runs red with blood."

Kirov paled.

A silence fell on the council of chiefs.

Ala broke the stillness. "My chief, what does this mean?"

Kirov's voice seemed to come from another world, "The war that we feared has come. The Soviet Red Army has destroyed our fellow tribesmen—those who chose to remain in the Coldwater River Valley." He bowed his head, whispering prayers to the God of his childhood.

Ala's normally husky voice fell to a whisper, "Will our children be safe here in this new land?"

Kirov's raised his face, "I hope... I think so. We are...."

He broke off. He turned to face Ala more directly.

"You asked if our 'children' would be safe. Do you mean the children of our tribes?"

Ala smiled deeply. She placed her hands on her stomach. The tigress had become a Madonna. "Yes; that—and another thing. Mighty Kirov, you have given me a second child."

Her mate's jaw dropped. The other chiefs pounded the ground with their feet in applause.

In the noise, the confident words of Tol the Traveler went unheard. "Truly, mighty Kirov is the greatest magician in all of Pellucidar. If the Soviet Red War Party comes to our land, he will kill them all!"

*Acknowledgements*

The world of Pellucidar, created by Edgar Rice Burroughs 1913~1964, is trademarked by Edgar Rice Burroughs, Inc (ERB). The characters "Edgar Rice Burroughs", "Viscount Greystoke", "David Innes", "Abner Perry" and "Bowen Tyler, Jr." created by Edgar Rice Burroughs 1912~1917 and are trademarked by ERB. The "International Astronomic Society" created by Edgar Rice Burroughs 1913 and is the intellectual property of ERB. Various historical and literary events are used fictitiously. The "International Geographic Society", "Universal Encyclopedia" and "E*cyclopedia" created by Lee Strong 2009~2017 and are copyrighted by ERB. All rights reserved.

THE WILD ADVENTURES OF

EDGAR RICE BURROUGHS® SERIES

**LEE STRONG'S** heart was captured by the dinosaurs found *At the Earth's Core* in 1962—and he has been a Burroughs reader ever since. Lee also worked for the US Department of Defense (DOD); changed international policy with a single report; deployed to Kuwait; saved taxpayers $5 million; and reformed the $2 billion DOD Personal Property Program. *A Soldier of Poloda* was Lee's first novel. This is the first of two Pellucidar novels with more to come.

**Lee's motto:**
More Adventure!
More Excitement!!
More Burroughs!!!

**DOUGLAS KLAUBA** is an award-winning illustrator. Doug was born and raised in Chicago, and is a graduate of the American Academy of Art. His paintings have been included in the art annuals of *Spectrum: The Best in Contemporary Fantastic Art*, the Society of Illustrators, and *Imagine FX* magazine. His painting, "Mercury Jack," exhibited in the Spectrum Show at the Museum of American Illustration and another of his paintings, "Da Vinci's Dream" was awarded Best in Show at the 2005 World Fantasy Convention. A poster of his painting, "Stella 7" can be seen hanging on Howard Wolowitz's bedroom wall on the hit television show, *The Big Bang Theory*. Doug was Artist Guest at the 2016 Dum Dum, and previously provided interior art for *Tarzan Trilogy*.

PUBLISHED BY
Edgar Rice Burroughs, Inc., Tarzana, California

## About Edgar Rice Burroughs, Inc.

Founded in 1923 by Edgar Rice Burroughs, as one of the first authors to incorporate himself, Edgar Rice Burroughs, Inc. holds numerous trademarks and the rights to all literary works of the author still protected by copyright, including stories of Tarzan of the Apes and John Carter of Mars. The company has overseen every adaptation of his literary works in film, television, radio, publishing, theatrical stage productions, licensing and merchandising. The company is still a very active enterprise and manages and licenses the vast archive of Mr. Burroughs' literary works, fictional characters and corresponding artworks that have grown for over a century. The company continues to be owned by the Burroughs family and remains headquartered in Tarzana, California, the town named after the Tarzana Ranch Mr. Burroughs purchased there in 1919 which led to the town's future development.

www.edgarriceburroughs.com
www.tarzan.com

# Sci-Fi

**BOOK SERIES #5**

## A Soldier of Poloda

**By Lee Strong**

FURTHER ADVENTURES
BEYOND THE FARTHEST STAR

Worlds at War! American intelligence officer Thomas Randolph is teleported from the World War II battlefields of Normandy into the belly of the evil Kapar empire on the planet Poloda. The Kapar's only passion is to conquer and destroy the outnumbered Unis forces who had been engaged in a century-long struggle to survive. Rechristened Tomas Ran, the Earthman now understands that the same fierce determination to defeat Hitler must now be used as a weapon to defeat the fascist Kapars—a merciless foe bent on global domination.

Available at www.ERBurroughs.com/Store

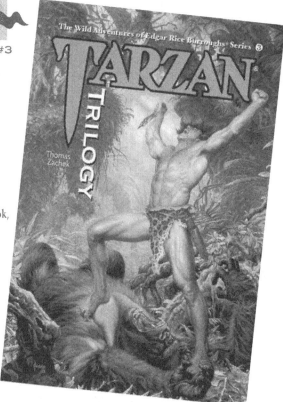

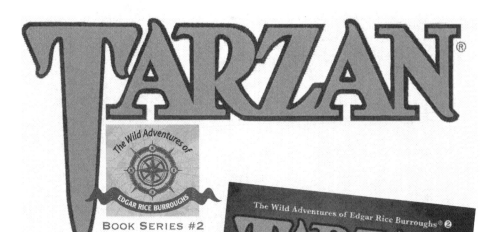

# KING KONG VS. TARZAN

Made in the USA
San Bernardino, CA
20 October 2018